# WICKS
## AND
# WINGS

# WICKS AND WINGS

SARAH C DAVIES

Paperback ISBN 978-1-7635688-3-9

Cover Design by Lemon Design Studio
@lemon.design.studio
Editing by Sarah Davies & Megan G. Mossgrove
Line editing by Mossgrove Writes
Proofreading by Sarah Davies & Megan G. Mossgrove

*To the readers who need courage to write their own story.*
*This is for you.*

_Author Note_

While this book does not focus on the following incidents, they may
trigger some readers.

Fighting scenes
Crude words
Adult themes
Loss of family

Please keep this in mind as you read.

# WICKS AND WINGS

## SARAH C DAVIES

## One

## FOUR WORDS TO SAY

A bead of sweat rolls down my temple, falling to its death on my shoulder. If only I could still the flickering tremor in my fingers. I'm usually calm, but not currently. Currently, I'm filled with anxiety and excitement. Which feeling is which, I'm unsure. They both offer the same symptoms: a hot sensation that starts in the pit of my stomach, burning its way through my body until it finally passes and I can breathe again.

With the stakes at hand, I need to push those feelings aside. I can't afford to entertain them, because tonight I'm going to be a free man.

As soon as I get this damned door unlocked.

"If we don't hurry up, we'll be spotted and there will be no hope for any of us," Roan mutters under his breath.

The copper-haired elf stands on lookout, his hands fidgeting in his pockets. He, too, was usually calm and collected, but when your brother's life and your own are on the line, it's hard to keep your shit together.

My fingers jimmy the lock. Sweat coats my palms. "I've almost got it," I hiss in response.

"Sepehr better have his bag packed ready to go, because as soon as that door opens, I'm out of here."

My gaze flicks to Roan briefly. I can see the worry etched on his face. It's a feeling I know all too well. We both want to be free—Sepehr too.

Well, today we're making that happen.

We're going to escape this prison we were handed as young boys. We are finally going to live the life we choose.

At least I hope. For me, things might look a little different.

Distant voices waft down the dark hallway, sending my heart into another erratic episode. Roan is right, if we don't hurry, our dreams of leaving this hole will be smothered by the sulphurous hand of Donovan—the man who could have been a father figure to me. Instead, he chose to be the devil in my own personal hell.

"Saint . . ." Roan hisses under his breath.

I can feel the pressure in my body building. There is so much riding on this. Roan and Sepehr are my brothers. Maybe not through blood, but through a bond that goes so much deeper. A kinship formed through having each other's backs time and time again. I would die for them.

But not today. Tonight we will live.

Finally, the lock clicks, sliding to the left with a metal thud. Without a second thought, I stand, grabbing the cold, bronze door handle, and push the door open.

Sepehr is standing in the middle of the room, a grin plastered on his face and a brown leather bag slung over his shoulder. "Did someone say it's go time?"

Roan steps past me to drag Sepehr into a rough embrace. "You got my note?"

"Well, obviously. My bag is packed, isn't it?" Sepehr smirks with a shrug.

It was good to see him. It had been four days since I'd laid eyes on him. That's the thing with Donovan. If you slip up even once, you're beaten and confined to the room we liked to call the *'We Fucked Up'* room.

I move to Sepher's side and gently clap him on the shoulder. His warm-brown, almond-shaped eyes find mine. "Glad to see you in one piece Sep, though that bruise looks nasty."

The long-haired elf shrugs, his glossy black hair tumbling over his shoulder. He brushes the back of his hand over his cheek bone. "I've had worse."

Roan clears his throat and throws a glance down the hallway. "We should really get going."

I nod and push myself into action. How we're going to manage this escape, I have no idea, but I would rather die trying than live for one more day in this place.

As the minutes tick by, it brings me closer to the part of me I'd rather not deal with right now. I can feel it moving. Calling to the night. It wants to be free from its own prison . . . To be free of me. So, time is of the essence.

The tension is palpable as Sepehr, Roan, and I slip through the shadows of the long hallway towards the stairway that will carry us to the main level of Donovan's estate. Amber, watery light leaks through the cracks of the manor's walls, hinting at the magnitude of time. I have to be free of these stone barriers—this prison—before sunset. Before I become somewhat useless to my brothers.

An eerie stillness fills the space. Every step we take down the winding staircase brings us closer to the freedom that we so desperately seek. Our boots barely scuff the step surface. Even with no light, I find my feet moving forward without thinking. I know this place better than anyone. I should, considering I've lived here for fifteen years.

Despite the night's impending approach, the dusk is still warm. Summer is fully upon us, and I welcome the touch of the cool stone beneath my hand as I drag it down the wall.

"Do we have some sort of plan?" Sepehr whispers into the inky darkness of the low lit stairwell.

"Yeah. Get out and don't die in the process," I whisper back.

"Oh, that's a great plan. Whoever thought of that is a genius."

Roan's white teeth slightly glow in the dark as he grins. "Saint must be a genius then."

I struggle to hold back my laugh. Trust my brothers to take the chance to poke fun at me in a time like this. "Thanks, I thought of it all by myself."

We move through the stairwell like shadows. It's how we were trained. Blend in, don't stand out, don't draw attention. Be one with our surroundings. So that's what we do.

With the hood on my cloak pulled down to rest just above my eyes, I reach the bottom step and hold up my hand, halting Roan and Sepehr.

This hallway leads to the main rooms. Thankfully, there are no guards—the only two we've seen so far are upstairs, face down on the floor outside Sepehr's room. Both would have quite the large concussion come morning.

"The hall is clear. Remember to stick to the shadows where you can," I whisper as I step into the narrow passageway. Both Roan and Sepehr follow me closely, the sound of our leather boots softly echoing in the small space.

"Did anyone happen to bring me a weapon?" Sepehr speaks in a hushed tone as we draw nearer to the danger.

I halt in my steps. "Glad you mentioned it. Here, have this." I reach down and grasp the hilt of the blade tucked in the top of my right boot. "Don't lose it. She's a keeper."

Sepehr grins at me. "Isn't that what you say about all of them?"

I shrug and return the smile. "Probably."

The end of the hall greets us and the feeling in my gut tells me that shit is about to go down. Whether I like it or not.

There's only one way in and out of this place, and Donovan isn't stupid enough to leave that exit unguarded. Well, to be fair, there are two other exits, but one is a deep plunge into the ocean from one of the upper balconies. The other is another spiral stairwell that leads to the ocean. That one has an iron grate below the surface that was blocked off years ago due to Donovan's paranoia and I really don't feel like dealing with that—especially when it's on the sea bed.

So the front doors it is.

I peek my head around the side of the entrance, glancing into the main part of the house that contains many different doors and passageways. As predicted, there are a few guards or henchmen—whatever Donovan calls them—stationed there, blocking the main corridor, their swords gleaming in the dim torchlight. Donovan must have placed some extra around the manor on his departure this morning. Who knows where he is going. Probably to restock his stash. He was partial to Lustre, the highly addictive drug only available from the Skimmers—ocean pirates who trolled the Veridian Sea. It reached our shores roughly six moon cycles ago—around one hundred, and eighty days. Now it's wreaking havoc amongst those who have heavy pockets. As for Donovann, I think the Lustre is beginning to affect his brain.

He is only going to be gone for a few days, but he's paranoid that people are out to kill him. I don't blame him for feeling that way. When you're the head of the criminal scene in Breydon, it doesn't surprise me that there are others out to get him. And if I'm being honest, he deserves whatever comes his way.

I'm done with him.

The last debt collection I'd gone on with Sepehr hadn't ended well. The male succumbed to a watery grave at the hands of one of Donovan's henchmen. Donovan hadn't even batted an eyelid when we told him the news, simply saying, *"You reap what you sow."*

Sure, I've done my fair share of teeth breaking, stealing, threatening—but taking someone's life? That only happens when I'm trying to save my own.

This escape has been in the works for a while. I need to be free.

"This will be easy, boys." I grin. "We'll dive right in there, slash some kneecaps and run out the front door in a blaze of glory."

"Sounds so simple." Roan huffs humorously.

"Right? I thought so myself."

On the outside, I'm calm. I'm grinning. I'm oozing confidence so my brothers can see that everything is going to be fine. But on the inside, my stomach is in knots. I'm trembling. Screwing this up could be deadly and I'm not interested in letting this hellhole be my final resting place. I won't let them see that, though. Because I have to get them out of here alive. We have to live a free life—together.

It will be easy enough to do now that Donovan isn't around to watch our every move. The guards won't be expecting the escape, either.

I turn to face them both. Roan's emerald-green eyes are steady, but I know he's afraid, and who wouldn't be? Sepehr's silver orbs travel over my face, communicating emotions he'd rather not say out loud. We all know what is at stake. But we are in this together. They both watch me, waiting for me to speak. But what can I say? I don't want to sprout promises I may not be able to keep.

I pull my favourite dagger from the belt around my waist and point it at them. "I have four words for you: Don't. Fuck. It. Up."

The boys grin and nod. That's the only pep talk we need.

The breath I suck into my lungs is filled with a weight I can't explain. It could be my last, so I savour it for a moment before I let it out and all three of us burst into the room.

What unfolds is utter chaos and my blood sings. I wasn't only trained to be a shadow, I was also trained to be a weapon. My blade comes down and slashes across an unsuspecting guard's face. The look in his eyes is one of pure shock as crimson beadlets spray across my vision. The guard screams and clutches at the wound. There's a small chance I caught the corner of his eye—that's going to hurt.

I don't have time to think as another henchman rushes towards me with his sword held high. I duck under the swinging blade just in time, dropping to my knees and sliding across the floor. My hand darts out behind me, catching the male's leg with my dagger. His cry confirms I got him right in the muscle. He won't be running after us anytime soon.

Metal clanging against metal sounds through the room and from the corner of my eyes I can see Sepehr and Roan are dropping bodies left, right and centre.

We are so close to getting free.

The last guard goes down with a swift kick to the gut from Roan and we race towards the looming front doors that lead to the life I've only ever dreamt of. Freedom is so close. I can taste it.

There's only one more obstacle. Four henchmen are stationed at the front door and they hear us coming, so we no longer have the element of surprise. Yet, let's not discount the weapons we were created to be. And when you put three weapons together what do you get?

A clusterfuck of chaos.

Everything around me stills as I move towards the men. Roan flies in from my left and Sepehr glides in from my right. Both of them are weaponised dancers. Their elven heritage makes them quick in their movements and light on their feet.

I'm a little jealous of just how beautifully they move. Bodies chiselled from stone, created to fight and protect.

All three of us dance to the song of violence as we fight for our freedom. It's all or nothing at this point and nothing isn't an option. I sink my blade two inches above the outside of the man's knee, avoiding any major arteries. Before I swing around towards the next male, sweeping his legs from under him and slamming the hilt of my blade into his skull. Blood sprays across my cloak. It's not followed by pain, so it's not from me.

I hurriedly glance at Roan and then Sepehr. Thankfully, they're still standing. So I keep fighting. I'll keep fighting until we are running into the sunset as free men.

As I twist out of the way from a descending blade, my shoulder collides with the stone wall and I grunt as a hot pain shoots through muscle. There's no time to nurse it though. I have to keep going.

I push through the throbbing ache and twist back around, catching the man off guard with an uppercut from the hilt of my dagger. I swear I see a few teeth go flying with the crimson spray of blood as his head snaps backwards, knocking him flat to the ground.

The breath I drag into my heaving lungs feels a little lighter, like it knows how close we are to the deliverance on the other side of the huge wooden doors.

Roan is the first to reach them. He jiggles the iron handle protruding from the left door and I have never felt so frozen in time before than I have in this moment right now.

I've been outside before—in fact, I practically live outdoors. It's my job to help collect debts that are owed to Donovan. For fifteen years I've been his lackey, alongside Sepehr and Roan. I know Breydon city better than anyone. But leaving the confines of the manor always comes at a price. I'm only ever allowed out with an escort and only ever with one of my brothers—never both.

A tactic to keep me emotionally chained to the manor.

Donovan had drilled it into me every damn day for the last fifteen years. *"You know the price your brothers will pay if you run, Saint."*

Roan fumbles with the handle, his hands trembling as he works to twist the rusty knob. The adrenaline from fighting is catching up to him.

"Ro . . . We are running out of time," I murmur as I take a step towards him.

A horn blares in the distance, signalling reinforcements. The sound of rushing boots growing louder with every second.

Sepehr spins, facing the sound of dread. "We're out of time!"

Roan starts to panic. "I'm trying! It's stuck!"

We don't have time for this. We didn't come all this way for a door to be our defeat. I gently shove Roan to the side. "Move!"

I listen to the sounds of the iron grating against the lock as it finally gives way and, with a sudden surge of energy, I kick the doors open.

Warm summer air hits me in the face, but I don't even care. My legs are already carrying me down the long cobblestone road towards the large iron gates that keep Donovan safe—or so he thinks—from the outside world. I don't even stop to see if the henchmen are chasing us. I know Sepehr and Roan are beside me and that's all that matters as we reach the gates and scale up and over.

Donovan's estate looms behind, torches flaring as guards pour out in pursuit. It's too late though. I'm free. And I am never going back.

Dark forest stretches before us. It's the only thing that separates us from the city down below. If we get through the forest, we can flee into the labyrinth of homes and hopefully blend in with the crowds.

I take the lead, heading into the dark web of trees and underbrush. The scent of pine on the wind. My inner beast starts clawing at me. Demanding to be let out in the habitat it craves. But I don't give in yet. I still have time until the sun sets.

Sepehr pulls up beside me, his breath coming in shallow gasps. "How far do we need to go?"

"Far enough that they give up—or lose us in the density."

Roan groans and pulls back. "I can't—can't keep this pace. My leg . . ."

I stop and take a few gulps of air as I glance at his leg. Blood is seeping from a gash across his thigh. Without a second thought, I grab my blade and cut a strip of fabric off the bottom of my cloak before tying it above the wound, slowing the blood. "Yes, you can. Focus on putting one foot in front of the other."

Roan nods, his eyes thanking me for the temporary medical assistance.

After running for what feels like hours, we finally reach a clearing on the outskirts of Breydon city. We aren't safe yet, but we stop for a moment to catch our breath. I'll admit I didn't think this far ahead. My goal was to get out in one piece. That's it. I hadn't thought about what I might do if we actually did make it out alive.

Sepehr's usually put-together appearance is dishevelled as he looks to me with his hands on his hips. "We can't stay together. It's too dangerous."

Roan's head flicks around, his voice panicked. "No! Splitting up will just make it easier for them to pick us off."

He has a point. But so does Sepehr. As individuals, we could hide easily, doing what we do best. Blending in. But being on our own also makes us an easy target. The thought of not being with my brothers sends a pang through my heart.

I've been with them every day for the last twenty or so years. We've been through everything together.

I run my hands through my hair as I try to think. The pain in my shoulder blasts through my body as I lift my arms. I hope I haven't broken something.

Loud voices from travellers coming to and from Breydon city send a chill up my spine. It's not the henchmen, but I can't help but shudder at the thought of being found so soon after the escape.

All of what we just went through has to be worth something. So I make the call. "It's the only way. We'll cover more ground, and it'll be harder for them to track us. Besides, Donovan won't even know we're missing until he returns home in a few days. It gives us a great head start."

Sepehr nods. "We will meet again when it's safe, three moon cycles from now—ninety days—at the orphanage."

Roan wipes his hand over his face. "How will we know it's safe?"

I can tell he's worried. I wish I could take that worry from him. But this is something we need to face. The unknown.

I rest a hand on his shoulder and squeeze it gently. "You'll know. Just keep your head down until then. Make sure you get that gash looked at once you're far from here. That tourniquet will help, but you might need stitches."

Roan nods, his copper waves glinting under the moonlight. "Be safe. Both of you. And in Saint's own words, *don't fuck it up.*"

A feral grin spreads across my face. We did it. We're free and we are about to find our way in the world.

"Bring it in." I chuckle, holding out my hand.

Sepehr grins, taking a step towards me as Roan joins in. The three-way fist pump is our thing. Together, we face the world, but for a small window in time we are going to have to go it alone.

"We're gonna get through this," I hum.

Both of them offer me a smile but remain silent, slipping into the shadows as if they were born from darkness itself. Sepehr disappears one way and Roan reluctantly heads in the opposite direction.

I wait in the forest, ensuring neither is followed, before I turn on my heel and head towards the south in what I hope is the liberation my body needs. Glancing down, I look at the insignia on my shirt. A coiled serpent wrapped around a jagged crown. With my blade, I cut it free, throwing it to the ground. I want no proof tying me to Donovan. I refuse to be chained to anything that symbolises him.

Alone, in the silence of the night, my heart hardens a little. "One step closer to true freedom . . . I hope."

# TETHERS

I've been running for two weeks. Hiding. Lying low or blending in with the shadows, anything to keep me from bringing too much attention to myself. Except for stealing. That I can do without a single soul noticing.

Never do I take more than needed, though. Greed is a one-way ticket to getting caught and I don't have time for that.

I'd travelled mostly through the nights, clutching my bag in my talons as I flew through the skies. Yet now, the throbbing pain in my shoulder reminds me I should do a lot more walking and a little less flying.

It's frustrating that I haven't covered as much ground as I would have liked due to the injury. The first week I walked most of the way—sleeping in the treetops every second night or so. Even in my owl form, I can still feel the pain. The second week, I was able to push myself a little harder, but now the pain has returned. I think I've overdone it. I'll have to rest and heal—lie low until it's time to find my brothers.

I hope with every fibre of my being that they're both safe and have found somewhere to blend in. And fuck, I hope Roan got his leg looked at and didn't bleed out somewhere in the woods.

Warm orange sun rays pierce through the clusters of pine and oak as I make a beeline for the town in the distance.

Meadowbrook. The town of plenty—or so I've heard.

I've never been here before, though I know Donovan's sulphurous tendrils still reach this far. I'll need to keep a low profile, but given the distance between here and Breydon, there is probably a little room to breathe. I could find some work and keep my head down for a couple of weeks. Save some coin.

Early morning farmers are already out in their fields, toiling at the soil before the heat of the day sets in. A bellowing sound makes me reach for the knife hidden at my waist. Herds of cows are slowly making their way into large green pastures. Probably free from this morning's milking.

Milk. My stomach grumbles. I ate the last chunk of bread last night before I shifted, before my owl form took over and tried to find a squeaky little mouse to devour. Thankfully, I found none.

My brown leather boots scuff at the dry dirt path that carries me through Meadowbrook's gates, to the centre of town. Despite the sun only just arriving, the marketplace is crowded. Bakers have opened their doors, letting out the scent of their goods with their fresh loaves displayed in windows. Stall holders call out their prices, their baskets filled to the brim with summer fruits and vegetables.

My attention catches on the black grapes, and my stomach redoubles its groaning.

Surely the fruit folk could spare a few juicy morsels for a hungry man like me. I mean, look at me. I'm practically starving.

Meadowbrook feels different to—home—not that Breydon is especially home-y. It's usually teeming with all kinds of folk: half-orcs, elves, humans, the odd siren every now and then, shifters. Not that I've noticed any in a while. They're hard to spot, usually only identified by a certain ring design on their finger. It's almost as if we don't exist.

Folk in Breydon are always rushing about and the streets seem narrower, making it unpleasant to wander the city. Though it makes it easier to pick the odd pocket.

Here in Meadowbrook, it seems more peaceful. There are still all kinds of folk and it's still busy, yet the smile on their faces seem real—genuine. As if they're all drinking from a fountain of joy that I never learned about.

A pair of female elves walk arm in arm as they giggle behind pretty smiles and ribbons. The woven baskets they carry are empty. I'd say they're on their way to gather berries in the forest before the sun sours the sweet flesh.

Wooden wheels creak behind me. I twist, spying a green half-orc running along with a handcart full of cabbages. A cream apron tied around his waist. On his way to the inn, no doubt.

So far, no one has looked at me sideways.

Except that guy.

The clanging of metal halts as the burly blacksmith eyes me. He squints a little too long. I can feel the energy pulsing between us. Now is probably a good time to keep moving. This is the kind of attention I'm trying to avoid.

It would probably help if I keep my arms covered, too. I tug my worn, cotton sleeves all the way to my wrists. The black ink etched into my skin is a lot for some folk.

I flick my gaze towards him again as I move away from his workstation. He breaks the stare and goes back to work. Mental note taken. Stay away from the guy with the beard, big heavy tools and probably an iron fist—by the looks of his arms.

Sure, I could take him on in a fight. I'd just hate to see him lose. And I can't afford to cause a stir.

From the corner of my eye, I spy a stall filled with one of my favourite kinds of fruit. Grapes. There was always an abundance when Donovan threw his ridiculous parties. As a young boy, I would sit under the table with a plate piled high. Especially if they were black grapes.

The sweet memory of the juice against my tongue causes it to twang. Sidling up to the stall, I catch the eye of the fruit vendor. His bright smile greets me as I step closer to the table. "Morning. How much for some grapes?"

As he shuffles closer, my hand grazes the edge of the table, pulling a small bunch of the juicy orbs under the palm of my hand. I'm aware to keep the attention of the stall holder the entire time I'm sneaking a few into my pocket.

"Two coppers for the green, three for the black. Fresh from the vineyard this morning," he exclaims heartily as he reaches for a brown paper bag.

With a handful of black grapes secured in my trouser pocket, I fish in my jacket for two copper coins. "Thanks, I'll take some green ones. Say . . . I'm looking for somewhere cheap to stay for the next few weeks. Know of any places that won't empty my pockets?"

The vendor chuckles as he hands me the bag. "Not much in this town comes cheap, stranger, but . . . there's a room above the stables on the far side of town. Ain't fancy, but it's got a roof, and the stable master won't charge you more than a few silvers a night if you don't mind the smell of horses."

I dip my head in thanks. "Better than rain on my head. Appreciate it."

Sleeping in a stable is ideal. There will be little interaction with townsfolk, and I highly doubt the horses will mind my company.

As I turn to leave, the man ushers me closer, leaning forward, lowering his voice slightly. "Word of advice—keep to yourself. The stable master's fair, but he doesn't take kindly to troublemakers. And there's always an eye watching, even when you think you're alone."

His words send a shiver down my spine. Does he know something I don't?

"Care to share whose eyes I should avoid?"

The man raises a brow, a smile dancing on his lips. "Stay out of trouble and you'll never need to know."

I offer him a lopsided grin. "Trouble and I go way back, but I'll behave. Thanks for the tip."

More and more villagers flood the marketplace, signalling it's time to make myself scarce. I'll head to the stable, talk to the stable master and then form some sort of plan to make some coin. I'm going to need it if I plan on staying around for a couple of weeks. Unfortunately, I can't steal all my food and lodgings. That would certainly draw some unwanted attention.

Maybe I could offer handyman services. I'd always been good with a hammer. More than once I'd helped the ladies in the orphanage to fix broken doors, windows, floorboards. You name it, I'd most likely fixed it.

I glance at the row of shops on either side of the street. Some vendors have already opened their doors, while others were still arriving. A woman to my left waters a hanging basket of red geraniums, while another sweeps a shop doormat.

What would I do about tools, though? It's not like I carried a toolbox around with me. Perhaps I could offer a 'you provide the tools and supplies, I'll provide the service' kind of deal. Surely there would be small odd jobs around people's homes that carpenters didn't have time for. That kind of service would get me into homes as well, where I could see what kind of precious goods Meadowbrook is filled with.

Some say the lake beds here are laden with precious gems. Though they can only be found through mining, and that's not something I know how to do.

Maybe amongst people's belongings, I might finally find an enchanted shifter ring. If I found a ring, I could stop shifting as soon as the sun sets every night and I could actually live my life. Talk about quality of life improvement and staying free from the iron grip of Donovan—the dream.

Perhaps I could finally allow myself to hope that I might find the love of my life and settle down. Although, I would need to be firmly out of Donovan's mind before I could even consider that. I'd need to be wholly free and able to control my shifting before I would feel safe enough to invite love into my orbit.

I slip down a side street, heading for the stables. As soon as I can discard my cloak and bag, I'll explore the rest of Meadowbrook. But for now, the sun's bite is setting in and my shoulder is giving me grief. It might even be nice to shut my eyes for a moment, catch up on some lost sleep since fleeing Breydon.

It takes me a good chunk of time to walk to the other side of town. Sweat trickles down my back by the time I reach the stables. Summer has never been my favourite time of the year. I prefer the colder months. Ones blanketed in sheets of powder-white snow, where my breath turns to puffs of cloud each time I speak. Where I can hide somewhere warm and sketch to my heart's content.

There hasn't been a lot of time for that lately, either. It's alright though. Things will change soon. They have to.

The scent of manure and hay floats in the air. I've definitely found the stables. My feet carry me through the sturdy wooden gates, past corrals towards the large wooden structure where I see a woman sweeping the cobblestone path out the front. She's tall and slender and as I step closer, I spy elven ears poking through her shimmering, pale-pink hair. She glances up as I approach, smiling while she sweeps.

"Can I help you?"

I flash her the most confident grin I can muster. "I'm looking for a place to stay and was told there was a room here?"

"You'd best talk to my husband about it," the woman nods. "You'll find him in the back pasture tending to the horses."

So far, so good. At least the information about the room was accurate. Now to find the husband and to win his good graces, so I can finally put this bag down.

It doesn't take me long to find him. He isn't hard to miss: about seven feet tall, the size of a small house.

Not really. But he is large, has tusks, and his skin is pea-green. A half-orc.

I approach him warily, but with the same smile I offered his wife in hopes it works just as well on him. His dark-brown eyes scan my appearance. At this moment, I'm thankful my sleeves are still pulled down. No need to go scaring the guy off with my big muscles and pretty skin.

"Excuse me, are you the stable master?"

The towering half-orc wipes his hands on a rag. "Depends who's asking."

"Name's Saint. Heard you've got a room to rent upstairs. I'm looking for a place to stay for a few weeks—quiet and out of the way."

Dark brown eyes look over me again. "Room's not much more than a box with a bed. No meals. No fires. And I don't tolerate noise or trouble. You good with that?"

I nod. "Sounds perfect. How much?"

The stable master grunts, folding his arms across his broad chest. "Two silvers a week. Pay up front. And if you break anything, you fix it, or I'll break you."

The funny thing is, I actually think he could break me. I'm not stupid enough to test that theory either. So I reach into my pocket, draw out two of the last four silver coins I have, and hand them over. "Fair enough. I'm not here to cause problems. Just need a place to lie low for a bit."

Green, stubby fingers inspect the coins before he slips them into a pouch. "Hmm. You look like the kind of man who's seen trouble—and maybe brought some with him. Don't bring it here."

Little does he know, the last thing I want to bring is trouble. Trouble means Donovan. And I don't plan on returning to that life ever again.

I hold up my hands and offer him my best smile again. "Not planning on it. Just a quiet place to sleep, that's all."

The stable master grunts again, motioning towards a creaky wooden ladder leading to a loft. "Room's up there. Key's on the hook by the door. Keep it locked—don't trust everyone who comes through these parts."

"Thanks. And for what it's worth, I'll keep to myself."

In a voice that is gruff but not unkind, the half orc calls after me. "Good. And don't go scaring the horses. They're more valuable than you."

I have no doubt about that. Most things are.

Pausing mid-stride, I send a smirk over my shoulder. "Noted."

As soon as my body hits the small wooden bed in the loft, I fall asleep. I sleep right through lunch and almost dinner too, only waking hours later as the sun is setting. From the stillness of the stables below me and the soft sound of horses munching on food, I'd say I'm alone.

It's so peaceful. So quiet. I could literally fall back on this cot and go right back into slumber, but my stomach is growling again and I know my owl form will wake me soon. Perhaps I should wander around town a little, gather my bearings, and see the layout of the place a little more.

Hopefully, with the setting sun, villagers will scurry to their homes, leaving me space to wander without drawing too much attention to myself.

I stand, brushing the dust from my trousers. I could definitely use a bath too. Those lakes sound inviting right about now. My body would appreciate a good soaking. Standing here thinking about it isn't doing me any favours though, so I tuck my bag securely under the bed. It's not like I have an abundance of personal belongings, but the little I do have is very important to me.

The iron key is heavy in my palm as I turn to lock the door behind me. I pocket it and descend the rickety wooden ladder. As my boots hit the ground, I glance around. There isn't a soul to be seen. Just the furry rumps of horses peaking over the tops of the stable. They were certainly beautiful colours. The half-orc was right. Definitely more valuable than me.

My stomach shoots a pang of hunger through me. I have to eat. Heading back down the cobblestone path, I jump the now locked entry gate and travel back towards the town.

I'm only halfway when I come across a direction sign that is labelled 'Lake'. The other side of the sign says 'Town.' Something about seeing the large body of water intrigues me. It's not like I haven't seen a lake before. Donovan's estate is surrounded by the sea. However, the sea is always angry. It never stills. And even though I thrive on chaos when it comes to fighting, another part of me longs for peace.

A lake demands peace. I want to see it for myself. I can always head to the town for food later. With the decision made, I turn left and head in the direction that my heart is calling me.

The lake is much closer than I anticipated. As I reach the top of a small hill, my breath is stolen from my lungs for a brief moment of time. Meadowbrook's lake stretches vast and serene, its surface a mirror for the fiery hues of the setting sun. Streaks of gold and orange dance on the water, interrupted only by the occasional ripple of a fish breaking the surface. Around the lake's edge, the world is painted in dusky purples and deepening blues, the fading light casting the surrounding willows into soft silhouettes.

I want to capture it so I will never forget. Too bad my sketchbook is back in the loft. I'm running low on charcoal sticks as well. Still, this sight is too mind-altering to not capture its beauty. I'll have to come back when I can. Perhaps if I earn enough coins, I can invest in some watercolour paints, because this image needs to be absorbed into paper with as much colour as I can provide.

A few lingering villagers dot the shoreline and I find my feet carrying me closer to the water's edge. Never have I seen something so beautiful before. I want to dive in and immerse myself in its cool current, but it might be wiser to wait until I am alone.

My knees crack as I crouch, my eyes catching the glimmer beneath the water's surface. The lakebed sparkles faintly, its treasures not hidden but flaunted—a bed of stones, polished smooth by time and water. Deep greens, oceanic blues, and the occasional fiery red gleamed faintly, like stars trapped underwater. These weren't the kinds of stones that paid a hefty sum—no—those were hidden much deeper beneath the lake bed. Only miners could reach them. But the shiny ones on the surface were just as beautiful to look at. No wonder this town is thriving. Maybe I could take a dip or two and collect a few stones for myself.

Sounds of townsfolk carry along the breeze. I glance ahead to see a small group of people gathered at the water's edge. Not wanting to be seen, I stand and move to stay hidden in the shadows of what appears to be a wooden boat shed. Straining to hear their conversation, I can't help but be drawn to the sound of a woman's laughter. It's the kind of sound you'd imagine from snowflakes sparkling in the moonlight. If that was even possible.

She turns to her left and I catch her profile. Her nose is the perfect proportion, and the way the corner of her upturned mouth carries towards her eye has me grinning to myself. Her laughter is infectious. A messy bun of chocolate brown hair sits atop her head, with stray pieces framing her face.

In my mind, I am begging her to turn towards me. I want to fully see this delicate creature that has caught my attention, but fate has yet to be kind to me as she grasps the hand of the woman she's speaking to and hurries off towards town.

My heart follows her, yet my feet remain with me.

To go after her means walking through the group of people she was with. No, it's best if I go back the way I came. Who knows, maybe I'll bump into her again.

I turn on my heel and set off for town. Silver coins clink in my trouser pocket, in tune with each step I take. I need to eat a decent meal and then I must find work or I'm going to be starving and have no money for stable lodgings.

My assumptions of the centre of town being a little more quiet this time of the evening is correct. A lot of the stalls have closed, leaving the inn or tavern the only place I might find a hot meal. Though I don't wish to linger in either of those places long. The tavern is the closest option, so I head inside and order the biggest slice of bread, topped with stewed meats and cheese that they offer. Thankfully, it's early enough that the room isn't filled to the brim with patrons yet.

A happy-looking human woman hands me my order and I thank her, then head back out into the centre of town.

The first bite of the hot food has me groaning. If only I had enough coin to order twelve of these. I savour each mouthful as I walk along, heading back towards my lodgings for the night with the sound of laughter from a dark-haired beauty still ringing in my ears.

Not even this meal compares to her.

Most of the stone and wooden stores are closed. I find myself relaxing a little. No one seems to be looking at me oddly and I haven't seen anyone I recognise either. In a perfect world, Donovan has forgotten about me and my brothers and in two and a half moon cycles, we can regroup, starting our new lives together somewhere peaceful.

One can hope, right?

Just as I finish the last mouthful of food, I see a faint orange glow coming from a shop just up ahead. Someone must be working late.

Too curious for my own good, I stop just outside the shop window, peering into the amber-washed room. Clusters of candles dripping wax of all colours litter a table in the middle of the room. A chandlery, no doubt.

Movement catches my eye and I step back, out of the window light and back into the shadows on the street. A figure emerges from the back room, stopping at the desk to flick through a book.

It's her. The woman from the lake.

My heart jumps inside its cage made of bone and flesh.

The orange gleam of the flames casts little dancing shadows in the room and over her skin. Warm, honey-coloured skin. What I'd give to see her closer. Something about the way she carries herself intrigues me. I want to know her—and I've never really wanted to know any woman before. More accurately, I'd never really had the opportunity.

I run my eyes over the shop. It doesn't seem to be in the greatest shape. The sign is fading, with patches of paint missing, and one of the glass window panes has a crack running diagonally across it.

I could fix that. Could she be my first customer? Should I take the risk of looking like a fool and visit her tomorrow, offering my services as a handyman?

If I want to pocket some coin, do I have much of a choice?

She closes the book and her gaze flicks up. At first, I'm worried she spots me. My heart stills for a second time today as I nervously await her reaction. Yet, I don't think she can tell I'm there in the dark. I allow myself to breathe again. It's probably best to move on.

Tomorrow, I'll return with the hope she won't turn me away. Because I have an unexplainable pull towards her, like my heart has made a decision, and I didn't even get a choice.

# Three

## BLUE EYED STRANGERS

The heavy weight of my small world lifts from my shoulders the moment I slip into the water. It embraces me like a second skin, cool and crisp in the early morning light. The sun has just risen, yet its pale rays cut through the surface above, painting golden streaks in the crystal water.

It's cold down here, darker the deeper I swim. Despite the depth, I can still see all the glittering precious stones on the lakebed. Blues, greens, purples—every colour of the rainbow. I'm quite partial to the blue stones. They remind me of my father's eyes.

Perhaps I shall stay here longer than intended. Perhaps no one will notice I am gone. Perhaps I'll find some form of freedom down here.

Icy cold water rushes along my body, reminding me that I'm alive. That I can't hide from the bitter pain that gnaws at my chest day and night, like a leech sucking me dry. No matter how many times I pour salt on the wound festering in my soul, it will not heal.

It refuses to.

Vibrating gills located on my ribcage suck in the icy cold water, filtering out the oxygen I need to breathe under the surface. I could stay here for hours. Tumbling through the reeds. Seeing how long I can keep my body flat against the pebbled floor. Pretending I don't have a care in the world.

If only I had the time.

But time moves on. It doesn't wait for anyone. Not even the heartbroken.

I flick my tail into motion, propelling myself towards the surface. The miners will be waiting for me. They won't be able to harvest precious gems from the lake bed with clogged pipes. And seeing as I'm the only siren currently available to do it, I throw myself into the task, determined to earn whatever coin I can. Being beholden to another wasn't my choice.

But when have I ever had a choice?

Ahead, pipes loom like skeletal fingers reaching into the lakebed. I wrinkle my nose at the sight. I've been doing this job for a year now. Ever since my father passed.

With a flick of my tail, I reach the pipes to inspect them. It's clear how bad they are, all choked up on silt and debris. Someone should think about installing some newer ones. These are too poorly designed to handle the amount of use they get. I swim closer, trailing my fingers along the rusting metal.

I sigh, releasing a cloud of tiny bubbles from my parted lips. A smile tugs at the corner of my mouth as I watch them rush to the surface, sacrificing themselves to the air as they break free.

The sooner I finish this job, the quicker I can start my second one.

The first pipe is the worst—its intake is almost completely blocked with algae and tiny jagged stones. I peer into the dark opening, pulling at the stubborn knots of plant matter. The algae resists at first, slimy and tangled, but I've done this a thousand times before so I know how to work around it. With a rough tug, my fingers slice through the toughest strands with ease, and soon, the mess begins to loosen.

Jagged stones are trickier to deal with, lodged so deep that I have to brace myself against the pipe to push them free. My muscles strain as I shove, the rough edges biting into my palms. Finally, with a satisfying crunch, the blockage bursts loose, and a gush of water rushes into the pipe, sending another, larger stream of bubbles spiralling upward.

My mind numbs as I move from pipe to pipe, the twitch of my tail holding me steady as I work. Fish dart around me, curious and quick, their silver bodies catching the light as they pass.

With the last pipe clear, I pause, letting the lake settle around me. The water is calm now, the pipes humming with a sound I know all too well. It's almost a comfort to hear them. Down here I can fully be myself. No one can hear me—or see me cry. Not that I've done that for a while.

I break the surface, sighing softly as I tilt my face to the pale orange sky. The air smells clean, untouched by the work of the day. I stay in the water for a moment, looking back at the rippling surface of the lake. It's time to face the day.

Without another thought, I pull on the invisible thread inside my chest. The one that connects me to my human form. I gently ease it towards my heart, internally asking my siren form to allow my legs to appear. She listens with eagerness. The shift is always strange, a mix of exhilaration and discomfort. I concentrate on the pull of my human body, the bones in my tail tingling as they begin to break apart and reshape.

The weight of my pale limbs leave me breathless. I float for a moment, disoriented, the burden of my body unfamiliar after so long in the water. A flock of birds race across the sky above me, kicking me into action.

As I reach the water's edge and begin to stand, my periwinkle cotton dress suddenly reappears, soaking up the liquid on my skin. Its hem drags in the water as I wade towards the shore, each step slow and deliberate as I adjust to the solid earth beneath me. My toes sink into the soft silt, and I steady myself, brushing wet hair away from my face. Warm, morning air kisses my damp skin as I step onto the grassy bank, droplets trailing down my legs. A large sheet of cloth is folded neatly on top of my leather boots. I always bring it with me so I can dry myself down.

Once I've squeezed all the water from my hair, I twist it up into a knot on top of my head. Sometimes I wish I had inherited my mother's curls, but unfortunately I received my father's straight hair. At least it's glossy.

I take a deep breath, gather my bag and start towards town, but not before I send a friendly wave to the miners back on the shoreline. They shout their thanks and I offer them a gentle smile.

Once again, I tell myself that today is going to be a good day. I'll get loads of orders done and maybe—just maybe my to-do list will look a little smaller.

With a bounce in my step, I hurry along. Father's shop isn't going to open itself and the candles will only get finished if I actually do the work.

Don't get me wrong. I love making candles. I just wish I had time to make the designs I wanted to, not just the ones my father always insisted on. *"People want candles to burn, to light their homes. We aren't an art shop, Juni. We don't have the time."* The debt made sure that was true. There was never time to stop and question the process. Now, with just me in the shop, I can't afford to question any of it. I keep my head down. Nose to the grindstone. Wicks in the wax—.

"Morning, Juniper!"

The sound of Maggie's voice brings a smile to my face. She's been a wonderful friend to my mother for as long as I can remember.

I turn and wave. "Hello, beautiful Maggie!" There's no time to stop and chat, so I keep moving. There's a good chance I'll see her later today anyway. Since my father passed a year ago, she's made it her business to check in with my mother almost daily. It definitely helped my mother's grieving process.

Which in turn I suppose has helped mine too . . . A little.

Cobblestone streets glisten with morning dew as I scurry along. The air carries the faint scent of baking bread and damp earth. It won't be long until the sun dries up the dew and I'll be wishing I was back in the lake, immersed in the deep waters, cool and hidden from the heat.

Vendors shuffle into place, their carts creaking under the weight of goods—fresh produce, bolts of fabric, bundles of herbs. The chatter of early risers blending with the distant clanging of Theon's—the blacksmith's—hammer. Above me, swallows dart between rooftops, their sharp cries a playful greeting to the day. Meadowbrook is alive, not in a loud or flashy way, but in the quiet hum of people and purpose. It feels like the town itself is exhaling, ready to embrace whatever the day might bring.

I reach the chandlery. Instantly my eye is drawn to the raised wooden slats on the step, worn with age and missing nails. I sigh as I look over at the cracked glass in the front window. So many things need attention, yet no one in town is interested in such small jobs, or they are too expensive, and I myself don't have the time. Papa always took care of the handiwork around the shop, and home. He was so good with keeping on top of it all, if only he'd been just as diligent with money. Too many times he'd borrowed more than the shop could pay back—his dream was for it to succeed, so I'd do anything to keep his dream alive.

Glancing up at the worn sign, I can still make out the image of a thin cream candlestick sitting snugly inside a bronze holder. Father painted it himself the day before he opened the chandlery. I've been meaning to get it touched up. I can barely make out the words anymore.

*Fairchilds' Candlesticks*

The whisper of my last name falls from my trembling lips. The name bestowed upon me the moment I was born into the world.

With a quick brush across my nose, I force the tears back down. I don't have time to cry today. There is too much debt to repay.

I turn the iron key, pushing the door open as I step inside. The scent of beeswax, lavender and honey greet me, a comforting smell that reminds me of the long day ahead. A morning of unclogging pipes, and then making candles until dinner time. Some days, I wish my life was different. That perhaps I could stay in bed all morning, or spend time in the garden more often. Maybe I could sit down, design new candles, and scents, then actually make them. But my life isn't different and there's nothing I can do about it. Mama needs me, and this shop is the only thing we have left of my father. His life's work.

I just have to figure it out.

As predicted, the mountain of orders that await my arrival is overwhelming. Yet, each time a customer wandered into the shop throughout the day and ordered more, I couldn't say no. How could I? It didn't matter how I felt towards the labour at hand. Money was a necessity—especially when the business owed as much as it did. My father hadn't intentionally left my mother and I with this burden. Yet, he'd done it all the same. And with mama's bad back, it was only I that could carry the load.

I sigh, dragging my finger down the page to see how many orders I have to finish before day's end.

The bell above the shop door rings. I glance up to meet my sweet mother's gaze. Her dark-brown hair, the same colour as mine, is peppered with greys. Twin orbs of sparkling green light up when they see me.

"You forgot to eat breakfast before you left this morning"—she smiled, holding out her hand—"and now it's past lunch time."

I take the paper-wrapped parcel, opening it with gentle fingers. Inside is a baguette of wholemeal bread, stuffed with all my favourite fresh, homegrown greens: lettuce, tomato, rocket and even some sliced cucumbers. She'd even remembered a small wedge of cheese.

"Thank you, Mama. In my rush out the door, I simply forgot."

Mother squeezes my arm as she moves past me to take her place in the back room. "I know, my love."

She does the books for the shop and I'm ever so grateful. There is already enough I'm dealing with.

"How were the miners this morning?" mother calls from the back.

"Oh, the same, really. Appreciative of my skills."

"Do you think you might stop soon? Allow yourself some time to do things that you love to do?"

I huffed softly to myself. "You know I can't."

Mother pokes her head around the side of the door and looks at me with a softness that tugs at my heart. "Juniper Fairchild, you're twenty-five years old. You're allowed to have fun. Your father's business isn't going to crumble in one day."

The use of my full name is a mix of pride and sadness.

My shoulders feel heavy as I shrug. "I know. I just want to get on top of things. There will be time for fun later."

The light in mother's eyes dims. She presses her lips into a thin line and nods.

I know she means well. But if we don't get through all of these orders on time, I'm going to have unhappy customers and then the debt will climb even higher because no one will want to order from us.

Now is not the time for dwelling, so I shove the wave of emotions clawing at my chest further down inside my soul. They can stay there for a little while longer. I'll deal with them later.

Right now, candlesticks need making.

The scent of melted beeswax and lavender fills the shop as I dip the wick into the pot, the molten wax clinging to it in smooth layers. My hands move in a practiced rhythm, the motion almost meditative as I hang the candlestick to cool and prepare the next.

Across the room, mother sits at the counter, her glasses perched on the bridge of her nose as she scratches away at the ledger with her quill. The faint sound of numbers being whispered under her breath mingles with the soft crackle of the fireplace. She rubs her back, unaware that I can see the pain she masks behind her smile. This is why I have to keep going. I don't have a choice. Without Father's shop, we would've sold our house months ago and who knows where we'd be living—what we'd eat.

I don't mind making candles, in fact, I always loved working for Papa. But he was resistant to change and now that he's gone, I've found I'm more like him than I realised.

My aching heart dances across the room and draws my mother into a warm embrace. It's comforting to have her close.

"The numbers are looking great this month, Juni," she murmurs. Her face is lined with concentration.

I drop my gaze back to the candlestick in my hand. "Doesn't mean we can afford to slow down."

She doesn't lift her eyes from the paper, scratching some more numbers in ink. "Have the wicks arrived yet?"

My heart drops to my stomach. I've been waiting for over a week for the supply of wicks. It wasn't like this particular supplier to be late.

I wipe the back of my hand across my damp forehead. The fire keeping the wax melted is too warm for this time of year. "It hasn't arrived, no, and I'm concerned."

"Have you contacted them?"

"No, I was waiting until today to see if perhaps I was worrying over nothing."

Mother nods, checking another page. "Without that shipment we won't make it through the orders scheduled for next month."

It's true. And despite what the books look like now, doesn't mean they wouldn't turn pear shaped in a heartbeat.

The bell above the shop door jingles and I scurry out the front, wiping my hands on my apron. Thoughts of wicks will have to be shelved for a moment.

I put on my bravest smile, ready to greet more customers, but I'm pleasantly surprised with who skips through the door. Dove smiles, her energy lighting up the room like the first rays of dawn. Her petite frame is bundled in a patchwork dress that she's obviously made herself, because it looks nothing like what the dressmakers in town sew. She's always been crafty like that, even when we were young girls making flower crowns and seashell necklaces.

"Good morning, my favourite lady!" she chirps, her silver eyes glinting mischievously as she reaches the front desk. I can't help but grin at her appearance. She's the quirkiest elf I know with her pixie-cut hair, dyed a soft blue.

"Morning, Dove."

"It always smells so delicious here. What is it? Lavender? I want to bottle the scent and carry it everywhere I go. We shall call it *ambience*." She leans casually against the counter, her sharp ears twitching slightly as she picks up on the scents wafting through the shop.

Folding my arms across my chest, I lean on the counter to match her height. "I promise to save you any candles I can't sell."

The gleam of joy in Dove's eyes radiates. "You're the bestest friend I could ever ask for, Juni."

I offer her a small smile. Her words don't settle in my soul happily. No, they churn about my stomach, fighting to be free. I don't feel like I'm the best. I'm aware that there have been many times in the last year that I've abandoned our friendship. Though not intentionally.

Dove places her hands behind her back and strides around the room, looking at all the coloured candles I have on display. As I watch her I can already tell why she's here. I'm just waiting for her to say it.

"Juniper Fairchild. You're coming out with me tonight, no excuses. The tavern's got music, dancing, and—oh!—new cider. It's practically a crime if we don't go."

There it is. The reason she's here. I can't help but grin. "Sounds tempting, but I can't, Dove. I've got so many orders to finish, and the festival's coming up. I'll never catch up if I take the night off."

Dove groans dramatically, flopping onto a nearby stool. "You're killing me here! Do you ever stop working? You're turning into one of those serious shopkeepers who forgets how to have fun."

I try not to laugh. She's trying ever so hard to be cross with me.

With a sigh, I shove my hands into my apron pockets. "I am not serious. I just . . . Have responsibilities. Big difference."

"Uh-huh. And when's the last time you did something just for you? Something wild? Hmm?"

Mother pops her head around the corner. "I heartily agree with you, Dove!"

"Oh, Mama Fairchild! I didn't know you were here!" Dove exclaims as she jumps from the stool to take mother in a gentle embrace.

"I've tried to encourage her to do something for herself as well. But it seems as if our Juni is as stubborn as her father was."

I roll my eyes at both of them. "Well, when either of you have the load of an entire shop on your shoulders, then we will see how you act."

Mother's eyes soften. I can tell I've touched on a sore subject. She's told me before that she feels guilty that she can't help me more.

"You both know I need to stay here," I add softly.

Mama injured her back a few years ago, which makes it hard for her to stand, though she does as much as she can from a stool. She takes care of so many things at home, so really, the work evens itself out.

I return to the back of the shop, calling over my shoulder. "Now, both of you leave me to my work."

Dove pokes her head around the door and rolls her pretty silver eyes. "Fine, but don't work too hard, Juni. I expect you to have at least one fun thought while I'm gone. Just one!"

"I'll try my best, Dove. No promises."

Mother moves to close the ledger with a soft thud, gathering her bag before turning to face me. "Well, I think that's enough bookkeeping for one day. I'll see you at home later, sweetheart."

I hope the smile I offer her masks my internal pain. "Thanks, Mama. Don't wait up—I'll be here late."

She walks to the door with Dove, turning to look at me one more time. "Don't overdo it, Juni. The work will still be here tomorrow."

The laughter that escapes my lips is soft. "I know, but it won't get done by itself either."

Two of my favourite people leave and the shop is once again quiet except for the crackle of the flames. I spend the next few minutes re-dipping the batch of candles I'm working on and hanging them to drip dry. My thoughts travel back to the missing wicks. The supplier is over a week's ride away in a town called Stone's Ridge. Perhaps I should write them a letter. Surely there's an explanation and it will all be sorted before I know it.

A lovely orange glow from the setting sun pierces the window, travelling along the floor and up my skirts as I enter the front of the shop again. The writing paper is stashed under the front counter.

The scratching of my ink pen on the textured surface sends a tingle through my brain and down my spine. Sounds like this make me feel peaceful. It's odd, but I like it.

I've just finished my inquiry letter when the doorbell jangles again. I glance up, thinking it might be Dove returning to torment me some more, but the figure is framed by the sun. The silhouette is much too tall and broad to be Dove.

They step forward, further into the shop, and I can finally see a face. One that I've never seen before, and I feel like I know most people in town.

Warmth spreads up from my neck into my cheeks as the male's eyes travel over me. Blue, like sapphires. Framed with dark brows and lashes. His hair is blond though, the colour of pale wheat. The sides are cut close to his skull, but the top is longer—messy—as if he's just run his fingers through it.

His square jawline is clean shaven, which draws my eyes to the ink markings on his throat that disappear down into the collar of his dark grey shirt.

How long I stare at him, I'm not sure. Time seems to have stopped. I know it's rude to stare, but the longer I look, the harder it is to find my words. My heart is doing something weird in my chest and no matter how many intentional breaths I take in, it refuses to slow down.

I finally clear my throat, clasping my trembling hands behind my skirts. "Can I help you?"

The male takes a turn about the room, his fingers lingering on a pile of forest green candlesticks. "I was just admiring the craftsmanship—though I have to admit, the view is far more captivating." His eyes flick up to meet mine.

I feel an instant flush creep into my cheeks, embarrassed that he's staring at me so intently, but I can't seem to look away.

I clear my throat. "Did you need some candles?"

He shakes his head.

My brow knits together. "So, what do you need?"

He runs his tongue along the inner seam of his bottom lip. "I'm here to offer my services."

"What kind of services?" My words come out less confident than I hoped they would.

He wanders back to the front desk, shoving his inked hands into his black trouser pockets. My eyes linger on his body for a moment as they travel up to meet his sapphire-blue eyes again, which are raised in intrigue.

What am I doing? I'm gawking at this male like I've never seen a man before. Well, not one like this at least. Practical Juniper would be slapping me so hard right now, telling me to get it together.

"Handy work. Fixing things. You provide the supplies. I provide the labour." His voice is deep and smooth. Like the polished obsidian stones I find on the lakebed. Dark, sleek, and flawless, with an almost mesmerising quality. "I noticed the sign on your shop is faded and there is a pane of glass in the window that has a crack through it," he continues.

I find myself nodding. Still staring at his face. Now that he's closer, I can see the silver ring in his septum. There are two more, one in each earlobe. And he has three straight lines marked into his skin to the side of his left eye, just above his cheek bone. There aren't many folk around here who look like this. The way his ears are rounded too, tells me that he isn't elven. At least I don't think so.

"Oh, umm, yes. I've been meaning to get those fixed."

"I could do it for you?"

His scent washes over me. Patchouli and cedarwood. Who is this stranger? And why am I nodding again? How is his presence unexpectedly disarming and different from anyone else I've met before?

Shifting from one foot to the other, I stumble over my words. "I don't have a lot to offer in the form of payment, but I could spare a few copper coins?"

He nods, a smile playing at his very nice looking lips.

Goodness, why am I looking at his mouth!?

"What about food?" His smooth voice slips over me and I feel warmth pool between my legs. I will be giving myself a serious scolding later for behaving this way. I usually keep myself so put together.

"Sorry, what did you say?"

That boyish smile tugs at his lips again. "Can you cook?"

I nod. "I wouldn't call myself a chef, but I haven't killed anyone yet." My hand slaps across my mouth. What is wrong with me? And what would Mama say? It's as if all my common sense flew out the door the moment the stranger walked in.

"Seems as though payment has just been sorted then?"

I'm not sure the shop can afford any extra outgoings at the moment, even if it's in dire need of some tender loving care. Yet, I can't seem to stop my words from tumbling out. Especially when only just this morning I'd been thinking of the much needed shop repairs.

His eyes glitter as he smiles. I can't help but smile back, easing my hand away. "Well, I suppose copper coins and dinner in exchange for some help could be arranged?"

"I thought you'd never ask."

I swear if I looked in a mirror right now, my face would be beet red. Never in my life have I ever met someone so confident in themselves. I think it's confidence. I mean, how would I know? I don't even know the guy.

"I suppose if you're to do work for me, I should know your name?"

He pulls a hand from his pocket, extending it towards me in greeting. "Saint . . . Saint Everhart."

As soon as my fingers brush his honey-coloured ones, a current runs up my arm and stabs me in the heart. Like an invisible rope that has attached itself to my soul without even asking for permission. His sapphire eyes lock onto me, holding me in place. I can't even find my breath.

My hand squeezes his for a brief second. "Juniper."

"It's nice to meet you, Juniper." His eyes flick to my lips and back up. Suddenly, I feel quite self conscious. I must look a right mess with my wax covered apron. Not to mention the loose hair strands sticking to my clammy skin.

"Would the price be dependent on the list of repairs?" I pose.

Saint shakes his head. "Tell me what you need done."

I wipe my forehead with the back of my hand, desperate for some relief from the heat in the room. "Shall I write you a list of things that need repairing?"

Saint nods. "That would be great—I love lists."

I quickly scribble down all the things I can think of, realising just how much I've abandoned the shop. Maybe it's a good thing that this stranger has come along. "Here." I hold the list out to him.

He scans it quickly before picking up the pen to scribble on the back. Saint hands the list back to me. "These are the supplies I will need. Also if you have any tools I could borrow, I'd appreciate it."

"Of course. Let me show you what I have." Before I can question myself, my feet carry me out into the back room.

The sun is just starting to dip, casting gentle shadows over the small courtyard behind the shop as I push open the back door. The faint scent of beeswax and herbs fades, replaced by the heaviness of the summer evening air. Saint follows me out, hands stuffed in his pockets, his gaze curious as it sweeps the cluttered workspace.

"So," I say, brushing my hands on my apron, "you'll need nails, a saw, a set of chisels . . . what else?"

"Wood glue, maybe a hammer. And a rasp if you have one," he replies, his voice steady.

I nod, leading him towards the storage bench tucked into the corner. "I have most of that already. My dad . . . He was always the handyman around here." My words falter slightly as my eyes drift to the wooden rack mounted on the wall. His tools.

It has been a whole year since they'd been touched by his broad, rough hands. For months, I couldn't even bring myself to touch them. The sight of his careful organisation too much to bear. But now . . . now they'll finally have purpose again. A part of him still lingering in the work they'll do.

Saint's gaze follows mine. "Those his?" he asks gently.

I nod, swallowing down the threatening tears. "They haven't been used in a long time." I force a small smile and look up at him. "But I'd rather see them working than gathering dust."

The male with the pale wheat hair and sapphire eyes gives a quiet nod, his expression unreadable but somehow softer. "I'll take care of them."

I shake my head, clearing my thoughts. I don't have time to open that floodgate of emotions. Especially in the company of a stranger.

A very . . . Very good looking stranger.

I gesture to the bench, clearing my throat as I pull out a drawer filled with nails and sandpaper. "The only thing I can't help with is paint," I admit.

For some reason, I just couldn't bring myself to re-paint the shop sign. Too afraid that I might mess it up. So why was I letting Saint do it? Something in me just wanted to trust him. Maybe it was the confidence in his stride and the way he held my gaze. The gaze that I was struggling to keep mine from.

Saint leans his sculpted-from-marble figure against the back door frame. "I can source paint."

"That would be wonderful," I say, fiddling with my apron. "And when can you start?"

"Would tomorrow morning be alright?"

I nod. "And dinner?"

Saint, straightens, folding his inked hands across his broad chest. "How about after half the list is done? That way, you can see my work."

He is standing close—too close. Yet, I don't move away. Looking up into his eyes, I nod again. "I'm alright with that."

"Great." Saint shifts his weight on the door frame. "So, boss, anything about the shop I should know?"

I bite down on the urge to smile, but it's a losing battle. There's something about him—something effortless—that tugs at a side of me I don't usually let slip free. I'm not one to be so bold, yet with him, it feels inevitable, like he coaxes it out of me without even trying.

"Only that it gets hot inside during the day, so I wouldn't bother fixing that pretty hair of yours." I instantly regret the words as soon as they leave my mouth.

A smirk tugs at his lips. "So you think I'm pretty?"

The audacity of this man has my heart doing somersaults. "I think I'm going to regret this in the morning."

Saint chuckles in response.

I clear my throat, hoping he doesn't notice the warmth rising in my cheeks. Suddenly, I'm aware of the time and how late it's getting. I still have a mountain of orders to get through, so I break the spell he's cast upon me with his suave character and spin on my heel, heading back inside without a sound.

Saint follows, closing the door behind us.

The front of the shop is dim, the setting sun taking its brightness with it. It's time for me to light some candles and lanterns so I can continue my work. I'll wait until Saint leaves. My hand won't hold a flame steady while he is in the room.

Patchouli and cedarwood waft over me as he walks past, making his way to the front door. It takes all of my self-control not to breathe him in. Because that's weird, right? Only someone not in their right mind would do that.

Saint pauses at the door, turning as his hand rests on the brass handle. "So, I'll see you in the morning then, Juniper?"

I nod. Forgetting my words again.

A smirk spreads across his face. "I'll let you get back to your candle-dipping."

His playfulness reaches inside my chest, beckoning my heart to come out and play. And for a split second, I let it. "And I'll let you get back to . . . what exactly is it you do?"

Saint huffs, apparently amused. "Careful, Juniper. You almost sound curious."

With a wink, he disappears into the fading light.

I stand alone in the shop. My heart is beating from my chest. I clutch it with a hand, leaning the other against the edge of the counter. Trying to catch my breath. What in all of this green earth just happened? One part of my mind whispers of trouble, that I should be careful.

The other part doesn't want to listen at all.

Four

## TRUST IS A DANGEROUS THING

Small glass jars filled with coloured paint clink inside my leather satchel as I walk to the chandlery. Surely it was okay to steal them if it was doing a good deed for someone else, right?

It's no big deal. The stable master clearly isn't going to miss it. I found them at the back of the cupboard in the loft—covered in a thick layer of dust. They haven't been used in a long time.

Morning sun washes the streets in golden light. I keep myself moving, eyes to the ground, not making contact with the few townsfolk who pass by. I'd risen early, not wanting to be late to meet Juniper.

Besides, it's not like I took everything from the cupboard. I left the rusted horseshoes, a bunch of rope, and the small carved wooden horse, forgotten by someone years ago. The moment I spotted it my chest felt heavy.

Suddenly, I was back in the orphanage, staring at other kids clutching toys they refused to share. I never had one of my own—nothing to call mine except the hunger twisting my stomach. Back then, I used to dream about things like that horse—a little carved figure, something to hold on to when the nights got too long.

All of that was in the past now.

I move through town as effortlessly as I can, and as my feet carry me towards the shop, my heart climbs higher into my throat. The sheets on my bed were in knots this morning after all the tossing and turning I'd done after shifting back. I tried to go back to sleep, but it was pointless.

A certain woman has consumed my mind.

I step aside as someone approaches on my right. There is a fine balance of being friendly and drawing unwanted attention. I'm grateful the blacksmith is on the other side of town. I hadn't made my acquaintance with that bearded fellow from when I first arrived, and I didn't plan to.

The chandlery came into view. I slowed, taking a few deep breaths. The physical effect Juniper has on me is not something I'm used to. I'm used to women of the night throwing themselves at me for a few scattered moments of pleasure at Donovan's parties. Usually I flash them a grin, tell them how pretty they are and sometimes take them to bed. But it never meant anything. Just hollow hearts trying to find some form of comfort in one another.

But with Juniper, I want to *know* her. I want to dive into her soul and fish out every thought and secret that makes her who she is.

The bell jangles as I push the door open. It is quiet inside, but I know she's here. Honey and vanilla betray her presence.

Her boots sound on the wooden floor as she appears from the backroom, tying a cream apron around her waist.

*By the light.* She is fucking perfect.

Eyes the colour of a sun setting over a meadow: moss green edges bleeding into sunburnt orange. They hold me captive like invisible chains wrapped around my feet, forcing me to be still. Her chocolate hair is braided, hanging down the middle of her back.

"Morning." I manage to fumble over the words.

"Hello."

Her voice is soft, as if she's afraid to speak, and for once, I have lost my words.

I clear my throat and take the list from my pocket. I must have read it a thousand times on my way back to the stables, running my fingers over the words she'd written. There must be something wrong with me. Never have I ever experienced these feelings towards a woman before.

Not that I'd ever really been allowed. Or maybe I didn't allow it, because allowing someone close to me put them in Donovan's line of vision.

The last place I want someone I love to be.

Rocking back on my heels, I shove my hands into my pockets. "Shall I get started on the list then?"

Juniper nods and ushers me out the back. The tools are already laid out on a nearby table—sturdy, well-used, and cared for despite the dust that lingers on them. I run my fingers over the smooth handle of a hammer, appreciating its satin finish. Her father had taken good care of them. I want to ask about him, but it seems as though it's not something Juniper is comfortable with yet, so I remain silent on the subject.

Back at Donovan's estate, whenever we weren't collecting debts, he'd make us repair the house, carriages, broken furniture—consequences from his wild parties. I'd find myself longing for those moments, it meant he would leave me and my brothers alone. It was peaceful, even if it was only for a while.

"Thank you," I utter, finding her gaze.

Her cheeks flush and I bite the inside of my cheek to still the grin that wants to spread across my face. I don't want her to feel uncomfortable with me here, so I pick up some nails, and break the trance that has settled over us.

Juni brushes past me, returning to her candle station, but not before she throws me a glance over her shoulder. "If you need me for anything, I'll be here."

I nod, offering her a smile.

Yesterday, when she'd taken me into the back courtyard, I noticed the hinges on the back door groan, but she hadn't added it to the list. It would take me no time at all, so I start there, oiling and tightening until the sound fades. Then, it's onto a set of shelves in the front of the shop, one corner sagging under the weight of too many jars. I brace it with a few nails and a supporting beam I find in the back. The steady rhythm of work is oddly satisfying—measuring, cutting, hammering.

By midday, I've patched the door, reinforced the shelves, and even mended the stool Juniper kept wobbling on whenever she reached for the high shelves. She hasn't stopped once. It makes me wonder how she manages to find the time to eat.

She was correct in saying how hot it gets in the shop. I feel for her, with the heat of summer and the fire keeping the wax hot. No wonder she told me not to bother with my appearance.

I wipe the sweat on my brow with the back of my hand just as Juni appears at the back door, shading her eyes from the hot sun beating down. "I was about to pour some tea and mother sent scones with me this morning. Would you like some?"

She doesn't need to ask me twice. I place the tools down and run a hand through my hair. The idea of food has me ravenous. "Yes, please."

I follow her inside, making sure to keep my eyes ahead. As much as I would like to stare at Juniper, I'm not sure she'd welcome it, and I'm pretty sure it would count as stalking.

The back room is no cooler than outside, and there's no breeze to relieve the heat. I place a stool near the door, sitting across from Juni, the chair creaking under my weight. The room smells of beeswax and . . . *Her*. It's such a comforting smell. It reminds me of my younger years at the orphanage. I used to help snuff the candles out each night, alongside Roan and Sepehr.

I glance at the scones—golden, crumbly, with a smear of butter melting on top—and my stomach growls before I can stop it.

Juni holds out the plate for me. My eyes flick to her, drinking in her flushed, honey-coloured skin splattered with almond freckles. Beads of sweat cling to her neck, travelling down her chest, and disappearing between her breasts.

My trousers tighten, and I inwardly scold myself. I need to get my thoughts into check and my eyes on her face.

No, that's not working either. Even her face, with her perfect pink lips, makes my dick harden. Calm down boy, we don't even know if she's single.

"Thank you," I murmur, reaching for one. She pours tea into mismatched mugs, steam curling up between us.

"Careful, it's hot," she warns, handing me a cup.

I take it anyway, the ceramic warm in my hands. "So, this is what you do all day?" I say, taking a bite. The scone is soft and buttery, with a hint of sweetness from whatever jam she's used. It tastes like the home I only ever dream about.

Juniper eyes me above the rim of her cup. "Amongst other things."

She's guarding her secrets, and who can blame her? She doesn't know me. Though in the perfect world, I'd do something about that.

"How long has the shop been open?"

"Ten years." Juniper smiles weakly. "But I've only been working here for seven."

Her eyes become dimmer. Like she's left the room, but her body still remains. I have the urge to brush the strands of hair framing her face, but I keep my hands on the plate I'm holding.

"You said it was your father's?"

Juniper comes back from wherever she went in her mind. "Yes, it's . . . Was his."

I sense that she is struggling with the topic of conversation, so I pivot. Maybe she needs some of my charming humour. Something to feel lighter. To help her forget whatever is troubling her. Even if it's only for a moment.

I clear my throat, shifting my weight as an idea forms. "You know," I say, keeping my tone light, "this place really needs a candle that smells like . . . I don't know, wet boots. Or burnt toast. Something classy."

Her head snaps up, a flicker of confusion in her vivid eyes before her perfectly pink lips twitch. "Wet boots? Really?"

"Absolutely. Think of the market potential. Every fisherman in Meadowbrook would be lining up for one." I place the plate down beside me, pretending to be serious. "We could even add a hint of lake water for authenticity. Call it 'Dockside Elegance.'"

I am fighting back the urge to laugh out loud. I sound absolutely ridiculous right now, but if it brings her some joy then I'll keep talking.

Juniper blinks, then laughs—a soft, startled sound like she wasn't expecting it. She shakes her head, the shadows in her expression easing just slightly. "You're ridiculous."

"Ridiculously right, you mean." I grin, straightening up. "Come on, you know you're considering it."

Her smile lingers this time, faint but genuine. It's enough to make me lean in a little closer. "See? That's better," I say. "The shop could use more laughter. And fewer wet boots, probably."

Juniper rolls her eyes, but the tension in her shoulders softens. Whatever was weighing her down, at least for a moment, it doesn't seem so heavy now.

"On a serious note, what's your favourite scent?"

She sips her tea, her eyes darting to the shelf lined with lots of little brown glass bottles. "If I had to choose, I would probably say lavender or bergamot."

I offer her a smile. "They're good choices."

We sit in silence for a moment, the kind that feels easy, not awkward. I watch her take a slow sip of tea, her shoulders relaxing slightly.

"Thanks," I say eventually, holding up the half-eaten scone.

"For the scone?" she asks, a playful glint in her eye.

"For the scone, the tools . . . the job," I say, setting the mug down. "Not everyone would hire someone they barely know."

Juniper shrugs, though her cheeks flush faintly. "Guess I have a soft spot for strays."

I snort, shaking my head. "Well, keep feeding me like this, and I might stick around longer than you hope."

"Wouldn't be the worst thing." She slaps her hand over her mouth in surprise. She did that yesterday too. Shocked at her own words.

Before I can answer, the doorbell jangles, signalling a customer. Juniper scrambles to her feet, rushing out the front, the tails of her apron flying behind her.

I down the last scone, and return to my to-do list. Grinning, the entire time.

Throughout the day, I observe Juniper's work. She moves with a quiet intensity that I can't stop watching. Her hands are steady, precise, dipping wicks into molten wax with the kind of care that speaks of plenty of practice. The way she tucks wisps of hair behind her ear without breaking rhythm, or how her voice softens when she greets a customer, makes her seem like she belongs in this space, as if the shop is alive because she's in it.

It's not just the work—it's her dedication, her passion. I recognise the weight of responsibility in her movements, though hers is different from the kind I've known.

Back in the orphanage, it was all about survival, making sure the younger ones didn't suffer. The loneliness and lack of parents was enough to make your heart break over and over. As I got older, I always did my best to comfort them, to put a smile on their face.

But with Donovan, that was completely different again. Working for him sometimes had its perks. His wild celebrations would mean I was well fed for a few days and could feel the pleasure of a woman from time to time. It also meant he'd leave me and my brothers alone in the days following as he recouped.

Juniper's devotion comes from something deeper—a love for what she's building. Watching her work, I can't help but feel fascinated. There's something about her I've yet to understand, something that draws me closer every time I look.

It's late afternoon as I finish removing the cracked window pane and replace it with a thin board of wood I found out in the back courtyard. I'll have to order some new glass from someone in town. At least for now, the window isn't a safety hazard.

I'm just securing the board into place when I hear someone approach behind me. I can't help but hold my breath. My instincts tell me that someone from Breydon could turn up at any second. And I really don't feel like fighting right now, especially in front of Juniper.

With a quick glance over my shoulder, I'm relieved to find I don't need to fight anyone. An elderly woman shuffles past me and into the shop. She leaves the door wide open, which allows me to hear the conversation between her and Juni. I pause my work, curiosity getting the better of me, and step closer to the doorway.

Juniper's boots click against the wooden floor. "Mrs Olive, how is your husband?"

"Oh he is fine, thank you, Juni. He loved the candle you made him so much that I've come to order some more."

Laughter that sounds like snowflakes—clear and light—drifts out the door. I catch it with my mind and store it away. Saving it so I can play it over and over later.

Juniper catches my eye across the room and my heart does a double flip inside my chest. That invisible thread that tied itself to her the moment I laid eyes on her grows taunt. I try to look as though I'm inspecting the doorframe instead of her. When I glance back, she is focused on Mrs Olive.

"I'm so pleased he likes it," Juniper replies, her tone laced with kindness.

There's a pause, and then the shuffle of coins being exchanged. "I'll be sure to start on them as soon as I can."

Mrs Olive thanks Juniper and leaves. As soon as she is gone, I see Juniper's face drop. It's as though adding more orders to her pile is the last thing she needs to do. Perhaps *she* needs the help more than the shop.

With a sigh, she heads out the back.

It strikes me then how different her world is from the one I've known. My dealings have always been cold, calculated—a ledger to balance, a debt to collect. No one ever thanked me, and I never gave them a reason to. But here she is, giving her cheer and warmth without expecting anything in return.

I finish up and retrieve the tools I was using. There are a few things left on my list and one of those is painting the sign, but I'll have to finish that tomorrow.

My mind lingers on the last few weeks as I cross the room. "Hey, I've finished . . ." I call, rounding the corner with haste.

I don't have time to stop before I collide with Juniper and the wooden box full of cream-coloured candlesticks.

My quick reflexes grapple at the box, but it's no use. The sound of wax smashing against the floor fills the room, shards of candles scattering everywhere like broken glass.

"No!" Juniper cries as she crumples to the floor.

"I—I didn't mean to scare you," I say quickly, but it's too late. Her shoulders slump as she surveys the wreckage.

I feel like such an idiot. I should have called out. Warned her that I was approaching. This is not a great first impression at all.

Her fingers tremble slightly as she picks up a piece of shattered candle. She doesn't say anything, but the way her jaw tightens and her chest heaves makes it clear she's holding back tears.

"I'm so sorry," I express, crouching beside her. "Are you alright? Let me help clean this up."

Is it so odd to think about how much I want to gather her in my arms and hold her until she stops shaking? She's like a leaf trembling in an autumn wind. Her face is pale and her perfectly pink mouth is pressed into a thin line.

I don't know how to handle someone so delicate. I'm used to breaking things instead.

"It's not just the mess," she says quietly after a moment. "These were part of a big order. A wedding this weekend. They needed to be delivered this evening, and now—" Her voice wavers, and she stops.

My stomach twists at the sight of her so defeated. "Okay, so here's what we'll do," I say, as I start to sweep the mess into my hands. "I'll help you make more candles if that's what it takes, or I'll deliver the ones that survived so you can focus on the replacements. Whatever you need, we'll fix it."

Juniper hesitates, her gaze flicking up to mine. I swallow as I take in her beautiful eyes. I can't remember the last time I saw eyes like hers. The way the orange in the centre of her iris bleeds out into the moss-green is breathtaking.

"You would help me?"

I flash her my most charming grin. "Of course. I'm the one who caused this mess in the first place. It's the least I can do."

Juniper doesn't answer me right away. She simply stands and moves over to the wooden table to the left of the room. I let her have some space, cleaning up the mess I accidentally created. Trust me to go and ruin a good thing. She might not even want me to work for her after this.

The pile of broken candles is finally cleaned, but she still hasn't spoken a word. I want to know what is running through her mind, but I'm afraid that if I open my mouth, I'm just going to make it worse.

So I wait.

She turns to face me. My hands are shoved into my pockets as I warily await her scolding. For a long moment, she just looks at me, her eyes searching my face like she's not sure what to do with me. Finally, she nods, her voice barely above a whisper. "Okay. You can deliver them, and I will make some more."

I nod. "Just tell me where to take them, and I will do it right now."

There was plenty of time before the sun disappeared. It set later and later in the summer months. I wouldn't be turning into an owl for a few more hours. Thank the heavens.

Juni pushes off the bench and heads out the back. Without saying anything, I follow her. I'm thankful that the bite of the sun has lessened as I step into the back courtyard. I spot the wooden cart she points to.

"You can use this."

The cart has seen better days. Chunks of wood are missing from the sides, A few too many nails are rusty and need replacing. It also seems to be the only mode of transportation that Juniper has. "Do you always use this?"

She nods. And I note the emotion in her eyes. I'm not sure if it's because of the accident or perhaps the cart holds memories I've yet to discover.

"The candles need to be delivered to the lemon-coloured cottage by the grocers in the middle of town. Do you know the one?"

I shrug, but offer her a smile. "I don't, but I'm certain I can find it. Now what boxes do you need me to carry?"

Juniper shows me the stack and I load them into the cart. I don't know where I'm going, but I'll figure it out. I have to.

She hovers as I lift the cart to start pushing it down the side of the shop. "Can I trust you with those candles?" she asks.

Now's not the time to bear my soul to the stunning woman in the periwinkle dress standing in the doorway of the shop. So I do what I do best. I flash her a smile over my shoulder. Because it feels strange to be trusted—especially when I haven't earned it yet. "Trust is a dangerous thing to give someone like me. Lucky for you, I'm on my best behaviour today."

# Five



## THAT LATE AFTERNOON ORANGE GLOW

Yesterday was emotional. Having Saint in the shop while I worked was a comfort and an inconvenience. A comfort because he made me laugh, something I hadn't done nearly enough of lately. But he was also a maddening inconvenience— because, honestly, how was I supposed to focus when he looked like that? Every stolen glance was a test of willpower, and I was failing spectacularly.

Perhaps today would be different—though I highly doubt it.

Movement at the door demands my attention. I glance up from the order sheet in my hand to see the groom from the wedding candle order poking his head through. I wince internally. He is going to complain about his order, I just know it.

"Morning Juni. The candles were perfect. The delivery guy told us what happened, and there is really no need to panic. We ordered more than we needed to, so don't pressure yourself to make more." He smiles.

Relief washes over me. He's happy? I still feel like I need to replace the broken ones. "Are you sure? I plan on making another box today."

The groom shakes his head. "It's fine really, oh and tell your delivery guy thanks again. He's really something."

I feel my brows pinch. He's talking about Saint, right? Did he do more than deliver the candles? My heart starts to quicken in my chest. Was I about to make amends for a stranger's behaviour? Maybe I shouldn't have trusted Saint at all. He had told me that trust was a dangerous thing to give him.

"I apologise if—"

"There is nothing to be sorry for, Juni. He helped us hang lanterns in the back garden. Given his height and all. He was very helpful."

My shoulders dropped as I let out the breath I was holding in, offering a genuine smile. I'm impressed, to say the least. Not only did he deliver the cart full of candles, he went above and beyond by being helpful. Perhaps my mind is worrying over nothing. Just because he's a stranger doesn't mean he's untrustworthy.

"Well, I'm so pleased he was of help to you. Please tell Trinity I said hello."

The groom nods, sending me a friendly wave as he walks away. It shouldn't be long before Saint arrives, so I head to the back to check my complexion in the small oval mirror that hangs on the back wall.

I don't know why I'm worrying about what I look like. It's not like I'm looking for a distraction in the form of the male figure—Saint being that male figure. *By the light,* what a beautiful figure it was. Tall, lean, muscular . . . Warm skin.

I catch my thoughts, putting them into a sack in my mind. I tie it tightly with thick rope and then scold myself. I was spiralling out of control. Plus, I'm probably not even his type. I'm sure he likes pretty girls—not ordinary looking women like me. What did it matter, anyway? Beauty didn't unclog pipes or keep a shop running day and night. It shouldn't matter what he thinks of me. I need to stay strong. I am strong. I just need to focus on the candles and not let myself get distracted by whatever he's doing.

So why am I fixing my hair in the mirror and why did I wear my rose pink dress that I usually only wear on special occasions?

Deep down, I think I know why. There's a small part of me that notices the way he looks at me—like he might actually like what he sees. Or maybe I'm imagining it, and he's just being polite.

With a sigh, I let my hand fall to my side. There's no time to dwell on this. I have candles to dip, money to earn, and debts to settle. And somewhere in all of that, I still need to post the letter to the wick supplier.

A knock sounds out the front, pulling me from intrusive thoughts. I know it's Saint before I round the corner. It's like my heart can tell when he is near. Which is such a strange thing to experience. Never have I felt this way before. A mix of fear and excitement every time I look at him.

This morning is no different.

"I thought I'd announce my presence, so I don't startle you again." He grins.

Warmth creeps into my cheeks, and inwardly I'm once again scolding myself for not being stronger. A few seconds is all it takes for my body to respond to his glance.

Eyes the colour of glittering sapphires find me. I'm like a snowflake in late winter, melting as soon as the sun touches it. How does he do it? How am I already sucked into his orbit? Floating around like a helpless star in the night, waiting for the sun to rise.

*Get it together Juni.*

I clear my throat and walk towards the front counter, breaking our gaze. "I appreciate it. I can't afford to lose any more candles."

Saint huffs softly. My eyes lift to find him smiling at me. *By the light.* I have no hope of getting anything done today if he keeps looking at me like that. I need to put him to work.

With graceful strides, Saint crosses the room to brush past me. Cedarwood and patchouli follow him. I grip the edge of the front desk, closing my eyes.

He heads for the back door, only stopping to glance back at me when he's halfway outside. "Candles made it safe and sound, but the cart wheel's another story. Needs mending before it falls apart completely."

I let out a sigh, straightening my back and brushing a stray strand of hair out of my face. Of course, it does. "I know," I admit, trying to keep the frustration out of my voice. "It's been on the list for weeks, but it'll have to wait. I can't afford to fix everything at once."

The words feel heavier out loud than they do in my head, and for a moment, silence hangs between us. He glances towards the open door, where the cart is sitting, and then back at me.

"I could take a look at it," he offers, his voice softer now. "Might be able to patch it up until you're ready to replace it."

Why is he being so nice? What have I done to earn his compassion? Perhaps it's only a front and his true intentions are yet to be revealed. That cautious voice inside me stirs, urging me to stay guarded. I know I *should* listen, but I don't want to—not when he looks at me like that. Like he's seen into my soul and he's not afraid of all the sadness he finds there.

"Thank you," I manage to whisper. "Though don't go out of your way."

Saint shrugs, flashing that boyish grin that sends my heart into an erratic state. "It's no trouble, really. Especially if it earns me a warm meal at the end of the day."

Dinner.

I push down the flicker of panic rising in my chest. I hadn't forgotten, not really—I'd just chosen to tuck it away. Cooking wasn't exactly my strong suit, and Mama and I didn't live in Meadowbrook's finest house. It was small. Too small, maybe. I couldn't help but glance at Saint and wonder if he'd even fit comfortably in the space, given his height. He had to be close to six feet tall. Father wasn't the tallest, so our home never needed elevated ceilings.

It's been years since I've invited anyone into my personal life. So why now? Why am I taking this step with a stranger?

Suddenly, the candles in my hand are very interesting to look at. I fiddle with them, trying to centre my thoughts before I look at him again. "I can't promise it will be worth writing home about."

Saint shrugs, drumming his fingers on the wooden door frame. "Just as well they don't need to know." There is a light in his eyes that I can't explain. Glowing brighter each time we exchange words. I can't help but smile at him.

He winks and disappears around the corner. I finally drop my shoulders, sucking a breath into my lungs. If I'm going to get through this day, I need to focus.

Dinner would be here soon enough.

Late afternoon brings that orange glow—that I love—to the front room. The way it dances through the glass window, morphing itself across the wooden floor, makes it feel as if the room is full of flickering flames.

Quite fitting for a shop filled with candles.

I'd managed to keep to myself most of the day, serving customers and dipping candle after candle. It's relaxing work, even if it is tedious. Unfortunately, the wicks still haven't arrived, which means I need to get the letter into the post on my way home.

Saint spent most of his time out the back. He seemed to prefer the outdoors over the confines of the shop, and I can't blame him. It was too hot anyway. He was painting the sign— which he refused to show me, saying I had to wait until he was finished. I didn't know whether to be calm or worried. But I settled on calm. There was no point fretting about something that I had refused to do myself.

Leather boots scuff against the wooden floor behind me. I find myself feeling flustered already, knowing he's about to be close enough for me to see the flecks of sapphire-blue in his eyes.

"I think I've done all I can do today, Juniper. I need to let the paint on the sign dry before I can finish the final touches." Saint hovers beside me, looking over my shoulder as I continuously dip candle sticks. Twisting slightly, I glance behind me.

His nearness sends a shiver up my spine. I let it wash over me. Filling all the dry, empty cracks of my soul that have gone so long without water.

I turn to face him. "You can call me Juni, if you like."

Saint's gaze slowly travels over my face, resting on my mouth. Instantly, that unfamiliar warmth pulses low in my stomach. I look at his lips too and wonder what they would feel like on my own. Here I go again, losing all control.

"Tell me, *Juni* . . . How does one make a candle?" Saint asks, a curious tilt to his voice. "It's fascinating seeing all the different shapes and sizes."

My body warms at the use of my name. Usually, only people I know call me Juni, but it felt so natural to offer the nickname after hearing him say my full name all the time.

I smile, setting down the wick I've been threading. "Well, it's quite the process. Though each candle follows a different set of rules."

Saint nods, folding his arms across his chest as he leans his hip against the counter. "And what are all of the candles you're working on?"

His blond hair falls across his forehead, and I instinctively want to brush it from his face. However, he would most certainly think that was too forward of me, so I keep my hands to myself.

Needing to focus on something else, I turn back to the table and start pointing at the bunches of candles hanging from a rack. "Some are for weddings, some for ceremonies, and others just for people who like their homes smelling better than their livestock."

That earns a chuckle from him. "Fair enough. So, what's the secret? Magic wax? Enchanted wicks?"

I roll my eyes but can't help grinning. "No magic. Just patience and a lot of practice." I walk over to a small rack and pick up one of my carving tools. "See these? I use them to make designs—flowers, initials, patterns, whatever people ask for." I gesture to a row of carved candles on the shelf, their intricate designs catching the light. "Though, I don't take too many orders for them, as they take longer than simple candlesticks, and father always said people prefer them simple and reliable, so it's almost silly of me to offer anything else."

He steps closer to get a better look, his brows lifting in appreciation. "That's impressive, though. I'd probably end up with a stick figure if I tried."

I laugh, the sound surprising even to me. My cheeks warm at the sudden outburst of joy. It seems as though Saint seems to bring out that dormant side of me. "Stick figures don't sell well, I'm afraid." I move to the pot of wax warming on the fire. "And over here, this is where the dipping happens. You have to layer it slowly to get the right thickness."

He watches as I demonstrate, dipping the wick into the boiling wax, pulling it out in one smooth motion. "You make it look easy," he says, his voice low and soft. "I'm pretty sure I'd drop that thing right in and end up with a lump of wax instead of a candle."

I turn to face him. Only to discover just how close he is. I swallow the desire coiling in my chest, shoving it down as far as it will go. "Just as well you're good at using other tools."

A grin tugs at the corner of his mouth. And as my mind catches up, I've realised what I've just said. He is going to think I'm the most daft woman in all of Meadowbrook—or Sapphire Vale, for that matter.

Not wanting to make a fool of myself anymore, I quickly douse the fire and lock the back door. "We should probably go. I need to post a letter on my way home."

# Six

The walk into town earns Saint and I some side glances from the townsfolk. I can sense it makes him a little uneasy. The way he keeps his head down low and his inked hands shoved into his trouser pockets is a dead giveaway. Perhaps he just doesn't like the attention. To be honest, neither do I.

As soon as I have this damn letter posted, we can leave.

It feels heavy in my hand, like it's the tipping point of whether the shop will thrive or fail. I do hope it's the former. It would be devastating to see my father's business crumble to the ground. All his hard work—and mine—wasted.

This letter must get to the supplier in time, because I am running out of wicks.

I flick my gaze up at Saint. He strolls beside me silently, though his shoulders and jaw are stiff. He's observing our surroundings with close intent, almost like he's waiting for someone to jump out at us.

"Is everything alright?" I murmur.

He glances down, drawing his mouth up into a faint smile. "Of course. Why do you ask?"

I shrug. "You seem tense?"

Saint pulls a hand free from his pocket, running it through his hair. "I'm fine. New towns are just—new—and I've never cared much for crowds."

I offer a gentle smile. "I know what you mean. I like the quiet too."

"Afternoon, Juniper!" a stallholder calls out. I offer them a friendly smile paired with a wave, but keep walking. I'm too tired for more conversation.

My shadow in the form of a man trails behind me as I round the corner. I can see the post shop ahead. It's a few buildings down from the grocers, which reminds me. Mama asked if I would stop by and purchase some green brussel sprouts. She was more than excited when I told her that someone was coming for dinner.

Hopefully, I won't regret it.

It doesn't take me long to post the letter and purchase the brussel sprouts. Then, with a quickened pace, I hurry home. Saint walks beside me, his stride easy. The late afternoon sun bathes Meadowbrook in warm golden light, and I can't help but glance around at the familiar streets—the cobblestone roads I know like the back of my hand, the way the shop windows reflect the light, the hum of townsfolk going about their business. It truly is a beautiful place to live.

As we near the edge of town, I spot Theon—the blacksmith—on the other side of the street. He's smoking a cigar as he strides along. I raise a hand and wave. "Hi, Theon!" I call out.

He glances up briefly, his dark eyes meeting mine. For a moment, he seems like he's about to respond, but instead, he gives me a quick nod and a tight smile before glancing at Saint, and continues his journey. The cigar in his hand raises, ready for another drag, as though he's decided his leisures need more immediate attention than a simple hello.

I lower my hand, biting the inside of my cheek. "Perhaps he's in a hurry," I mouth, trying to sound casual, though the dismissiveness stings a little.

"Doesn't seem like much of a people person," Saint remarks, his tone neutral but carrying a hint of curiosity. "Friend of yours?"

"Yes," I say, my gaze still lingering on Theon's forge as we pass by. "I've known him since I was a child. We've been friends for a long time."

"Hmm." Saint's response is noncommittal, but I feel his eyes on me. I wonder what he's thinking, but I don't ask. Instead, I focus on the sound of our footsteps on the road and the weight of the sky growing softer and pinker as the sun sinks lower.

I feel my whole body relax the moment I push open the front gate to home. It squeaks on its hinges, a loud reminder that I need to fix that too.

Saint seems to hesitate behind me. So I usher him in with a hand. "I promise the garden won't bite."

His gaze flicks to mine as he steps through, and I can feel this invisible pull towards him. I need to stop it. I need to focus on my job and how I'm going to manage to keep the shop afloat with the mountain of debt my father left me. Not the way Saint's inked hands are running over the forget-me-nots in the garden bed. Or how his fingers delicately brush the tall, blue delphiniums reaching their long stems out to catch our garments as we stroll past.

He seems to linger on them longer than a male would. Perhaps he's not seen these sorts of flowers before?

Saint tarries by the morning glory vine that is strangling the garden arch. All the sapphire-blue blossoms are blooming. Despite its abundance and the way it likes to take over everything in its path, it's one of my favourites. As well as the cornflowers.

"If I get attacked by an angry carrot, I'm out of here," He grins.

His blue eyes find mine and I can't help but smile. He has this way of making me feel like the sun follows wherever he goes—perhaps it always has.

My foot pauses on the bottom step. "I'll come too."

I swear the smile dancing on my lips is bigger than usual. Before Saint can respond, the cottage door flings open—also squeaking on its hinges—and mama steps outside. Her face is beaming with joy as she hobbles closer.

"Mama, this is Saint. He's been working at the shop. Fixing things."

"Juniper Fairchild allowing someone to help?" Mama teases. "It's unheard of."

I roll my eyes, but can't help but smile.

Saint stretches out his hand. "Mrs Fairchild, it's lovely to meet you."

Mama shakes his hand, her gaze laced with softness. "Please, call me Kamari. Mrs Fairchild is for old folk."

Mother never cared much for formalities. It's why everyone loves her so much. She is so accepting and kind to everyone.

Saint grins. "As you wish. Your home is lovely."

He's being polite. Sure, our home isn't horrid, humble at best, but it is kind of him to say so. I need to step away from his closeness. His scent is making me feel light headed—in a good way.

I clear my throat, handing mama the brussel sprouts. "Got these like you asked."

Mama takes the sprouts with a smile and ushers us both inside. At a quick glance around the room, I can see how hard she's worked today to make the house look as respectable as possible. Hopefully that won't cause her back to flare up later.

The smell of roasted vegetables and freshly baked bread fills the small dining room as I head into the kitchen. It's been such a long time since we've hosted someone for dinner that I truly don't know what to do with myself.

Perhaps I should offer him a cool drink? It is summer after all, and the walk from the village causes a light layer of sweat on anyone's forehead. I don't bother asking him. I simply take a cup from the cupboard and fill it with the fresh lemonade mama made earlier today with the lemons from our garden.

Heading out into the dining room, I find Saint chatting with her. She's showing him the latest quilt she's been stitching. Saint is pretending to be very interested. Where has he come from? Who is he? And how is he in my house sharing dinner with mother and I? I have so many questions racing through my mind and yet, those answers aren't going to find themselves. I know for certain that I need to do some digging before allowing my interest to linger any more than it already has.

I walk up to Saint and hand him the lemonade. His fingers brush mine momentarily and a shiver travels up my arm, into my heart. "Thank you, Juni. Is there anything I can do to help with dinner?"

I'm not sure if he genuinely wants to help, or if it's just a coping mechanism for uncomfortable situations. Perhaps it's both.

Mama raises an eyebrow at me, clearly surprised. I step in quickly. "Actually, the fire in the hearth could use some attention. Could you stoke it, Saint? The poker's just by the woodpile."

Relief flickers across his face, and he nods. "On it," he says, moving towards the fireplace.

Good. Now I can breathe for a moment. The table needs setting, and the sprouts need to be drowned in butter, garlic and cream. It's the only way they're edible. I don't know why my mother insists on eating them. Horrid things, really.

As I set the table and finish putting the final touches on dinner, I can't help but steal a glance towards Saint. He kneels by the hearth, prodding and poking at the burning embers, bringing them back to life. We certainly don't need the fire in summer, but it's the only way to boil the water for our meal. The golden light of the fire catches the planes on his face, softening its usual sharpness.

But it's the small, almost invisible wince as he adjusts his position that catches my attention. He rolls his shoulder once, twice, before reaching for another log. Something about the gesture tugs at me. Maybe he's injured himself doing all the work at the shop but is too humble to tell me about it.

"Juni, can you hand me that serving tray, please?" Mama asks, pulling me from my thoughts.

I hand her the tray but steal another glance at Saint. The fire is well and truly alive now. He stands, dusting his hands on his pants as he steps back. He catches my eye and gives me a faint smile, as if to say, *job done*. I feel my cheeks warm.

"Thank you," I murmur, my voice softer than I intended.

He nods, looking a bit more at ease, though that shadow of tension still lingers in his posture. I make a mental note to ask him about it later.

Dinner of roast chicken, steamed greens, brussels and baked potatoes is a success. Mama always does a wonderful job with cooking. Hopefully, this is the kind of payment Saint was hoping for. He seems to have enjoyed it.

"Ladies, this was delicious." Saint grins.

"Eat as much as you like. It's not every day we have company for dinner."

Mama smiles, offering him a second helping of chicken. "I can't remember the last time Juni brought a male friend around."

Saint raises a brow as he fixes his gaze on me. "How surprising. I thought she would have the men flocking to her door."

Heat seeps up my neck, flushing my face.

"Oh she does," Mama replies, her voice filled with humour. "She just isn't interested in any of them. In fact, she's had Theon—the blacksmith—pining after her for years."

"Mama!" I scold. "I'm sure our guest is not interested in my love life."

Saint cocks his head to the side as he folds his arms across his chest. "On the contrary. I'm quite fascinated, to be honest."

A second wave of heat washes over my body. Saint's gaze never leaves mine. The air is thick with something I can't explain, and I find myself needing to get some fresh air. All this talk of love leaves me flustered. But her words are true. I'm not interested in anyone—right now.

Theon has been a wonderful friend through some of my toughest years. He's kind, gentle, caring, and thoughtful. Yet he always had a habit of scolding me. Like that time, I wanted to pick berries in the forest and when he found out, he scolded me for going alone. I knew the risks, but Theon never understood that I didn't have a choice. Nevermind that he never offered his company. I know he means well, but he's just always felt like an older brother to me.

Plus, he's not really my type. I prefer . . . I don't know. I don't even know what I want in a lover. I just know my focus is on my father's business right now. Love will have to wait a little longer.

"Well, moving on from all of that. Shall I fetch us some tea?" I'll do anything to shift the focus at this point.

Mama rises from the table, her plate in hand. "I'll do that. Both of you sit."

As we sit alone, the remains of dinner scattered between us, Saint leans back in his chair, a smile dancing on his lips. "What were you saying about not being the greatest chef? You lied. Dinner was amazing."

I fiddle with the napkin on the table. "That's because Mama cooked most of it."

"Perhaps it was your finishing touches that brought the entire meal together though. Maybe I'll come back again," Saint says, his blue eyes sparkling with mischievousness.

I raise a brow, hiding my grin as I fiddle with the napkin again. "Maybe? Please, you've already cleaned your plate twice.

If I'd known you could eat like a horse, I'd have changed the payment options."

A chuckle escapes Saint's lips. It's a beautiful sound. The kind you want to trap so you can listen to it over and over. His charm is infectious, and I don't want to admit the effect it has on me.

"Juni, have the wicks arrived yet?" Mama's question interrupts our banter, and I'm grateful. Saints gaze is so intentional it has me feeling things I know I shouldn't. The sudden reminder of reality helps to break the desirable tension pulsing between us.

"No, they haven't. But I did post them a letter today."

Mama enters the room again, a tea tray in hand. "I wonder what is keeping them," she says as she places it down on the table. "If you don't hear from them soon, you may need to go to Stone's Ridge yourself."

I nod. "I know. I'd rather not, but I may not have a choice."

Saint shifts in his chair, accepting the cup of tea mother has poured for him. The look on his face is unreadable.

"So, Saint, what brings you to Meadowbrook? Are you planning to stay long?" Mama asks.

He offers her a small, easy smile, but I catch the way his fingers drum lightly against the table. Something has unsettled him. I can feel it.

"Just passing through," he says with a shrug. "Needed a change of scenery, I guess."

Mama nods, blowing the top of her tea. "Well, it's a good town to land in. Though you might have noticed my daughter keeps herself far too busy to enjoy it properly." She nudges me with her elbow, grinning. "You could learn to slow down, Juni. Life isn't all work, you know."

I roll my eyes. "Someone has to keep the shop running. And speaking of Meadowbrook," I say, eager to change the subject, "did you hear the Flannigans are selling their house? They're moving to Rosewood."

Mama's brows shoot up. "No! Really? That's a shame—they've been here for as long as we have."

I nod, pretending not to notice Saint's leg bouncing under the table. "I've always loved their house. It's so quaint and the garden is beautiful. I wish I could buy it."

Saint glances at me then, his tapping slowing for a moment as his expression softens. Mother chuckles, breaking the silence. "You'd fill it with candles and still find a way to work too hard—just like your father."

I smile before resuming my tea drinking. Mama chats away with Saint, but I can't help noticing the way he deflects every question, keeping his answers light and distant. It makes me wonder what he's hiding—and why he seems so restless. But for now, I hold my tongue.

Saint shifts in his chair. "Is it rude of me to ask how Mr Fairchild passed?"

Instant pain clutches my heart. Strangling the life from it. I hate talking about my father's death. Mama is the one to share his story—not me though.

"It was twelve moon cycles ago," Kamari begins, her hands folding neatly in her lap. "My husband, Vern—Juniper's father—was on his way home from the woods. He'd been gathering firewood all day, trying to stockpile enough for winter. He was always doing that—working just a little harder, pushing himself a little further."

Her voice falters for a moment, and I instinctively reach across the table to rest my hand on hers. She pats it, offering me a faint smile. I know it's just as hard for her to talk about it as it is for me.

"That night, he never made it back to us," she continues. "The cart he was pushing was full, the front wheel needed repairs, and the road from the woods to town isn't forgiving. When they found him, the cart had tipped on its side, the firewood scattered. They said he'd just . . . stopped walking. His heart gave out."

Saint doesn't say anything immediately. His eyes flick to mine, as if searching for some way to navigate the weight of my mother's words. I force a smile.

"I'm sorry for your loss," he says finally, his voice low, sincere.

Mama nods. "Thank you. It's been a while now, but some days it feels like yesterday. He was a good man. Loved his family more than anything." Her gaze drifts towards me, soft and proud. "That's where Juniper gets it, you know. Her drive, her stubbornness. She's her father's daughter through and through."

"Mama . . ." I hiss, my cheeks heating.

"Anyway, enough about that!" Mother smiles and rises from the table. "I don't want to put a damper on the evening. You two head out into the garden. I will clean up here."

"Are you sure?" Saint murmurs as he stands.

Mother ushers us out the door. "Of course, and Saint. Please visit again."

He grins at her, flicking his gaze towards me. "I will if Juni lets me."

I feel the warmth in my cheeks as he looks at me. A piece of me doesn't want him to leave.

"You can come back as long as you don't eat everything."

"Cross my heart," Saint throws back at me.

The sun is getting lower in the sky, the hues around me turning from warm oranges to lilac as we stroll towards the garden gate.

"I wanted to ask before, but why are most of the flowers in the garden blue?" Saint asks, his voice curious as his eyes travel over the blossoms.

I stop by the cornflowers, picking one. "My father loved flowers and my favourite colour is blue. So I planted them in memory of him."

Saint takes a step towards me, picking a cornflower too. I'm taken aback when he reaches out to tuck it into my hair just above my ear. "It's the prettiest garden I've ever seen."

I blush at his boldness, his words making my cheeks even redder, I'm sure. "Thank you," I manage.

Even though I've only known him for a small amount of time and there is a great deal I've yet to learn about him, he's already left a mark on my soul. I just hope it's the good kind.

Saint glances up at the sky as he rolls his shoulder.

"I noticed you doing that before. Is everything alright with your shoulder?"

"I think I slept on it funny. It'll be fine."

The smile he offers me is genuine, so I let the matter rest. "Where have you been sleeping? The inn?"

Saint shakes his head. "Over at the stables. They have a loft there. I like the quiet."

My mind travels to Grim, the half-orc, and his wife Alice. He and my father had been great friends. Lovely folk. But surely, sleeping in a stable isn't the most hygienic choice—dust, hay, and the unmistakable scent of horses clinging to everything. And yet, somehow, Saint never looks unkempt, nor does he carry the scent of the stables with him.

We reach the gate. He strolls through to the other side and clicks it shut behind him. I don't know what to do or say next, so I place my hands behind my skirts and look towards town. Saint doesn't say much either, but he does keep looking towards the skies as if he's waiting for something to drop from it. Perhaps he is just eager to leave and is too polite to say so.

I shift my weight; the silence stretching thin.

"I should probably call it a night," I say, brushing my hands on my skirt. "I've got an early start tomorrow."

Saint straightens, his gaze flicking to me before nodding. "Yeah, I need to head out, too. Thanks for dinner . . . and, uh, everything."

"Of course. See you tomorrow to finish the list?"

"Right. Tomorrow." His voice carries a strange tightness as he pushes off the gate, but then he flashes me that crooked smile of his. "And if I get to work too early, I'll be sure to bring coffee to keep you awake."

I roll my eyes, the hint of a smile tugging at my lips. "I'll hold you to that."

"Good night, Juni," he says, giving me a wink before walking away.

I watch as he strides down the road, his pace brisk, almost hurried. My brows furrow as his figure disappears into the fading light. Something about the way he left feels . . . odd. But I shake the thought away, turning back towards the house.

At least I've held up our part of the payment agreement. Hopefully, he will deliver on his end.

# AN ENCHANTED RING

Is it so wrong to want something that's not yours to have if it means you can finally be free? Something so beautiful it steals your breath? The one thing I've been searching for, for so long, and that I'd finally found.

Smooth gold, glinting in the firelight. The flat oval surface on top holding one tiny red ruby—half the size of a grain of rice.

The moment I spotted it at dinner last night, the restless years of searching finally came to an end. Relief and anticipation curled in my chest—I could finally have my happy ending.

Kamari is a shifter. That much is clear. But did that mean Juniper was one too? I've never seen her wear a ring, never sensed the same restrained energy in her. Perhaps not.

I brush my fingers over the paper surface of my sketchbook. I trace around the curved edges of the image.

It's more beautiful than I thought it would be. I knew it was an enchanted shifter ring when I laid my eyes on it. In my years of limited research on my own kind, I'd come to learn that shifter rings are rare—coveted, even. They were generally worn on the pointer or index finger, so as to not be confused for wedding bands. They're a birthright, given as a symbol of identity and grounding. Lose it, and the cost to replace it could feed a family for years. I've never been able to afford one for myself.

If I was given one at my birth, I've never seen it—not in the orphanage, and certainly not in Donovan's estate. I would know, I've searched for it.

The sun had risen just above the horizon about an hour ago. I'm exhausted. After shifting last night, I slept little, my owl form taking over my reflexes more than I liked. My shoulder aches from all the flying around I've done. And the few moments I managed to find some sleep, I was woken by the noises of the forest.

I need to find refreshment for my body this morning, or the day will most definitely drag. Perhaps I should wander to the lake for a cool dip before I head over to the shop and finish painting the sign.

Shutting the sketchbook in my hand, I sigh, staring at the loft ceiling. The bed is much too small for my tall frame, but at least it's a safe place out of the constant eye of the townsfolk. And the stable master barely glances my way. So I really can't complain.

The last thing I need is any of Donovan's men turning up and spotting me. If they found me, I'd try my best to run, but with this constant ache in my shoulder, I'm not sure I could outrun them for long.

I'll do anything not to return to that hellhole. I won't stand for being beaten and locked away, treated like a misbehaving child in need of discipline. I need to break free from that existence once and for all.

Even though I've never met my parents—I don't even know what they look like—I'm sure that it wasn't the life they wished for me. Same with Sepehr and Roan too. We weren't meant to be slaves to a man whose selfishness could rival the devil's.

The bed frame creaks as I sit up and swing my legs over the edge. It is happening, my life is changing, yet in ways I didn't anticipate. I've been searching for a shifter ring, but I wasn't expecting to find one here in Meadowbrook. Following the natural progression of my life from bad, to really bad, to hopelessly complicated, it belongs to the mother of the girl that my heart is whispering about.

How am I supposed to steal the ring and skip town when the eyes of a meadow sunset haunt my every waking moment?

The sketch I'd been working on—before I drew the ring— falls open. I run my eyes over it. Her face had taken shape under the strokes—her wide, thoughtful eyes, the curve of her perfectly pink lips, the way her hair tumbles over her shoulders. I've sketched countless things over the years, but this feels different. Personal. Intimate. Dangerous.

It's Juni, an unexpected development. The woman who has no idea what she's doing to me. My hand tightens into a fist as my mind drifts further, wandering where it shouldn't. I imagine what it would feel like to touch her—how her skin might warm under my palms, how her lips might part when I kiss her. What her moans would sound like if I took my time with her, learning every secret, every soft place, until there was nothing left between us but need. Until she knew only my name . . . and I hers.

I exhale sharply, the restlessness in my chest clawing for release. This is torture. I'm not the kind of man who gets to *want* things, let alone *have* them. But her? For once, I want something selfishly. If there's even a chance she might want me too . . .

I close the book quickly, pressing the pencil into the spine as if I can bury these thoughts with it. But the image of her—her face, her voice, her everything—burns brighter in my mind.

My face feels dry as I run my hand over it. I need to get to the lakes before the miners arrive. I want to soak in the cooling waters, rehydrate my parched soul—and body. It would be good to wash my hair too.

I pack my sketchbook away. This morning's quiet time with only paper and pencil had been therapeutic. Exactly what my hands had needed.

The loft door clicks quietly shut behind me. I climb down the ladder—which creaks under my weight—before I stroll down past the horse stalls, stopping to scratch a few muzzles that poke above the doors. Warm brown eyes of a dappled grey find me, and it's almost like I know what he's thinking. One of the bizarre side effects of being a shifter. Animal instincts . . . I would know.

I head out of the stable into the early morning. The air is fresh in my lungs as I drag it in. There's no need to make a decision about the ring right now. As long as I don't see anything suspicious in town, I can probably afford to stay another few days. At least until I've finished everything at the chandlery.

Grey and red squirrels dart across the path as I stroll towards the fork in the road. The faint glow of dawn paints the horizon in shades of gold and pink. Left will take me to the lake and right will take me into town, past Junipers' house. My boots crunch against the gravel, but my mind is far from the present. It drifts back to last night, to the dinner table with Juniper and her mother.

I'm positive I've never experienced anything like that before.

It was so . . . foreign. Sitting there, surrounded by warmth, hearing the easy laughter between them, sharing a meal that wasn't eaten in silence or under the weight of expectation. It wasn't just the food or the firelight; it was the way her house felt—cosy, lived in. There were no cold marble floors, no heavy drapes that blocked out the world. No harsh laughter from my so-called father figure. Just a simple comfort that I hadn't realised I was starving for.

And yet, as I walk, the unease creeps in. Being free of Donovan's mansion feels like I'm finally breathing fresh air after years underground. But there's a part of me that's still bracing for it all to be taken away. Like Donovan's sulphurous tendrils are just waiting to stretch out and pull me back. Freedom is unsteady, like standing on legs that have forgotten how to walk.

I glance up as the lake comes into view, the water smooth as glass in the morning stillness. The sight tugs at something in me—a longing I can't quite name. For now, though, I'll hold on to that memory of Juniper's house. Of the way it felt. A small, stubborn hope sparks in my chest. Maybe, just maybe, this could be something more than just that . . . Hope.

The water is the perfect temperature. From the moment I dip my toe into the lake, I know it was exactly what my body and my mind need. Quickly stripping, I allow my nakedness to sink fully beneath the surface, letting it consume me. No one is around, so I had nothing to fear—or hide.

Once my lungs scream at me for air, I rise, flicking my head back as I break the surface. I sink back down, my head only visible as I tread water. There was nothing like this place back in Breydon. Nothing peaceful and quiet. Did I really have to leave soon and give it all up?

Movement, and a splash towards the middle of the lake catches my eye. A fish perhaps? It seemed too large to be a fish. Though who knows what truly lives out in the deeper parts.

A large tail rises from the water before slapping the surface and disappearing again. Colours of green, blue, black, and violet shimmer in the sunlight like polished, black opals. One of the rarest gems in all of Sapphire Vale. Given the size of it, it was most certainly not a fish. Siren perhaps?

I keep my distance, waiting to see if it will surface again. The water ripples, signalling movement. I expect the tail of my mystery creature to make an appearance again, but I'm shocked when I see what is attached to the other end.

Dark brown hair slicked back with water. Warm honey-coloured skin. Breasts covered in pale gold scales. A siren. I don't know where to look first. And even though she is a distance from me, her silhouette betrays her. It's Juniper.

I ease my body towards a clump of reeds on the lake's edge, not wanting to be seen. Well this answers my question from earlier. She's definitely not a shifter.

No, she's the most beautiful creature I have ever seen.

Sirens are a different kind of fae. They are known for their beautiful tails, their quick thinking in the water, and the strength they can harness. The childhood stories of them singing were no longer true, the power lost to time. It's been a while since I've seen one. Breydon is surrounded by the sea, but is located high up the mountain range, so there are few sea dwellers in the city.

Juni elegantly drags her hands through her long hair, squeezing all the water from it. The sun dances on her skin, making all the droplets look like liquid gold as they fall back into the lake.

She's a goddess.

I can't take my eyes from her as she starts to move towards the water's edge. She's a vision—just for me. It's just her and I at this moment.

Should I call out to her? No, I think she enjoys the quiet alone time like I do. She said she preferred the silence.

I'll wait. It looks like she's leaving, anyway.

The morning mist clings to the edges of the lake, softening the light as the sun inches higher. I should move, should turn away and give her privacy, but I can't. I'm rooted by the reeds, unable to function as Juniper steps from the water.

Her tail shifts seamlessly, the iridescent shimmer of her siren self melting away to reveal her human shape. A thin, blue floral gown clings to her as she emerges, her hair a cascade of straight dark tendrils down her back, dripping with lake water. Each step she takes is slow, deliberate, as though she's savouring the quiet moment before the day begins. I can't blame her. That's what I'm doing down here at the lake too right? Preparing myself for a day of looking over my shoulder—wincing each time I hear a loud sound, thinking I've finally been found.

The fabric of her dress darkens with every drop it absorbs, plastering itself to her frame, and I have to remind myself to breathe. She's like something out of a dream, untouchable yet achingly real. My chest tightens as I sink further into the water, careful not to be seen.

I shouldn't be watching. But as she brushes the hair from her face, squeezing the water free and returning it to its home, she gazes out across the lake. I can't help but think there's a kind of magic in her—one that has nothing to do with being a siren and everything to do with the pureness of her heart.

Now I have another image that needs to be sketched into my book.

# Eight

## THE FAIRCHILD CHANDLERY

It had been way too easy to slip the small baguette under my shirt outside the bakery. Even though some folk were probably still tucked up in their beds, the town was slowly waking. I suppose the baker is always the first to open his doors. At this time of the morning, no one would notice a small, missing baguette . . . Plus an apple that I'd picked from a branch hanging over a wooden fence on the way into town. The tree was heavily laden with an abundance of fruit. I highly doubt anyone was going to miss one apple either.

I take a bite, the crisp sweetness sharp against my tongue, and follow it with a chunk of bread. Around me, the town stirs to life, the streets filling with noise and movement. I should probably make haste. There's still no certainty that I won't be spotted by unwanted company.

Children dart between stalls, chasing one another with laughter that echoes off the stone walls. Shopkeepers haul crates of goods out to their displays, calling greetings to passersby or shooing curious hands away from their wares. In the market square, a woman argues loudly over the price of potatoes, her voice sharp enough to draw amused glances.

I'm suddenly back in Breydon amidst all the clamour and noise of the city. My heart begins to race in my chest, my eyes darting around, automatically looking for danger.

I chew slowly, skimming my attention over the waking bustle. It's lively, warm even, but as I step past the heart of the activity, I feel it—the prickling sensation that runs up the back of my neck like a warning. A glance here, a whisper there. A few heads turn my way, and I catch the edges of curious stares before they quickly look away.

What am I doing here? I was meant to be keeping a low profile, not strolling around the place as if I own it. If those sideways glances weren't enough to get me on my way, the thought of unwanted eyes spotting me does.

My feet carry me out of town as I mingle in the earlier morning shadows. I toss the apple core into a nearby bush, heading for Juniper's shop. As I pass a patch of wildflowers growing stubbornly against the stone wall of a house, I pause and pluck a single stem.

It's not long before I find myself outside the chandlery. As I stand on the other side of the cobblestone road, I watch as Juni moves about inside the shop. She hasn't seen me yet. She gracefully moves about the room, filling the shelves with coloured candlesticks. I can't help but smile, twirling the flower stem between my fingers.

The colours of the morning sun drenching the shop is breathtaking. Sweeping across the ground and over the stone building in hues of amber, citrus and marigold. Mentally, I paint the image in my head. Each brushstroke of oil paint brings the chandlery to life. If I wasn't on the run, I'd stay a while, and paint the whole town.

A young boy pushing a cart of carrots rushes past me, the noise of his cart wheels jostling me from my trance. I need to stop dawdling on the sidewalk. Juni will be expecting me.

I hurriedly cross to the other side, pushing the door open. The bell announces my arrival, and I wait for Juni to return from out the back. No need to go scaring her again.

The delicate scent of lavender and honey wafts through the room as she enters. She's wearing the blue floral gown I saw her in earlier, but her silky brunette hair is piled on top of her head in a messy knot of sorts. It only takes one look from her and my heart is in my throat. How am I supposed to steal her mother's ring and leave town when she's looking at me like that? As if she has waded through hell to find my soul, and drag it back into the light.

"Morning, Juni."

A gentle flush spreads across her cheeks. "Good morning. How's your shoulder?"

I offer her a grin. "It's healing up, but if you're looking for an excuse to fuss over me, I won't stop you."

The flush on her cheeks brightens and the corners of her mouth turn up. I'd do anything to see her smile. If it helps lessen the burden she carries or distracts her from her worries.

"There will be no fussing here, I believe you have a sign to finish painting?" Juni motions her head towards the back room just as the door to the shop opens. I don't wait around to see who it is as I slip into the backroom.

I can hear the gentle hum of voices as I place the flower I picked for Juni on her open ledger. The sun greets me as I step outside. It's going to be another hot day, but I am grateful for the large oak in the corner of the yard that offers me shade as I work.

Thoughts of Juni as a siren swim around my mind as I paint delicate brush strokes onto the wood. She was this delicate being, moving through the glass surface as if she was created from water itself. Yet, seeing her in her human form is just as breathtaking.

I gently release air from my lips. I really need to get a grip on my feelings. Juni is the dream I don't deserve—the dream that will always be just that . . . A dream.

Immersing myself into the artwork, I try to forget about the world around me. Each stroke of coloured paint is like breathing. I don't even need to think about it.

"Saint?"

The silent throb in my ears disappears as Juni's voice reaches me. I glance up to see her standing in the doorway. "Sorry, I was lost in another world."

She offers me a sweet smile. "I can see that. I've called you three times."

"Well, the fourth time is the winner," I huff softly, placing the brush down. "Did you need me for something?"

Juniper shuffles awkwardly before holding up the flower I picked earlier in her hand. "I found this in my book. Did you put it there?"

I shrug casually, picking up my brush. "I have no idea what you're talking about."

She eyes me warily, a smile dancing on her lips. "Well, whoever it was. I wish to thank them."

"I'll happily pass on the gratitude for you."

Juni rolls her pretty meadow eyes and disappears back inside. She smiled with the flower, my job was done for the day.

The hours pass by and I'm finally done with the sign. It feels so good to let myself sink into a project with no sudden commands to head into the streets and shakedown people for money. There was no one hovering over my shoulder, watching my every move. This freedom of being able to breathe is something I savour with every passing second.

Even if that means I have to keep moving from town to town. Away from Donovan. But hopefully towards Sepehr and Roan, and hopefully with a ring.

That's what I want, right?

I've never cared for anyone but my brothers. But the thought of leaving Meadowbrook—Juni, has me feeling things in my chest that I'm not sure I'm ready to admit out loud. She's placed me under a spell, and the funny thing is, I don't even think she realises.

While I wait for the paint to dry, I glance around the garden. The rickety cart sits in the corner with its crooked wheel. Probably in the same condition as the day Juniper's father passed.

It can't wait to be fixed. The next time someone uses it, they could injure themselves.

Without a second thought, I collect the hammer and some nails and set to work.

"You've done a beautiful job, Saint. You have such an eye for detail," Juni murmurs as she glides her fingers across the wooden sign. The sun begins its descent, it would only be a few more hours until it sets, so I wanted to make sure she was happy with all my work before I left for the day.

"I like to think my eyes work quite well."

Juni's cheeks flush again, and she shoulders my arm gently. "You know what I mean."

I grin in response. "I'll hang it before I leave."

Juni nods and heads inside. I follow her with the sign in hand. Once it's hung, she stands out on the street to view it. She doesn't say a word, but I swear I can see a tear glistening in the corner of her eye.

Something about this sign means more to her than it does anyone else. "Are you happy with it?" I ask gently, walking to stand beside her. We both look up at the sign as I wait for her to answer.

Juni brushes the stray tear. "It's perfect," she says, her voice quivering. With a hurried step, she returns inside the shop, and once again I follow her.

"Want to go find somewhere that we can scream out loud?"

She turns to me; her face crumpled in confusion. "What do you mean?"

I stroll to the counter and lean my hip against it. "You know, a place where we can scream all of our pain into the void. Let it rush through us and out into the world. Never to be ours again."

Juni sniffs, holding back the tears I know so desperately want to pour out. She is so strong and kind, why does she choose to suffer? Probably because holding onto the pain is easier than not knowing what's on the other side. She has to walk through it.

I know what it's like to lose a parent—two of them. And I don't know what's worse. Losing a parent you never met, or losing one that you only got to spend a small amount of your life with.

Juni fusses at the shelves on the wall, rearranging candles. "It's fine, really," her voice is tender. "Thank you, though."

Strands of her hair are tucked behind one ear, and the faintest smudge of red dye streaks her cheek. It's a little too easy to watch her, but I force myself to focus when she turns to me, her hands on her hips.

"I was thinking," she starts, her tone trying to be happy. "If you're still looking for work, there are a few things around my house that could use some fixing up."

I raise an eyebrow and fold my arms, a slow grin tugging at the corner of my mouth. "Careful, Juni. At this rate, I'm going to start thinking you're intentionally breaking things just to keep me around."

She huffs in amusement, but I catch the faintest twitch of a smile. "Don't flatter yourself, Saint. My house isn't in perfect shape, you've seen it, and I haven't had time to deal with it. But if you'd rather not—"

"Oh, I didn't say that," I interrupt, holding up my hands as if to defend myself. "I'm just wondering if you're trying to pay me in dinner again. Or is there some secret treasure chest hidden under your floorboards you haven't mentioned yet?"

Juniper huffs. "I'd pay you in something a little more substantial if I could, but I'm not exactly rolling in money right now. I promised ten copper coins and dinner for the first list. How about the same for the second?"

"That's all this humble man needs," I say, turning to rest my elbows on the counter, cupping my face in my hands.

"Well, it's settled then," Juni says as she reaches under the counter. I can hear coins clinking around. Her eyes find me as she extends her hand. On her honey-coloured palm sit ten copper coins. "The rest of your payment?"

I push off my elbows, standing straight. As my fingers brush her hand, little bumps race up my arm. Time slows around me as my fingertips feel her soft, silk-like skin. I hear the slight catch in her breath and our eyes lock on one another. She truly has me hypnotised. "Thank you," I answer. "When would you like me to start on the house?"

"Would tomorrow be alright?"

I nod, shoving my hands in the pockets of my trousers. Being this close to her, knowing the things I know, it's too much. I want to do things to this woman in a very respectfully disrespectful way—if she will allow me. Yet, I'll be leaving soon. Is there any point in pursuing anything with her?

"Tomorrow will be fine. Will Kamari be alright with it?"

Juni wipes her hands on her apron. "Of course, she loved having you over."

The heels of my boots squeak a little as I rock back on them. "Oh, she did? And how did her daughter feel?"

Perfectly pink lips form into a smirk as Juni resists the temptation to grin at my question. "Her daughter has no comment."

My grin grows bigger. "Oh, I do love a game of cat and mouse . . . Are you ready to lose?"

The smile I've been trying to coax from her since we walked inside finally breaks free, and it's glorious. "Don't be too confident. I run pretty fast."

An outburst of laughter erupts from my soul. Every now and then I catch a glimpse of the real Juniper Fairchild. And every time I do, it settles in my soul, finding its home there.

"Well, I'll see you in the morning then."

"See you in the morning."

I twist on my heel, not looking back as I head out of the shop. If I look back, I don't think I will be able to control myself. I want nothing more than to kiss her. To feel her tongue upon my own. To bury my fingers in her hair. To offer her a fleeting moment of time, where both of us can get lost in each other and forget the world.

My feet carry me to the stables, into the loft to collect my sketchbook and back out into the woods. It's safer to wait out here while the sun sets. Once I'm an owl, I can take refuge in the trees—where I can wait out the night, keep my talons to myself—where I won't harm anyone.

I need some time away from Juni—from the desire and dreams that I'll never get to have with her.

The forest is quiet, save for the gentle rustle of leaves from a scurrying ground dweller and the occasional birdsong. The sun's rays pierce the underbrush with streaks of amber. I've wandered further than I meant to, following an overgrown trail that led me here—to a pool so still and clear it looks like the sky poured itself into the earth. It's the kind of place you'd expect to find in the stars, the water serene and untouched, ringed by moss-covered stones and brown mushrooms.

I step closer, feeling like I've stumbled into something sacred, and drop my bag onto a flat rock by the edge. This place isn't meant to be rushed. I sit down, pulling out my sketchbook and charcoal, and before I know it, I'm sketching her—Juniper as a siren, the lines of her fins blending into the soft curves of the water.

I pause, the charcoal hovering above the page, and let my thoughts wander. The idea of staying here has been clawing at the edges of my mind, though it feels more like a fantasy than a real possibility. I imagine setting up a small shop, painting signs or making sketches for townsfolk. I could even illustrate my own book. Wouldn't that be the dream? Earning an honest living, building something that's mine, instead of running or hiding.

No debts. No Donovan.

But the reality presses in like a heavy stone bound to my chest, with rusted chains. I rub at my shoulder absently, the ache dull but persistent. Even if I could outrun Donovan, my shifting is still a curse that brands me, a constant reminder that I'm never fully in control. There's a very real possibility that my animal form could hurt someone—even kill them. What if it was someone I loved?

And then there's Kamari's ring. If I took it, I could finally have the life I've been chasing—free to exist without fear. It would cost me nothing but a little guilt.

Except it would cost me wouldn't it? It would cost me . . . *Her.*

I glance down at the sketch of her, incomplete but already perfect. The way she looks at me . . . It keeps me here longer than I should be. But leaving feels so wrong, like something I'm not ready to do.

I close the sketchbook and exhale, my gaze lingering on the glassy surface of the pool. For now, I'll let the dream breathe a little longer.

*Nine*

## INKED HANDS IN POCKETS

The woman in the mirror is someone I hardly recognise. Since when do I furrow my brows so much? I need to smile more often or I'm going to get wrinkles sooner than I'd like.

Brush bristles drag through my hair, tugging the knots free. The one positive of having dead straight hair is that it doesn't take me long to fix. With a defeated sigh, I place the brush down, twisting my hair into a messy knot on top of my head. All I need is for it to be out of the way.

I glance at the pots of homemade beeswax lip balm, and the charcoal pencils that I use to line my eyes sometimes. They rarely see the light of day. Only when Dove drags me to the tavern—though it's been a while since I even did that. She likes to remind me almost daily.

My fingers tap against the lid of the lip balm. Why am I even sitting here at my dressing table bothering about my appearance? It's like Aunt Molly said all those years ago at the festival of lights, *"You've got to work hard for your money, Juni. You're too plain to have men flocking, you've got to carve your own path in life. Don't wait around for a husband to take care of you."*

She was right. I was too plain. Especially in my younger years. Round face, with a dimpled chin. And hair as straight as straw. Thankfully, I'd lost my baby face with time. I'd thanked the Creator the day my cheekbones became visible and my chest filled out.

Yet, none of that mattered now. A good job and food on the table were my focus. I'm the practical one, not the one that men desire. My fingers draw back from the rouge. I've never cared too much about what others think of my complexion, so why was I considering it now?

I stand, my slippers scuffing on the wooden floor as I make my way to my wardrobe. Pulling the doors open, I select a plain cotton dress. At least this lemon colour does a little to help my complexion.

Saint would no doubt arrive soon, and I need to finish writing his list. As I pass my dresser, I pick the small glass vial filled with my favourite oil—lavender and honey—and I dab a few drops onto my wrists before gently tapping them on either side of my neck. I may be plain, but I didn't need to smell bad too.

No sooner than I put the oil back, a knock sounds at the front door. It instantly sends my heart into an erratic state. Inwardly, I scold myself for acting this way. I still don't know who Saint really is. And despite the fact that I find him utterly attractive, I still need to keep my heart in check.

"Will you get the door, Juni?" Mama calls from the kitchen. She's been up for hours baking bread and preparing oatmeal. The house smells delicious.

I try to still my beating heart as I approach the door. Sweat coats the palms of my hands, so I quickly wipe them on my skirts. The doorknob feels cold as I twist it to the right. Horrid hinges squeak, rudely reminding me that I need to add them to the list as well.

Patchouli and cedarwood reach my nose, and a gentle sense of peace washes over me. It's a sensation I've not felt in such a long time. Like my heart knows where home is, but my mind has yet to catch up.

Eyes the colour of spring skies, peppered with flecks of sapphire, find me. Time slows. The world fades away, and it's only us standing on the porch of my home. There is no sound except the rhythmic drum of my beating heart. Can he hear it? Can he hear how my heart beats for him?

I try to distance my emotions from the logical side of my brain. Why does it beat for him? I barely know him, yet he is constantly in my thoughts.

Partially, it's because of the way he looks. What woman wouldn't melt under his intense stare? The way his pale wheat hair falls recklessly over his forehead. Or the way one corner of his mouth is slightly higher than the other when he smiles. Perhaps it's because he's covered parts of his skin in designs so intricate and detailed that he's become a walking art piece. Maybe it's the nose ring, or the earrings, for that matter? Maybe it's because everything about him is so masculine and strong, yet gentle and kind?

There's something about him—something untamed but oddly steady—that pulls at me in ways I don't entirely understand. It's unnerving, this feeling, this stirring of something I've always managed to keep tucked away behind practicality and purpose.

I'm not used to being noticed like this, not used to wanting someone to notice me. It's thrilling, yes, but it's also dangerous, like stepping into a current stronger than I can handle. My mind can be a witness to say I don't usually want things for myself, but I see the way he looks at me. And I would be lying if I said, deep down, I didn't welcome it. I want to know what his lips would feel like on mine. I want to know his body and how it would respond to my touch. I want to taste him. I want . . . I want *him*.

I fist the sides of my skirt, forcing myself to speak, to break the spell before I lose myself in it.

"Morning, Saint."

He leans his good shoulder against the door frame, clasping his hands behind his back, as if he doesn't have a care in the world. "Juni."

"Have you had breakfast?"

He shakes his head. "Came straight from the stables."

I shift out of the doorway, inviting him inside. "Well, I'm sure mother will feed you well enough. She's been in the kitchen for hours baking."

Mama was more than pleased when I told her Saint would be working on some things around the place. It seems as though she's already grown a soft spot for him. And despite my logical brain's objection, I sort of have too.

Saint moves past me. My eyes have no control as they flutter shut at his nearness. It's almost like I can feel the heat from his body, though I'm probably making it all up in my head.

"Did you sleep well? How is your shoulder?" I ask, moving towards the dining table to retrieve the list. I jot down *'oil front door hinges'* while I wait for Saint to respond. His voice is closer than I expect when he answers, sending a shiver down my spine.

"It's healing day by day. Thanks for asking." He leans over me to glance at the list on the table. "Seems like I'll be busy today."

"Yes, I need you to fix the broken rocking chair in Mama's room, plug the leaky roof in the greenhouse, adjust and oil all the door hinges, fix the front gate—"

"Is this a repair job or a quest? Because I think I'm going to need a map and some extra supplies," Saint drawls.

I spin to face him with a light laugh on my lips. His nose is inches from mine, our breaths mingling. My eyes don't miss the flick of his gaze on my lips. Or the way his feet seem to gravitate closer to me. It would only take a second for my hand to grip the back of his neck and pull him closer.

"Saint. You're here!" Mama's sweet voice interrupts our moment.

I step back, placing distance between us, but not before Saint's hand brushes mine.

"Morning Kamari. Ready to keep me entertained all day while Juni abandons us?"

Mother chuckles as she places her tea tray down. "We are going to have loads of fun."

With a gentle smile tugging at my lips, I move towards the coat stand by the front door and collect my bag. "Now, don't you have *too* much fun without me, and if you need any tools, they're in the shed."

I look at Saint. In return, he looks at me with a smug grin on his face. One I've become accustomed to. "Noted." His voice is laced with amusement.

Mother giggles like a silly schoolgirl while she pours the tea. "Juni, I placed some scones on your bag don't forget to eat it when you get to the shop."

My hand lingers on the front doorknob. I eye Saint one more time. He's smiling at me with a glint in his eye. Why is he helping so much? What does he want from me? What does he want from this town? I can't shake the feeling that there is more to him than he's letting on.

And perhaps it's time I find out.

"See you at dinner."

One hundred and twenty-three candles have been dipped this morning, with hundreds to go. A sigh escapes my lips. The round wooden stool behind the front counter calls to me. I listen. My feet are aching, begging me to ease them from the weight of carrying me.

I suppose taking a break is a good idea. While I sit, I can eat my scones and look through my orders. Let's hope I can cross some off.

Well-worn pages crinkle as I open my ledger. While I'm grateful for each transaction that helps pay the bills, it's still overwhelming to see pages upon pages of orders. But I have to keep going. I have to keep making money. I'd missed last month's debt payment, but I'd sent a letter telling the lender that it would be included in this month's payment. I couldn't let them down, all the more so because who knew what type of people they were.

Debt holders didn't have sparkling reputations. I definitely don't need to deal with that.

I jump out of my skin when the bell above the door jangles. For a brief second, I don't want to look up. I don't want to take another order. But what choice do I have?

My eyes find a friendly face, allowing the rush of heat to dissipate quickly. It's Theon. I haven't seen him since that time in the marketplace when I was with Saint.

"Afternoon, Juni Bear." Theon offers me a grin. His brown eyes are kind, yet troubled.

The childhood nickname brings a smile to my lips. He's called me that ever since we were children looking for frogs down by the lake at dusk. He's always been such a steady friend. Most of the girls in town are always trying to get his attention. With his wavy brown hair, neatly trimmed beard and arms the size of small tree trunks, he's certainly a handsome man. I think he secretly loves their attention.

"Been busy at the ol' forge?" I ask, closing the ledger.

The scent of embers and metal follow Theon wherever he goes.

He leans his right hip against the front counter, angling his body towards the front room. Something is bothering him.

Theon sighs, his broad shoulders dropping ever so slightly. "Work has been busy lately. I was on a break, and I thought I'd come by. Sorry about the other day."

"It's no bother. I figured you had a lot going on."

Theon turns to lean against the counter, arms crossed and brow furrowed in that way that always makes him look like a disapproving older brother. "So, who's the blond guy?" he asks.

I feel my own brow scrunch. This is not what I thought was on his mind. "Do you mean the person you saw me in town with?"

Theon nods slowly.

I offer him a light shrug. "That's Saint. He's just helping out around the shop. Fixing things, you know."

The look he gives me says he isn't convinced with my answer.

"Helping out?" Theons voice is gritty, almost annoyed. "You sure that's all he's doing?"

My back straightens. His response is more accusation than it is a question. "What are you suggesting?"

Theon glances at me before fiddling with an invisible who-knows-what on the countertop. "There've been reports of things going missing around town lately."

Something in my gut reacts. Doubt. But just because I had my suspicions about Saint, didn't mean I was going to make allegations against him.

The stool scrapes across the floor as I stand. Rolling my eyes, I cross to the shelf to arrange some jars of scented wax. "Come on, Theon. Just because someone's new doesn't mean they're up to no good. Not everyone's a thief."

"I'm just saying, Juni." His tone is softer but still firm. "You don't know anything about this guy. He could be trouble."

I turn to face him, hands on my hips. "And I suppose you've got him all figured out just by looking at him?"

He shrugs but doesn't back down. "Call it instinct."

A small part of me agrees with him. Theon's always had good instincts. Yet, he wasn't always right. He was human, after all.

I huff, shaking my head. "You've been overprotective since we were kids. I'm not thirteen anymore, Theon. I can handle myself."

He doesn't look convinced, but he lets the subject drop with a mutter, "Just be careful."

"Don't I always?" I offer him a reassuring smile. "Now, break time is over. I have so many candles to dip and I'm sure there's a horse out there who needs a new shoe."

Theon strolls to the door, pausing after it opens. "We should go to the tavern sometime soon."

I nod softly. "I'll see what I can do. Perhaps Dove can come too."

Theon raises a hand in acknowledgment, but doesn't say anything else. I let out a breath as the door swings shut. He's a good guy—he means well. I know Mama would love it if Theon became a part of the family. But—I just . . . I just don't feel for him that way.

I'm not even sure what that way even feels like.

I'd definitely had fun a few times with some of the local boys. A few kisses here and there with Elliot—my childhood neighbour. My first time was with him in an old barn. We were seventeen. He'd been sweet on me for a while and I was so excited that someone thought I was pretty. It was awkward and neither of us knew what we were doing. Of course, he'd moved away a few weeks later, and I'd never seen him again.

It's been eight years since then. In that time there'd only been one other. Wesley—a friend of Dove's. We'd dated for a few months, it was fun at first, new, and exciting, but I knew deep down that he wasn't the one. Then when Papa died I'd pushed anyone who might be interested away—friends alike.

My thoughts travel to Dove and Theon. I want to spend time with them, I truly do. I just find it hard to balance the shop responsibilities and social connection. But what if I'm not doing the right thing by focusing so much of my time and energy into the business—perhaps I too need to find happiness.

I glance outside the shop window towards the sun. I only have a few hours of light left before I need to get home. I should finish the candles. It's what Papa would want. If I can hang on for a little longer, we might be okay. If those damn wicks would arrive. No word back from the supplier, either. Looks like I'll be making a trip to Stone's Ridge by the week's end.

Before I continue dipping the next batch of candlesticks, I need to load the boxes of finished ones onto the handcart.

I put the ledger away, heading through the back room and outside. The summer sun heats my skin instantly. I can't wait for autumn. Cooler weather, golden brown leaves, and the promise of winter. My favourite season.

The cart is in the corner of the yard, where it usually is. I prepare myself for the struggle I know I'm going to face as I wheel it to the back door. I am pleasantly surprised, though, when it doesn't squeak, and it doesn't wobble. My gaze darts to the front wheel. The whole cart moves as if it's brand new.

My mind instantly travels to Saint, and his obviously skilled hands. He fixed it without me knowing. Didn't even ask for extra payment. Why? Or the better question. Why me? Theon was wrong. Saint isn't stealing things around town—he's helping. I can't let my or Theon's suspicions of him get in the way of the trust that is building between us.

Tears build in the corners of my eyes. Papa built this cart with his own hands. He was always busy making something. Everything in the shop was made by him, and all of it was so special.

Saint doesn't even realise the small part of me he's healed by fixing the cart. I need to thank him at dinner tonight.

Mama is in the vegetable garden amongst the short rows of cabbages and carrots when I return home. The sun is setting, bringing with it a golden blanket to place over Meadowbrook, tucking us in for the night. Ready for the moon to take its watch.

Saint is holding a wicker basket, walking alongside Mama as she hands him freshly picked vegetables still covered in soil.

Neither one of them notices as I linger at the gate. Mother's smile almost reaches her ears. Saint must be weaving his charm and she's falling for it hard. Who can blame her?

He has a way of making me feel good. A way of saying it's okay to laugh and have fun without saying the words. I know that it is, but I haven't done it freely in so long.

I want to give in to him. I want to fall into his world and find out everything about him, but something is holding me back. Theon's words? The shop? My own heart? Perhaps all three?

Sapphire-blue eyes find me across the garden. Saint winks and my heart jumps in its bone cage inside my chest. I'm being invisibly pulled towards him, and I don't have a choice but to obey.

The gate doesn't squeak or swing awkwardly on the hinges as I open it. Good to see some items on the list have been done. I have no reason to doubt they wouldn't; Saint hasn't disappointed me yet. In fact, he's done the opposite.

Mother waves to me as she scurries inside with the fresh vegetables.

Saint strolls my way, inked hands in pockets, looking quite pleased with himself. He falls into step beside me as we walk the garden path.

"How was your day?"

I place a little distance between us. It's too hard to think when he is close. "It was fine, thank you. Busy—as usual."

Saint huffs softly. "I expect nothing different."

Warmth spreads into my cheeks. Do I truly work too hard?

"Did you fix the wheel on the cart?"

A small rock skitters away as Saint kicks it. "I don't know what you're talking about."

The grin on his face says everything—he's just being coy.

"Well, whoever left the flower on my book and fixed the cart wheel, please tell them I am very grateful."

Saint catches my eye, smiling softly. "Will do."

I reach the bottom step of the front porch. I'm halfway up when I feel the warm pressure of a hand on my wrist. Pausing, I turn to face Saint. We are eye height like this. My pulse quickens at the nearness of his body, those sapphire flecks taking hold of my heart with no intention of letting go.

He fishes something from his trouser pocket, placing it in my palm.

"I've finished the list," Saint says, his hand lingering on mine longer than it ever has before.

I don't pull back. I like the way his skin feels on mine. It's calloused from a hard day's work, but there is something gentle in the way his hands move. They're intentional, as if they have a mind of their own. Or perhaps they've been trained to be smooth—to move like thieves in the night, hiding in the shadows.

The paper crumples in my hand. "I see everything has been marked off." My eyes find him. "Thank you."

Saint shrugs lightly. "I mean, I did it because I like Kamari's cooking."

My cheeks feel warm, and I can't help but smile. "Too bad I'm cooking tonight?"

His brow lifts. "Should I alert the healer now?"

I scoff. "Only to administer some aloe vera to the burn you've inflicted upon my ego."

Saint grins. Our eyes say everything, yet our mouths remain shut. Internally I'm screaming. Why am I flirting with him? I shouldn't be. He's going to leave after dinner and I will probably never see him again. But I can't seem to help it. He brings it out of me in such a subtle way that I don't even realise it's happening until after the words have slipped from my mouth.

I take a few steps backwards, reaching the porch, now a head height taller than Saint. His eyes follow me. "Are you coming?"

The smirk I've come to loathe and love creeps along his face. I roll my eyes and walk towards the front door. "You know what I mean, Saint. Now hurry up, I need someone to peel the potatoes."

Dinner had been more than enough. Lamb steaks, mashed potatoes, steamed greens, and a side of thick gravy.

Mother slowly stands from the table. I can see the pain flash across her face. Her back must be giving her grief. "Well, you two can clear the table. I'm off for a walk."

"Be careful, mother."

She tugs her shawl free from the coat rack by the door and turns back to me. "Juni, did the wicks arrive?"

I shake my head and sigh. "Unfortunately not."

Disappointment hovers over her. "It looks like a trip to Stone's Ridge is at hand."

"I know. We'll talk about it when you're home."

Mama nods, closing the door quietly behind her.

The room is silent for a moment, only the sound of the crickets singing their later afternoon song.

Saints' low, smooth voice washes over me. "Can I help clean up?"

I nod, rising from the table to collect the plates. He follows me with an armful of things. I fill the sink with warm soapy water and Saint begins to wash the dishes. We don't talk a lot, but the air around us is tight. Like so many words want to be said, but none seem to form.

The kitchen feels smaller somehow with Saint in it. He's leaning over the sink, paying close attention to every detail on the dishes. Making sure each one is perfectly clean before he places it aside to dry. It's not long before he's all done, wiping his hands on a towel that looks much too small for his inked hands.

I brush past him, reaching for the iron kettle hanging above the fire. He steps back at the same time, and suddenly we are in each other's way.

"Excuse me," I mumble, trying to squeeze by.

"Sorry, let me—" he pauses mid sentence, his hands lightly finding my waist as he moves to let me pass.

I can't breathe.

His touch is like fire burning through the thin cotton fabric of my gown—hot, leaving devastation in its wake. The air between us thickens, making the room feel warmer. His inked hands linger—just a second too long—and I glance up, only to find his gaze locked on mine. He's looking at me in that way again. The look that is going beyond my face, beyond my mind, reaching deep into my soul. My breath catches as his fingers dig into my skin, the pressure of them sending a shiver all over my body.

"Saint . . ." My voice quivers.

He pulls me closer, so our hips touch. "Yes, Blue?"

He's too close, yet not close enough. His grip tightens, and I lean into him. Why is he calling me Blue? Do I care? Not really. Not right now. Not when all I want is for him to kiss me. Kiss me until I don't know up from down.

"I—" My voice falters, so I clear my throat and try again. "I just need to get to the sink."

Saint's lips curve upwards. Forming into that maddening smile that makes me weak. "Of course."

I slide past him, the fabric of my skirt brushing against his leg. My hands fumble with the teapot as I lift the lid, ready to top it up with water. I try my best not to notice how his eyes track my every move.

The tension builds until I force myself to break it. "You missed a spot," I throw over my shoulder, nodding to the plate on the drying rack.

Saint chuckles softly, a sound that feels like it was created just for me. He can't see my face, so I allow myself to close my eyes and take in a breath. Perhaps Mother should have stayed, to force us to behave. Though I can't shake the way his hands felt, warm and steady, like they belong on my skin.

I walk to the fire, placing the iron kettle back. Anything to place some distance between us.

"Where did your mother slip off to at this time of day?" Saint hums, his back towards me.

I quickly calculate my answer. "She often visits my father's grave at night," I reply. "I don't like it when she goes there alone, but she insists."

Saint places the dish down to dry, turning to face me. After wiping his hands, he folds his arms across his broad chest.

"She likes to be alone . . . You know?" I continue on.

He looks at me, like he still has questions, so I continue, "Mama doesn't yell it from the rooftops, but she's a shifter. In the evenings, she likes to stretch her legs . . . If you know what I mean?"

He doesn't say anything straight away—just nods, but I see the way his face changes. I can't read his thoughts, so I let the conversation drop.

"Did you want to stay for tea?"

Saint glances towards the window. "I think I should get moving. I've already overstayed my welcome."

My heart sinks at his answer, but I don't let it show on my face. So I simply nod and move to the front door. "Well, let me walk you outside."

We move together, like a dance, as we wander the garden path to the front gate. The warm summer breeze is flirting with us as it darts across our path. I reach the gate and push it open.

Saint strolls through, turning to lean against it once it's shut. The sun is so low now. It's almost dusk. Where has the time gone? I've been having so much fun that I hadn't noticed just how late it was getting.

He's got that restless energy about him again, one foot planted, the other ready to pivot, his body half-turned as though he's already halfway gone. He's always standing by a door. Makes me wonder what haunts him. What is chasing him that he's so afraid to speak it aloud? His eyes dart over his shoulder, scanning the empty road like he's expecting someone—or avoiding someone.

"Still worried that a carrot is going to bite you?" I tease, trying to break the tension.

Saint smirks, a gentle huff escaping his lips. "If it does, I'll be sure to bite back."

I return his smile. "So, what's next for you?"

"What do you mean?"

My shoulder lifts and drops as I shrug. "Well, is this goodbye? Will you be leaving town or will you stay and find more work?"

He doesn't answer right away. So I don't force him. Choosing to wait instead.

Saint shrugs, his answer aloof. "Look for more work, I suppose. Long enough to figure out what I want next."

I nod softly. "If you need to borrow tools, you're welcome to any I have. And if you come by the shop in the morning, I'll get those copper coins for you."

Is it so wrong that I want to keep him around just a little longer? Even if it's just until I leave for Stone's Ridge? I haven't felt a connection with someone in such a long time that I'm not sure I'm ready to let it go yet.

Saint reaches across the gate and picks a blue cornflower. My world slows as he places it in my hair, just above my ear. "I might take you up on that, Blue."

There he goes with that nickname again.

"Thanks for everything," his voice is low, smooth. "I'll see you around."

All I can offer him is a smile as he turns and walks off.

My hand has a mind of itself, brushing the flower above my ear as I watch him go, with a slight rush to his step, as if he can't wait to melt back into the shadows. I note the slight tension in his shoulders and wonder if he's carrying a weight that is not his to bear.

# Ten

## YOU DON'T BELONG HERE

Once again, breakfast is a handful of stolen fruit and a loaf of bread. I'm grateful for the meals shared at Juniper's house. If it wasn't for her, who knew what state my health would be in?

The sleepy town is starting to awaken. My cue to head out, keep my head down, and stay out of trouble. Even though the days passed by and there were no signs of Donovan's men, it didn't mean they weren't still looking for me.

I slip down a side street lined with storefronts. A butcher, seamstress, apothecary, and a cobbler. A few folk are gathered outside the cobbler's, huddled together in a small group. Humans, elves, and a half-orc. Their voices are loud enough for me to hear as I walk down the opposite of the road.

"There are tales bleeding from Breydon's borders about degenerates on the run. Some of the debt lord's lackeys? And

Mrs Harisson said the wheel for a cart went missing, just vanished from her shed. It bodes ill."

My pulse quickens, and I slow my pace, keeping my head down.

A male with pointed ears shoves his hands into his pockets. "Probably best to keep your valuables under lock and key, just to be safe."

"There hasn't been that kind of folly around these parts in some time," the half-orc mumbled.

Half of my mind screams that they're talking about me. Especially the part about Breydon. I knew it was too good to be true—that Donovan would leave me be. Well, if it's taken this long for the tales to spread, I should still have enough time before anyone might show up.

As for the stealing? Surely not. I've taken some measly fruit and a loaf of bread or two . . . Oh, and some paint. That can't possibly be the talk of the town. Who would even notice? No one ever has before.

Though hovering in the shadows, eavesdropping on conversations not intended for my ears isn't going to find me in the good books, so I hurry along.

After the second meal spent at the Fairchilds', I was pleased Juniper confirmed my suspicions. Kamari is a shifter. She has a ring. And I need it. All it would take would be sleight of hand, out the door, and into the night.

I need to figure out what I'm going to do, and I need to do it fast. Usually, I do as I please within reason. So why am I hesitating now?

Perhaps it has to do with a certain dark-haired siren that I can't seem to keep from my thoughts. She has my heart twisted in knots. I see how she struggles, how her mother does. I know what that feels like to struggle in life because it has shaped every corner of my existence. For once, I want to help not hinder, but I know that if I can't get my shifting under control, I won't be a help . . . I'll become the hindrance.

"It's just one ring. Kamari will survive without it," I mutter under my breath as I stride along. Surely given her experience in being a shifter much longer than I have, or having parents who possibly taught her how to control it will keep her safe—and Juni.

For a moment, I balk at my thoughts. They've lost so much already. Why is it so hard for me to make a decision this time? My freedom lies on the hand of a woman whose personality is bright enough to make the moon hide her face. Why don't I take it and leave?

My teeth ache, and I realise I've been gritting them in my frustration. Even far from Donovan's grasp, he still holds power over me. I just want to *live*. To be rid of my past life, and start brand new. I want to find love, companionship—stability. I don't want to always be looking over my shoulder.

Perhaps I don't deserve any of that though. Perhaps my sins will be the shackles around my ankles for eternity. Reminding me daily that someone like me doesn't deserve any of those things.

This has been my thinking for many years.

Until Juni.

She's the first woman who hasn't thrown herself at me and I'm captivated by it. Not because I wish she did, but because it makes her different from the airheads that do. She has determination and goals. Even if I can see that they are weighing heavily on her. Juni. She's different. She's lonely and so am I. I can feel it.

There's also no denying the way she looks at me, or the way her breath hitches when I'm close. She might not outwardly flirt with me, but I know she feels the tension between us, because I feel it too.

If only we had a chance.

The peach in my pocket suddenly doesn't appeal to me. Not with all of these thoughts rushing through my mind at the speed of light. If I could, I'd build a wall, shut them out, hide away from the intrusive thoughts—just for a while.

I round the corner of another street just as a hulking figure steps into my path. At first I think it's the stable master, but I quickly realise it's the male that Juni knows—the blacksmith—and the look on his face tells me he has a bone to pick.

Even if I wanted to avoid him, I couldn't. These laneways are notoriously narrow.

"Something I can help you with?" I say, trying my best to behave.

Theon folds his arms across his chest, obviously trying to look as intimidating as possible. Little does he know I don't intimidate easily.

"I've got a few questions."

I shove my hands into my pockets. "Ask away," I say, tilting my head just enough to make it clear that I am unfazed by his tough guy act.

Theon's eyes narrow. "Who are you, really? What's your game?"

My shoulders lift and fall. "I'm just a guy trying to get by. Doing some odd jobs here and there."

He's not pleased with my answer. I can tell by the way his weight shifts to the other foot and his face becomes darker.

His thick brows pinching in the middle. *What is this guy's deal? What did I ever do to him?*

Theon takes a step closer. "You don't belong here," his voice is low, "and I don't know what your angle is, but let me make one thing clear—stay away from Juniper. And her mother."

Ah. There it is. This is about *her*.

The corner of my mouth pulls up, and I smirk. The kind that I know annoys guys like him. "I'm sorry, but I don't think I need your permission on who I can and can't see around here."

"You don't *need* it, but if I catch wind of you doing anything to hurt them—anything—you'll regret ever stepping foot in Meadowbrook."

I let the threat hang in the air for a moment before replying. "Big words. Are you always this welcoming, or is it just me you don't like?"

Theon shifts his weight again. His umber eyes fixated on me. He's not a happy man. In fact, I should be careful. Would hate to see anyone get hurt. Anyone being him—not me.

"Let's just say I don't trust men who show up with a smirk and shifty answers." His tone is sharp, but his posture gives him away. He's not just pissed—he's protective. His shoulders are square, his feet planted like he's ready for a fight. One that he will not win. I can guarantee. He might have strength from all the metal work he does for a living, but I doubt he has spent his life defending himself from the world.

I can fight in my sleep.

Pulling my hands from my pockets, I stand straighter, showing my height. "You're worried about Juniper, aren't you? That's so sweet."

That riles him up quickly. Internally I am laughing, but I shouldn't be. Yet he is so easy to tease.

"I'm not worried," Theon snaps. "I'm warning you. She's been through enough without some stranger strolling in, acting like he's got a right to—"

"To what?" I cut him off, stepping just a little closer, lowering my voice. "Fix her fence? Paint her shutters? Or maybe you mean share a meal with her family? That's what's got you so worked up?"

Theon's jaw twitches, and for a second, I think he might actually take a swing. So I mentally prepare myself for defence, but then he just shakes his head.

"I don't know who you think you are, waltzing into our town with your smug smile, but if you so much as breathe wrong near her, you'll regret it." His voice is quiet, but the threat is as sharp as a knife.

I meet his stare, unblinking. "Noted."

For a moment, we just stand there, the air between us tense. Then Theon leans back, his glare still locked on me.

"I'm watching you," he says finally.

"Good to know," I reply, flashing a grin as I turn away. But even as I walk off, I can feel his eyes burning into my back. This is really not a great start. I've only been here for a short amount of time and I'm already making enemies.

Theon is clearly in love with Juni. Even a blind rabbit could tell. I feel for him—just a bit—because after the small conversation I had with her in regards to him; I don't think she feels the same way.

Even the time Kamari mentioned him at the dinner table, Juni was quick to dismiss any romantic notions her mother might have. I smiled to myself. It must be nice to have a mother worry about your future. I wish I knew what it was like.

With a sigh, I head towards the chandlery. I promised Juni I would come by to collect payment. The stable master was expecting it too. And I definitely don't need to anger two burly men in the one town.

The sun is above the horizon now, the heat of the day already setting in. When would it end or better yet, when would it bring the storms? I feel like it hasn't rained in forever.

I'm nearing Juni's shop when an old lady waves at me. "Hello, young man!"

She's short and round, her shoulders wrapped in a light purple knitted shawl. For someone who is trying to stay out of the public eye, I sure do seem to be attracting people today.

"Is everything alright?" I cross the street, glancing around at my surroundings, marking all the exits. You know— just in case.

"You're the handyman Kamari was talking about, aren't you?" she says, stopping in front of me.

I raise an eyebrow. "Depends who's asking."

"My name is Mrs Flannigan. Kamari's neighbour from down the road." Her cheeks are rosy red, and her smile bright. "She said you've been helping around town and I've got some repairs that need doing. You see, my husband is busy with work and we are selling our house soon. My usual lad has been extra busy these days. So I'm in a bit of a pinch."

Mrs Flannigan finally takes a breath. For a moment there, I thought she was going to faint on me.

"What kind of work?" I ask, crossing my arms.

"A few shutters need reattaching to the house, the postbox is falling off its post, the front gate is squeaky—you know, odd jobs. The kind that carpenters in town don't have time for."

I have a multitude of thoughts running through my mind as she chatters away. I pick up keywords like *'cat'*, *'moving'* and a few others that sum up her whole life story, really. But what I'm most consumed by is what answer I'm going to give her. Do I take the risk and stay here a little longer? Earn a little more coin? Or do I steal the ring and come nightfall, leave Meadowbrook for good?

My fingers run a path through my hair. "Because I'm new around here, I don't have a lot of supplies. So if you can provide them, I can provide the labour and the tools for a small amount of coin."

"Fair enough," Mrs Flannigan replies. "I'll have my husband collect what you need and have it ready at the house for you. Can you start tomorrow?"

I offer her a grin, accompanied by a nod. "I'll be there bright and early."

She flicks me a smile, turning on her heel. "Not too early! I like my sleep."

A soft chuckle escapes my mouth as I watch her shuffle away. The town, the people—everything feels so tightly wound together, like stepping on the wrong thread might unravel it all. And yet, somehow, I've been pulled into the weave of a beautiful tapestry.

Now, I truly must get to Juniper's. Because I know for certain I'm going to need to borrow some tools.

The chandlery comes into sight. The familiar glass window, with the newly painted sign out the front. It almost feels like

I've known this place in a past life, or perhaps my heart just finds peace here.

A small cluster of dandelions grow from between some cobblestones. I lean down, picking a few. A tiny bit of sunshine in the form of a flower—for Juni.

I take a deep breath. She isn't at the front desk, so I have a few seconds to collect my thoughts before I step inside, because I know when I do see her, the air will be knocked from my lungs, I'll find it hard to think and my hands will want to do things that they shouldn't . . . Unless they've been invited to.

The bell above the door jangles, announcing my arrival, like it always does, but I don't wait for Juni to come to me. I stride out the back with a smile on my face. Yet, I'm not met with pretty eyes and perfectly pink lips in the form of a grin.

Instead, I find Juniper hunched over the workbench, her shoulders shaking as she cries into her arms. The sight stops me cold. She tries to muffle her sobs, her hand clenching a piece of cloth like it's the only thing holding her together. Juniper—so strong, so in control, always carrying the weight of the world on her back. But today? Today she's just a sad woman, crumbling under the weight of responsibility she works so hard to carry, with a broken heart that I want nothing more than to take into my hands and tuck away inside my soul.

"Juni?" I step closer, my voice soft, careful, like I'm approaching a wounded animal. "What's wrong?"

# Eleven

## SMOOTH AND STEADY

I'm so lost in my spiral of emotions that I don't even hear the door to the shop open. I don't hear footsteps across the floor, either. But I do hear *him*. His voice, as smooth as velvet. Warm and comforting as it rolls off his tongue. How embarrassing for him to find me like this. With a blotchy face, red nose, and a tear stained dress.

I quickly wipe my sleeves across my eyes and smooth my hair down before I turn to face him.

Saint takes a step towards me, concern etched across his face. "Is everything alright?"

His eyes beg me to tell him everything. To share with him the inner parts of my lonely soul. I want to . . . I want to share it all with him, but I'm so scared. Scared that he won't like what he finds there, leaving me to feel even more lonely than I already am.

He takes another step. I think I can hold it all together, but I can't. As soon as he tucks the dandelions behind my ear, I'm a mess. Fresh tears fall from my eyes and sobs rack my body once again.

I don't even care for what is proper or not right now. The scent of patchouli and cedarwood touches my senses as I lean forward to rest my forehead on Saint's chest. Between sobs, I breathe him in. Trying to find a way to ground myself, to get a hold of my emotions.

Warm, gentle—yet strong—arms slowly encircle me. Saint holds me as each wave of emotion washes over me. He doesn't probe or push me for answers, he simply stands and holds me. After what feels like forever, the tears finally subside. I don't know how he does it, or what it is he's actually doing, but with him I feel—I feel safe.

Once I catch my breath, I pull back, looking up into his face. He lets me go as I ease from his embrace. "I'm so sorry you had to walk in on that so early in the morning."

His infectious smile tugs at his lips. "It's never too early to purge away the pain, Blue," Saint whispers. The pad of his thumb brushes a stray tear from my cheek. "Now, tell me. What do you need right now?"

I reach for the cloth that I was using to cry my soul into earlier, and wipe my nose. "What do you mean?"

Saint shoves his hands in his pockets, obviously unsure what to do with himself—or me. His eyes travel over my face, and suddenly I want to hide it from him. "Do you want help, or do you want someone to vent to?" His voice is soft but sincere.

My brow pinches. I'm not sure anybody has asked me what I wanted in—forever. Do I even know what I want right now?

Something about the way he looks at me unlocks a part of my heart that I keep hidden away. And before I can stop, all the words come tumbling out in a messy, unorganised kind of way.

"I need help *and* someone to vent to. The Festival of Lights is in a few days and I still have so many orders to finish. It's all so overwhelming. It feels like no matter how many candles I dip, it's never enough." I shake my head, trying to ignore the lump forming in my throat. "I've got debts hanging over me, Saint. Debts that don't care how tired I am or how much I'm struggling to keep up."

Saint's brow furrows, and he straightens, taking a step towards me again. "Debts? I didn't realise it was that bad."

"Nobody does. Well, Mama knows, and she tells me that everything will be okay, but she doesn't know that for sure, and I can't let Papa down." My heart is pounding in my chest as the words form out loud. I've said it. A small part of the continuous ache inside my chest has finally been freed. I don't want to disappoint my father.

"Well, I may not know how to dip candles effortlessly like you do, but I'm willing to help in any way I can," Saint offers.

He's so close to me. The sapphires in his eyes glitter in anticipation as he awaits my reply.

I brush a stray tear from my cheek. "I can't afford to pay you." The words come out softer than I intended. I'll be surprised if he even heard me. It's hard to admit that I can't even afford to pay someone to work with me.

"I'm not asking for money, Blue." Saints' warm voice washes over me. "Let me carry some of the weight?"

The lump in my throat that's been threatening to erupt builds again. He's offering to help me without payment?

Why? Why do I deserve his assistance? I don't want to believe that he might have other intentions, like Theon says. Nothing in his eyes tells me I should be careful, but my mind can't help but keep a small distance between us. Just for now.

"Are you sure?"

Saint nods, placing his bag down on the countertop. A small, brown notebook peeks out from the top. The leather is worn, as if he's owned it for a long time. "If it makes you feel better, I'll never say no to a decent meal?"

"Dinner as payment again?"

He turns to face me, hands on hips. "I thought you'd never ask. Now, put me to work."

The room feels warmer than usual. I can't quite tell if it's because of the close proximity between Saint and I, or perhaps the sun is being extra cruel today. Usually, I find some peace to my chaotic mind while I dip candles in the familiar rhythm, but today my nerves are all over the place. The wick shipment is yet to arrive and there's been no word from them either. The thought of travelling to Stone's Ridge alone also pounds at my head.

"Like this?" Saint beckons from beside the pot of molten wax.

I glance up, catching him holding two candlesticks, the wick making a rainbow shape across his thumb as he holds it above the pot. His face is pinched, focusing so hard that I struggle not to laugh.

My skirts make a swishing sound as I move to stand beside him. "Relax your arm a little. Let it sink under the wax and then pull it back up in a fluid movement," I say, placing my hand over his to steady it. Our fingers brush and I swear my face is the colour of a tomato.

"See?" I murmur. "Smooth and steady. Don't rush it."

Saint catches my gaze as he waits for the wax to drip free. "You're a tough teacher," he teases. "I think I'm getting the hang of it though. Watch out, I might start up my own business—move in on your territory."

I squint my eyes, but can't help smiling. "You wouldn't dare."

He hangs the candle across the wooden drying rack and turns back to me. "Are you sure about that?"

Everything about him pulls me into his orbit. The way his voice sounds, the teasing, his blue eyes, the patterns marking his skin that beg my fingers to trace over them. Yet, all of this excitement scares me. Enough to keep my hands to myself and my thoughts inside my head.

I roll my eyes but can't help the smile tugging at my lips. "You'd probably just end up setting something on fire."

"Fair point," he admits with a chuckle, his voice vibrating so close to me that it sends a shiver down my spine.

Piles of orders beckon for my attention, so I turn my lingering gaze from the ridiculously beautiful man at my side and return to my candles. The hours seem to pass by in a blur as Saint and I move together through the small space. It's almost like a dance that forms between us . . . Like he's done this a thousand times before.

He moves with fluency and ease, dipping, hanging, and re-stoking the fire beneath the pot of wax. Beads of sweat gather at his temples, glistening like molten gold. Saint drags his arm across his forehead, wiping it away. In one fluid movement, he hangs the candle he's just dipped, tugs the bottom of his shirt loose, and pulls it up over his head. It falls to the floor in a silent heap.

I'm transfixed, can't tear my eyes away. Who knows, I'm probably drooling too.

Black ink paints pictures onto his skin. From the tips of his fingers, down his arms, and across his back and chest. Even his neck is etched with patterns. Three faint vertical lines sit under his left eye—a marking of some kind. No patch of skin is left untouched. Everything about him is so different—so beautiful. Like he comes from a different world. One that I've not been a part of before, but one I'm willing to visit.

Saint catches me staring and I almost die internally. Here I am gawking at him when there is much work to do.

"Do you mind if I take my shirt off? It's awfully warm."

I tear my eyes away, finding something on the floor to look at. "Of course not, do what you like. This heat is horrid."

Saint chuckles lightly and returns to the candles. What is wrong with me? None of these orders will be completed today if I keep getting distracted and I'll have no one to blame but myself.

The box of wicks I was using is now empty, so I walk across the room to climb the ladder to the top shelf. Hitching my skirts up, I reach the top rung to grab the last box I have. There is no denying the fact that I'll be making a trip to Stone's Ridge next week—if I want to stay in business.

As I'm descending, my foot slips. I let out a small squeak from the sudden shock of losing my footing, but before I even register that my ass is about to hit the floor, warm, solid hands grip my waist, steadying me.

Heat from Saint's hands tear through my body, and pleasure rips down my spine like a lightning bolt. I suck in my breath and freeze. As I glance over my shoulder, his intense gaze catches mine. "If you wanted to leave me breathless, Blue. There are safer ways to do it."

My cheeks flush with warmth. I've climbed the ladder a thousand times before. Why today of all days, must I slip?

I clear my throat, trying to regain my composure, but Saint's hands are still tightly wrapped around my waist. Making it very hard to concentrate. "Thank you—"

"You keep this up, and I'm going to start charging a rescue fee. Payment in smiles only, of course." Saint winks, his hands loosening their hold as I slowly step down the last few ladder rungs.

Smoothing my skirts down, I flash him a weak smile before turning to the bench to place the box down. Little do I remember that Saint's bag is there and I'm only rudely reminded when I accidentally knock it, and some of the contents go flying—the brown leather book included.

It topples to the floor, landing face up, pages spread wide open. I feel like such a clutz today, and it's so unlike me. Saint must think I am completely out of it. I try to fix the mishap by reaching for the book. In my attempt to rectify the situation, it's not until the book is securely in my hand that I see the image that is sketched onto the paper. The detailing is immaculate. Down to the very last scale. It's me— in my siren form.

My brow pinches. How—?

Saint reaches for the book. "Sorry, I shouldn't have—"

"Wait," I say, twisting away from him so I can study the image longer. When has he seen me? Is he watching me? I don't know whether to be offended or flattered.

"This is . . . This is me?" I say, my voice slightly trembling.

Saint reaches for the book again. "Juni, I—"

"Are you watching me?" My eyes find him.

"Not as much as I'd like to." His smirk returns, but the look on my face doesn't change at his words.

His hands fall to his side in defeat. "It was one time, down by the lake, I saw you."

"And you didn't say anything?"

Saint runs a hand through his hair, lost for words—for once. "What was I supposed to do? "Hey there Juniper, I'm taking a bath. I see you're here too.""

His eyes dart around the room and I sense that he feels just as silly about the drawing as I do about almost falling off a ladder. I look at the picture again. It's breathtaking. He truly has a gift. How can I be cross at him when he's captured me in a way that I've never seen myself before?

I close the book. "You told me that you could only draw stick figures. How untrue that is. You have a talent, Saint."

His gaze drops to the floor.

"Have you thought about opening your own shop? Painting and drawing. Even sign making," I continue softly, holding the book out to him.

He tucks it securely back into his bag before turning back to face me. "Wouldn't that be the dream?" His voice is soft, forlorn even, like he's dreamt of that for so long, but is convinced it will never come true.

I can't help but study his face as he takes silent steps towards me, like a predator stalking its prey. I move to step back, but my hip bumps the edge of the bench.

Saint's eyes twinkle. "Careful Juni, you keep staring at me like that, and I might have to fetch my pencils. Make you sit there while I sketch you again."

Anyone who could hear my heart right now would insist I go and see the healer. Because it is thumping inside my chest in a way that would make even the Creator concerned.

"Who said I'd mind?" My voice comes out softer than I intended, yet Saint hears every word.

He leans in closer, his lips almost touching mine. My heart beats wildly in my chest as I am bathed in his scent. Saint is going to kiss me . . . And I'm going to let him. I shouldn't, because making my life complicated is the last thing I need to do right now. But this invisible tether I feel connecting us together is too strong. I *want* to know his touch. I want to know what it's like to touch *him*. To dig my fingers into his skin as he drags his mouth across every inch of me. I want to taste *him*. To run the tip of my tongue up his vine covered neck. I don't think I've ever *wanted* anyone like I want him.

His lean, muscular body is golden from the afternoon sun, filling the room through the wide open back door. There's no chance I'm looking away now.

Saint's eyes drop to my mouth, and I let go of the thoughts hammering at my mind. My eyes flutter shut, waiting in anticipation for the kiss from his lips.

And just like that, the moment shatters as a log in the fire collapses with a loud crack, sending a shower of embers into the hearth. I jump, laughing nervously, and Saint steps back, the tension easing just slightly, though his eyes still sparkle with a desire that I too feel.

"By the way," he says casually, as if he hadn't almost kissed me, "I saw Theon in town earlier. He seems like a great guy."

I spin, turning my back on Saint as I try to tamp down the rush of heat to my face. "Oh, you did?"

Saint's boots scuff across the ground as he returns to the pot of wax. "He gave me the impression that you and he were an item."

I huff, trying my best not to roll my eyes. "Far from it. He's just a friend. Really, he's just overprotective," I say, glancing over my shoulder.

A smirk pulls at the corner of Saint's lips as he folds his arms, leaning against the counter. "Overprotective, huh? So, he keeps a close eye on you?"

"You have no idea," I sigh, pulling some wicks from the box. "He means well, but sometimes it's . . . Suffocating. I don't need protection. I can take care of myself."

Saint chuckles.

I squint, throwing a glance in Saint's direction. "What?"

"Can you?" Saint teases, his grin turning into something softer, more thoughtful.

"Can I what?"

Saint adds some beeswax chunks to the vat. "Can you take care of yourself? Pretty sure I just saved you from falling off a ladder."

I fold my arms across my chest, trying to look grumpy. "It was one time."

A glorious sound erupts from the male across the room, and as I return to the wicks, I can't stop the smile from spreading across my lips. Saint's laughter is like liquid gold.

"Are you sure Theon's just a friend to you? He seems pretty invested," Saint murmurs.

My words get stuck in my mouth. Theon is just a friend. He always has been, but perhaps I mean more to him than I've allowed myself to believe. My cheeks burn as I shoot him a look. "Yes, I'm sure. Why? Jealous?"

Saint's smirk widens. "Just curious if I should be worried about him throwing a hammer at my head the next time I walk into your shop."

Laughter escapes my lips, and I slap my hand over my mouth, stifling the giggle that wants to run free. We need to get the focus off me and onto more important things. Like—Saint.

"I can assure you that no one is bursting through my front doors wielding violence." I begin to tie weights to the end of the wicks, ready for dipping. "Speaking of Theon. He came to see me at the shop the other day."

Saint's eyes darted to me for a brief second before returning to the candles. "So he does keep an eye on you."

I shake my head. "It's not like that. He was just concerned."

"About what?"

"There are reports of things going missing around town. He wanted to make sure I wasn't having any issues."

His eyes return to me, but his expression remains neutral. "Are you having any issues?"

*If* Saint was stealing things, surely his body language would give him away? Unless he's really, really good at acting.

I shake my head again. "No, not at all—well, not the issues Theon is talking about, anyway."

A small huff escapes his lips as he returns to the candle dipping. He doesn't seem to be even slightly bothered about the accusations on the tongues of the townsfolk. So I shouldn't be bothered by it either. I return to weighting the ends of my wicks. There is no need to fill my cup with other folk's problems, not when I have so many of my own.

"Enough about that, though. What about you? Is there a significant other in your life?"

Saint shakes his head, and I find myself relieved. We almost shared a moment that I've not yet forgotten, and probably never will. It could have been more than awkward should I discover that he's involved with someone.

"I travel too much for love to find me."

His words find a place in my heart, yet it's not a pleasant feeling. It's hard, lumpy, and if it had a colour, it would be grey. There is so much I've yet to learn about him, but he doesn't seem to let people in easily. It's going to take some work on my end.

"Have you travelled all your life?"

He glances at me, accompanied by a small shrug. "I've been to places, but I'm boring. Let's talk more about you."

I sense that his life is not up for discussion right now, so I let the matter rest. Though his elusiveness just intrigues me even more, making me want to pry into his past. Perhaps he just needs to feel safe before he can open up his heart.

The pile of weighted wicks grows. "What do you want to know?"

"Can you just shift into your siren form whenever you like?" Saint's voice is casual, but his gaze flicks to me with curiosity.

Gathering the pile of ready wicks, my feet carry me across the room. I place them beside Saint. "I can. Though I still require my legs to be submerged under water to do so."

"What does it feel like? You know, when you . . . Shift."

I tuck my hands into my skirt pockets and rock back on my heels slightly as I consider how to put it into words. "It's hard to describe. It's like—" I trail off, searching for the right comparison. "Imagine being submerged in water, and instead of just floating, it's like the water becomes a part of you. Every nerve wakes up, and my body becomes alive. An invisible pull tugs and I answer. And when it's time for me to change back, I simply thank it and ask it to let me go."

Saint hangs a dipped candle on the rack, and tilts his head, a faint crease forming between his brows. "Does it hurt?"

I shake my head quickly. "No, not at all. It's the opposite, really. It feels natural, like slipping into a second skin. My legs feel . . . constrained on land sometimes. But in the water? Everything just flows. It's like I'm more myself as a siren than I am as a human."

He stays quiet for a moment, his gaze trailing to the floor, then back to me. "That sounds . . . incredible," he says finally. "But doesn't it freak you out? That pull you mentioned—like you're not fully in control?"

I meet his eyes and shrug. "I used to fight it when I was younger, but now? I've learned to balance it. The pull doesn't own me; it's just a part of me."

His lips tug into a boyish grin. "You make it sound easy. Most people would probably panic if they had no control."

A soft laugh escapes my lips. "Well, I'm not most people, am I?"

Saint reaches across me to fetch another wick. "No," he says, his voice lower, softer. "You're definitely not."

I feel the heat returning to my cheeks, and it's not because of the fire, or the summer sun. "What about you and that book of yours? Are you going to show me what else you've been sketching?"

His gaze travels to his bag before coming back to me. "I could, or I could keep making these candles for you so that we get them all done in time. Which would you prefer?"

I huff, rolling my eyes in protest. "You're no fun."

Saint grins, and I find myself grinning right back. I'm like a small pebble teetering on the edge of a very steep hill. One move in the wrong direction and I'm going to find myself falling . . . hard.

# Twelve

BERRY PICKING

The sky is still pale blue as I leave Mrs Flannigan's. The birds are calling to one another, saying it's time to find their rest place for the night. The air has lost its heat. Yet the sun won't set for a couple more hours. There's still time to return the tools I'd borrowed before my owl shift. Juni had been more than accommodating when I'd asked her if I could borrow them for another job.

Three silver coins clink in my pocket as I walk down the lane, past Juniper's house, and towards the chandlery. It's enough to pay for my boarding, and put some food in my stomach. But it won't be enough to sustain me for long. No matter how strong the pull is to stay in Meadowbrook and get to know Juni further, I really need to start making some plans to move on.

Get the ring and get out.

Laughter to the right draws my attention. Two males with pointed ears cross the street. My heart jerks towards them. It reminds me of the two brothers I'm currently missing. Sepher and Roan. I may have found a small comfort in my new friendship with Juni, but that didn't mean I'd forgotten them.

Where are they? Are they safe? Only two moon cycles to go before it is time to re-group. To form a plan for the future. One where we would all hopefully be free of Donovan.

Though that future isn't quite the future I dream of anymore. I'm tired of the rough, survivalist way of living. I want to build a home. I want to form long term connections. I want to place my roots in the ground, and stay long enough to reap the harvest.

My heart craves the grounded life that I know someone with meadow eyes can give me.

Her name is Juniper Fairchild.

Yet, what I *need* to do and what I *want* to do are two very, *very* different things. And one of those things doesn't get me *her*.

With a heart that's coming undone at the seams, I trudge my way to her shop. She'll be closing soon, and I'd like to return the tools before she leaves.

My eyes are forever darting here and there. Mapping my surroundings. The locksmith walks across the street, toolbox in hand. The moustache on his pale face resembles the hands on a clock. Two young girls with ribbons in their hair are playing a game in the dirt out the front of a pale blue house. Something to do with jumping and a rock. The joy on their faces tells me that the game is most enjoyable.

I smile in their direction, though they are oblivious to my presence. Oh to have the bliss of a child's mind. Not a care or responsibility in the world. I presume it would be nice. I never got to experience it.

Hair on the back of my neck prickles. I sense someone watching me. Not wanting to make a scene, I search without changing my pace. If Donovan's men have finally found me, I don't want them to know that I know. A familiar figure catches my eye. Broad, steely umber gaze, and a beard. Theon. He spots me, yet I pretend I haven't noticed. I have no desire to speak with him today, so I put one boot in front of the other and keep my head facing forward. His judgement is not my problem.

A smudge of forget-me-knot blue appears in the doorway of Juni's shop. When she told me of her debt, I hoped to the *stars* that it did not lay with Donovan.

She has a basket in hand, and she's locking the front door. Is she leaving already?

My pace quickens. "Juni!" I call.

Her head turns at the sound of my voice. Sunlight bathes her figure, and I catch my breath. Her hair is down today. Usually she keeps it in a pile on her head, or confined to a braid. And even though she's beautiful, no matter what style she chooses, I do love it when she wears it down.

Perfectly pink lips form a sweet smile. "Saint, I wasn't expecting you."

I hold up the toolbox. "I wanted to return these before the day's end."

"Of course." She nods.

"Are you heading out?" I glance at the basket she's holding.

Juniper pushes the front door and heads back into the shop, with me close behind. I catch her scent. Honey and lavender. So sweet I want to taste her.

She throws a shy glance over her shoulder. "I was headed out into the forest. My jar of wax berries is empty, and I need more."

I fight the urge to breathe her in as I pass by, heading for the back room to return the tools. "Were you going alone?"

Juni doesn't answer until I've placed the tools down and returned to her side. "Well, yes. I always go alone."

"And it's safe?"

She offers me a small shrug. "I suppose. Though I don't have much of a choice. There isn't anyone who can go in my place, and the sun has not yet set, so I'll be fine."

The thought of her being in the woods alone does something to my soul. I don't like it. Who knows what is lurking in the shadows? Lycans, or even Galanthors—mythical beasts that still roam throughout Sapphire Vale. Remnants of the magic from gods long forgotten. Yet, traces of the magic still reside in certain creatures. I'd seen the odd one here and there in the past years on my travels from town to town collecting debts. You can never be too careful while travelling through the forests.

"Would you like some company?"

Juni's brow pinches ever so slightly. Like she finds it hard to believe that someone might actually want to spend time with her. "Don't you have more important things to do?"

I offer her a grin. "What could be more important than wax berries?"

A slight pink flush creeps up into her cheeks. "Well, I'm sure there are—"

"Blue."

Her eyes find me.

"Lead the way." I gesture towards the door.

Juni tucks a strand of dark brown hair behind her ear as she hesitates by the door. I lift my brow and nod towards it. "Are we collecting berries here or in the forest? Because I'm pretty sure they don't grow on shelves."

The flush on her cheeks deepens, and the smile on her face widens. But as soon as it appears, it fades. "I just . . . I just don't want to be a burden."

I glance towards the sun out the window. There is still plenty of time, so I take a step towards her. "Who said anything about a burden? Think of it as a business transaction. You have food and I'm hungry."

A gentle huff escapes Juni's lips. "At this rate, you might as well move in."

The idea of waking up under the same roof as the stunning woman in front of me sends a sharp pain straight into the vessel inside my chest. It also sends blood straight to the lower regions of my body—imagining Juni in the early mornings, all dopey from sleep. She would look utterly divine in a cotton nightgown.

Taking a step closer, I lean down, my lips barely brushing her ear. "Now, that's a dangerous idea, Blue."

The forest swallows us into its cool embrace, the canopy above turning the sunlight into fractured streams of golden light. A refreshing break from the heat of summer.

Juni walks ahead of me, her wicker basket swinging gently in her hand. Her steps are light and purposeful as she leads the way. I can't help but watch the way her hair catches the dappled light as it spills down her back. Each strand is like spider silk that's been dipped in chocolate.

"How far into the woods are the berries?" I say, breaking the silence.

She glances over her shoulder. "Just through that shrubbery over there."

"You seem to know your way around the forest quite well? And here I thought you were a water creature."

Juni huffs softly. "Just because I'm a siren doesn't mean I only love the water." Her hair picks up in the breeze. "There's something peaceful about the forest, too. My father and I would come here almost daily, gathering firewood or coloured herbs."

Pain is the undertone lacing through her words. It's hard for her to be out here in the woods, doing a task that she used to do with her father. My heart aches for her. I may not know the pain of losing a father, but I do know what it feels like to never know one at all.

"Just as well he taught you the right berries to pick, because if it were left up to me, anyone with a candle would be dead."

Juniper giggles, and my knees nearly buckle at the sound. She's as delicate as a snowflake in winter, yet she shines brighter than the sun.

I shove my hands into my pockets, but keep a close eye on our surroundings. Every crackle of leaves underfoot, or distant bird call sharpens my senses. I'm also aware of the sun's position. I need to be away from Juni and the public eye before I shift. My owl form has been feeling agitated lately, so who knows what kind of behaviour it will display tonight.

"Oh look, is that what we are looking for?" I halt, pointing at a bush covered in pale yellow berries.

Juniper turns to follow my gaze. A small smile dances on her lips, and she covers it with her hand. I hate when she does that. Hides her smile. She should have it painted on posters all over town so people can see just how beautiful it is.

"Only if you're looking for a way to poison someone."

My brow lifts. "I could have sworn they were wax berries. So, what *do* they look like?"

Juniper encircles the basket in her arms, and with a gleam in her eye she tugs her head in the opposite direction of where we are standing. "I'll show you. They're small, clear and grow in clusters. Almost invisible if you don't look closely."

I fall into step beside her. "And what exactly do these berries do to the candles?"

"Well, after I boil them, they release a liquid that looks almost like stardust. I add them to the beeswax to give the candles a shimmer when they burn." She stops by a bush and crouches down. "Something my father taught me."

I quietly drop to my knees beside her, and sure enough, there are clusters of clear berries no bigger than a green pea, covering the bush. With gentle fingers, I begin to fill her basket. The scent of earth and greenery fills the space between us.

Juni flicks her gaze towards me before returning to plucking berries.

"You know," I say, leaning in just slightly, "if you wanted me alone in the woods, you could've just asked."

With a snap, her head turns towards me and she playfully gives my arm a shove, causing me to nearly lose my balance.

Her cheeks are pink again. "Keep talking, and I'll leave you out here to find your own way back."

I release the hearty chuckle brewing in my stomach. Before I know it, the basket is half full. After a few more bushes, it's completely over flowing. The sun is lowering in the sky, and I know I need to make my way back to town soon.

"Let me take that for you." I offer, as I reach for it. Our fingers brush in the exchange, and I hear her breath catch. Without a doubt, I know she feels the crackle of something between us. I see it behind her eyes everytime her gaze meets mine.

What am I doing? Leading her on? All for what? To gain her trust so I can steal her mother's ring? For once, it feels good to help people, rather than steal from them. The way I was made to be isn't how I have to stay. Yet, I *need* that ring. Without it, my inner beast grows restless. Every time I shift, it controls me more than I control it. One day, I might shift and hurt someone I love—or someone innocent. I don't want to live the rest of my life as only half a person. I'll never be able to lie beside the woman I love at night, or to hold future children when they wake from nightmares.

I would *be* the nightmare. What kind of life is that?

Juniper is the first person who I can see laying beside me every night. The mother of my future children. But none of that will happen if I steal her mother's ring. Will it?

Am I capable of being more than . . . this? A thief?

We walk in step beside one another. The forest is peaceful, though I'm keenly aware of the dangers it holds.

"So tell me, was your father a siren, too?"

Juni nods. "He was magnificent. His tail, midnight blue. He used to clean the pumps out for the miners like I do now."

A breeze whips around us, playfully dancing with our hair and clothes. "Do you enjoy—"

The sound comes suddenly—a rustling in the bushes just ahead. I freeze mid-step, the woven basket of wax berries balanced on my hip. Juniper's head tilts, her brow furrowing as her gaze flickers towards the source. A large holly bush, thick with thorns to the left of the path.

"Did you hear that?" she whispers, her voice low and cautious.

I nod, setting the basket down and stepping closer to her, instinctively shielding her with my body. The rustling grows louder, frantic now, like something struggling. It doesn't sound big, though. Whatever it is, it's stuck.

Juniper grabs my arm. "What is it?"

"Stay here," I say, my voice steady. Not that I think she'll listen, but I still need to say it.

I take a step towards the brush, parting the leaves. Thorns snag at my shirt, digging into my skin. The shrill cry grows louder. Finally, I see it. A spotted chestnut robin. Its poor feathers are tangled in the snarl of brambles, wings plastered against a thick, thorny branch, its tiny chest heaving with effort.

"It's just a bird," I call over my shoulder.

Juni hurries to my side, and a cloud of honey and lavender washes over me. "The poor darling. We have to help it," she murmurs, crouching beside me.

Very slowly I reach out, trying not to spook the bird further. My fingers tremble as they work carefully through the brambles, untangling the sharp vines from its fragile wings. It flinches, but I shush it quietly, murmuring nonsense under my breath. Juniper leans closer, her presence oddly calming.

"Gotcha," I whisper as the last thorn loosens. The bird quivers in my hand, its tiny claws gripping my fingers for a moment before it flutters free disappearing into the canopy above.

Juniper exhales, a small smile playing on her lips. "That was kind of you."

I shrug, brushing off my hands on the sides of my trousers. "I know what it feels like to be trapped."

Her meadow-meets-the-sunset eyes find me, and her brow creases ever so slightly. "What do you mean?"

The atmosphere is becoming sombre much too quickly. I should have kept my mouth shut.

"You know," I grin. "The daily grind. Work, eat, sleep."

Juni sighs beside me. "Don't I know it."

"You certainly do, and that's why we need to get these berries back to the shop. Those candles won't dip themselves." I collect the basket in my arms once again, and we begin our journey back into Meadowbrook.

As we walk, I can't help but glance at her out of the corner of my eye, the soft curve of her body. The way her nose turns up slightly at the tip. Her perfectly pink lips. Everything about her lingers in my mind far longer than it should.

I would love to be the one carrying her basket for the rest of her life, and yet there's an underlying fear that my involvement might disrupt the peace she's built. Will she ever want me when she finds out the darker side of my soul?

Some might even ask, how do I even know anything about love? But that's just it. When you don't have something your whole life—it's all you think about.

# Thirteen

## RASPBERRY PINK SLIPPERS

Early morning sun drenches my face as I sit on the back step of the shop, drinking my tea and eating the breakfast scone Mama had packed for me. Cleaning out all the pumps in the lake earlier made me hungry. The back of my head drops against the wooden door frame as I lean all my weight on it. I close my eyes and savour the peacefulness before I have to get up and open the shop.

No wicks. No letter. I was treading water. Without them, next month's orders would have to be cancelled, and then I'd be in more debt than I'd like to admit to myself.

Sitting here on this step wasn't going to get those orders finished, though. With a sigh, I get up and throw out the dregs of my tea leaves onto the grass. One foot in front of the other, I tell myself.

Like clockwork, I turn the front door sign to open and head to my desk to study today's list. The morning sun has barely reached across the floorboards when the door bursts open, the bell above it jangling loudly. A mountain of a man stomps inside, his face flushed red as if he's been stewing all night. My heart sinks immediately—Mr Kent. Wonderful.

"Where's my order, girl?" he bellows, slamming his hands down on the counter hard enough to make the candle displays wobble.

"I'm working on it," I say, keeping my tone as calm as I can manage. My hands tighten around the edge of the counter. "You'll have it by tomorrow, like I promised."

"Tomorrow's no good!" he snaps. His beady eyes narrow, and I can smell the faint trace of ale on his breath, though it's barely past breakfast. "I needed those lantern candles yesterday. How hard can it be to pour a little wax? Too busy playing shop, are you?"

Heat rises to my face, anger mixing with the knot of anxiety in my stomach. "I've got more orders than just yours, Mr Kent, and I'm doing my best."

I wanted to offer him a refund so he could take his business elsewhere, but if I did I'd be low on coin, and either way he'd spread ill rumors about the shop, meaning I'd potentially lose customers. No. I had to be firm, no matter how red in the face Mr Kent was becoming. I'd told him I couldn't guarantee the timeline.

"You watch that tone," he growls, leaning closer like he's trying to intimidate me. "I'm paying you good coin, and I expect—"

The door creaks open again, cutting him off mid-rant. I glance over his shoulder and my body stiffens as Theon steps inside, his broad shoulders blocking the light for a moment.

"What's going on here?" Theon's voice is calm, but there's a sharp edge to it as he takes in the scene.

"None of your concern," Kent barks, glancing back with a scowl.

"Oh, it's my concern," Theon says, stepping further into the shop. His presence seems to fill the room. "You're yelling at Juni, and I don't take kindly to people shouting at my friends."

I can see the way Theon's fists curl at his sides, though he keeps them relaxed enough not to escalate things. "Everything is fine here, Theon. Thank you."

"She's got a job to do," Kent mutters, though his bravado falters under Theon's steady gaze.

"And she's doing it," Theon says evenly, his voice low and pointed. "Now, you've made your complaint. How about you let her finish that job instead of wasting her time?"

"Me?! Wasting *her* time?!. The candles were meant to be delivered yesterday!" Kent roars, going red in the face.

Theon takes another step towards the enraged male, and I grit my teeth. This is not helping. "Theon, please! I have it handled!"

"I'm sure Juniper has very valid reasons as to why she has not delivered your candles yet, so why don't you shut up and let her speak," Theon rumbles.

Mr Kent's beady eyes glare between us, but after a tense pause, he huffs and stomps towards the door. He turns back to jab a finger in my direction. "Tomorrow. No excuses."

"It's a pleasure, as always, Mr Kent!" I call after him.

The door slams behind him, rattling the glass panes.

"Charming," Theon mutters, watching him go before turning to me. "You all right?"

I nod, though my heart is still racing. "I'm fine. Thanks for stepping in, but it really wasn't necessary."

He shrugs, leaning casually against the counter. "Didn't seem like he was gonna back off on his own. You shouldn't have to deal with that kind of thing alone."

"I can handle it," I say, brushing my hair back from my face.

I appreciate Theons chivalry but truly, I could have handled it on my own. I don't need rescuing . . . Do I? Am I that helpless that men think they can walk all over me?

My chest expands as I take in a deep breath, trying to calm my nervous system. There was no point dipping candles with an unsteady hand.

"I've been worried about you since we last spoke," Theon utters.

I reach for an apron, securing it around my waist. "Why?"

"Because I've seen that Saint guy hanging around and I don't like it, Juni."

My brow pinches. Since when did Theon get a say in who I keep company with? He doesn't own me. "I can assure you, there is nothing for you to worry about."

Theon isn't convinced. He straightens, folding his arms across his chest. "There's rumours coming out of Breydon, about a dangerous criminal on the loose. What if it's him?"

I place my hands on my hips. "Do you have proof?"

With a huff, Theon runs a hand through his hair. "No—"

"Then stop making accusations. You don't know him at all."

Frustrated brown eyes find me. "And you do?"

My vision tunnels. My heart pounds in my chest. I can't say that I know Saint either, but I'd like to think my moral compass knows when it meets friend or foe. So far, there's been nothing in Saint's actions to warrant a I'm-a-dangerous-criminal sign slapped across his forehead.

I shake my head, taking in a deep breath to steady myself. "I don't know him, but I think I'm a good judge of character. Now, please, can we stop talking about Saint?"

Theon huffs, shoving his hands into his pockets. "Fine, but just know, I'll be the first to send the law his way if he steps out of line."

I nod. "Thanks Theon, but I'm sure everything will be fine. I have to get to work now."

With a silent nod, he heads towards the door, pausing halfway out. "I'll be here if you need me." And with that he leaves.

I watch from the counter as his back disappears around the corner. Frustration tugs on my heart. I recognise that Theon nature is to be protective, it's always been that way. It's how he shows care, but I'm overwhelmed with everything, and I don't need him to act like I can't handle myself, or that I need rescuing. Everything is fine.

Even if it's not.

It's past midday when I finally take a break. I look at the hundreds of candles hanging on racks from the ceiling, all the way to the floor. I'd be lying if I said I wasn't impressed with myself. All of Mr Kent's candles were drying and would be ready for packing this afternoon. He couldn't be angry at me now.

I flop down on the stool, taking in the scene before me. My mind travels to Saint. The last time I was in this room with him, he almost kissed me. My eyes flutter shut as I try to picture the scene again. I imagine he's right in front of me, his hands on either side of my shoulders as I lean back against the counter.

First, he tucks hair behind my ear before he traces a finger across my cheek. His thumb rubs across my bottom lip, causing my lips to part and my heart to race. He leans in further, his scent of patchouli and cedarwood washing over me. I breathe him in, anticipating the moment his lips will touch mine.

I can't remember the last time someone made me feel like my body was on fire—certainly not Wesley—and I can't help but wonder what it would be like for Saint to bend me over one of these benches.

My hand reaches down between my legs, the ache there longing to be touched. It's been so long since I felt the touch of a man. And Saint's is the only one I crave. I cross my legs over my hand, forcing myself to pause. What am I doing? Why am I fantasising over someone when I know it's foolish to get involved when I don't have the energy to offer them more than a kiss?

I shouldn't be getting attached to any part of him. He's travelling through, and I don't have time for love. Besides, what if I let him in and he disappears from my life?

But I *want* to kiss him. I want to feel his hands on my body. I want us to explore each other together, even if my mind tells me no. The vessel in my chest feels tethered to him, and it's telling me yes.

He was so gentle with that bird yesterday, despite his rough exterior. Perhaps he would be gentle with my heart, too?

My hand has a mind of its own as it returns to exploring the warmth under my skirts. Though I'm rudely interrupted when the bell above the door jangles again.

Feeling flustered, I scramble from the stool as I straighten my dress. I need to stop this tomfoolery right now. I'm a sensible woman, so I'd better start behaving like it.

I poke my head around the corner to find the sunshine on my dark days.

Dove.

Her silver eyes light up when she sees me. "It's been far too long since I saw you last." She darts across the room, pulling me into an embrace.

"It's been a week," I chuckle.

Dove pulls back. "Like I said, far too long."

I move to the front counter, and Dove follows. She chats away about her work, and how busy it's been. I happily listen as I tie ribbons around clusters of candles. Her face lights up with joy as she talks about the latest fashion, and who's wearing what.

She finally takes a breath. "Juniper!" she says, drawing out my name like she's singing it. "You are coming to the tavern with me tonight. No excuses."

Placing down the ribbon, I groan quietly. "Must I?"

A frown forms on her lips. "You promised you would soon. Please?"

It's true. I did promise that. And it's been too long since I spent some quality time with her. Her big, beautiful eyes plea as she waits for me to answer.

My mind flickers to Saint—his teasing grin, the way he's taken up space in my thoughts far too often. A distraction might not be such a bad idea.

Still, guilt bubbles in my chest. And my thoughts flicker from Saint to my father. He always taught me to put responsibility first, to work hard and never let things slide. Would he think I was being frivolous?

"It's not like you're abandoning the shop," Dove presses, sensing my hesitation. "One night won't ruin your business, I promise."

I chew on my bottom lip. She's not wrong, and deep down, I know I could use the break. Maybe stepping away from everything—even just for a few hours—might help me breathe.

"All right," I say finally, holding up a finger. "But straight after work. And we're not staying out late. I mean it, home before the sun sets."

Dove lets out a squeal, clapping her hands together like she's won a prize. "Deal! You won't regret it, Juni. I'll meet you at the tavern!"

Before I even have a chance to say another word, she whirls out of the shop, leaving the room silent once again. Maybe this is exactly what I need—a chance to feel normal for a change, to remind myself there is more to life than candles. Still, the weight of responsibility lingers, a quiet voice in the back of my mind.

Just one night, I tell myself. Then it's back to work.

I stare at myself in the mirror. I'd at least tried with the different colour rouges on my dressing table. I'm not sure if I've done the best job, but I do feel a little prettier. My hair is a different issue entirely. It's too straight to do anything with, so I leave it brushed and loose.

A soft knock sounds at my bedroom door. Mama pokes her head around the corner, a smile gracing her face. "Oh yes, that is perfect."

My hands float over the fabric of my shell pink dress. I usually only wore this on special occasions. Tonight seemed fitting.

Mother reaches for my brush and drags it through my hair. "You have such lovely tresses, Juni."

I catch her eye in the reflection. "I wish it was curly like yours."

She smiles softly. " We all want what someone else has. Your hair is perfect for you."

Mama places the brush down and gives my shoulders a squeeze. "I'm so glad you are going out. You deserve it. Perhaps you'll find love tonight."

I spin on the chair to face her, a humorous huff escaping my lips. "I highly doubt it, mother dear. Besides, I definitely don't have the energy for that. Nor is anyone who actually lives here interested in me."

She opens her mouth, but I quickly hold my finger up. "And no, I'm not interested in Theon. He's a great guy . . . He's just not *my* guy."

Mother picks up a pink ribbon from the dresser and places it on my hair, deciding if I need something extra or not. "What about Saint?"

My cheeks flush at the mention of his name. Trust my mother to not let the matter rest. She decides I don't need the ribbon, placing it back down. "Perhaps you should pursue things with him?" She continues.

The room suddenly feels warmer than it should. Probably because all the focus is on me and my nonexistent love life. I stand from the chair, brush my skirts. Mama's right, this is the perfect dress. The neckline runs low across my chest, blending into off the shoulder sleeves that are peasant shaped, cuffing at my wrist with pearl buttons. The skirt is gathered at my waist, ending just above my ankles.

I reach for my dyed raspberry-red leather slippers. "I don't think he is looking for love, nor will he be in town long enough to find it."

"Are you certain?"

"Well, I guess not. But even if he was interested in me—"

Mama's brow lifts. "And how do you know he isn't?"

My shoulders rise and fall. "I think he's the kind of guy who likes to keep things casual. Besides—I don't have space for love. Especially if it's not long term," I murmur, slipping my shoes on.

She doesn't answer, but when I look up, I see a small tear glistening in the corner of her eye. "Mother, what is it?"

She sits down on the edge of my bed, her hands clasped together in her lap. "I wish I could help you more, Juni. If my back wasn't so bad—I hate that you are carrying everything on your own." Her voice is soft.

I pause, turning to face her. The weight in her words tugs at something deep inside me, but I force a smile and kneel down beside her. "Mama, it's okay. I don't mind working hard. It's what we need to do to keep the roof over our heads, right? You've done so much already. It's my turn to take care of us."

Her eyes glisten as she reaches out, brushing a hand over my cheek. "You deserve more than this. More than working yourself to the bone."

I lean into her touch, closing my eyes for a brief moment. "I'm fine," I insist, gripping her hand and squeezing it gently. "We'll be fine. I promise."

She tries to smile, but it doesn't quite reach her eyes. "You're a good girl, Juniper. Too good."

"Maybe," I tease lightly, standing and twirling for her. "But for tonight, I'm just going to be a girl having a little fun. Don't wait up, okay?"

Her chuckle is soft but genuine, and as I head for the door, I glance back at her. The lines of worry on her face haven't disappeared, but for now, I'll let her believe that everything is okay. For both our sakes.

There is no need for a coat, as the summer heat still lingers in the air. I close the door behind me and make my way to the front gate. Smiling as it swings open beautifully without a sound. The walk to the tavern is pleasant, and I find myself growing more excited with each step. I'm glad Dove insisted I go out. For a few hours, I'm going to pretend that I don't have a care in the world.

Even though the sun is still in the sky, townsfolk are scurrying home to their beds, warm dinners, and leisurely time before the stars come out to play. I offer the odd smile here and there as I make eye contact, though none of them are Saint.

I wonder what he's doing right now, or even where he would be? Perhaps he's found more work somewhere, or even left town. Surely he would say goodbye first, though? I definitely owe him at least two dinners, so I'd say he's around here somewhere.

The Wildflower Tap is already bustling with life as I near it. Patrons trickling in through the large swinging doors. My heart beats a little faster as I walk up the steps and enter the tavern. Dove spots me before I see her. She comes flying at me in a flurry of colour. She's always wearing something she's created from the scraps at the seamstresses. Tonight, it's a mix of yellows and blues.

"You're here!" Dove grips my hand, dragging me towards a table to the left of the room.

The smell of spiced cider, roasted meat, and wood smoke wraps around me like a cloak. A burst of laughter erupts from a table near the fireplace, where a group of men are already deep into their drinks. The air is thick with voices—some shouting over each other, others conversing in corners.

"There are already so many people here," I loudly say over the noise.

Dove grins. "Isn't it so exciting?"

My gaze wanders around the room before it rests on a cloaked figure in the corner by the front doors. His back is against the wall, but there's no missing the colour of his eyes despite the distance. Saint is here—at The Wildflower Tap.

Suddenly, I'm very aware of my outfit, my face, my hair. Was it all too much?

I smile at him, and he returns it but doesn't make a move to come over. Should I invite him?

"Who are you looking at?" Dove's voice interrupts my thoughts.

Clearing my throat, I reach for the pitcher of water on the table. I pour myself a cup and take a drink before nodding my head in Saint's direction.

Dove follows my gaze. "Hello, sir. Who is that?" she hisses, turning to face me again.

My cheeks feel warm as I make eye contact with Saint again. He takes a swig of his ale, and I feel like we are having a silent conversation with just our eyes.

It's Dove's turn to clear her throat, and I realise I've been staring this entire time. "He's just a guy who's been helping around home and the shop."

"No guy that looks like that is 'just a guy,' Juni."

I flick my gaze to Saint again. He's still looking my way. I agree with Dove though. He's definitely more than just a guy, but who exactly?—is the question.

"You're practically glowing when you look at him! Why are you holding back?" Dove leans across the table so she doesn't have to shout.

"Because tonight is about you and me. Now, let's have some fun."

Dove sends me a knowing look. "He could be fun?"

A grin forms on my lips. "Stop . . . I barely know him."

"Oh, come on, Juni! When was the last time you had an orgasm with another person? And Wesley doesn't count. He was terrible in bed."

My jaw drops open. "Dove! . . . He wasn't terrible in bed!"

She gives me a side eye as I playfully swat her arm.

It was true, Wesley was terrible in bed. Or perhaps he just wasn't confident enough. Either way, it's been a while since I found pleasure in a man.

The evening draws on, and I find myself having more fun than I imagined I would. The plate in front of me is nearly empty, crumbs and smudges of sauce the only evidence of the hearty stew I've devoured. I wipe my fingers on the edge of my napkin, leaning back in the creaky chair as Dove waves for another round of ale. The warmth of the tavern has seeped into my skin, and the tang of the drink lingers pleasantly on my tongue.

"You're slowing down on me," Dove teases, nudging my arm with her elbow. She downs the rest of her mug and slams it on the table, grinning. "Can't have you fading this early, Juniper. The night's just getting started."

I laugh, shaking my head. "I thought we agreed on not staying out late?"

"That was before I got you out of your house." She grins at me, her cheeks rosy from the drink, and when the fiddler strikes up a lively tune, she's out of her chair in an instant.

"Come on!" She grabs my hand, pulling me up before I can protest.

Saint hasn't left the chair in the corner of the room, just as his gaze never leaves me. The ale has definitely gone to my head because I find the courage to let myself be free as the music picks up. It's infectious, and I can't help but pick up my skirts and tap my feet to the beat.

Dove twirls around me, a smile plastered on her delicate face. The heat in the room intensifies, but I don't care. For a moment, the worries that usually press on my shoulders—debts, responsibilities, expectations—melt away.

She catches my hand, spinning me again, and I throw my head back with laughter. I'm not sure if it's the ale, the music, or the sheer joy of the moment, but for the first time in what feels like forever, I let myself have fun.

Saint watches as I dance, causing that heat to build down low in my stomach. It's not like me to act this way, but my body has a mind of its own at the moment. I'm dancing for me, but deep down I know I'm dancing for him, too. I want him to notice me. There may be other males dancing around Dove and I right now, but I only have eyes for *him*.

The room around me narrows until it's only Saint and I. He watches intently while I dance. Letting the music wash over my soul, like it's been starving for water. Time slows. Who knows how long I dance for. I only know when the trance ends.

Saint finishes his ale, winks at me and disappears out the front door, like a spirit, as if he was never truly there to begin with.

Sounds rush around me. My feet stumble across the floor, and I no longer feel like I'm riding on a cloud. Instead, I'm weighed down by reality.

Of course he left. Why would he be interested in me? I'm no one. Not the prettiest girl in the room, or the funniest. What do I have to offer anyone? I should be ashamed of myself for letting the drink go to my head. I've probably embarrassed myself. Besides, I'm not worthy of that kind of interest—especially from someone like Saint, who is free-spirited and capable of so much more than plain Juniper Fairchild.

The evening has been wonderful, just what I needed, but it's time to return to the real world. Where I have a bed that is calling my name, and a mountain of orders to return to in the morning.

# Fourteen

## PERFECTLY PINK LIPS

I want to stay and watch her. I want to be the one spinning her around the room, and joining in on the fun, but dancing would only bring more attention to myself. Being at The Wildflower Tap was a risk in itself. When Mrs Flannigan had paid me handsomely, I'd wanted to treat myself to an ale or two. It's been weeks since I allowed myself that pleasure. So I'd come early for a quick pint.

Seeing Juniper walk through the door was certainly a surprise. One I was not expecting. I didn't want to disrupt her evening, so I stayed at my table, watching closely. I watched her interacting with her friends. Laughing with her mouth and her eyes. *By the stars* her eyes. I want to drown in them. I love watching how she carries herself, how her energy fills the room.

But as soon as the menfolk began their descent on both Juni and her blue-haired friend, jealousy got the better of me. I didn't like the way they grabbed at her, placing their sweaty palms on her small waist, drawing her closer.

Watching them lit a fire inside of me that would soon rage if I didn't leave. So that's what I did.

Now I stood outside, leaning against a large oak planted in the town square. Some of its lower branches conceal me. The perfect position to be able to watch the comings and goings of townsfolk also visiting the tavern. Summer heat sends a warm breeze through the tree canopy. The sun will soon set and I'll have to disappear for a while—until dawn. But I'll stay right here for as long as I can—until Juni leaves. I want to make sure she gets home safely.

My gaze stays focused on the town around me. Theon appears from down a side street, heading for the tavern. Thankfully, I'm out of his view, though I do hope his presence at the tavern doesn't keep Juni much longer. Something about them being together drives me crazy. It shouldn't. But it does. Juni is convinced she feels nothing for him, but that doesn't mean Theon won't try to change her mind.

I shove my hands into my pockets, leaning my good shoulder against the tree trunk. I'm grateful there's little to no pain on my other side. All of this downtime has allowed my injured shoulder to heal, and now that it has I have no reason to stay.

Do I?

Melodic laughter spills into the dusk as Juniper and her friend tumble out the doors of The Wildflower Tap. I take a step back behind the trunk, not wanting to be discovered.

Juni piles her hair on top of her head with one hand, fanning her face with the other. "The heat was too intense after all that dancing."

Her friend nods in agreement. "Did you want to stay at my house tonight?"

A chocolate waterfall of hair spills down Juni's back, and I imagine running my fingers through the silky tresses. Fuck. She is so beautiful. The dress she's wearing is driving me wild. The way it fits her body like a second skin does something inside my chest. My heart twists, lurching towards her like it's trying to crawl into the space beside hers.

My hands fist in my pockets as I strain to hear her answer. I want to get her alone. I want to tear the dress from her body, explore every inch of her skin with my lips.

Juni reaches for her friend, pulling her into an embrace. "Thanks Dove, but I'd best get home to Mama. Tonight was wonderful."

Relief washes over me. She was going to walk home alone. Perfect.

The women part ways. Yet I haven't made a move to follow Juniper just yet. Thoughts hold me back. If I go after her, it will be the end of all self-control.

Perhaps it's best if I don't follow her. Don't offer her my heart. Because I know I don't always choose the right thing, but she does. She's the sensible one working hard, making a living for her and her mother. Here I am floating about, stealing and concealing my true identity. I'm complicated, and her life is already so full.

I watch her walk towards home.

However, if I stay, I need a ring. But it can't be Kamari's ring, and there aren't any other shifters around here that I've seen. So if I'm being honest with myself, there is no point in staying if I can't control my shifting.

Frustration tears through my body. I'm done missing out.

I push off the tree and follow her.

The evening sky bleeds orange and purple as I trail a few steps behind her, keeping my presence quiet. The soft thud of her boots against the cobblestone road is the only sound between us, apart from the occasional chirp of a bird settling in for the night.

As she turns to head down a side street, I catch a whiff of her scent, and I'm done for. There's a shortcut where I will meet her at the other end. I slip down the alleyway with hurried feet. A small space between two buildings allows me to wait in the shadows for her. I hear her coming before I see her.

Just as she passes, I step from the shadows, collecting her arm in mine as I push her up against the wall of the weatherboard building behind her.

A squeal begins to form on her lips. My instincts take over, and before my brain can catch up, I cover her mouth with my hand. Silencing her. The instant her warm breath collides with my palm, a sharp jolt runs through me. Her body goes rigid, her eyes wide, her breath quickening beneath my touch. For a moment, I think I've gone too far—I hadn't meant to scare her.

Then her meadow eyes find me. Her pupils are dilated, but there is something else there, not just the fear of my sudden appearance. Something I'm struggling to name—something deeper—wild, even.

I see the way she is looking at me—like she's trying to piece me together. She stays still beneath my hand, not fighting, not trying to pull away. Instead, she seems to be . . . Waiting.

My body is so close to hers. I can feel her heart thrumming in her chest. She's not fearful anymore, she's curious.

Fuck.

She wants this too.

My breath catches, and my chest tightens. I'm not supposed to feel this way. I'm supposed to be leaving town—leaving her. Running away, hiding, doing as I'm told. It's all I know how to do.

Yet that undeniable pull between us tightens. I can't deny it. It's like gravity is shifting, tilting the whole world on its axis, and Juni and I are about to collide.

I didn't think my heart could beat this fast, but as soon as Juniper's hands melt between us, gripping the front of my shirt, it beats erratically. Almost jumping right out of my chest.

My hand slowly releases her mouth, my thumb dragging across her bottom lip. She doesn't move, or say a word, just flicks her gaze between mine and my mouth. I lean in closer. She's inches away from me. I should stop, pull away, but the thought of her slipping from my grasp feels like a mistake—like I might never get another chance.

One hand grips her waist, tugging her closer as the other sits flat against the wall over her head. Her breath catches, and I'm done for. My body betrays me as my trousers grow tighter. With a soft groan, I lean forward. "Ju—"

"Juniper!" Theon's voice suddenly echoes down the alleyway.

Instantly, my body stiffens. Juniper tries to peer around my frame. "Is that Theon?"

"Unfortunately, it is," I growl under my breath. Trust him to show up at the worst possible moment. Was he following Juni home from the tavern too?

Juni doesn't move. It's like she's waiting for me to decide how this is going to play out. *Fucking Theon.* I could flatten the bastard in the blink of an eye, but I highly doubt Juni would appreciate that.

Perhaps I could steal a kiss before slipping away.

Footsteps grow closer as Theon approaches, and just as he comes into view I take a few steps back. Instantly, I feel the absence of her warm body. It's safe to say I am thoroughly pissed.

Theon folds his arms across his chest, a scowl on his face. "What is going on here?"

My jaw tightens as I exhale through my nose, shoving down the sharp irritation rising in my chest. I'm still fuming from the last time he cornered me in the street, and now he's here again, stomping all over a moment that was none of his fucking business.

"What's it to you?" I mutter, refusing to step any further from Juniper.

Theon's glare flickers between us before settling on her. "Are you alright?"

She straightens, lifting her chin. "I'm fine, Theon. You don't need to—"

"What are you even doing out here with him?" he interrupts, his voice edged with suspicion. "You know people have been saying things, right? How do you think your father—"

At the mention of her father, Juni's eyes glaze over. I see the way her body flinches, and she begins to retreat inside her shell. Does Theon have a clue what he is doing?

"What the actual fuck?" I snap, crossing my arms. "Did you follow her all the way home just to bark at her like she's some helpless little thing?"

Theon turns on me so fast I almost think he's gonna swing. "I don't trust you."

"Yeah, I gathered that much." I smirk, tilting my head.

Juniper moves to stand in front of me. "Theon, please—"

"Stay out of this, Juni," Theon barks, not even looking at her.

Something in me bristles at that. No way does he get to act like she's not standing right here. I step closer, just enough to make my point, my voice dropping low. "You wanna pick a fight with me?"

Theon's nostrils flare. "I don't know who you think you are—"

"ENOUGH!" Juni cries out, shoving her body between us. "You're both acting like animals, and it's embarrassing."

I take a small step back, putting distance between Theon and I, but my fists stay clenched at my sides. I'm ready to defend Juniper and myself.

"Juni—" Theon starts.

Her head snaps towards him, her voice quivering. "Don't. You know better than to act this way. I'm ashamed of you."

Theon's shoulders drop as Juni turns her attention to me. Her eyes beg me to calm down. She doesn't want to see anyone get hurt. I do as she bids, taking another step back.

"Now, I am going home. No one . . . And I mean, no one follows me."

My once beating heart, filled with desire and want, is now shattering as I watch Juni spin on her heel and stride away. Her pink dress disappearing around the corner.

Theon shifts on his feet, and I'm quick to face him. "Happy now?"

"I warned you. If you hurt her—" he mutters.

I take a few steps towards him so my face is inches from his. "You'll what?"

"Just stay away from Juniper."

I huff a quiet laugh, shaking my head as I step back. Theon watches me like I'm a wolf eyeing the flock. Maybe I am. "Juni is her own woman, I'll leave her alone when she tells me to."

Theon curls his fists. I've hit a nerve. There's no stopping the smirk rippling across my face. Voices and distant laughter drift through the air. People are coming out for the evening, and if anyone catches us like this, it's going to cause some sideways glances. Something I don't need.

He takes a step towards me, like he's chomping at the bit, fighting the urge to unleash his rage on me.

I meet him halfway. "Everyone can see you're in love with her, but does she return your love? You pine after her like a lost dog, but she doesn't need a dog—another mouth to feed."

His eyes darken. "I'm exactly what Juni needs."

I release a low chuckle. "Only Juni knows what she needs. And if that's me then you're going to have to pry her from my cold dead fingers."

Theon, frustrated and furious, steps into my space, our faces mere inches apart. The anger in his eyes is matched by the burning rage inside my soul. "You might want to be careful with your next move," my voice drops to a low growl. "You have no idea who you're messing with."

I'll fight him if I have to. If it means he'll stay out of my business. But I don't need the law bashing down the loft door at the stables while I sleep, and I certainly don't need to re-injure my shoulder again. Not when it's healing so nicely. So I keep my fists to myself—no matter how hard it is.

However, I stand my ground. My gaze never wavering.

Theon's upper lip curls in disgust as he starts to back away. "There are rumours that some rogue lackeys from Breydon are on the run. You sort of fit one of the descriptions."

Dread fills my stomach, sinking like a weight, but I keep a straight face. I can't afford to make a scene. "I have no idea what you're talking about."

Theon eyes me. "You'd better be on your best behaviour . . . I'm watching you."

"You've said that before. Usually, I like to have dinner together first." I grin.

With a snarl, Theon abruptly turns and disappears, leaving me alone in the street. I glance towards the sky. *Fuck*. The sun has almost set, and I don't want to shift in town. This evening hasn't turned out how I thought it might.

Sounds from the village melt the further I hurry away. Even though I don't like not being in control of my body, shifting is probably what I need to do. To spend some time in the trees, soaring and escaping reality for a while.

Because right now, my mind is in turmoil. I'm at a crossroads, and I need to decide what to do. I'm not ready to give Juni up yet, but if anyone shows up from Breydon, I'm going to have to give her up, anyway.

Perhaps I need to leave Meadowbrook. Just for a day or two. Let the dust settle. Juni could get some peace, and Theon will get off her back.

It's decided. I hurry back to the loft and write Juniper a note. Then before my shift happens, I dash to her house. Placing the note in the latch of her garden gate. No movement in her cottage can be seen from where I stand, but there are red shoes at the front door. She made it home safely. My heart feels a little at ease as I disappear through an overgrown laneway and head into the forest with my bag over my shoulder.

Just a day or two, then I'll come back for the ring.

# Fifteen



## WHEN DEBT COMES KNOCKING

The lake is still. The early morning mist curls over the glass surface like a breath. My arms ache from hours of clearing debris from the pumps, yet it's satisfying seeing them hum back to life.

Ice cold water spills over my skin, pulling my hair in every direction. It feels so good to lose myself in the world underwater, even if it's only for a while. Down here, I'm Juni, the siren, clearer of pumps. I don't have any other responsibilities. Perhaps I should stay down here—swimming with the fishes.

On the surface, I'm Juni, the candlestick maker. The breadwinner. The companion. The daughter. The friend. The woman who is slowly sinking under the weight of all her problems.

I tug free the last string of weeds that have found themselves lodged in the pipe shaft. It hums to life again. Satisfied that my job is done, I kick my fins into motion and head to the very bottom of the lake bed.

As I lay with my back against the pebbled surface, I look at the world above me. It's a shimmering kaleidoscope of gold, blue, and green. I suck water into my amphibian-like lungs that allow me to switch between breathing air and water. My body absorbs the dissolved oxygen while I'm submerged.

I could stay here for a while. Where it's quiet and cool. I should be on my way to the shop, but my mind is elsewhere.

On Saint.

On the way he caught me unawares, and it was only for the briefest moment that I was afraid. Once I knew it was him, my body came alive, aching for his touch. For the way his gaze lingered on my lips, the rough scrape of his voice as he whispered my name. Even now, the thought of him is driving my body wild. Desire pooling in places that it hasn't in such a long time. But it was the way he looked at me before Theon arrived that won't leave me alone. Like he actually wanted me. There's no denying that I wanted him too.

Then Theon had to go and ruin it all with his overprotectiveness. Creating an atmosphere of toxicity, disrupting my very pleasant evening. How does he keep showing up when I need him the least?

A school of silver minnows dart above me, their scales reflecting the sun, making them look like streaks of liquid silver travelling through the water.

I close my eyes and sigh, trying to stay submerged in the peace of the lake. Saint is not a part of my plan. But I want him to be. How do I make it so?

After finding his note on the gate this morning, my heart feels heavier. He is gone, only for a day or two, but clearly his run in with Theon had ruffled some feathers. I don't blame him for needing some space. The note said he'd found some work out of town and would be back in a day or two. I think it was more than that, though.

Who knows if he will even return? I wouldn't blame him if he didn't.

If he does come back though, perhaps I could ask him if he truly needs to leave. Perhaps I could help him start his own trade of painting shop signs. He could use the space at the back of the shop, and we could turn the small shed into storage for him.

I shake my head at the silly notion forming in my head. How would I know what Saint wants? I barely know him at all. Yet, I'd like to.

Frustrated with all the thoughts swimming around, I push off the lakebed and rise to the surface. The morning sun warms my skin as I drift towards the shore. Miners are already lining up to start their morning panning for precious stones. A few see me, sending me a wave of thanks as I retreat from the water.

With a soft utterance of thanks, I tell my siren self to let go. It releases me with ease. A tingling sensation washes over me as my legs form. The weight of them makes me feel clumsy as I stumble from the water. At least the refreshing dip in the lake was a good start to the day. Who knows what awaits me at the shop, besides the large pile of orders.

My feet carry me to the chandlery, and before I know it I'm unlocking the front door. The familiar scent of beeswax, honey, and lavender wash over me. A comfort and a sense of dread riding on it. I set the sign on the door to open, tie a white apron around my waist and begin making a fire.

Time seems to pass by quickly, and I'm startled when the bell above the door jangles, announcing my mother's presence. Her bright-green eyes find me from across the room as she holds up a bundle wrapped in lilac chequered cloth. "I brought us morning tea. Scones and plum jam."

I smile at her before resuming reading the ledger spread open in front of me. It slipped my mind that she was coming in this morning to do the bookkeeping. "How's your back this morning, Mama?"

She bustles past me to the back room. "Fine, Juni dear. Nothing I can't manage."

The quill makes a soft scratching sound as I mark the orders I've completed so far. Mama sits at the counter, spectacles perched on the bridge of her nose as she flips through the ledger. The scratch of her quill also fills the quiet shop, accentuated only by the occasional creak of the wooden chair beneath her. Even though I should be concentrating on what I'm doing, I can't help but glance her way every few seconds. Trying to read her face. She mutters under her breath and my heart sinks. It's not looking good and I know it.

I try to put the worry from my mind as I move into the display area of the shop. Dusting some candles, and checking what coloured sticks I need to dip next. The only way this feeling of heat in my stomach will disappear is if I keep my mind and my hands busy.

"Juni?" Mother calls.

I brace myself for bad news as I pop my head around the side of the entryway. "Yes, Mama?"

Her eyes glisten as she exhales and nods. "You're doing a great job."

Relief loosens the tight knot in my chest, but it doesn't last long. Mother taps her quill against the page, her expression now serious. "As long as there are no interferences," she continues, "and we can get our hands on more wicks, we'll be able to make the next debt payment on time."

I sigh, wiping my hands on my apron. "That's a big if."

"So, you've not heard anything?"

My eyes drop to the floor as I shake my head. "Unfortunately—"

The door to the shop opens. I spin on my heel with a smile plastered on my face, ready to greet the customer.

Three hulkling shadows step into the shop and my heart once again sinks to the bottom of my stomach. Theon is here, with—two strangers. None of them look pleased. I know they aren't the law, as they don't wear colours I recognise, but I notice the emblem stitched on the front of their jackets. A coiled serpent wrapped around a jagged crown. These don't look like friendly folk.

I square my shoulders, trying to look confident. I'm still mad at Theon and don't particularly want to speak with him right now, but obviously I don't have a choice. "Good morning, gentlemen—Theon—how can I be of assistance?"

The two strangers waltz forward with a sway that doesn't sit well in my stomach. Before the day's end, I'm going to need more than one cup of lemon balm tea to calm my nerves. "We're here to remind you of the debt that you owe."

My vision tunnels, and my heart thuds inside its bone cage. I think I might even pass out. We will need to close the shop. I'll have to start packing to sell the house. How will Mama cope with losing father, and now her house? Will we have to move to a different town?

"Juni?" Theon calls my name. "Juni, are you alright?"

I swallow, my heart kicking up a notch. I knew this day would come, eventually. I'd only missed one payment, but I was going to make up for it with the next. I thought if I kept my head down and worked hard, I'd get away with it. But not this time. Soon they wouldn't ask politely. They'd start demanding, perhaps become threatening.

I nod slowly, keeping my expression neutral. "I'm fine. I appreciate the reminder and I can assure you that I will have payments as soon as possible. Is that all you're here for, or do you need something else?"

Mother's stool squeaks. "Is everything okay, Juniper?" She senses something going on. I know it. Yet none of this needs to involve her.

"It's fine, Mama," I call over my shoulder.

My gaze flicks to Theon, who looks at me like he's sorry he's barged in here. What is he doing with these men, anyway? Could they not find father's shop on their own, so he assisted them?

The shorter male of the two, the one with the ring in his bottom lip, and the shaved head takes a step towards me. "We've heard that you might know the whereabouts of someone we're looking for."

My brow pinches together. "And who might that be?"

The male with the scar across his left cheek fishes for something in his trouser pocket. He holds up a crumpled poster in front of me. It's a sketch. My heart almost stops working. I'm definitely going to pass out now, but I can't. I won't let them see my reaction.

It's a picture of Saint.

I swallow down the fear crawling over my skin. "Who is he to you?" My voice quivers, as I try to keep my limbs from shaking.

Theon steps around the men to stand closer to me. Usually I might find it somewhat of a comfort considering how intimidating these debt collectors are, but after his behaviour recently, it's not a comfort at all.

"Come on, Juni." Theon encourages. "Tell them where Saint is."

"Yeah, be a good girl for your man here and tell us where he is," the man with the scar across his face grunts.

I keep my lips tightly sealed, though my gaze doesn't waiver.

The shorter of the two men folds his arms across his chest. "Just you and your Mother here, huh? Shame. Doesn't seem safe." The smile he offers me sends my stomach to the floor. It's wrong—evil.

My attention fixates on the men before me, as I try to muster up the words to defend myself—the shop.

Look at them lording their sex over me like they're superior. Thinking their stares and broad figures will make me feel small. I'm tired of men doing that in my life. My father never treated women this way, and always taught me my worth. So I squared my shoulders again. "I have no idea where he is."

The men look agitated, and the air in the shop feels heavier than usual, thick with unspoken tension as the two men glance around. Their eyes flick over the counter, the shelves, the workspace behind me—searching. But they won't find him. Saint isn't here.

Theon shifts his weight to the other foot. "But you know where he is staying, right?"

I shake my head. "I have no idea. I haven't seen him all day, nor do I know where he's staying."

Even though I had no idea why these men wanted Saint, something inside me told me to be careful. They were looking for trouble, and I refused to play a hand in it. For the sake of the blue-eyed stranger who'd taken up residence in my heart, and for the sake of my mother, I would play the ignorant woman. It shocked me how easy it was to lie. Despite the warning about the debt I owed, I would not speak out.

Theon steps closer again. "You saw him last night, Juni."

"So did you!" I spat back. "Do you know where he is?"

I had him there. The two men stole a glance towards Theon, who was beginning to look a little red in the face. "I haven't seen him, and I'm not the one who spends their days with him."

The shorter male takes a step closer to the counter. "Just so you know, he's wanted for murder."

My fingers grip my skirts as I steady the shaking in my body. I refuse to bend the knee to their intimidating tactics. How can I believe anything they say? A morsel of fear that they speak the truth blossoms in my chest, but I shove it down. Until I speak with Saint myself, he is innocent in my eyes.

"Fine, all I will say is he said something briefly to me yesterday about leaving town and heading north, and I haven't seen him since."

The taller male grunts in frustration, and Theon eyes me warily, like he doesn't believe a word I'm saying. I keep my gaze locked on all three of them, hoping that my confidence will be enough to send them away.

"Can we check out the back? Make sure you're not . . . Lying?" The taller male with the scar across his cheek motions his head towards the back room.

I scoff, folding my hands across my chest. "I don't have to say yes, but I will, only to prove the point that I have no idea where Saint is."

He roughly pushes past me, but I stay close on his heels. Mother's brow pinches as we all step into the back room, and I try to have a silent conversation with her. "These men here are looking for Saint, but he's not here, is he, Mama?"

She's quick to shake her head. "Haven't seen him for a few days."

Internally, I smile, she's not one to feed someone to the wolves ever, especially not if she doesn't know the full story. And until I find Saint, and have my own words with him, I'll remain oblivious.

With a satisfactory grunt, the men walk back into the front of the shop. "If you see him, send us word." The shorter man flashes a yellow grin my way. My stomach curdles at the sight. "Oh, and about that late payment, don't think Donovan hasn't noticed. Because he has."

Dread washes over me. I can physically feel the colour draining from my face. "I know when my payments are due."

"Oh, we're sure you do," the taller man says. "But sometimes, people need a little incentive to stay on schedule."

I glance at Theon. My heart is cracking right through the centre. He brought them here. He brought this dread to my doorstep. He may not know what he's done, but once these men are gone, I am going to give him a piece of my mind.

The shorter man tsks. "Let's hope the next payment is on time." His eyes gleam as they settle on me. "Because if it isn't, well . . . Donovan doesn't like to be kept waiting."

A slow, creeping chill spreads through me.

The taller man leans in slightly, just enough to make the warning feel more personal. "Miss Fairchild, let's just say . . . if you don't pay what's owed, we'll have to find other ways to make up the difference."

I hate the way my pulse hammers at his words, the unspoken implications laced between them.

The shorter man grins. "See you soon."

With that, they turn on their heels and leave, strolling out as if they hadn't just poisoned the air with their presence. The door shuts behind them, but it does nothing to quiet the storm in my chest. My gaze lingers on Theon's back, and my heart feels heavy.

Mother rushes to my side the moment the door closes. "You did so well, Juni. What horrid men, and what is Theon doing all caught up with them?"

I shrug, fighting back the tears that want to spill. "What are we going to do, Mama?"

I find her warm gaze, and she pulls me into a solid embrace. We both stand silently in the front of the shop for a moment, allowing the nerves to settle.

Mother pulls back, cupping my face in her weathered but soft hands. "Saint is a grown man, he can take care of himself, but if you see him, you might want to warn him."

"That's just it, Mama." My voice shakes. "Saint left town for a few days, and I don't know when he is coming back."

"Well, maybe they will be gone by the time he returns." Mother squeezes my hand and heads back to the stool. "As for those wicks, I think you will have to leave for Stone's Ridge—tomorrow."

I spin to face her. "And who will look after the shop, Mama?"

"I will." She beams.

The fire crackles and pops, reminding me that there is so much to remember and do. Would Mother even know the process well enough?

My hands find their way to the top of my head, where I clasp them together and pace around the room. I was truly hoping I'd hear word from the supplier and I wouldn't have to go to Stone's Ridge all by myself. Dove can't come with me, she works every day. I refuse to ask Theon to go with me. He will be lucky if I ever speak to him again. And Mama certainly can't. So that leaves me. Stone's Ridge is a week's ride away, too. I can't afford to take a traveller's wagon, so I'll have to walk.

With a groan, I flop down on a spare stool. "And who will help you?"

Mother shrugs. "Wilson, from the dairy farm. He's been looking for extra coin, and he's a hard worker. Together, we will get it done."

"How can we afford that?" I say softly.

Mama shrugs her shoulders. "He's young, his father caught him vandalising Mr Tucker's barn, and he's been handing him off to businesses around town to make up for it. We won't work the boy for free, but I think if we ask Mr Tucker he'd be happy to have more work for him. And we don't have much of a choice, do we?"

"And what of the festival in a few days? Do you think you will get all the candles done on time?"

Mother nods eagerly. "I will make sure of it."

I groan softly. "And your back? You will be in so much pain."

Mama reaches out to squeeze my knee. "We all have to make sacrifices Juni, I will do my part happily."

I shake my head, deep down I know I don't have any choice. If I want to keep food on the table, a roof over my head, and Donovan away from the shop, I need those wicks.

I grip the letter tightly in the pockets of my skirts. My eyes dart around, making sure I'm not being followed. Saint is still out of town, but I know he's been staying at the stables run by the half-orcs.

After Mother left for the day, I was determined to finish as much work as I could, because tomorrow I was leaving. However, I needed to get a message to Saint if he came back while I was gone. So here I was, scurrying to the stables to deliver said letter.

The sun is low in the sky, and I'm grateful that some of the shadows conceal me, making it harder for eyes to follow. Solid gates, as thick as tree branches, loom before me. I hurry over to them and squeeze through the gap, not bothering to undo the latch.

Horses of all colours and breeds scatter across the paddocks. Tails swishing, muzzles snorting as they chase away the pesky flies. The stable master, also known as Grim, looks up from the chestnut horse he is grooming as I approach. He wears a smile on his face, his tusks jutting over his bottom lip. "Juniper, how are you?"

"Hello Grim," I say, with shortness of breath. "Is Saint around?"

I know he's not, but I just want to be certain that he wasn't lying to me about leaving town.

Grim exhales through his nose. "No." His gaze sharpens. "He in trouble?"

I shake my head quickly. "No, nothing like that. I just wanted to leave him a note."

He watches me for a moment before jerking his head towards the loft. "Go on, then."

I flash him my best smile and head towards the large, red stable on the hill. It's been a while since I've visited—not since Papa passed away. Growing up, I used to come here all the time when Father and Grim got together to swap stories over rum and a pipe. I'm almost certain I've left toys here when I used to play in the loft.

I climb the narrow steps; the wood creaking under my weight, and push open the door. Dust lingers in the air, catching in the late afternoon light that filters through the single, grime-streaked window. The space is small—smaller than I remember.

And the bed—if I can even call it that—is barely a bed at all. The thin mattress looks like it's seen better days, the blanket folded so neatly that it doesn't seem like it's been used at all. It makes something twist deep in my chest.

Has he even been sleeping?

I swallow hard and step forward, placing the folded note on the small table by the bed. My fingers hover there for a moment longer than necessary before I pull away.

I don't know if he'll see it.

I don't know if I'll see him again when I return.

All I can do is hope.

Before I leave, I reach for the small door on the only cupboard in the room, and I pull it open. My breath catches when I see a small, carved wooden horse on the shelf. It sits proudly beside some old tins of paint that are covered in layers of dust. My fingers brush the horse, picking it up for a brief moment. This was the horse Grim carved for me. I'd left it here many moons ago, in the hopes that one day a child would find it, and it would become theirs to play with. I hoped that it would bring joy, like it did with me.

I smile softly, placing the horse back down. The door shuts quietly, and then I'm down the ladder and back outside the stable.

A pain rips through my chest. What if last night was the last time I saw Saint? My last words had been, *"No one follows me home."* Tears threaten to spill again. Will he be here when I return? Will I ever see him again?

I wave to Grim as I hurry back down the lane to the gates. I don't want anyone to see me crying, especially over a male whom I know so little about. Yet, I can't help it. As soon as I'm safe and near to home, the wave of emotion crashes over me, and I allow it to break. This is why I shouldn't let my heart get close to people. Because they leave, and I'm left here—shattered and alone.

It was my fault though, so I can only blame myself. I should have kept to my candle making and leave the relationship building and the adventures to the folk who could afford to do it.

Stone's Ridge calls, and I must answer.

# Sixteen

## BLUE FORGET-ME-NOTS

Lavender scented paper crinkles in my hand. My heart is pounding in my ears. Did I read it correctly? Reading isn't my strongest ability, not that I announce that to listening ears. It's embarrassing. Someone of my age struggling with words. I can make out most, but longer ones, containing more than eight or so letters, become a chore. The letters jumble together and it's hard to let them roll off my tongue.

I've only been gone for one day, and now that I'm back, everything has changed. I read the letter again. My hand trembles as it grips the paper.

*Saint,*

*I've left for Stone's Ridge, I'm not sure how long I will be gone. Hopefully, only two weeks. I hope to see you when I'm back, but if not, thanks for everything.*

*Juni*

*P.S. Be careful out there. Two men came into the shop looking for you. They didn't seem like friendly folk. I sent them north.*

I thought staying away would be good for both of us, but in truth, it was the last thing I should have done. If Donovan's men hurt her in any way, I would never forgive myself.

Watery morning light spilled through the grimy window of the loft. Surely she's only been gone for a few hours. If I leave now, I could catch up to her before nightfall, before I—

Fuck.

I need that damned ring. I can't follow her into the woods, and then disappear at night while I shift into an owl. Especially when my owl form feels like I'm becoming more and more animalistic with each and every shift. I don't want her to see me so out of control. I also need to get out of this town. The small sliver of hope that maybe—just maybe, Donovan had given up on finding me was shattered. Who was I kidding? As if he would ever stop searching for the sons who made him the most coin. I will never be free of him.

The letter falls to the bed in a whispered heap as I drag my hands through my hair. Five strides is all it takes to walk from one side of the loft to the other, as my pacing intensifies. I'm torn. What. The. Fuck. Am. I. Doing?

My boots scuff against the dusty wooden floor, my hands now resting on my hips as I bite my bottom lip. Of all the things consuming my mind right now, Juni wandering off into the forest alone is my greatest concern. I won't allow it. She *needs* to be protected. Not because she's a woman, but because even the bravest of men would fear Galanthors and Lycans.

I have to go to her, but I'm not leaving this town without that ring. Without a second thought, I grab my bag and shove my very little belongings into it. Sketch book, pencils, my compass and the few apples I'd snatched from an orchard on my way back to Meadowbrook. Juni's letter—that smells just like her—goes into my trouser pocket, and the wilted sprig of blue flowers goes into the breast pocket of my jacket.

I glance around the room to make sure it's how I found it before I close the door quietly behind me. Who knows if I will return here again?

Grim is taking horses from the stables to the pastures. I offer him a wave, catching his attention. He stops and turns the horse, walking back towards me.

"You're back? Juniper was here last night looking for you."

I nod. "I got her note, thank you."

Grim stands beside the horse, one hand on his hip. "Is everything alright?"

Not wanting to show any signs of alarm, I smile and offer him the loft key. "Absolutely, it's just time for me to move on. Thanks for everything."

Grim's brow twitches, but he doesn't question further when he reaches for the key. "You're welcome here anytime you need a place to stay."

Something in the half-orcs invitation warms me. It's rare that I'm ever invited back to a place, or welcomed into the warmth of someone's home. My heart twists towards the stable master. "Thanks, Grim."

The green skinned half-orc nods, before walking off with the dappled grey horse. I take one more look at the place that I'd called my home for the last few weeks. It was exactly what I needed at just the right time, but now it was time for new adventures. Ones that were going to take me on paths treacherous to my soul, but ones that needed to be trodden all the same.

The 'open' sign hangs on the door of the chandlery. Though I can see through the glass window that it's not Juni at the counter, it's a young male with fiery-red hair. Kamari potters beside him, their attention held on the ledger that I always see Juni with.

Anger tugs at my chest. Why would Donovan's men even come to her shop? How would they associate me with her? Have they been watching us this whole time? A puff of air escapes my lips. There is no way Donovan's dense men were watching me. They don't have the brains for that.

I need to get in there and find out exactly what happened.

The street is clear as I step out from behind the tree. I steal across the road and enter the shop. The bell above the door barely finishes jangling before Kamari's eyes are on me.

"Wilson, will you stir the wax over the fire for me? I need to serve this gentleman," Kamari chirps at the red-haired male with a smile.

Wilson eyes me quickly before disappearing out the back.

"Where is she?" I ask.

Kamari sighs as she sits on the stool behind the counter. "She left for Stone's Ridge before dawn this morning to go to the wick supplier."

"And you let her go alone?" My voice comes out harsher than I intended.

"What would you have me do, Saint?" Kamari uses her free hand to rub her temple, and that's when I notice she isn't wearing her ring. It's not the first time I've seen her without it, yet this time it just feels more intense. Like fate is finally being kind to me. "I have no husband, no sons to accompany her and if you know Juni, she is a determined woman with a mind of her own. She and I knew this was coming."

I push down the unease clawing at my ribs. "What happened?"

Kamari hesitates, then sets down her quill. "Two men came in. Debt collectors from Breydon." Her mouth tightens. "We missed last month's payment. They seemed upset, but I think it was more than that."

My world shrinks as Kamaris words register. Debt. The debt that Juni owes belongs to Donovan. I had hoped with everything inside of me that it didn't—but of course it does. He has his sulphurous tendrils in every town he can sink them into, poisoning everything he touches. I should've seen it sooner. Should've known. But I never thought to ask her who she owed money to. Never considered that the weight she carried, the strain in her voice when she spoke about making ends meet, was because of him.

A slow, simmering anger coils in my gut.

Because now, it's not just her problem. It's mine too.

I fold my arms across my chest, trying to blanket the fire building in my soul. I'm surprised there isn't smoke pouring from my nostrils at this point.

"They threatened her?" My voice is flat, but I can feel the heat behind it, creeping up my spine.

Kamari nods. "A reminder, they said."

I flex my fingers, jaw tight. I should've been here.

"Who brought them to the shop, and how did they know to look for me there?"

Her eyes dull a little, the light fading from them. It was almost as if she didn't want to say the words out loud. "Kamari—" I urged.

She drops her shoulders with a gentle sigh. "Theon."

Heat rips through my body. I'm going to fucking *kill* him. He's interfered with me one too many times.

A warm hand stretches across the counter to grip my arm. The pounding in my head calms for just a moment. Kamari's bright green eyes are filled with concern. "Is everything alright?"

I exhale through my nose, forcing the heat back down. "I'm fine." A lie, but there's no time for anything else. "I just don't think it's safe for her to be out there travelling alone."

Kamari nods. "I agree, but without those wicks we can't fulfil orders, and if we can't do that—then we will be worse off."

It tears me up inside at how hard Juni works to keep her father's business alive and food on the table. She pours everything she has into it—her time, her energy, her damn heart—all to honour his legacy and make sure her mother is taken care of. But who is taking care of her? Kamari does what she can, keeping the house in order, offering quiet support, but it's not enough. It's not nearly enough. Juni carries the weight of it all on her own, and I can see it wearing her down, even if she won't admit it. She's stubborn, too proud to ask for help, but that doesn't mean she doesn't need it. And gods, if there's one thing I know for sure—it's that she deserves better than this.

Juni needs support, someone who will have her back. Someone who will stand beside her through times good and bad. Is it so wrong of me to hope that I could be that someone?

Probably.

She's the wick—ever burning, lighting the way, and holding steadfast, while I am the wing—drifting wherever the wind takes me. Even if I could imagine a life together with her, with Donovan around, she would always be in danger.

I shake my head softly. "What matters is that it's not safe for Juni to be traveling alone." I head for the door. "I'll go after her."

Kamari's eyes water as I turn back one last time. "Thank you, Saint," she murmurs. I offer her a faint smile as I leave the shop. If I hurry, I will catch her, although there is something I need to do first.

The window slides open with barely a whisper. Just as well I oiled the hinges. I slip inside, careful with my footing, my breath steady despite the fact that I shouldn't be here. I don't want to touch anything I don't have to.

Familiar smells greet me in the silence of the room. Boxes of soap, washing baskets, and a small pile of linens tell me that I'm in the washroom of the house. It feels so wrong to be here, but I can't let that bother me. I need to do this.

I move quickly, silent as I make my way down the hall, ignoring everything that isn't necessary. I'm not here to snoop. I'm here for one thing.

The bedrooms.

I hesitate in the doorway of hers.

It's small, but perfectly her. A bed in the corner of the room is covered with white and pale blue linens. A floral cushion sits on a dainty cream-coloured chair by the window, and a sturdy, round wooden table next to that. I wander to the dressing table, grazing my fingers over the hairbrush, and small pots of rouge. There is nothing fancy about her room, but it feels intimate, and suddenly I feel guilty for being in here. The air is laced with the scent of her—warm, familiar, something soft beneath the sharp edges of my guilt. Maybe, when it's all said and done, she'll forgive me.

I push forward, slipping into Kamari's room instead. It takes me a minute to search through the drawers of the dressing table, my fingers grazing over a green box. I flip it open, and there it is—the ring. Its thick gold band wraps around, joining together in an oval-shaped surface.

I close my fist around it, exhaling slowly, before I shove it into my pocket. Instantly, it feels as though it's burning a hole into my trousers, but I have no choice. I need it. With this ring, I can finally live my life, free of shifting every night. Free to roam the world, choosing to shift or not. Surely Kamari and Juniper will understand.

A heavy feeling settles in my stomach. Unease begins to creep its way up my throat, but I can't focus on it. If something were to happen to Juni out there in the woods alone—

I can't even finish the thought.

The coast is still clear, so I slip through the silent and unmoving house. One glance towards Juni's room, then I get out. I slip back through the window, moving fast, quiet, disappearing into the back garden before anyone knows I was ever here.

The town is well and truly awake as I hasten through the streets. For once I don't care if I'm seen or folk notice me. I'm leaving anyway, but not before I give someone a fucking mouthful.

Clanging of metal reaches my ears before the blacksmith comes into sight. I don't hesitate.

The moment I step into the blacksmith's shop, my gaze locks onto Theon, and the anger I've been carrying—boiling just beneath my skin—erupts. He barely has time to register my presence before my fist crashes into his nose.

Bone crunches under my knuckles, and I imagine his nose shattering into hundreds of tiny pieces. That's gonna hurt.

Theon staggers back, knocking into a rack of tools with a loud *clang*. He lets out a sharp grunt, hand flying to his face, blood already trickling between his fingers.

"What the fu—" Theon straightens, blinking away the shock, his expression hardening as he wipes the blood from his face.

The tension between us is palpable.

"You sent her out there alone," I growled, stepping closer. "Do you have any idea what kind of risk you put her in? What if something happens to her? All because you thought bringing Donovan's men to find me was a good idea."

Umber eyes darken as Theon stands taller. His stance doesn't faze me. I've killed men larger than him.

"You may not like me, but those men are the ones Juni should be protected from—not me," I mutter.

Theon exhales through his nose, still pinching the bridge to stop the bleeding. "I was just trying to protect her—"

"Well, all you've done is put her in danger. You've put Juniper on Donovan's radar. His men will be watching her now, hoping they'll find me."

Confusion washes over Theon's face, his voice louder than I'd like it to be. "*You're* the danger. *You're* wanted for *murder.*"

It's true that my hands aren't clean. I've roughed people up—some worse than others. I've broken bones, emptied pockets, and taken things that never belonged to me. But I've also never killed anyone who wasn't trying to kill me first.

I'm not proud of it, but when you only know one method of living, it's hard to see a different way. Harder still to believe you deserve one.

Survival doesn't come with a rulebook. And for someone like me, mercy has never been a luxury—it's been a risk.

A few folk pass by peer into the blacksmith. I wait until they move on before answering. "I'm wanted for standing up to the man everyone else is afraid of. I won't be his weapon anymore."

Theon's brow pinches in confusion. "But—"

I take another small step towards him closing the gap between us so I don't have to speak loudly. "I have been on the run for weeks. Hiding from a man so wicked that he will use anyone and anything to get what he wants. Including Juni, if it means punishing me."

"I didn't know—"

"Of course you fucking didn't, because you only think of yourself. Do you even love her?"

Theon's eyes narrowed, his jaw tightening. "And what do you know about love? You're a rogue, not a man who knows how to love someone."

My lips curled into a cold smile, my temper rising once again. "I know enough. I'd never have allowed her to go off alone if I loved her. I'd be with her, protecting her, not standing here acting like this is some kind of game."

"Why didn't you say you were on the run from Donovan?" Theon hisses.

My face is inches from Theon, so close I can see the frustration burning in his eyes. I don't know if it's because of me, or because he suddenly realises the weight of his actions.

"You never gave me the choice." My voice is low. "One look at me, and you'd already decided who I was to you. A problem—someone who only knew how to destroy things, not protect them."

Brown eyes study me for longer than I like. I ready myself for a fight, but Theon's shoulders drop. "I just wanted her to be safe, and to me, you weren't safe. I never meant to put her in harm's way."

The heat building in my gut simmers, but I don't let it rise. I'm wasting too much time standing here arguing with the buffoon of a man in front of me.

"How can I fix this?" Theon sighs.

My head shakes. "You can't—but you can lend me a horse."

My mind flicks to the wilted stem of blue forget-me-nots in the pocket of my jacket. The flower name alone was all the invitation I needed. She doesn't want me to forget her. She came to the stable to find me, and tell me, but I wasn't there.

I take a few steps back. "I'm going after her."

## SUMMER HEAT BRINGS THE RAIN

The road is well worn. Many horses, feet, and carriages have travelled this way. I'm grateful it's easy to follow. One of the fears hammering at my mind is the potential of getting lost in the woods, not knowing where to go. I'd never left the safety of Meadowbrook on my own before. Any trips out of town were always with my parents.

Not this time, though. I'm all alone.

I shift my backpack, the weight of it evident by the way it was cutting into my shoulders. I'm not used to lugging something so large for long periods of time.

Mama helped me pack: cheese, dried meat, a few slices of fresh bread and a small, brown, wax covered paper full of blueberries. It wasn't a lot but it would be enough to get me through until I reach the next town before nightfall. She'd also insisted I take Papa's old dagger. Just in case.

Golden summer sun shines through the trees like floating ribbons winding their way through the air. I rub the back of my neck; the heat is taking its toll on me. Mother had insisted I wear trousers, a blouse, and a cloak. Even though it's much too warm, it would protect me from the elements and any pesky insects that might find me a tasty morsel.

By the sun's position in the sky, it is noon. I've been walking since before it had even risen. Probably wasn't the wisest idea, considering the creatures that potentially lurked in these woods at dawn and dusk. However, I needed all the time I could manage to make it to Fernwell before the moon decides to wake.

Instinctively, I reach for the small pouch of coin inside my trouser pocket. Mother had also made sure I had enough to pay for my lodgings each night. It was a loan against ourselves. More debt that I will have to make up for. At first I'd refused, but Mother insisted. She didn't want to think of me camping under the stars amongst who knows what. To be fair . . . neither did I.

Thoughts of a blond-haired man accompany me with every step I take through the woods. Will he ever return to Meadowbrook and see my note? The letter he'd left said he'd be returning in a few days, but perhaps that was his way of saying goodbye. Giving me hope, but also letting me down gently. Yet, how could I forget the almost kisses, the way his hand would brush against my knuckles as he walked past. Or the way I'd catch him looking at me, like he *wanted* me.

Is a future with Saint even possible? He's a nomad. He's always been clear that he was only passing through. Perhaps we are simply not meant to be.

I shake my head, wiping the back of my hand over my forehead. I need to stay focused. For now, Saint is gone and I have something important to do. Maybe one day we will cross paths again. Maybe then we can be free to explore each other.

Perhaps if I'm lucky, he will be there when I return home.

A flock of pigeons race through the forest canopy, the sudden rush of wings startling me. I halt, grabbing my chest in the hopes it will still my thudding heart. I was not made to walk these woods alone, not when I barely know how to use a knife. Though what choice do I have?

Mother doesn't force me to work, and she certainly helps where she can, but I know that if I don't do it, we will have to sell everything, and then be left with nothing. We will have to start over, and I'm just not sure I'm ready to do that.

The road is quiet, save for the soft rustle of the trees swaying in the morning breeze. My mind drifts to Saint again—his sharp eyes, his infuriating smirk, the way he makes me feel seen in a way no one else has before. I shake my head again, forcing myself to focus on the path ahead. If I'm going to get to Fernwell, I need to be thinking about my surroundings and not the male who invades my dreams most nights with his sapphire stare.

I glance ahead. Then I see it.

A figure stands in the middle of the road, cloaked by the harsh shadows of the midday sun. My breath quickens, and I slow, heart pounding. Heat floods my body as a wave of panic washes over me. Bandits? A Galanthor? A Lycan? I swallow hard, fingers twitching as if that might somehow make me less of a target. But as I step closer, the shape shifts into something else entirely.

A deer.

Just a deer.

My shoulders drop, and I pause for a moment. Gathering myself. The tension in my chest releases on a shaky exhale. I can do this. I can be brave. It's only a deer.

The doe lifts its head, ears flicking in my direction before bounding off into the sea of trees. I place my hand over my heart, willing it to slow down. Suddenly, I'm all too aware of just how alone I am out here. What if it hadn't been a deer? The thought makes the hairs on the back of my neck stick up.

I need to get out of this forest, and the only way to do that is forward, so I pick up my pace and hurry along. Minutes pass by. My heart has found a somewhat normal pace, so I slow down. Perhaps I should sit a while, eat some blueberries, and allow myself a moment to breathe.

I glance around, spotting a patch of soft, green moss clinging to a decaying log off the side of the road. Lowering myself to sit upon it, I groan, and the backpack falls to the forest floor. My body is aching in places I didn't even know existed. I pull the pouch of berries from my satchel and begin to eat them. The taste bursts on my tongue—sweet and juicy. The smaller, hard ones are my favourite. I chew slowly, allowing my body to regulate its system. The trees around me whisper gently in the breeze, the scent of damp earth grounding me.

I've only eaten a handful of berries when I hear the snap of twigs behind me. I don't wait for the creature to sink its fangs into my neck. If I'm going to die, I'd rather face my killer front on.

Blueberries spill to the ground as I leap from the log, my hand reaching for the blade at my hip. My mind begs me to run as fast as I can. Scream for help. Anything other than just standing here frozen to the spot, but I can't move. My feet simply will not budge.

I'm not sure my heart can take this constant up and down of emotions. My body begins to tremble as I face the looming shadow seeping from the woods.

It has to be a Galanthor. The size of it is too large to be a Lycan. I expect to see an owl-like head, the body of a bear and claws dripping with ruby red, ready to tear me apart limb from limb.

I shudder at the thought.

Yet, it's not a creature of monstrous proportions snapping its maw at me.

It's a beautiful chestnut horse, and . . . Saint.

I don't know whether to scream or cry at the sight of him— loose blond hair falling across his forehead. Eyes so blue that even the sky is jealous. On his back, he carries his satchel, which means he's either returning to Meadowbrook or he's come to find me. Wait, a horse? . . . Where did he get a horse? He's approaching me slowly—no—cautiously, almost as if he's not sure I'd welcome him.

My fingers unclench from around the hilt of my blade. I'm not going to need it now, and I'm so relieved.

"Hello, Blue," Saint purrs as he pulls the horse up in front of me. He slips from its back, landing with a thud.

With a pinched brow, I reach for him, grasping his arm to make sure he is real and I'm not making it up in my mind. "What are you doing here?" I manage to whisper. "How . . ."

Fear no longer laces through my blood, making my heart race, instead it's relief, and his scent. I pull my hand away, shaking my head.

Saint runs a hand through his hair, grinning in the way that makes my knees weak. "I got your letter, and then I went to the shop and Kamari told me everything."

The surrounding forest is quiet while it waits for my mind to catch up with his words. It still doesn't explain why he is here.

I angle my head to the side. "You do realise you're not supposed to sneak up on people in the woods?" I ask, arching a brow. "Unless you want to get stabbed."

"I like to live dangerously, besides I couldn't leave you to wander these parts alone, and it just so happens that I have business in Stone's Ridge too."

"Oh? Doing what?"

Saint scuffs the ground with his boot. "I need to see someone about a potential job."

His answer seems legit, yet there is so much he's not saying. I can see through the shadows of his words. He's hiding behind that boyish smile, and I want to know what exactly it is that he's keeping locked behind his lips.

I stoop to pick up the fallen berries before brushing them off and placing them back inside the little pouch. "Those debt collectors were after you. Said you were wanted for murder."

Saint takes a small step towards me. "I can assure you that I have not been going around murdering people." He rolls his eyes playfully, the smile never leaving his face. "I just owe some debt as well, and those folk like to be dramatic."

Is that the truth? Or is there something he's not telling me? Those men had been so insistent on knowing where he was. Warning me that he was a dangerous man. So far I've yet to see proof, but it makes me cautious all the same.

"How did you find me so quickly? I thought you were going to be out of town for a few days?"

Saint shoves his free hand into his trouser pocket. "Miss me already, Blue?"

A light laugh escapes my lips. "To miss someone, you have to actually like them."

My cheeks warm as his eyes find me. The grin on his face grows deeper. I can't help but smile in return. Saint cocks his head to the side, a smirk playing on his lips. "So, you're saying you don't like me?"

I shake my head, but I can't help the corners of my mouth turning up. "I'm saying I don't miss you."

Deep, warm laughter rings through the trees, the sound of it jolting me into action. I step forward and clamp my hand over his mouth, silencing him. "Do you want all the Lycans to hear us?" I whisper fiercely.

My hand lingers on his mouth, his warm breath licking at my palm. Saint's eyes darken as he flicks them down to my lips and back up to me. I'm impossibly close to him, and this situation feels all too familiar.

I pull away, taking a step back. "Unless you want to be a Galanthor's next meal, I suggest we keep our voices down."

Saint chuckles softly, glancing around the quiet forest. "Well, I promise to keep my voice down if you admit that you missed me . . . Just a little bit?"

There is no denying that I missed him, because I did. It has only been a day since I've seen him, but the thought of never seeing him again really left a mark on my soul. I'd missed him more than I'd like to admit to myself, but I don't want him to know that just yet. At least not until my heart can trust him a little more.

I reach for my backpack, placing it over my shoulders. The weight on my back makes it ache once again. Yet, it's a weight I have to bear—like many others.

Once my feet are stable, I turn to face him. "Okay, maybe I missed you a little bit."

Saint's grin grows wide again. "Does that mean you like me a little bit?"

I roll my eyes as I take a few small steps backwards. "Perhaps."

"Where are you going?" Saint asks, clicking the horse on.

"I need to get to Fernwell before night's end, as much as I'd like to stand around talking all day." I grin, my gaze never leaving his.

"Are you sure you'll be alright?"

I nod. "Of course—why wouldn't I?"

Saint tilts his head. "Because for a while there, it looked like you were about to start talking to the trees for company."

"I was not—" I huff. "You shouldn't spy on people from the bushes."

He chuckles again. "Maybe I could accompany you, make sure you don't get eaten by a Galanthor."

My eyes flick to my surroundings before finding him again. It certainly would feel better having some company than walking these woods alone. "How thoughtful of you."

Saint grins. "I have my moments." His gaze flicks down the road, then back to me. "So? Are we going?"

I hesitate, but why? Is it because those men warned me that Saint was dangerous? Was it the silent pleading in Theon's eyes when he insisted I tell them where Saint's whereabouts were? Perhaps it's because being in such close proximity with him is going to make it very hard for me to keep my eyes to myself?

Yet, there is something about the way Saint just stands there, waiting, not pushing, that makes my resolve waver. He lets me decide what I want. He's done that a few times, and it hasn't gone unnoticed.

He takes another step towards the road. "It's fine," he says, with a casual tone. "I can leave you here in the woods. I'm sure it's safe. The deer seem friendly enough."

I glare at him. "That was one deer."

He shrugs with a chuckle. "Maybe you'll get lucky, and the next set of eyes watching you won't belong to something with fangs."

With a huff, I cross my arms. "Where did you even get a horse?"

Saint strokes the chestnut's glossy neck. "Borrowed it from a friend."

"You have friends in Meadowbrook?"

Blue eyes find me. "Theon, to be exact."

My face scrunches in disbelief. In what universe is that even possible? Theon has made it very clear that he does not like Saint. And I'm pretty certain that Saint feels the same way about the blacksmith. "How did you become friends all in the space of one morning? I've only been gone a few hours."

Saint chuckles. "Let's say I can be very—persuasive."

I shake my head. I don't need to hear anymore. I'm sure there's a very logical reason for all of this, but right now, all I care about is not having to travel on foot the rest of the way. I'd thank Theon once I was back in Meadowbrook.

"Do you think he can take both of our weight?"

Saint nods, his hand outstretched, beckoning me closer. "I'm certain he can."

As I reach his side, Saint eases the bag from my back, securing it to the saddle. Once again, my body thanks me for the offloaded weight. I put one foot in the stirrup, and two hands at either end of the saddle, readying to pull myself up. Warm hands grip my waist, sending a shiver up my spine. I glance over my shoulder at Saint. "Thank you," I whisper.

He helps me into the saddle, pulling himself up behind me once I'm settled. My back presses into his chest. The warmth of his body is immediate, solid and unwavering. His arms brush my waist as he adjusts the reins, and it takes all of my self control to not settle into his embrace. I swear I can feel the heat of his breath against my temple.

The horse shifts beneath us, and instinctively I grip the saddle, my other hand gripping his thigh. It's hard under my hand, like it's been carved from the finest marble. Yet, even between the fabric of his trousers, I can feel warmth—softness.

Saint stills for a fraction of time. My pulse stumbles. Should I move my hand?

"Careful, Blue. I might begin to think you like me more than just a little."

Heat blossoms in my cheeks, I slowly pull my hand from his thigh and place it beside my other one on the pommel of the saddle. "We can't have that now—can we?"

He chuckles as he nudges the horse into a walk. With every sway of the four legged animal, we move together—his chest rising against my back, his arms caging me in, the rough fabric of his coat brushing my bare skin where my sleeves have slipped. Each shift, each breath, each unspoken moment coils tight between us.

Perhaps travelling with him is going to entail its own dangers—and not the kind that involves creatures of the forest.

"Are you nervous?" Saint murmurs.

I turn my head slightly, glancing over my shoulder. "Of leaving Meadowbrook? Or possibly running into unwanted company?"

Saint shifts in the saddle, and I have to hold my breath. He's so close—too close.

"All the above?"

I nod softly. "A little," I whisper.

His grip around me tightens. "I promise to keep you distracted as much as possible, but as far as the monsters go—I'm just as afraid."

My body twists in the saddle as I turn to face him. His face is so close to mine. I'm certain my eyes are as wide as dinner plates as I stare him down. He's being humorous, isn't he? I hope he's not totally useless when it comes to creatures of the forest, because I know I certainly am.

It only takes a moment for his laughter to ring through the forest again. "I promise to keep you safe, Blue."

The hours pass by quickly thanks to the fact my mind isn't on the road ahead, but the warmth of the male behind me. As we ride into Fernwell, the sky is streaked with dusky violet and warm amber, the last traces of sunlight slipping behind the trees. The town is smaller than Meadowbrook, its streets narrower, its buildings clustered closer together, yet it's still alive with energy. Lanterns flicker in the twilight, casting a golden light on the cobblestone roads, and the scent of roasting meat and mulled cider lingers in the air.

Despite its smaller size, Fernwell is bustling. Merchants linger at their stalls, haggling with late-evening customers, while laughter spills from a nearby tavern, where a trio of musicians plays a lively tune. Children dart between the buildings, their voices carrying over the hum of conversation.

Saint shifts in the saddle. His body feels more tense here than what it was in the forest. He's uncomfortable—I can feel it. His fingers tighten around the reins in his grip. My hands itch to reach for his. To hold them in my own—a small offer of comfort.

I glance over at my shoulder briefly. His eyes find me, softening when I smile. "Fernwell is smaller than I thought it would be."

"Small doesn't mean quiet." His voice is casual, but there's a knowing edge to it. His eyes leave mine to scan the crowds, almost like he's searching for someone. Perhaps the debt collectors? I don't blame him. I wouldn't want to run into them again either.

We pass a dressmaker's store. The stone building is covered in green, creeping ivy, and the glass window in the front has two mannequins in it. Both display frilly dresses, one pink, the other a butter yellow. I smile as I think of Dove. The shop reminds me of her. She'd like it here in Fernwell.

Saint's arms tighten slightly. "Shall we find an inn for the night?"

I nod. My body is aching, and I'm most definitely ready for a good soak in a hot bath.

We weave through the streets, searching for an inn, and I can't help but marvel at how alive this place feels. I thought Meadowbrook was lively at night, but here, even in a town half its size, the night is just as alive.

Saint pulls the horse up outside a stable, and with ease, dismounts the chestnut. I slip down after him, my boots crunching in the gravel as I land. I wait by the side of the building as he speaks to the stable master. Soon he joins me, and we move across the street to the inn.

It's cosy as we step inside. Some sort of casserole must be simmering on the stove in the kitchen. I can smell the mix of stewed meats and spices. My stomach growls. Those blueberries definitely weren't enough to appease my hunger.

The room is filled with warm light, gleaming from the wall sconces. Dancing shadows form on the walls as patrons bustle about. Some dancing to merry tunes sung by the local bard, some returning to tables with arms full of golden ale. A few females with breasts spilling from their cotton blouses cinched at the waist by colourful corsets balance themselves on the knees of burly men who seem all too pleased to hold them. Laughter is on the lips of nearly every figure I see. It's infectious. I can't stop the grin that begins to form across my lips.

Saint's warm hand finds me, breaking the trance that I'd been lost in. He tugs me along and I follow as he heads towards the front desk.

An elf greets us. Her skin an umbre, reddish-brown. Her glittering violet eyes capture my attention, as do her pearly white teeth and hair the colour of red velvet. "Are you dining with us tonight, or would you like a room?"

Saint releases my hand, fishing for something in his trouser pocket. "Boardings, please."

The elf opens her ledger, dragging her finger down the page to find an empty slot before she fills the space with scribbling from her quill. "One room for the lovely couple."

My face warms at her assumption. My gaze flicks to Saint, who makes no move to correct her, yet a smirk graces his lips. I step up to the counter, clearing my throat. "We are just friends. Is it possible to get a room with two beds?"

Violet eyes flick between us. "Of course, my apologies. Here is the key, it's the third door on the right as you head up the stairs."

Saint drops two silver coins onto the counter and then nods in appreciation towards the elf. I offer her a smile as we head to the stairs. I suppose he got the money to pay for lodgings from that out-of-town job he did. I do have enough to pay for myself—perhaps I should let him know.

The room is small as we enter, but I'm grateful that there are two beds as requested. I wander over to one of the small cots and place my bag down, turning to look at Saint. He's watching me from across the room. He knows just as well as I do how it feels to stay in the same room. Something I had not anticipated when I left Meadowbrook this morning.

He runs a hand through his hair, dropping his bag to the ground. "Shall I fetch us some dinner?"

I nod softly. "I'll freshen up."

He sends me a wink as he quietly disappears from the room.

It's quiet—peaceful. I allow a few deep breaths as I make my way to the small washroom adjacent to the sleeping area. It's also cosy, housing a round wooden tub, large enough to fit one body. A small sink and a waste pit. There's a small fireplace with a bucket of water bubbling away. At least I'll be able to soak in a warm bath.

I close the door behind me and undress. After filling the bath to the perfect temperature, I sink under the bubbles the lavender soap created and I let my body relax.

It's not long until I hear movement in the room. Saint must be back. I sink under the surface. One more dip and then I would let him freshen up.

The room is warm when I return. Saint glances up at me as I walk through the doorway. A wooden tray of steaming food in his hands. "Did you want me to empty the bath? Or—"

"Surely you're not that grimy," he teases.

Heat blossoms over my cheeks. "I'd like to hope not."

A soft huff escapes from his lips as he drops into the seat across from me and starts tearing a piece of bread apart with his fingers. The scent of roasted meat and fresh bread fills the air, and my stomach tightens. Not just from hunger, but at the simple act of sharing a meal with Saint. It feels like we've done it together all our lives.

As we eat, he leans back in his chair, watching me with that easy, unreadable expression. "So, how do you feel about leaving the shop in someone else's hands?"

I sigh, wiping a crumb from my lip. "I trust Wilson and my mother to get things done, but I can't help but worry. The shop's been my whole life since . . ." I trail off, not wanting to say it out loud.

Saint nods as if he already knows. "Since your father passed."

I clear my throat and force a small smile. "Yeah. I haven't left Meadowbrook since then."

He tilts his head slightly. "Does it feel strange?"

His question dances on my mind as I poke at the food in my bowl. "A little. But . . . It's also nice. I want to see the world, you know? I'm sure there's more beyond Meadowbrook. The whole of Sapphire Vale to explore. Yet, I can't stop thinking about the shop."

Saint nods. "I'm sure it's very normal to feel that way. But— if you'll allow me, I'd like to help ease some of that worry."

My brow pinches. "What do you mean?"

He leans across the small table, resting his chin on his forearms as he looks up at me through darkened lashes. "I'll allow you to think about the shop for ten minutes a day," he drawls. "But for the rest of the day, I want you to only think of me."

A smile breaks out across his face, and before I can stop myself, I'm laughing. I pinch a piece of bread and throw it at him. It hits him square in the forehead. "You're too conceited for your own good."

Saint grins, leaning back in his chair. "This conceited guy needs to bathe. Don't fall asleep while I'm gone."

He brushes past me. I struggle not to close my eyes and breathe him in as he does. "You'd better hurry then. My body is already fighting me."

A warm chuckle reaches my ears. I turn in my chair to glance over my shoulder. He hasn't fully closed the door and I can't help but watch him for a moment. Through the narrow opening, I see the bare stretch of his back, the candlelight casting flickering shadows over the scars that mark his skin. I wonder what he's done to earn such painful reminders.

He stands still for a moment, rolling his shoulder slowly, testing for pain. His fingers press into the muscle as if searching for something beneath the surface.

He is breathtaking. A body carved by the one who created the world. Rippling muscle from his legs, all the way to his neck. Black vines cover his upper body, and an owl resting on top of a skull is inked into his left arm. My breath catches. I feel the warmth building between my legs. He has a way of making my body come alive and I'm not even sure he realises what he does to me.

My gaze flicks to his hands. Slender, yet sturdy. I imagine them tracing patterns over my bare skin, finding all my secret places as if he is searching for treasure and I am his map.

Saint exhales and glances towards the door—toward me.

I snap my head down, heart hammering, pretending to be far more interested in my half-eaten food than I actually am. Guilt prickles in my chest. I shouldn't have looked. I'm on my way to find my wicks, not ogle a male.

Swallowing, I put my plate back on the table, suddenly not as hungry as I was before. The bed in the corner of the room beckons me, and I need to rest my aching bones.

It creaks softly as I climb under the covers. Turning onto my side, I face the door and the ridiculously handsome figure in the washroom. I close my eyes, trying to ignore the heat pulsing through my body.

Water sloshes against the side of the bath, and within a few minutes, Saint enters the space. I crack one eye open to see him stroll across the room; a towel strung low across his hips. I swallow the lump of desire rising in my throat. His stomach is defined by bumps of silken skin trailing their way down, forming a v-shape that disappears beneath the towel.

I've never been one for crass words, but if I was to use them, now would be the time. He's *fucking* perfect.

He needs his personal space, so I close my eyes, no matter how hard it is.

Soon the world starts to fade away as my body sinks into the soft mattress, sleep calling to me.

Light footsteps dance across the floor, coming to rest at the side of my bed. The scent of lavender soap washes over me, and I know Saint is close. I pretend to sleep, intrigued by what he might say or do.

The air around me freezes as I feel his fingertips brush a few strands of hair off the side of my face. He's so gentle, despite having rough, calloused hands from all the handy work he does.

"Sweet dreams, Blue," Saint whispers, so low that I almost miss it.

I feel his absence as he moves away, the sound of his bed creaking as he climbs under the covers. The glow of the oil lamp is snuffed out, leaving the room in darkness, and I finally allow myself to breathe.

Thunder in the distance rumbles, and a sleepy smile stretches across my face as I drift off to the sound of water droplets hitting the slate roof of the inn.

It's about time the summer heat brought the rain.

# Eighteen

## SILENCE IS SUFFOCATING

Unrelenting heat from the sun beats down, never letting up or hiding its face to allow some respite. The heat is affecting Juni too. I see it in the way she keeps wiping the back of her hand across her brow. It probably doesn't help that we are sitting so close together.

She fits so beautifully in my arms. The perfect height for her head to rest just under mine. It takes all self control not to pull her against my chest, to bury my face in her hair, inhaling her very essence.

It also took all self control not to lift the covers and crawl into her bed last night. I'd finished in the washroom, and on my return, Juni was fast asleep. Seeing her peaceful face adorned with a very faint smile, pulled on that tether I felt in my chest any time she was near.

Last night had been the first night in all my years alive in this world that I'd slept in a bed. My body has been able to relax for hours on end, never shifting, simply resting. It'd been the greatest sleep I'd ever experienced.

The ring works.

Which only makes the weight of it in my pocket even heavier.

It was possibly the first night in a long time that Kamari didn't sleep in her human form. I knew it wouldn't kill her, and by the time the sun comes up, she'd be human again. Hopefully, in time, I could be forgiven.

I highly doubt Juni will ever offer me another smile if she finds out what I've done. Usually not a care for others' opinions dares to tarry in my mind, but it's different with Juniper. I want to tell her everything. I want to share all my secrets. I want her to sink her fingers into my mind and pick it apart until she knows everything about me.

She can't find out, though. Not yet anyway. Perhaps once we're far enough from Meadowbrook she'll have no choice but to keep travelling to Stone's Ridge. If I can just get her safely to the wick supplier, maybe—just maybe she will understand why I had to take the ring.

Under the canopy of the trees, the heat still finds its way to sink its teeth into my skin. Even though last night's rain had brought some relief, it didn't last long.

I shift my weight, gritting my teeth when Juni's soft curves settle back against me. "I think there is a stream nearby. Would you care to freshen up?" I ask.

We'd been riding for most of the morning. I for sure could use a dip and some light refreshments. I had a few peaches stashed away in my satchel, the stall holder back in town had plenty to spare, and wouldn't know a few had mysteriously gone missing.

Juni dropped her head back, closing her eyes. Her hair brushes across my arms, and even though I can't feel it through the fabric of my jacket, I already know how soft it would feel.

"Anything to escape this heat," she groans.

I chuckle softly, pulling the horse to the right of the road. The underbrush fights us as we carve a path to the stream's edge. I bring the horse to a stop and slip to the ground. A quick scan of our surroundings, and once I'm confident there is no immediate danger, I help Juniper down.

Her breath catches when my hands grip her waist. Slowly, I lower her to the ground, yet when her feet touch it, she doesn't pull away. She simply lingers, her meadow eyes travelling over my face. I fight the urge to bring her lips to mine, even though that's all I want to do.

I clear my throat, releasing her waist, and take a step back. "I think it's safe enough here, but you can never be too careful, so if you see or hear anything, make sure you tell me."

She nods, offering me a small smile before she heads to the water's edge. I secure the reins to a nearby branch, joining her.

"Full body or just feet?" I steal a glance to the crystal blue waters gently rushing by. It's not a large stream, yet it would be refreshing all the same. Deep enough to allow our bodies to sink under the surface.

Juniper eyes fill with a sparkle that has me all hot and bothered. "I'm game if you are?" She shrugs off her cloak, dropping it to the ground in a heap.

For a moment, I think she's going to strip completely, yet she throws a smile over her shoulder before she wades into the stream. I watch, mesmerised, as she dives headfirst into the water. One second, she's there—the next, it swallows her whole. But as the ripples settle, she resurfaces, and I forget how to breathe.

Her siren form shimmers under the dappled sunlight, water streaming down her smooth, honey drenched skin. Clinging to the strands of her chocolate hair that stick to her shoulders, and delicate neck.

Perhaps I'm still in the inn—dreaming—because the vision before me is certainly one from another realm. Perhaps some place like the stars.

I should move, but I can't. All I can do is watch, heart hammering as she floats effortlessly in the water.

"You're staring," she teases, a smirk tugging at the corner of her mouth.

I huff out a breath. "Can you blame me?"

A blush creeps into her cheeks as she slips under the surface once more. I waste no more time standing on the water's edge, gawking. Without another thought, I strip off my shirt, then my boots, discarding my trousers next. I have no issues with Juni seeing me naked, but she might, so I wade into the water and dive under before she surfaces.

The cold is a shock at first, a biting contrast to the summer heat, yet it feels heavenly. I kick off the riverbed until I break the surface, dragging my hands through my wet hair. When I open my eyes, Juni is there, floating inches away, watching me.

I want her. All of her. But I will wait. I'll wait until she gives me the signal that she wants me just as much. Too many people in her life have taken her choices from her. I don't want to be one of them.

And if she decides she wants to experience pleasure with me, I'll willingly give it to her until she's a wet, trembling heap in my arms.

I tread water, letting the current push and pull me, but I don't take my eyes off her. "You keep looking at me like that, and I'll start thinking you're up to no good."

She tilts her head, lips curving. "Me? Never."

Before I can blink, she dives. A flash of movement, then she's gone. Deep ocean blues and magnetic forest greens, blending with inky black glimmer, as the sun's light catches on her tail. Black opal in the form of a siren. I twist in the water, searching, but she's too fast. The next thing I know, something tugs at my ankle, and I lurch forward with a curse.

Juniper pops up a few feet away, laughing, her wet hair clinging to her face. Her laughter is intoxicating. I want to hear it every day for the rest of my life.

We stare at each other for a moment, the sounds of the birds in the trees, and the water trickling by. She's looking at me like she has a thousand questions, but doesn't know which one to ask first.

"Tell me about the women you've loved," she murmurs, her mouth skimming the rippling surface. "I imagine you've broken a few hearts over time."

I arch a brow. "Are you asking about my love life, Blue?"

She shrugs, feigning indifference. "Maybe I am."

Cool water laps at my skin as I maintain my position. How much do I tell her? Is there any point? She'll hear my truths, and I'll be left here alone, watching her walk out of my life, never wanting to be a part of it again.

Yet, I have to give her something.

I exhale, glancing towards the treeline. "There've been flings. Nothing serious."

She studies me, her expression unimpressed with my answer. "Why not?"

I flick water at her. "Because my lifestyle didn't allow for it."

Juni wipes the water from her cheek, rolling her eyes. "That's a vague answer. If you don't want to talk about it, you can just say so."

I shrug lightly. "It's more that I don't have a lot to say. Travelling . . . Drifting—whatever you want to call it doesn't allow me to get close to people."

She narrows her eyes, swimming nearer. "How about now?"

"That's pretty close." I grin. "But I think you could get even closer."

I'm thankful she's not under the water right now, because if she was, she'd find a very hard surprise waiting for her. And to be honest, I'm not sure either of us is ready for that yet. Even if it's all I can think about.

For a moment, we just float there, the world quiet except for the gentle lapping of the river. Her gaze flickers to my mouth, but she doesn't move away.

Neither do I.

A flock of birds overhead breaks the trance we're in, and Juni glances towards the skies. It looks darker than this morning. It's quite possible a storm is rolling in.

"We should get going," I murmur.

Juni nods, flicking her tail as she propels away from me. I'm not ready to wake from this dream, but if we want to make it to the next town before nightfall, we should really get a move on.

I hold my breath, sinking under the water one last time. When I surface, Juni is already out of the water. Her dress has returned and only her hair hangs in damp tendrils down her back.

She fetches her bag, rifling through it before taking out some brown paper bundles. I use this moment to climb out of the water, quickly changing back into my clothes. Glad that the water has made them damp, because when the breeze travels over me, it keeps me cool.

Juniper's gaze finds me, but she quickly looks away, as if she doesn't want to be caught looking. She settles on a log under the shade of a tree and unwraps one of the bundles to reveal a wedge of cheese.

"Want some?" she offers, breaking off a chunk, and holding it out.

I take it, popping it into my mouth with a nod of thanks. Then I reach into my own pack and pull out a peach, rolling it between my palms before holding it out to her. "Trade?"

Her eyes flick to the fruit, curiosity sparking. "Where did you get that?"

I shrug, biting back a smirk. "I have my ways."

She huffs a laugh but accepts the peach, turning it over in her hands before taking a careful bite. Juice dribbles down her chin, and she wipes it away with the back of her hand.

I sit beside her, finishing our food in easy silence. Nothing but the sound of birds as company. After a moment Juni stands, heading for her bag on the saddle once again, where she pulls out some rolled-up parchment. She returns to my side. As she smooths the paper over her lap, I realise it's a map of Sapphire Vale.

A sour taste forms in my mouth and my stomach churns. I've never been great at reading, but reading maps—I'm even worse. Mainly because all the town names are usually so long winded in their pronunciation.

Sweat beads at my temples. I hope she doesn't ask me anything about it. Yet fate still isn't kind to me. I finish my mouthful of cheese. "Where did you get that from?"

Juni glances up at me. "When you fetched the horse this morning, I asked the innkeeper if she had one, and she did."

I nod before turning my focus to the peach in my hand. Hopefully she's content enough to look at it, and I can keep another secret to myself.

"Have you been here before?" Juni points to the map.

With a quick glance, I shake my head but remain silent. She's not satisfied to leave it there as she points to another place. The words jumble in my mind, and I struggle to recall the town name. I force myself to look, but the markings blur together, shifting in and out of meaning. My jaw tightens. Maps have always been a mess of scribbles to me—too many lines, too many letters, none of it making sense fast enough.

Juniper, oblivious, starts tracing a route with her finger. "I think we should take this road here—"

I snap before I can stop myself. "I'm sure you can figure it out yourself, Blue." Leaving the log, I make my way over to the horse, feeling horrid.

My hands fiddle with the saddle. I can't bear to face her yet. I don't want to see the pain I've potentially caused, as it forms in her eyes.

"Is everything alright?" Juni's voice is soft—too kind for how I've just treated her.

With a sigh, I turn to face her. "I'm sorry. I shouldn't have snapped like that."

Juni pushes the map to the side as she stands and makes her way over to me. Sheepishly, my gaze stays locked on the ground until I feel her small hand grip my forearm. "What is it?"

My eyes meet hers. I'm lost in the orange that bleeds into the green around the edges of her irises. I'm not used to someone responding with such gentle kindness. "I'm not— I'm not good with maps," I admit quietly. "Or reading. It takes me too damn long to make sense of it. Little to no education in my youth."

Gentle pressure on my arm draws my gaze as Juni squeezes it. Understanding flickers across her face when I look at her again, and to my surprise, she just nods. "Then I'll do the reading for the rest of the trip." Her tone is light, like it's the simplest solution in the world. No pity. No teasing. Just fact.

I nod in appreciation. Perhaps there would be time for me to explain further, but for now, we must get back on the road.

The closer we get to Breydon, the more tense my body feels, as if it knows what waits for me there. Donovan and his never ending, soul-sucking grip around my throat. My eyes are forever scanning our surroundings, keeping a close watch for unwanted creatures—or people.

As the sun dips lower in the sky, I'm aware that we need to pick up the pace if we are to reach the next town before nightfall.

A dark, looming mound in between the trees in the distance catches my attention from the corner of my eye. "Woah," I urge the horse to a stop.

"What is it?" Juni throws over her shoulder.

I lean closer, my lips almost touching her ear. "Galanthor."

Juniper stiffens in my arms. I draw her closer, reassuring her that she has nothing to fear.

"Where?" she whispers.

I point, and Juni's gaze follows. Her breath quickens at the sight. The Galanthor lingers in the distance, half-hidden in the trees, its hulking frame blending with the deepening shadows.

Juni glances over her shoulder. "How did you even spot that?" her voice is barely a whisper.

"When you've lived the life I have, Blue, you learn to look for the dangers," I reply. "We can't stay here. If it catches our scent, we'll become its dinner."

Juni nods, and we move on, slow and steady. No sudden movements. No giving it reason to follow. Only when the creature fades into the trees behind us do I let out a quiet breath.

But we're not in the clear yet. If we don't keep moving, we won't make it to town before nightfall. And I have no interest in setting up camp out here—not if I can help it.

I push the horse into a canter once we have put a safe distance between us and the Galanthor, but we don't make it far before there is trouble on the road ahead of us.

An elderly couple stands beside a wagon, its front wheel cracked, the entire thing leaning awkwardly to one side. The man rubs his temple, the woman wrings her hands, and I know exactly what's coming.

Juni shifts in the saddle, already looking at me expectantly. "We have to help them."

I hesitate.

If we stop, we lose time. And if we lose time, we'll be riding through the forest after dark, which isn't exactly my idea of a good time. Especially after spotting the monstrous creature behind us. But leaving an old couple stranded out here feels—wrong. Even for me.

I exhale sharply and swing off the horse.

Once I hit the ground, I look up at Juni. "Stay here."

"You'll be stuck out here all night if you don't fix that," I say, stepping towards the wagon.

The old man sighs. "Aye, we know. But my hands aren't what they used to be."

I crouch beside the wheel, inspecting the damage. It's bad, but not beyond fixing. "I can fix it, but it's going to take me a little while."

The wheel proves to be quite stubborn, and despite Juni's, and the elderly couples' help, it takes more time than I hoped to fix it. Finally, with adjustments, some muttered curses, and a well-placed shove, the wagon groans back into place.

Golden sunlight filters through the trees, signalling the sun's descent. We are running out of time. The ring in my pocket feels heavy, a constant reminder of who I am, and what I've done.

The couple thanks me profusely. I shake the male's hand. "See that you get somewhere safe before nightfall. We spotted a Galanthor a few miles back."

A gasp sounds from the woman, and I offer her a smile, though I doubt it will do little to settle her nerves.

As we ride away, Juni glances at me. "That was kind of you."

I don't meet her eyes, but I can't help the feeling churning in my gut. Like I'd done something right for once. "You must be rubbing off on me."

With a light laugh, we push through the forest, travelling as fast as we can. I'm not sure how long we ride for, but the closer the sun gets to the horizon, the more fearful I become. I need to get that ring on my finger or I will shift. Yet we are still so far from the village, all because I had to go and be helpful.

Pulling the horse to a stop by a small clearing, to the left of the road, I clench the reins in my hands. We're going to need to camp for the night.

Juni spins in the saddle. "We're not going to make it to the next town, are we?"

My lips press into a thin line as I shake my head. "Are you alright with setting up camp here?"

She glances around, then back at me. "What's a journey without a little adventure . . . Right?"

Thankfully, Juni has a small canvas tent packed in her bag. The fabric is worn but sturdy, and between the two of us, it doesn't take long to assemble. Then I move on to bringing a small fire to life. She busies herself retrieving food from her bag, but I can't keep the agitation at bay. My fingers itch to reach into my pocket, to slide the ring onto my finger before the sun disappears completely. My pulse picks up as I steal a glance at the horizon—the sky darkens in slow gradients, streaked with deep purples and burnt oranges. Dusk is slipping away, and soon, night will swallow the forest whole.

I clench my jaw. *I can't wait until Juni is asleep.*

The thought rattles in my skull, growing louder with each passing second. The longer I sit here, the more unbearable it becomes. Perhaps I could quietly slip it on now, right here by the fire. Maybe she won't even notice.

If she finds out, though. I will have to tell her everything. Am I ready to do that? Am I ready for her to never look at me the same again—or at all?

I don't have a choice. I flick my gaze over to Juni, she's busy breaking some chunks of cheese for us, so I shove my hand into my pocket, slipping the ring on. It's snug—verging on tight, just like it had been last night, but it was perfect for now.

Juni walks towards me, offering some bread and cheese. With my ringless hand, I take it from her before settling on the ground beside the fire. She moves away, sitting opposite me.

The food tastes bland in my mouth, and I struggle to swallow. This is why we aren't a balanced fit. She is all that is good. I'm all that is bad. I steal, lie, inflict pain. Where Juni helps, cares, and loves people.

Around us, the forest begins to settle into the night. My instinct is to run, to disappear into the maze of trees. Hide away where she won't see me. When you've spent twenty-six years of your life shifting at sunset, it feels so wrong to just sit. Yet, I will my body to stay put. The ring worked last night, so there is no reason it won't now. I just need a distraction.

Juniper seems to be lost in her own world when I glance at her. "I don't think I've asked you this before, but do you have any siblings?"

She looks over at me, a soft look upon her face. "I don't. It's just me and Mama now. How about you?"

I offer her a slight shrug. "It's only me too . . . At least I think? Do you have grandparents?"

Juni swallows down some food before answering. "I did yes, though both sets now rest alongside Father."

I drop my gaze to the fire, trying to find the right words. She's suffered loss too, possibly more than anyone I know, yet there is still love inside her soul. I can see it in the way she speaks to her customers, her mother—me.

"The elderly couple from earlier reminded me of my grandparents," Juni continues softly. "It felt good to help them."

Darkness shrouds the forest. Tiny pin pricks of glittering stars disappear behind angry storm clouds. Yet the sound of thunder is absent. The golden glow of the fire sends light in a parameter around us.

A subtle huff escapes my lips. "Even if it meant we now have to spend the night in the forest instead of a warm bed at an inn?"

Juni pops a blueberry into her mouth. I watch her lips close around it, and I almost need to look away. Everything she does is so innocently perfect. I imagine her lips doing something else, making it very hard to bring my attention back to the conversation.

"We have a better chance of outrunning a Galanthor than they did. I'm more than willing to sleep out here in the forest, if it means they are safe."

I chuckle, easing back against the tree behind me. "It's true. Especially with how quickly you darted away from that deer earlier."

A soft blush creeps into her cheeks. I can't stop the smile rippling across my face. "You're never going to let that go, are you?" she exclaims softly.

Her eyes find me across the fire. It's a moment that could be so powerful, reading her silently. Instead, I drop my gaze, feeling guilty as I run my hand through my hair. I just have to get through tonight, then I will take the ring off and she will be none the wiser.

"Saint?" Juni's voice is soft, but there's hesitancy there.

A prickle runs down my spine as I meet her gaze. She isn't looking at me, though. Her eyes are fixed on my hand, the one hanging loosely between my knees. "Do you usually wear a ring? . . . It looks just like my mother's. Where did you get it?"

A weight slams into my gut. Heavy. Sinking. My throat tightens like it's been lined with gravel, and for a moment, I can't breathe. The truth surges up, demanding to be spoken— but I shove it back down, swallowing it like poison where it will sit for the rest of my pathetic life. Before I have time to stop myself, a lie tumbles from my lips. "It's nothing. A keepsake from a trade I did."

I hope it's enough to quench her interest as I shove my hand back into my trouser pocket.

She doesn't believe me. I can see it in the way her brows pinch, the way her gaze flicks from my face to my hand like she's peeling back the layers of my lie. "I've never seen you wear it before. It looks so familiar. Is it new?"

I nod, shoving some cheese into my mouth. "There are probably hundreds around."

She chews, slowly, too slowly, brushing the crumbs from her lap before standing. Then, in the quiet, she says the words I was dreading. "Let me see it."

A sharp bolt of fear grips my ribs. My fingers curl into my palm, as if the ring itself is burning me.

*Fuck.*

Without a doubt, the colour has drained from my face. This is wrong. All so horribly wrong. Why did I have to go combing my hair, flashing the ring for her to accidentally see? I wanted to punch myself in the face for being so daft. My mind races for an out, any out, but there's nowhere to run.

I scramble to my feet. "It's really nothing, Blue."

She isn't convinced, as she snatches for my hand. I want to pull away, but it's only going to make me look more guilty. So I let her study it briefly before easing my hand away. "See, nothing special."

The silence is suffocating. Her eyes find mine, and it's not curiosity I see there—no—it's pain and confusion. This is it. The moment I've been dreading. I'm about to break her heart, and I'd chosen to do it.

Her voice shakes, not with rage, but something worse. Something raw. "Don't lie to me, Saint. I've seen that ring my whole life."

The world tilts. My lungs constrict.

I could lie again. I could run. I could twist the truth into something palatable. But she deserves better than that. I open my mouth to speak, but she silences me with her stare.

"Did you—did you take it from my Mother? . . . From my home?"

# Nineteen

## THE TRUTH IS SHATTERING

Distant lighting flickers through the forest, illuminating the trees in a ghostly flash before plunging everything back into darkness. Very faint thunder follows what feels like hours later. Slow and distant, a low growl rolling across the sky. It should have come sooner. Perhaps it did. Maybe time has stopped, unravelling at the seams, leaving me stranded in this endless nightmare.

Saint's eyes search mine, the look on his face unreadable.

"Well?" my voice quivers.

He runs a hand over his face, and the ring catches on the firelight again. My stomach sinks, anticipating his answer. *Lie again, Saint. Lie. Because the truth will shatter me.*

He takes a hesitant step towards me. "Juni—I can explain."

I bite the inside of my cheek to stop the flow of tears threatening to spill. The taste of metal coats my tongue.

Theon warned me, and I didn't listen. Now, my mother was paying the price.

"You—you stole it?" My fists curl at my sides. "After I trusted you—defended you . . . You stole it? Do you even know what it is?"

The air around us shifts. Not because of the incoming storm—no—it's in the way Saint is looking at me like he *is* the storm. His voice is cold—distant. "I did what I had to do."

My brow pinches, and I swallow down the lump of emotion in my throat. "What you had to do? That's your excuse?"

I'm angry that all I want to do is cry. This is all my fault. I shouldn't have let his eyes, his hands, his smile, his smell or his voice fool me. "That ring is vital to my Mother's well being. Without it, she . . . She—"

Saint steps close, his eyes boring into mine just as more lightning ripples across the canopy above us. "She what? . . . She shifts for the night and turns human again?"

I flinch at his words, pulling away. "And that doesn't bother you. Why do you even need her ring?"

"Because I'm a shifter too."

The forest around me ignites in an instant, flames devouring the trees until all that remains is a wasteland of ash and soot. The air is thick with the ghost of what once stood, a hollow space where life used to breathe. Everything is grey. Lifeless. Empty.

My mind has sent me here—this desolate, ruined place—so I can catch my breath, but there's no relief to be found. Only the pounding of my heart, the crackling of something inside me splintering apart.

Saint is a shifter?

The words don't make sense, and yet, they fit too well. Like a missing piece I never realised was gone. There aren't any shifters in Meadowbrook. At least, none that I've ever known.

Except for Mama.

Devastation twists my stomach into knots. Why did he have to take her ring? Why does he not have his own? Why is he so desperate to not shift that he took it from her, even though he knew what it would do to our relationship?

I spin, walking away from him, but I don't get far before I need answers, so I turn to face Saint again. "So you decided to steal her ring? Why me, why us, why this?" My voice cracks. "Do you even care about anyone but yourself?"

His jaw tightens. I see the flex in his jaw. "You think I wanted this? You think I enjoy being the villain in your story? I don't have the luxury of playing the hero, Blue, not with the situation I'm in."

"What do you mean? How long have you been planning this?" My voice rises with intensity. "Are you even going to Stone's Ridge or are you just looking for more things that don't belong to you?"

Thunder rumbles overhead, closer than before, a low growl that vibrates through the air and settles deep in my chest. The wind picks up, sending a shiver down my spine as the trees around us sway, their branches creaking in protest. Petrichor washes over me. The earthy, fresh scent that rises from the ground when rain falls on dry soil. It was coming.

Saint drags his hands through his hair, letting them rest there, as if trying to steady himself. His jaw is tight, his expression unreadable, but I can feel the tension rolling off him in waves. The storm above is nothing compared to the one I'm drowning in. Lightning flashes in the distance, illuminating the hard set of Saint's features.

"If you'll just let me explain. I need it . . . And once I've done what I need, I will give it back." His hands drop to his sides, but he makes no move towards me. And I'm grateful, because I don't want to be anywhere near him right now.

I shake my head, biting my bottom lip in fear of crying. "To be honest, I don't want to hear anything you have to say."

Saint takes a step towards me. "Blue, please—"

I hold my hands up in front of me, stopping him in his tracks. A bitter laugh escapes my lips. "Stop calling me that. My name is Juniper."

The light in his eyes snuffs out. His shoulders drop, and I don't feel sorry for him. I should have never allowed him to work in the shop all those weeks ago. I should have listened to Theon.

"You made me believe you were someone worth trusting." My voice cracks this time.

Saint's dull blue eyes travel over my face, his expression softening for just a moment. "Maybe you shouldn't trust people so easily."

The first drops of rain kiss my skin, cool and sharp. The storm is almost here. But I can't look away from Saint—not yet. Not while he stands there, accusing me of misplaced trust. His arms are folded across his chest, his stance firm on the spot. My heart cracks, jagged and raw, but instead of shattering, it fills with something more unbearable than the grief it already carries. A quiet rage, simmering low, waiting for the right moment to boil over.

I step closer, my fists clenched. "You're right. This is on me. I saw the red flags. I saw the lies, the half-truths, the way you'd avoid real answers. But I ignored them because—" I pause, swallowing down the threatening tears. "Because I thought . . . Well, it doesn't matter what I think now. You have shown me who you are, and what you value." I wipe a stray tear that manages to escape. "And it's clear it's not making candles with me."

Saint flinches, but remains silent.

"I should have listened to Theon—myself. I saw all the signs. I saw the way you always stood near an exit, ready to run. I heard the whispers in town of things going missing and I . . . I was a fool for thinking there is something in you worth believing."

He shoves his hands into his pockets. "Maybe there still is. But believing in me won't get me what I need." His voice is low. "It won't fix what is broken."

Another tear slips down my cheek. "So you'll just break everyone else in the process?"

Saint takes a small step towards me—an olive branch. "You don't understand what it's like to have everything ripped away from you, to live every day knowing you're nothing more than a pawn in someone else's game."

I steady myself, not moving from next to the fire that is already dwindling from the lack of attention. "You're right. I don't know what that's like. But I do know you had a choice. And you chose to hurt the one person who would actually want to help you."

"You think I wanted to hurt you?" he says softly, guilt flicking across his face.

He's so close. Too close. I wish this was all a dream. That I would wake to find myself back in the inn, Saint sleeping peacefully and the warm sun bathing my skin. But the ache in my chest, and the tears slipping down my cheeks is proof that this is not a dream—it's a nightmare.

I shake my head, stepping back. My voice filled with a quiet anger. "I think you don't know how to do anything else. Do you even like me?"

Saint's eyes swell with pain. "I didn't take it to hurt you. I took it because I need my life back. I can't afford to let my shifting rule my life anymore. It doesn't mean there isn't something between us." His voice cracks, almost like he's pleading—hoping I will understand. But I don't. Mama took him in—fed him, and he turned around and stole from her.

I can't stand this anymore. I need to get away.

"There is nothing between us . . . There never will be and this is why. You're secretive. You do whatever you want. There are no rules or consequences. I can't have that in my life," my voice is low. "What good is getting what you want if it costs you everything else?"

Saint doesn't say a word.

I can't bear the pain anymore, so I spin towards the tent, stopping when I reach it to face him once again. "I will travel with you to Stone's Ridge and you will do what you need to. Then you will give me the ring back and I never want to see you again."

The canvas tent shakes as I rip the flap back, dipping my head to hurry inside before the outpouring of rain. I won't let him see me fall apart. He doesn't deserve to see my soul shatter.

My body crashes to the thin mattress on the ground, the ache in my chest greater than the sticks and rocks digging into my flesh. Outside the storm arrives. Howling wind whips around us, and I don't even care that Saint is out there. As the thunder rumbles, I allow the floodgate of emotions to open. Pouring my heart onto the ground.

As much as I want to be at home right now, I need those wicks.

I wish Papa were here. I wish he was at home taking care of Mother, and I didn't have to carry all of this weight.

If he was here, if the creator had taken me instead, none of this would have ever happened.

I feel like death incarnate. Sleep was not my friend. If it wasn't blusterous winds or heavy rain keeping me awake. It was the constant reminder of what Saint has done.

Sunlight seeps through the opening of the tent. I'm thankful that it kept me dry all night. Who knows how Saint fared. He dared not step foot in the tent last night. He knew what would await him if he did. I didn't want to go out and face him yet, but the quicker we reached Stone's Ridge, the quicker I could get rid of him.

Before the tears return, I get up, fold the blanket with the thin mattress, and head out into the morning. It takes a moment for my eyes to adjust to the light. They are definitely swollen.

I spot Saint almost where I left him. His body is slumped as he leans against the tree. Doesn't look like he slept much either. The ground squelches as I make my way over to Theon's horse. I fasten the mattress to the side of the saddle, and turn back to Saint. He slowly gets to his feet, his gaze never wavering.

"Junip—"

"I'd like to get along. We've already missed enough time." My voice is sharp.

His shoulders drop, but he doesn't press further. After he packs down the tent, he stays back while I climb into the saddle, and once he's behind him, he gives me as much room as possible. I suck in my breath when I feel his chest on my back. I hate that he feels so good, and how his earthy patchouli and cedarwood scent settles over me.

He's just a thief. Nothing more.

Sunlight streams through the trees, warming my skin. The underbrush is vivid green from the soaking it received last night. The rhythmic thud of the horse's hooves against the dirt does little to drown out the storm brewing inside me. I fight the tears that threaten to spill, keeping my gaze fixed ahead, unwilling to let Saint see me break again. The silence between us is thick, stretching for hours as we ride, neither of us daring to shatter it. The weight of what I know—what I've learned—presses against my ribs, making it hard to breathe.

I've lost track of time. I don't know where we are, or how long we've been riding. All I can think about is Mama back home and reaching Stone's Ridge. So it comes as a surprise when Saint suddenly brings the horse to a stop. I don't even need to ask why.

Up ahead, a river, swollen from the recent rains, rushes wildly beneath the worn wooden bridge. The water churns, frothing and crashing against jagged rocks. Saint adjusts his weight behind me, and I catch my breath. I need to get off this horse and put some distance between us.

He exhales. "That doesn't look very sturdy. And it certainly didn't look like this when I came through a few weeks ago."

The jarring reminder of him waltzing into town—taking what is not his to own—rips through my chest, and I can't scramble down from the horse fast enough. I'll walk the rest of the way if I have to.

"Juni, where are you going?" Saint calls after me.

I don't answer, I just keep walking.

His boots hit the ground as he hurries after me. "Juniper, wait."

A firm grip tightens around my wrist as Saint catches my hand. My head whips around to face him.

"It's too dangerous to cross here." His voice is steady, but his eyes are pleading.

I yank my hand out of his grasp. My blood running cold. "If you made it across last time. I'm sure it will be fine. I can swim, and besides, we don't have time to look for another route."

Saint doesn't try to reach for me again, but he keeps close. "You don't swim in rivers like this Juni, now just give me some time to figure this out."

My head shakes, sending my unbrushed tendrils over my shoulders. I don't want to wait. I want this to be over. I want to get the wicks so I can return home and pretend like none of this ever happened.

"You don't need to look out for me. I think we are past the point of pretending you care about me, Saint."

I don't need his help. I've been taking care of myself for a while now, why do I suddenly need him to do anything for me? If I hurry across, he will see how overbearing he is, and then we can both move on.

Saint stares at me for a long hard minute, before he spins on his heel, heading for the horse. I hear him utter a curse word under his breath. Behind me, the river rages on, but I swallow my heart and turn to face it, placing one boot on it, and then another.

The bridge creaks. Dread washes over me. If it's groaning under my weight, what will it do under the horses? I move cautiously, one hand on the rail, and the other clenched at my side. I'm not so daft that I don't take my time picking where I should place my feet.

Hoofbeats sound behind me. Saint has chosen to follow. I have no desire to look at him, so I keep my focus straight ahead. Almost there. Just a little further.

Then—*whoosh!*

Something slices through the air, embedding itself into the wooden planks just inches from my boots—an arrow. With a startled cry, I snap my head in the direction it came from. Two riders in the distance are gaining on us.

A second arrow flies through the air and lands near the horse. The animal startles, tossing its head, and my heart lurches into my throat.

There is no time to run. The horse rears in fright, its panicked whinny piercing through the chaos. My hands reach for the railing to steady myself as the beast's front hooves slam down onto the bridge with a sickening crack.

The wood beneath us groans and splinters, a deafening snap ringing out as part of the bridge shatters under the horse's weight. Fragments of wood and shards of broken planks explode around me, tumbling into the raging river below.

The horse lurches, scrambling for purchase, its hooves slipping dangerously close to the jagged edge where the bridge has given way. He rips the reins right from Saint's hands as he barrels past me, aiming for the other side. Hot, searing pain rips through my shoulder as the horse gathers me and knocks me backwards. The world tilts as my breath leaves my lungs.

Arrows are flying towards us, none finding their mark, but all I can think about is how I've lost my footing, and time has slowed as I fall through a hole in the bridge's surface. Heading straight for the roaring river below—its hungry churning waters ready to swallow me whole.

"Saint!" The cry leaves my lips, and I just hope that he hears it in time.

## BRIDGES AND BIRD CAGES

Juniper's cry pierces my soul. I whip around to find her clinging on to the bridge for dear life. Only a few fingers grasp the splintered wood. My hands burn from the leather that sawed through them as the horse bolted across the bridge, leaving gaping holes in its wake.

Arrows whizz past me as Drogos and Rigg draw nearer. *Fucking losers.* I know they won't kill me, Donovan will want me alive, but that won't stop them from injuring me—or using Juni as leverage, or worse . . . Killing her. I scramble for Juni, my legs finally making the connection with my brain.

"Saint!" she cries out again, and the small part of what's left of my already shattered heart gives way at the desperation in her voice. Just as my feet pick up traction, a searing hot pain rips through my upper left arm. An arrow catches my skin, tearing flesh as it finds its mark in a wooden bridge post a few feet from me.

I clench my teeth against the searing hot pain. A flesh wound—not life threatening, but as the blood soaks my shirt, the pain is a reminder that while Donovan holds power over my life, I will always be in danger. Juni too, but right now she is my only focus. I will not let her suffer because of me.

"We've got you now, you fucking worm!" Drogos cries over the raging waters. His face is contorted with rage as his horse plummets towards me.

I don't have a spare thought to offer him, so I throw him a wink as I dash for my heart, in human form, who is about to be torn from me.

"Juni!"

She barely has time to gasp before I lunge, grabbing hold of her wrist just as the bridge groans beneath us. My boots slide over damp, rotting planks, but I grit my teeth and dig in, yanking her towards me with everything I've got.

"Hold on!" I growl through clenched teeth.

Tears streak her face, and her eyes are filled with fear. A different kind of pain digs its talons into my heart, sending heat through my body. This is not the end for us.

Her shaking fingers grip my forearms tightly as I drag her body back up and onto the groaning platform. Before she's fully safe, I steal a glance towards the two dipshits on horses. They've come to a halt, but they don't advance closer. Drogos and Riggs hover at the other end of the bridge, their faces twisted with hesitation. They won't risk it. Hell, I wouldn't either. The whole damn thing is about to go down. They aren't that dumb to know they won't make it across.

The bridge groans, shifting to one side. It's now or never. I have to pull Juni free. She scrambles, her free hand catching the jagged wood as she tries to pull herself up.

With one final pull, I heave her onto the last stretch of stable planks. She crashes into me, breathless, her fingers clutching at my coat. No time to stop. No time to breathe.

"Move!" I bark, grabbing her hand and dragging her forward.

We run, feet pounding over creaking wood, the bridge swaying and cracking beneath us. Every breath burns in my chest. Every step could send us plunging into the raging river below.

Our feet land on the solid ground on the other side, just as a loud crack sounds through the air. Both Juni and I spin, facing the bridge as it finally gives way, disappearing into the white foam below.

My chest heaves, my gaze landing on the two men on the other side.

Riggs rips a well used, metal bird cage that had been secured to his horse's saddle. He holds it high in the air. "Look at what we brought for you?" His voice carries across the sound of roaring water. "You'll need this for when you grow those weird feathers."

I run one hand through my hair, the other resting on my hip. "Funny! I don't think I'm going to fit in there."

"Don't think for a moment that we won't find you again, little bird."

I clench my jaw, every muscle in my body coiled tight. I don't have a witty remark. Not yet. Not while my blood is still running hot from nearly watching Juniper fall into the furious, churning waters.

Drogos takes a step forward. "What's the matter, Saint? No smart words? You always have something to say when you're slinking in and out of places you don't belong for Donovan."

My fingers twitch, aching to wrap around his throat.

"Guess we'll catch up with you later," Riggs calls, flashing a smirk. "Can't run forever, shape-shifter."

The corner of Brogos' lip turns up in a snarl. Neither one pleased that once again, I have escaped their grasp. "This is not the last you will see of us, Saint!" he yells.

With the biggest grin I can muster up, I hold my middle finger up to them. "Nice seeing you both again."

Both imbeciles curse before scrambling for their horses. I watch them as they turn back on the path they came. It won't be the last we see of them, but having to find another way across the river will buy us some time.

I exhale sharply through my nose, forcing the tension out of my shoulders. It doesn't work. I can still feel it, coiling like a viper beneath my skin.

While the immediate threat has passed, I still have to deal with a stunningly beautiful, yet extremely hostile woman, who has taken it upon herself to hurry off in the direction of our escaped horse. A quick glance at the wound on my arm confirms I'm not going to die on the spot, but I should definitely attend to it soon.

Heat from the sun bears down on me, mixing with the sweat and adrenaline from the last few minutes. I swivel around, looking in the direction that Juniper went. Swallowing down the throbbing pain in my arm, I curse under my breath before striding after her.

"Juniper." My voice is firm, but she doesn't slow.

The horse is quietly eating grass at the side of the road. I gather his reins, being mindful of the leather against my palms. I pick up my pace, closing the distance between Juniper and I. "Juni, slow down."

"Why?" she snaps, throwing a glare over her shoulder. "So you can tell me more half-truths? Or maybe another convenient lie?"

I exhale sharply, raking a hand through my hair. "Damn it, will you just—" I lunge forward, grabbing her wrist gently but firmly, forcing her to stop. She whirls on me, eyes flashing.

"Why?" she hisses, pulling free. "Why did you take Mother's ring, and who do you actually work for?"

Tears well in her eyes—her pretty meadow eyes, shimmering like rain-soaked grass, and I know I put them there. I've inflicted pain upon something soft, something good. The weight of it presses against my ribs like a brand, searing into the marrow of my bones. I should be flogged for my sins, for every cruel thing I've done, for every moment I've let her believe I was someone worth trusting.

Yet, I have to make her see. I have to make her understand. Not for my sake, but for hers. If she walks away now, believing I'm nothing but a liar and a thief, then I've lost more than just her trust—I've lost the only thing that's ever made me want to be something more.

The horse is more than happy to be tethered to a branch in the shade. So I leave him there and turn my attention back to Juni.

"I tried to explain yesterday, but you didn't want to hear." My voice is low yet gentle.

She folds her arms across her chest, a thunderstorm settling on her face. "Well, I'm listening now."

My shoulders drop, and a small sigh escapes my lips. Now is not the time to be baring my soul, not when Riggs and Drogos are so close, but Juni deserves something. I want to fix this. I want her to look at me again like she has for the last few weeks, like I'm someone worth loving.

"I work for Donovan."

Her face doesn't change. "The debt collector?"

My hands raise in defeat. "Yes."

Confusion washes over Juni. Her brows twitch, as she tilts her head at an angle just slightly. "I don't understand."

There's too much to tell her right now, but if I don't give her something—some piece of the truth—she'll only hate me more. Time isn't on our side. With a storm brewing in the distance and Drogos and Riggs still hunting us, we can't afford to linger here any longer.

With a sigh, I shove my hands into my trouser pockets. "I was born in Stone's Ridge."

Juni's brow softens, but she remains silent.

"My parents died when I was a bairn. I don't remember them at all. Or even have a picture of them. All I know is I was given to the orphanage by some neighbours who found me, or so I've been told."

A slight breeze whips between us, warning of what is to come.

"Donovan took Roan, Sepehr, and I from the orphanage when we were eleven years old. I thought it was going to be a dream come true. My brothers and I would finally have a family, but that was not the case," I continue on.

"I thought you said you had no siblings?" Juniper's voice is filled with caution, like she's caught me in a lie again.

"I don't, but they are the closest thing I've ever had to a family," I quickly answer.

"Where are they now?"

My shoulders lift and fall. "I don't know. On the run like me, free from Donovan's grasp, hopefully."

Juniper's gaze washes over our surroundings—avoiding me as she bites her bottom lip. "So what does all of this have to do with my mother's ring?" Her eyes find me again.

Thoughts of my past fill my mind. There are too many things to tell her, so I try to filter them, only wanting to tell her what I need to say for now. I sift through the memories, picking out the pieces that matter most. The rest . . . The rest can wait.

If she still wants to hear them. If she still wants anything to do with me after this.

"I never got my own—well, I don't think I did. My shifting didn't kick in until I was twelve, so I had no need for one. I've spent most of my life surviving day-to-day, fulfilling Donovan's orders and evading danger. It left little time for me to research my heritage, but when I got the chance, I found out that shifters were given a ring from the faeries at birth. I presumed my parents would have had one for me. So, when I asked Donovan about it, he told me that he was never given one from the orphanage. I believe they still have it."

"Why didn't you go there first? After you ran away from him?"

I run a hand through my hair, then shrug. "I figured it would be the first place Donovan would look. I couldn't risk it."

Juniper chews her bottom lip. "So why Mama's ring?"

Very faint thunder rumbles in the distance. I glance at the sky. Grey, sullen clouds are forming overhead. If we don't move soon, we will never make it to the next town before the storm hits.

Dragging my hands from my pockets, I run them through my hair. "It's the first I've seen in such a long time. I took it because I need full control of my body. I need to not worry about shifting every night. I want to find my ring and then I will give Kamari hers back."

At the mention of her mother's name, Juni flinches. The small act tears another hole in my chest. "Why can't you just buy a new ring?" she murmurs.

I shake my head. "Unfortunately, it doesn't work like that. They cost a lot of money, and take time to make—of which I have neither."

"So why is Donovan after you? What did you do to him, and what will you do if the orphanage doesn't have your ring?"

My hands find their way back to my pockets, and I shift my weight. Thankful for the shade we're both standing under from the large Oak behind Juniper. "I didn't do anything. He just sees me as his property. Someone to make him money. I've made him look like a fool with my escape—he likes to be in control. As for my ring, I don't know, but I have to start somewhere."

"You're not looking for work in Stone's Ridge, are you?" Her voice trembles. "You're going to the orphanage?"

A sigh escapes me. "Yes."

Juniper's eyes well with tears again. Her face no longer clouds with anger, but betrayal still lingers. Her shoulders have dropped, no doubt letting go of some of the tension she'd been holding onto.

She fiddles with the sleeve of her cream blouse. "You could have told me all this. I would have helped."

The way she's looking at me has given me some hope that maybe—just maybe, she will forgive me one day—for all of this. And that tiny glimmer of hope is all I need to hold on.

I take the smallest step towards her—a peace offering. "I panicked, okay? I got into town and you were gone, and I panicked."

She shakes her head lightly, chocolate wisps framing her face that have spilled from the pile on her head, shimmering in the sunlight breaking through the leaves. "I can't share my world with someone who lies and steals." Her voice is barely a whisper.

A sigh escapes my lips. "I know—I know, Blue." My fists clench inside my trouser pockets. "I want to be different. I just never learned how."

Juni's gaze travels over my face and down my chest until it finally rests on my blood-soaked sleeve. "You're hurt."

"It's fine—"

She shakes her head, spinning to walk towards the tree. "No, it's not . . . None of this is."

I'm losing her again. I can see it in her eyes, and we're running out of daylight. I need to fix this, and I need to do it now.

My boots gravitate towards her. "I'm so sorry, Juniper."

She turns to face me, her eyes filled with pain. "Sorry for what? That you hurt me, or that you got caught?"

"I'm sorry I hurt you."

For once in my life, it's the truth. I've never cared before who my lies hurt, or how my stealing affects others. Then Juniper came along, and now everything is different. She is all that is good. She makes me want to be that too.

"Please say something . . ." My voice cracks.

Her eyes never leave mine, but I can see the war raging behind them—the push and pull of trust and betrayal, of anger and understanding. She stands rooted in place, as if the very ground beneath her is uncertain, shifting. She's fighting a battle in those meadow-green depths, one I can only hope I'll win. Because if I don't, I'm not sure I'll ever find my way back to her.

"I don't know what to say, Saint," she whispers.

"Say you don't hate me . . . Please?"

Her boots crunch against the ground as she takes small steps towards me. I hold my breath, fearful that if I breathe, she will disappear. She's walking towards me—not away—that's a good sign, right?

She stops in front of me. So close that I can smell her honey scent. "That's the problem. After what you've done, what you've told me, and despite what I probably should do. I don't hate you at all."

I don't hear the rumble of thunder in the distance, low and threatening like a beast stirring from its slumber. I don't notice the way the horse lifts his head, ears twitching towards the sound, sensing the coming storm. I don't feel the wind as it snakes through the trees, rustling the leaves in warning, or see the branches begin to sway, whispering secrets of the tempest that creep ever closer. All I can focus on is the weight in my chest, the way my world narrows to the person standing before me, and the silent cry in her eyes. I know the storm in the distance approaches. I know that Donovan's men are out there trying to find their way to us, but I can't break this moment.

She doesn't hate me?

I stay rooted to the spot. My feet refuse to move. She doesn't either. With a shaky breath, I let all my words out. "I'm tired of never winning, of never being allowed happiness. All the stealing, lying—I want that to be over now. But I refuse to let go of the one thing I want . . . You."

My hands find her, cradling her face as I crash my lips to hers. The moment our lips meet, her breath hitches—a delicate, fleeting sound that sends a tremor through my chest. The world around us ceases to exist, fading into nothing as I claim her mouth, tasting her like she's every wish I've ever dared to make.

A fire ignites deep within me, an unrelenting, consuming blaze that belongs to her and her alone. It sears through my soul, eternal and unquenchable, a flame that will never—can never—be extinguished.

Her hands clutch at the front of my shirt, holding on to me with everything she's got, as our lips become one. I don't even need to be invited in. Her tongue slips across the seam of my mouth, and I respond with fervour. *By the stars.* She's driving me wild.

Every fibre in my body is awake, as our tongues dance to the song of desire. I need the breath she is holding. It belongs to me and I want it back. Her fists clutch my shirt tighter as I drown in her essence. Only when I softly pull away do I open my eyes. I'm so afraid that I will find it all a dream.

Yet, there she is in front of me. Perfectly pink lips swollen from my touch. A feral desire in me awakes as I single tear steals its way down her cheek. I brush it away with the pad of my thumb. Never will I make her cry again.

Neither of us utters a word, yet a thousand unspoken ones pass between us in the space of a single breath. It's not enough.

I *need* more of her. I need the certainty of her, the warmth of her presence wrapping around the raw edges of my soul. She is the soothing water my parched, withered existence has craved for longer than I dare admit. And like a man dying of thirst, I want to drink her in until I am whole again.

Meadow green eyes, fractured with amber and orange, roam my face, landing on my lips again. I almost groan when her delicate hands slide around my neck to clasp behind my head. With a gentle tug, she draws me in, and once again I'm done for.

Juniper lets out the sweetest moan when our mouths collide. I struggle to stay upright as we nip, tug and bite. My cock is straining against my trousers, making it very hard to function properly. I gently walk her backwards until my hands find the rough bark of the large oak. There I grip her hips, drawing her into me as close as we possibly can, allowing the tree to take our weight.

Eager fingers dig into the back of my hair, and I wrap my arms around her waist, lifting her off the ground. Juniper's arms tighten around my neck as we stand beneath the protection of the oak. She feels so warm, and familiar, as if my soul has known that from the beginning of time it was her all along.

I pull my lips from hers softly, peppering kisses along her jaw all the way to her ear, where I gently bite her lobe. Her skin feels like silk, like the petals of a blue, morning glory blossom that's newly bloomed. Like the ones that grow over the arch in Juni's garden. She moans again as I nuzzle her neck; the sound makes my cock twitch.

Her boots whisper against the grass as I lower her to the ground, but I don't let go. My hands remain at her waist, unwilling to break the connection just yet. Her eyes no longer brim with confusion or pain, but doubt lingers in the shadows, a ghost that refuses to fade. It will take time—longer than I'd like—but that's okay. Trust isn't given; it's rebuilt, piece by fragile piece. And if it takes a lifetime to earn hers back, then so be it. I'll prove myself to her, over and over again, until there's no room left for doubt at all.

She reaches up to trace a finger across my lips. I fight the urge to close my eyes and groan at her touch. "So now what do we do?" she asks.

I lean down to kiss her forehead, lingering for a moment. "Now, we go get those wicks and my ring. Then we go home."

# Twenty-One

## THE OLD BARN

The sky is a bruised shade of grey. Purple, black and midnight blue. Silver flashes of lighting outline the cumulonimbus clouds, making them appear closer than they are, stretching as far as the horizon. All of this rain was going to make the grounds through the forest almost impassable.

We've been riding for a few hours, but after today's sequence of events, I doubt we will make it to the next town before the storm hits. Which is a shame, because I would love to get off this horse.

Saint sits snug against my back, his warmth a comfort. The taste of his lips replays over and over in my mind. I can still feel his velvet skin under my hands. The moment he kissed me, I was done for. I needed him like I needed air. Was it so wrong? He stole Mama's ring. He broke my trust.

Yet after hearing his story, and seeing the broken little boy in his eyes begging to be given a second chance . . . How could I not?

"We need to find shelter," Saint says, his voice cutting through the quiet between us. I throw a glance over my shoulder and nod, already scanning the landscape. It's as if he's reading my thoughts.

Deep thunder rumbles through the sky, rattling my bones as it seeps into the ground. Wind whips against my face as we pound the earth, flicking up mud behind us as we barrel along. Then, in the distance, just off the road, I spot it—a broken-down barn, its wooden frame weathered and sagging but still standing. It's not much, but it's better than nothing.

Saint sees it at the same time, and aims the horse for it. Long graceful legs cut through the underbrush with ease. To my left a loud *crack* sounds. A tree a few meters away is struck by lightning. Orange flames lick the air, but aren't alive long, the rain snuffing out the fire with a hiss. Half its branches explode with the force. "Saint!" I squeal in fright.

Splinters fly through the air as he twists, throwing his body over me, protecting me from any stray shards.

My heart lurches, beating faster as the storm descends upon us.

He urges the horse on, aiming for the barn. We will be safer inside than out here.

Thunder shudders through the sky again as we reach the decaying structure. Saint pulls the horse to a stop, and throws himself to the ground, practically dragging me with him. We break into a run just as the rain starts to fall in earnest. It comes in sheets, cold and relentless, soaking through my white blouse and hood in seconds. Saint is right behind me, throwing an arm over his head as we race towards the shelter.

By the time we reach it, we're drenched. I pull the rotting door open; the hinges groaning in protest, and scurry inside. Saint drags the horse in behind me, slamming the door shut. The space is small, musty with the scent of old hay and damp wood, but it's big enough to house all three of us, and at least it's dry.

I breathed out a laugh, wiping droplets from my face. "That was intense."

Saint smirks, wringing out the hem of his shirt. "For a minute there, I thought we were going to be burnt offerings."

A small huff quietly escapes my lips as I take off my cloak before folding it over a broken beam that is leaning against the wall. "I haven't seen this amount of rain in such a long time." My eyes find Saint from across the small space.

The sight of him soaked, his shirt plastered against his body like a second skin, warms me.

He shrugs lightly. "I'd wondered the same thing. Here—" He gestures to a dry patch of hay. "Sit, and I'll make us a fire."

I find the driest spot in the hay and slowly drop to the floor.

The storm howls outside, rain hammering against the warped wooden walls of the old barn. The wind pushes through the cracks, chilling the damp air around us. Saint retrieves his backpack from where it's strapped to the saddle, before dropping it to the floor as he rummages through it to find some flint and steel.

I watch him closely as he kneels on the dirt floor, brushing aside stray straw and gathering the driest pieces he can find. He braces the steel against his knuckles and strikes hard.

Sparks jump, flashing orange in the dim barn, but they die before catching.

With gritted teeth, he tries again. On the second go, he's successful. The ember catches, eating at the dried grass, curling the edges inward as smoke threads into the air. The small flame grows, licking at the twigs he carefully stacks around it. He adds a little more, feeding it just enough to stay alive.

He certainly knows what he's doing. Not that he's ever given me reason to doubt his skills. Yet as I think of Mama, and the betrayal I feel, I can't help but also see him in a different light. Like there is a haze that has settled over us. A sheer curtain keeping me from fully allowing him to come close.

Not yet anyway. I know for a fact that he hasn't told me everything, and no matter how good his lips taste on mine, or how delicious his hands feel as they grip my waist, I need answers.

A sigh escapes him as he sits back against a bracing pole. His body must be exhausted from the adrenaline it's endured today—I know, because I nearly fell in those waters . . . If it wasn't for him, who knows what would have happened? He's possibly suffering some shock from the blood loss, too.

I flick my gaze to the scarlet soaked fabric. "You should let me clean your wound," I utter.

He glances at the rip in his jacket before bringing his attention to me. He nods slowly. It's almost like he's not used to people taking care of him. They probably haven't. Fractures disperse through my heart as I think of Saint growing up in an orphanage. He's never known the true love of a parent—not like I have. What if no one has ever cared when he was injured?

Salty tears gather in the corners of my eyes. I'm so torn with wanting to rush to his aid, but also guard my heart.

Fighting back the urge to cry, I scramble to my feet, fetching my bag before I return to Saint's side. I didn't bring any bandages with me, but I did have two nightgowns. One was older than the other, it's fabric thin. I could rip the bottom off to use as binding. The white cloth is soft beneath my touch as I pull it from my bag. Saint watches me between full, dark lashes. Every time I catch his gaze, my heart doubles over in my chest. Warmth spreads into my cheeks as I remember how his lips felt.

I rip the cloth into a wide strip before dampening it with the water from the canteen. I'd be lying if I said I didn't want to kiss him again.

While I prepare, Saint shrugs his coat from his shoulders. He reaches for the hem of his shirt. It peels away from his damp skin, sticking slightly before he tosses it to the floor alongside his coat. His knees are drawn up, allowing his arms to rest on top, his hands hanging between them. The desire to look at his naked, muscled torso is too great. Everything about him is purposeful. From the finely cut muscles on his abdomen, his long slender arms chiselled from marble, the translucent, pale blue veins jutting from his forearms. All of him is exactly how he should be.

A glint catches my attention. Mama's ring. My stomach drops, but I don't let it show on my face. Saint is right. Mother won't suffer for not having her ring, but she will be losing her mind wondering where she placed it. And having to shift into a deer every night isn't something she's ever had to do. My heart aches for her. I know it's only for another week or so, and then we—I will return home with it—I hope.

Perhaps Saint will join me, perhaps he will not. I can't fully trust his words, but a tiny part of me hopes that he speaks the truth.

There's also a part of my heart that aches for him, too.

His gaze finds me, a small smirk dancing on his lips. My cheeks warm, knowing I've been caught staring at him. I drop my gaze, placing the wet cloth over the angry wound. Saint winces, a small hiss escaping his lips.

"Crybaby," I hum, a faint smile playing on my mouth.

His brows raise with a playfulness that I've come to adore. "Do you want to be shot by an arrow?"

I wince internally. He took an arrow to the arm, but didn't let it deter him from saving me. I truly thought I was to perish in those waters, and yet he'd come for me. Saved me from injury—even death—and I hadn't even thanked him yet. Perhaps I needed him more than I'd like to admit right now.

I inch closer to him, gently wiping blood from his arm. "Thank you." My voice is soft.

"For what?"

The sound of fabric ripping is almost drowned out by the storm raging outside. I wrap it around his arm, tying it securely. "Thank you for saving me."I trace a finger down a pattern marked into his skin.

It's as if my hands have a mind of their own. Dancing across his skin as if it belongs to them.

Desire races through my blood, quickening my heart. I want *him*. All of him. Every day that he will have me. Yet parts of my mind scream at me that I'd be a fool to let him into my life. What else would he steal? What lies would tumble so innocently from his perfect mouth? Can I have him and keep my guarded heart? What if his past is forever a stain marked on our relationship? Hindering a true and honest future that might blossom between us.

Saint's hand dips to brush my leg ever so slightly. "I will always do my best to never let anything happen to you." His eyes find me, and a part of my soul finds its way back into its rightful place. For a moment I come alive. The breath in my lungs is cool and fresh, reminding me that it's his air I breathe.

I offer him a small smile, like I believe him, as I sit back on my heels.

Outside, thunder rolls, deep and angry, shaking the earth beneath us. But here, in the fragile glow of the fire, we have a moment of quiet.

Fatigue washes over me. Today—no, this trip has not been anything like I thought it would be. I shift my body, settling as close to the fire as I dare, drawing my knees up to my chest as I wrap my arms around them.

Saint is staring into the orange flames, his body here, yet his mind is far away. Dare I dig into his past? Pry open his troubled thoughts and coax them into the light?

If I do . . . Will he tell me the truth?

"What was it like?" I ask softly. "The orphanage?"

The fire crackles, drying our clothing. Rain hammers at the roof with the odd drip sounding on the ground in the corners of the small barn.

Saint flicks his gaze at me, a look that's unreadable. He lets out a breath, leaning forward to rest his arms on raised knees. "It was hard," he admits, staring into the flames. "Crowded, strict. We were always hungry." A small smirk tugs at the corner of his perfect mouth. "But it wasn't all bad. Sepehr, Roan, and I . . . We found ways to entertain ourselves. We'd hide in the stairwells, trying to avoid chores. Sneak into the kitchens at night, stealing bits of bread and whatever scraps we could get our hands on."

Seemed like an accurate trait. My heart softens towards him. "Were you ever caught?"

"Of course." He huffs quietly. "But we got good at running." His smile fades a little. I watch as his mind wanders down memory lane. "That place . . . It wasn't perfect, but it had moments of light. More than Donovan's house ever did," he continues on.

I struggle to find the words. Yet my gaze never leaves his face. The pain in his voice louder than the storm outside. "And what was it like there?"

A muscle in his jaw tightens. "It wasn't a home. Not like the orphanage, not even close. We were tools meant to be sharpened and used. I thought I was free when he took us in—thought I had a place, a purpose." He shakes his head, exhaling sharply. "Turns out, I was just swapping one prison for another."

"I'm sorry you had to live in a world that made you believe you weren't worth loving."

Saint flicks his gaze towards me before returning it to the fire. "Maybe I'm not."

Another piece of my shattered soul finds its rightful place, and before I can question myself, I reach for him. His breath catches as I slide onto his lap, my hands snaking around his neck. Deep orbs of sapphire-blue stare at me through darkened lashes.

"This is a very dangerous place to sit, Blue." His voice is low—almost a purr.

It sends my stomach into a fluttering heap of knots. Many times I've thought about his hands on my body, and what his kiss would taste like. Now that I've had a morsel, I can easily admit that I want more.

My fingers draw patterns on his skin, gently scraping through his blond hair. "Why do you call me Blue?"

Saint tugs me closer, as his hands find their way to my hips, gently gripping the fabric of my olive green trousers. "Because your name means Juniper berry, which is blue, and it's the only colour flower in your garden."

A faint smile dances across my lips. "No one's ever given me a different nickname. I've always been known as Juniper, or Juni."

Saint tips his head back, closing his eyes as my fingers drag up the back of his head, drawing bumps to the surface of his skin. "Would you rather I called you something else?"

His eyes are dark when they return to me. Desire, like a thick blanket, wraps us in a cocoon.

"You can call me whatever you like . . . As long as you moan it." My body warms at my own words. It's like Saint has this power over me, awakening my soul from a sleep so deep that I didn't even realise it was in. His infectious charm and sense of adventure make me almost jealous. Perhaps just for a while I could put all the thoughts churning in my mind to rest, and just be here—in the moment—with him.

His brow raises in surprise, like he's just as shocked as I am.

"Juni—" ,he warns softly.

"Yes, Saint?" With a shift of my hips, I feel his cock twitch in his trousers. Heat rushes to my core, as his rigid length lays trapped between us. His eyes, his scent, his body, his face, his voice. All of it drives me wild.

His fingers grip my hips tighter, digging into the fabric. I wish nothing more to have nothing between us, but it's been so long since I've been with someone that I almost feel unequipped in the situation I've put myself in, but I don't want it to stop.

Saint leans a little closer. "You're making it very hard for me to behave."

I tilt my head towards him so our lips almost brush. "What if I don't want you to?"

He groans again, closing his eyes briefly. "I want you more than you know, but not here. Not in a barn. Our first time will be where it's safe and warm and where I can fuck you on every surface in the room." His voice is low. "A place where I can do all the things on the list I have planned."

Shivers ripple up my spine, sending my hips rocking in response to the vibration of his voice. My brow raises in question, heat coiling in my stomach. "There's a list?"

Saint nods very slowly—too slowly. "A long one."

Blush creeps into my cheeks. I don't know whether to be afraid or intrigued. "When do I get to see this list?"

I appreciate that he wants to explore this connection in a place that doesn't have holes in the roof, but if I'm honest, I'd have him right here—right now. Perhaps just a taste?

Eyes filled with *desire*, clouded in *want*, clear with *need* trace over my face, like he's fighting with all his might to keep his hands to himself.

No . . . This won't do. I rock my hips slowly as I bite the corner of my bottom lip. Saint's eyes darken even further— which I thought was impossible.

"Fuck it."

His mouth crashes into mine, one hand still gripping my hip as Saint reaches the other to cradle the back of my head.

I can't stop the whimper escaping as his tongue slips between the seam of my lips. I devour him like he's made from the nectar of honeysuckle blossoms.

His rigid length between us hardens, and I fight the urge to cry out at the feeling of my warmth dragging against it. Cupping my hands around his face, light stubble scratches my palms. I grip him tighter, not yet willing to let go of this blissful moment. Not even the rumbling of thunder outside, or the ferocious rain hitting the side of the barn, can steal my attention.

It's as if my hips have a mind of their own, as they begin to leisurely rock. I'd give anything to ease the ache that is building between my legs.

In a low voice, Saint moans against my lips, his hand dragging across my thigh to find my core. I tear my mouth from his, a cry releasing at the first brush of his fingers against the fabric of my undergarments.

"Is this what you want?" Saint whispers, one hand cupping the back of my neck, the other tracing circles over the lace.

I nod, my eyelids heavy, my cheeks on fire. "Yes," I manage.

Saint chuckles softly, his fingers finding the edge of the fabric. He teases, dragging them across the top, making my stomach quiver in delight. "Is that so?"

With a sensual thrust, I rock my hips harder, which draws a moan from him. The corners of my mouth tip up into a smile, one I know he can't resist.

"Very well," he whispers before plunging his fingers between my slick warmth.

A cry rises to my lips, but he swallows it with a kiss—raw, deep, and utterly consuming. The world narrows to the heat of his mouth, the steady, deliberate touch of his hands as they unravel me with a pleasure I've never known. A shuddering breath escapes me, tears pricking my eyes, overwhelmed by the intensity of it all. If time could stop, if I could live in this moment forever, I would.

His other hand drops from neck to seize my ass. He squeezes it, yanking me towards him as his fingers pump into me.

Who knows how long we find refuge in each other's arms. I put all worries aside, and just immerse myself in *him*, because when the storm breaks we will move on, and who knows what waits for us in the next town?

I buck my hips against his hand, knowing my climax is about to break over me. My hands tighten around his neck and shoulders—anticipating the ecstasy that is going to flood my body.

"Saint," I moan.

"You're so fucking beautiful, Blue." His fingers curl inside my warmth, his thumb tracing circles over my clit, sending a shock right through me.

His lips graze my jaw, a teasing bite that sends a shiver down my spine. His scent, the warmth of his breath, the possessive grip of his hands—it's too much, yet not enough. The storm outside rages, a blinding flash of lightning illuminating the barn as pleasure crashes through me like a breaking wave. A cry tears from my throat, swallowed by the thunder as I shatter in his arms.

Who knows where I go in my mind. Everything turns black, my ears ring, and my body feels numb—or on fire—I can't quite tell. All I know is, Saint is everything I ever wanted in a man, and I hope this is the beginning of us.

I pull back, gasping softly, my body boneless. Saint is silent, watching me as he traces the tip of his tongue over his top lip like he's making sure to consume every drop of our kiss. His eyes flick between mine and my mouth.

"Was that on the list?" My voice quivers.

His grin is feral as he slowly nods. "Yes, Blue."

With a smile, I trail my lips with soft kisses over his face, across his eyelids, and over the bridge of his nose. I feel Saint's body relax, like the tension of the last few moon cycles is leaving his body—like it is mine.

I bring my lips back to his, hovering just above them, teasing. His breath is warm, tempting. But he doesn't let me torment him for long. He closes the distance, capturing my mouth again—soft this time, slow and intoxicating. Warm fingers dance around my waist as they grip me tighter, crushing my breasts against his solid chest. We stay like this for a while, simply tasting one another, until I must breathe or I will pass out from all of this pleasure.

Saint rests his forehead on mine, both of us basking in the moment. He slowly pulls back, a drowsy look on his content face, but his hands don't leave my waist.

"Now I will behave," I whisper.

A grin forms on his mouth as he reaches up to run a thumb across my swollen lips. "Good girl."

Warm sun filters through the inn's lace curtain, drifting across the bed, and up my back. It brings relief to my aching bones. Yesterday had not been kind to me, but I hold on to the hope that today will be kinder. Just a few more days, and we'll reach Stone's Ridge. Hopefully, I'll find answers about my wicks, and Saint will get his ring from the orphanage. Where it leaves us after that, I'm still uncertain.

My gaze drifts across the rustic decorations before settling on Saint. He steps out of the washroom, hair damp, shirt hanging open, clinging to his body. We arrived late last night, exhausted from the ride. As soon as we'd booked a room, which I'd insisted I pay for, we both collapsed into bed.

I can still feel the way I fit perfectly against him, his arm wrapped around my waist, holding me close. It was the first time I'd ever spent an entire night with a man in my bed.

Part of me hopes it won't be the last.

He catches me staring. A blush creeps into my cheeks at the way he slowly saunters across the room. "How is your arm?" I say, slipping from the bed.

Saint stops in front of me to view his bandages. "It's not bleeding, and the pain is minimal. I'll survive."

I dip my head in acknowledgement before turning to retrieve my belongings. "You'll need to keep an eye on it, you don't want it to get infected."

Patchouli and cedarwood envelop me as Saint wraps his arms around my back, nuzzling his face into my neck. I pause, allowing him to hold me in the quiet of the room. His embrace is a brief escape from my responsibilities.

My eyes flutter shut while my heart skitters in my chest. I want this. I want him. I think I've wanted him the moment he stepped into the chandlery. But betrayal is hard, and even though I understand why he took the ring, I feel for my mother—I'm worried about her.

There is also the lingering thought that he will find his ring, I will get my wicks, and his wandering ways will take him far from me. I have a shop to save, and there are places he is yet to discover.

"Where are you?" Saint's warm breath tickles my ear.

I turn in his arms to face him. "What do you mean?"

His eyes travel over my face as he reaches up to tuck a stray piece of hair behind my ear. "You're here, but your mind is not."

My shoulders lift and fall in defeat. I'm not ready to allow my thoughts loose into the world, so I keep them bottled up, painting a smile across my lips. "I'm fine. Just thinking about all the riding we have to do today."

Saint relaxes his hold on me, but his solid arms rest lightly on my waist. I shouldn't want this, I shouldn't want *him*, but I do. Despite the emotional barrier still lingering between us that prevents me from fully letting myself give in.

"Are you in pain?" Saint asks, his fingers drawing patterns on my back.

I shake my head softly. "No. Though I might become one if we don't eat soon."

His deep chuckle washes over me like a hug. "Wouldn't want that now, would we?"

The absence of Saint's arms leave me feeling empty—perhaps something I should get used to, sooner rather than later.

We gather our things, leaving the comfort of the space behind us. Downstairs, the inn's common room is already bustling with early risers. Travellers and merchants gather around wooden tables, their voices blending with the clatter of dishes, and the crackling of the hearth over in the corner.

My eyes scan the surroundings, still aware of the danger that follows us in the form of two males. Thankfully, I don't spot either of them.

Saint places his hand on my lower back, the heat of it burning a hole right through the fabric of my blouse. He ushers me to a small table by the window, towards the corner of the room. A lace curtain obstructs our view, but I don't mind. It's probably best we don't put ourselves on display too much. I'd say Saint is thinking the same thing.

The innkeeper who greeted us late last night shuffles over to our table—plump woman with greying curls, and warm brown eyes. "How was yer' sleep last night?"

Saint offers her a smile she can't refuse. "It was delightful, thank you." He flicks his gaze to me, and my cheeks warm.

"Are ya wanting breakfast this mornin'? And are ya planning on attending the fair today?" The innkeeper continues, turning to catch the attention of someone hovering at the kitchen door. She holds up two fingers, to which the young boy with the large doe eyes and shaggy black hair grins and scurries out of view.

I turn to look up at the woman. "Fair?"

"Aye," she nods. "Happens every year. Traders, performers, all sorts of wonders. Starts in an hour."

Saint raises a brow. "Sounds like a good way to get pickpocketed."

I steal a glance at him and furrow my brows. He's just teasing . . . Right?

The innkeeper chuckles. "Only if you're daft enough to flash your coin. But there's good food, music, even a dance at sundown." Her gaze flicks between the two of us, a knowing glint in her eyes. "A fair's a fine place for sweethearts, you know."

The shaggy-haired boy returns with a tray in hand, on top is two plates filled with sausage, egg and some bread. Accompanying it are two pots of steaming hot tea.

I wait until the boy leaves before I respond. Heat creeps up my neck as I glance between Saint and the innkeeper. "We're not—"

Saint just smirks, sipping his tea.

"We're not going to be around long." I offer her a smile.

The innkeeper winks at me. "Well, if ya change your mind, you'll find it in the town square." With that, she bustles off to tend to another table, leaving me staring down at my plate.

I shove a bite of toast into my mouth, avoiding the male across from me. What was I about to say? That we aren't lovers? It's true, is it not? Yet, why did I stop myself? Perhaps for a moment I wanted to taste the idea on my tongue. Perhaps if I said it out loud it would make it so.

Saint leans back in his chair, stretching his legs out as he watches me pick at my food. "You'd like to go, wouldn't you?"

I glance up at him before reaching for my tea. I take a sip before answering. The warm liquid is life giving. "It doesn't matter what I want."

"How so?"

"We have to keep moving. I need wicks, you need a ring, and there are people after you," I say with as much confidence as I can.

Saint shrugs, the smirk never leaving his lips. "We've been travelling for days Juni. A few hours won't kill us."

I furrow my brow. "No, but Brogos and Riggs might."

He leans forward, resting his forearms on the edge of the table. "They won't be looking for us at a fair, Blue."

The toast becomes my victim as I slowly tear it apart piece by piece as the thoughts in my mind bounce back and forth. I don't break my gaze, but my lips are tightly sealed.

Saint's eyes are soft. "Juni, when's the last time you did something just for the fun of it?"

I shake my head, not wanting to admit that the last time I did something was dancing at the inn. Before that—who knows? The responsibilities on my shoulders take up too much space for me to allow anything else in.

I press my lips together.

"That long, huh?" He exhales, shaking his head. "You talk about survival like it's the only thing that matters, but what's the point if you never live a little?"

I don't bother denying it. Deep down, I know he's right. But that doesn't mean I have the luxury of doing whatever I want—not like him, anyway. He needs a ring so he can come and go as he pleases. I need wicks to keep the chandlery in business, so I can put food on the table.

However, this is not the time or place to have such conversations.

"Fine," I mutter, stabbing a piece of sausage with unnecessary force. "We'll go. But only if you promise that it's only for a little while and then we head out."

Joy dances across Saint's face, and my heart can't help but leap towards him. He's smiling that infectious smile. The one that I find impossible to resist. "Promise," he says with a wink.

# Twenty Two

## FAIRS ARE POINTLESS

The fair is alive with colour and sound, a world apart from the vivid greens and mottled brown roads of the forest. Lanterns sway in the breeze, green, blue, yellow and orange, lining the stalls brimming with trinkets, pastries, and woven fabrics. The scent of roasted nuts and melted sugar drift through the air, mixing with laughter, and the distant tune of a fiddle.

Being here reminds me of home. The heart in my chest twists. Meadowbrook would be having their festival, too. I left all the candle preparations to Mama and Wilson. Hopefully, they will get it done in time.

Most towns in this part of Sapphire Vale celebrated the ending of summer, and the welcoming of the new autumn season.

Saint and I wander through the crowds. I have one eye on the colours and sights, while the other is scanning for any signs of unwanted company. His hand brushes against mine, a fleeting touch that sends heat blossoming through me. I don't pull away—neither does he.

"Are you hungry?" Saint leans down to murmur in my ear.

I glance up to meet his blue eyes. It's so easy to drown in them, and as I drop my gaze to his perfect mouth, I'm reminded of our kisses in the barn. I offer him a smile. "I could eat."

A smirk breaks across Saint's face. "So could I."

There is no doubt my face has turned beet red. I don't think he's talking about food. My shoulder finds his arm as I shove him lightly. "You're insufferable."

His grin widens. "I try."

With his hand against the small of my back, we veer off to the left towards a stall selling popcorn. Saint purchases a bag that's coated in caramel, and offers it to me. I take a handful, popping a few in my mouth. Before I can stop myself, a small moan escapes my lips. The crunch is sweet and buttery, melting on my tongue. Despite my mind telling me I should be on my way to Stone's Ridge, I allow myself to enjoy the moment.

A gentleman wearing a fine suit coming towards us doesn't step to the side quick enough, his shoulder catching Saint's. Both men collide, spilling some popcorn onto the ground.

"My apologies, sir. Too caught up in the magic of the fair." Saint brushes away a stray crumb on the front lapels of the man's jacket.

The man snorts, unimpressed. "Be more careful." With a final glance, he adjusts his cufflinks and strides off into the crowd.

Saint watches him go, jaw tight. I reach up and squeeze his arm. "Maybe he's jealous of your popcorn."

He huffs lightly, a smile playing on his lips. "Maybe he's jealous that the prettiest girl at the fair is walking with me."

My smile falters, and my gaze drops to my boots. I should be happy, should let his words warm me, but doubt creeps in like a shadow. He's just being kind . . . Right? I've never thought of myself as beautiful, never had a reason to. So why does hearing it from him make my chest tighten in a way I don't understand?

We weave through the bustling fair, the sounds of laughter and distant music wrapping around us like a warm breeze. The caramel popcorn is nearly gone, and Saint keeps stealing pieces from my hand instead of the bag, smirking every time I swat him away.

Up ahead, a small boy steals a handful of roasted nuts from a distracted vendor's cart. His mother catches him in an instant, scolding him before marching away from the stall.

Saint chuckles beside me. "That was me as a kid. Always trying to sneak extra food from the orphanage kitchens."

I grin, nudging him. "Sounds like something you would do—taking things that don't belong to you."

He stiffens for a second, like the words hit somewhere deep. His smirk fades.

Laughter bubbles up from inside me, and I nudge him again. "Too soon?"

His eyes find me, and the look he gives me is playful. He exhales, rolling his eyes, but I catch the hint of a smile before he shoves another piece of popcorn into his mouth.

I keep putting one foot in front of the other. I should be encouraging Saint to leave the fair, but I just can't bring myself to do that—not yet. He was right about me needing to live a little.

The scent of lavender reaches me. I whip my head around to search for where it's coming from. My gaze lands on a stall selling candles, and my heart almost tumbles from my chest. I catch it just in time, tucking it away where I can keep it safe.

Saint must have sensed my hesitancy. He reaches for my hand and squeezes it gently. "Would you like to look at them closer?"

I nod, taking steps towards the stall. Candles of every shape and size are arranged on tiered wooden shelves, their wax carved with intricate designs—swirls, florals, even tiny constellations. Some are dyed deep blues and purples, others a soft cream, while a few glow like amber in the midday sun.

I reach out, trailing my fingers over the smooth ridges of one, my chest tightening. This is exactly the kind of work I've always wanted to do.

"Are these the kinds of designs you want to create?" Saint steps up beside me, hands in pockets as he eyes the display.

Silently, I nod.

"Did your dad ever have a stall at festivals?"

I shake my head, swallowing down the lump forming in my throat. My mind flashing back to my father's words so long ago. *"Fairs are pointless, Juni. The real money is in sticking to what we already know."* He never cared for the new ideas I had, or how we might be able to grow the business. And now that he was gone, there was no room for me to be creative, at least not until I'd paid off his debt.

Saint stays quiet, watching me as I lift a small, intricately carved pillar candle to my nose. "You need to make the candles you want to make, Blue."

I let out a small laugh, shaking my head. "Maybe when I'm not drowning in debt."

"Someday," he insists, and there's something in his voice—something certain, like he believes it enough for the both of us.

I tuck the memory away, along with the quiet hope it stirs in me, and set the candle back down. "We really should get moving."

Saint nods as he takes my hand, tugging me back through the crowd. It's time to return to reality.

With fresh supplies in our packs, paid for by Saint to my quiet surprise, we get back out on the road. After we've left the town behind us, he lets the horse set the pace as we ride through the forest, and open fields. The sun is still warm, which has me anticipating the cool evening air. Wind whips over us as we race along.

Saint's rigid body is becoming a comfort. Something that I will miss when we reach Stone's Ridge, when he finds his ring and I return home.

Saint leans down closer to my ear so that I can hear him above the constant pounding of the horse's hooves. "We won't reach the next town before nightfall. We're going to need to find shelter before the last light of day." I nod in agreement. A soft bed would have been preferred, especially if Saint was in it, but I'd slept in the tent before, so I could do it again.

We travel for another hour before spotting a small clearing nestled beneath the sweeping branches of a towering oak, just off the main road. The air is thick with the scent of damp earth and pine. Together, Saint and I erect the tent, and build a small fire. We eat in silence, savouring the quiet of the forest. The odd squirrel scurrying by, disturbing the peace.

My gaze finds Saint across the fire. He seems lost in his thoughts.

It's not dark enough yet to see the shadows from the fire dancing across the forest floor, but the flames still glint in Saint's eyes. He offers me a small smile.

"Are you nervous about returning to the orphanage?"

He hesitates, fiddling with a twig before tossing it into the fire. "A little."

"And what of Donovan? Do you think he will ever leave you alone?"

Saint shakes his head. "To be honest . . . I don't think so."

Silence drapes over us like a heavy cloak, thick with unspoken words. I wonder what thoughts linger behind those guarded eyes, yet I'm too afraid to ask. There's so much I want to ask—so much I need to know—yet none of it feels right. Still, how will I ever find the answers if I don't summon the courage to ask?

I settle against the trunk of the oak. "Have you ever wanted to find out more about your parents?"

Saint shrugs. "Sometimes I wonder if it's best I don't know."

He didn't shy away from my question, so I ask another. "Do you know anything about them?"

With a soft sigh, he leans back against the moss-covered log supporting his back. "Only their names."

I pause, waiting for him to continue, not wanting to push him further than he's ready for. Seconds pass by as I study his face. My body aches to be in his arms again, but perhaps now is not the time.

After a moment, his eyes find me, a smirk dancing on his lips. "Now, that's privileged information. I don't give that out to just anybody."

I quickly nod. Of course, a very sensitive subject must be approached carefully. I don't blame him for not wanting to share, so I look away, distracting myself with a trail of ants on the forest floor.

His voice is soft when he speaks again. "Evaine and Merek Everhart." My gaze flicks to his face, my brow pinched. "But you just said—"

"You're not just anybody, Blue." He smiles.

I can feel the invisible tether between us tighten as I draw my knees up, wrapping my arms around them. He opened the door wider to his past and invited me in. I smile at him softly. "Those are beautiful names."

The pain flickers back into his eyes, a shadow of something long buried but never forgotten. He never knew his parents, and keeping it that way is his shield, his way of surviving. I too, know the burden of hope and the weight that it carries.

Yet, I can't help but wonder—if he had someone to stand by him, to share the weight of the past—maybe uncovering the truth wouldn't feel so impossible.

Distant thunder rumbles. I look at the darkening skies. A storm is rolling in again. No longer do I want to feel the distance between us, so I get up and move over to sit beside him.

Saint's eyes light up as I place his arm around my shoulders. Even the toughest folk need to be embraced. He pulls me closer, and together we watch the fire sparks disappearing into the night sky. Lightning flickers on the horizon.

"Tell me more about Roan and Sepehr, your childhood." I glance up in time to see the corner of his mouth turn up.

"There was this teacher. Her name was Mrs Eggles. She was one of the strictest teachers in the orphanage, and boy did she hate animals—but no more than she despised all three of us. One afternoon, after discovering a particularly large frog near the riverbank while playing outside, Sepehr came up with a plan. He claimed this frog was destined to go into Mrs Eggles's desk drawer in the classroom. Now, Roan, being the practical one, didn't want to risk the thing hopping away, so he kept it in a box all day, making sure it wouldn't escape. That night, we snuck out of our room and put it in her drawer." The grin on Saint's face widened—as did mine.

"And what happened?" I ask eagerly.

A deep chuckle escapes his lips. "Let's just say that the next morning in class, when the frog was discovered, Mrs Eggles knew exactly who to blame."

"Were you punished?"

Saint huffs. "If you call scrubbing the mess hall every night for a week after dinner punishment, then I'd say so."

I rest my head against his shoulder, like it's a natural thing to do. Lightning flashes across the sky—closer this time. I do hope this storm passes quickly, and I do hope that the tent doesn't leak.

Saints fingers drag up and down my arm, awakening the smouldering fire in my belly that he alone took a match to. My thoughts travel to the *list*. Did he truly have one? Do I really want to know what's on it?

Of course I did. I'd give anything to have the chance at exploring pleasure with him. Too bad we are once again in the forest.

"What's your favourite memory growing up?" Saint asks.

My mind wanders into the past. "Probably fishing with my father."

Saint tugs me closer. "Tell me about it."

I stare into the fire. "When I was really young, before everything got hard, Father would take me out on the water. We'd sit in the boat at sunrise, the mist curling around us, and he'd hum this song—some old sailor's tune, I think. He always let me have the first catch, no matter how small. I remember feeling like I ruled the entire sea in those moments."

I feel the warmth of Saint's breath against my temple. "He must have been so proud of you."

My gaze finds him, offering a small look of appreciation. "He was my best friend."

Saint's arms tighten. I welcome his steady embrace. Talking about my father is never easy, but when I'm with Saint, it doesn't seem so scary.

A deep rumble shakes the ground, drawing his attention to the skies. "You should probably try to get some sleep." He gently nudges me towards the tent.

"What about you?"

"I'll sit in the tent opening, keeping watch. Don't want the horse to spook and run off," he murmurs, his gaze finding mine once again.

I nod, reaching up to run a thumb over his cheek. "Goodnight, Saint."

As Saint settles the horse closer under the tree, I gather our bags and shove them inside the tent, following behind. Once I'm settled, Saint places himself in the doorway, watching through the night.

I watch his back, my gaze tracing the tense line of his shoulders. They're slumped, weighed down, as if the world itself is pressing him into the ground. And in that moment, something shifts in me. I understand it—the weight he carries, the burden of a past too heavy to bear. Because I carry it too.

# Twenty Three

The forest is serene. Damp earth carries on the light fog covering the underbrush. A yellow breasted robin flits from branch to branch to my right. His sole purpose for the day is to find food and avoid larger fouls. That could be me—sitting high in the treetops, viewing the world below.

I glance at the golden band with the tiny red ruby on my left hand. Guilt washes over me for a brief moment. Was I leading Juniper into danger that wasn't hers to face? And if I was, how could I spare her from it?

Ever since I put the enchanted ring on, my inner beast had become quiet. I didn't quite know how to feel. It's what I'd been searching my whole life for, but now that I had it—even if it wasn't mine to keep—I suddenly don't feel like myself. Like half of me is missing.

Gone was the urge to burst from my skin. To rip it from my bones, discarding my human life to take the form of another for a while. To fly away from all the thoughts that consume me day and night.

Now . . . Now it was peaceful—too peaceful.

I've been living in chaos my whole life. Until *her*. Juniper has this way of covering my ears—blocking out all the noise. I flick my gaze towards the tent. She is still sleeping. Can't blame her. The storm had lingered for quite some time. Thankfully, the oak above us offered a good deal of protection. My eyes feel heavy, so I close them for a moment, leaning my head back against the log.

It brought me so much joy watching her eyes light up at the festival. I knew the risks of being in such a public setting. I knew the dangers that possibly lurked alongside us, but I also knew the freedom it would offer her from the weight she carried, even if it was only for a while.

I'd deal with Brogos and Riggs if they'd found us. Thankfully, we haven't seen them yet. Let's hope it stays that way. We're so close to Stone's Ridge. One more day's ride, and we'll be there. If I find my ring at the orphanage, I'll—actually . . . I don't know what I'll do. When I'd set out to find it, I hadn't planned on a beautiful woman accompanying me. Especially one who has quite quickly stolen my heart.

A breeze stirs the foliage around me. It's probably best if I wake Juniper. We need to get on the road. I want to reach Stone's Ridge before nightfall.

The ground is soft under my boots. All the rain we've had recently is really making the ground wet. It wouldn't surprise me if we came across a bog or two soon.

I pull back the tent flap and duck inside, the fabric sweeping against my shoulders. Keeping low, I crawl in, settling on my side with my head propped on one hand. My gaze lingers on Juniper, her chest rising and falling in a slow, steady rhythm. She looks peaceful—so peaceful that rousing her feels almost cruel. Yet time does not wait for us. With careful fingers, I brush a stray lock of hair from her face. She stirs, a soft breath escaping her lips, lashes fluttering as she slowly blinks awake.

"Is everything alright?" she whispers, sitting straight up.

I chuckle softly. "Yes, Blue. Although I'm sure the creatures of the forest think there is a Galanthor in this tent with all that snoring you're doing."

Juniper's eyes widen. "I don't—"

I collapse onto my back, laughter spilling from my chest, rich and unrestrained. She doesn't let me get away with the teasing, as she crawls over to me and straddles my hips, pinning me beneath her. Her hands press into the ground on either side of my face as she leans in, her glossy strands of hair cascading around us like a silken curtain. The world narrows to the warmth of her body, the weight of her presence, and the mischief dancing in her gaze.

Meadow eyes soaked in sun flick to my mouth. Perfectly pink lips hover above mine, and I'm reminded of how they tasted the first time I kissed her.

"Lost for words?" Juniper grins. "So unlike you."

A smirk tugs at my lips as she hovers over me, her hair tickling my skin, her weight pressing down in the most distracting way. But if she thinks she has the upper hand, she's sorely mistaken.

With a sharp twist, I grip her waist and roll us over, pinning her beneath me in one swift motion. A surprised gasp leaves her lips as her back meets the ground, her hands now caught between us.

"Now who's lost their words?" I hum, my voice low.

Her wide-eyed shock flickers into something else—something that makes my pulse stutter. I brace my forearms beside her head, trapping her in place, drinking in the way her breath hitches, the way her gaze flickers to my mouth.

"Saint," she whispers, but she doesn't sound like she wants me to move.

And *by the stars*, I don't want to.

I'd told her about the list—the one that holds all the achingly beautiful things I want to do with her. Yet I'd also told her I wouldn't do those things until we were somewhere more—comfortable. Here in this tent was definitely cosy, and she can scream my name as loud as she wants. But it doesn't feel right. I want our first time to be special.

"As much as I would like to stay right here with you—" I rub my thumb over her bottom lip, tugging down to part her mouth. "We should probably get on the road."

Disappointment flashes across her eyes, but only for a moment. She nods, and I reluctantly peel myself from the warmth of her body.

The morning drifts by as we move in practiced silence—folding the tent, kicking dirt over the embers of our fire, securing our packs. Once Juniper is settled on the horse, I pull myself up behind her, and we set off down the road.

We travel in silence for a while, letting the horse set the pace. The closer we get to Stone's Ridge, the tighter unease coils in my chest. What if the orphanage doesn't remember me? Or worse yet, they don't have my ring? What then?

I haven't set foot in that town since Donovan took me in. It doesn't hold bad memories, just . . . All of them. My entire childhood, locked away in a place I never thought I'd return to.

Sun streams through the canopy above. I'm grateful for the leaves and the shelter it offers us from the heat. Juniper shifts in the saddle. A wave of her perfume washes over me. I can never get enough of her honey soaked skin.

She glances over her shoulder. "You're quiet back there."

My eyes fixate on her profile. The way her nose dips just before the upturned tip, or how almond freckles dust her cheeks, complimenting her naturally blushed complexion.

An ache begins to form in my chest. She deserves more than this life has offered her.

I shrug lightly. "Lost in thought."

"Want to talk about anything?" Juniper asks before returning her gaze forward.

There is a mountain of things we could discuss, yet I'm not certain I'm ready to allow that part of me to see the light. Perhaps I'll never be. So I keep all my dark thoughts hidden inside the black box inside my head. "Nothing of great importance."

Juniper tips her face towards the sun, closing her eyes against the glare. "And what of things with little importance?"

A quiet sigh slips from my lips. How can I resist her? She wants me to let her in, to tear down the walls I've spent years building. But if I do . . . How will I know she won't run? Although she hasn't yet, even after I stole her mother's ring. So perhaps I could let her see over the wall . . . just a glimpse.

"I haven't been back to Stone's Ridge since I was a kid—I don't know how to feel."

Juniper drops her head, glancing over her shoulder again. "Ahh, I see. Perhaps distraction is what you need?"

The leather saddle squeaks as I shift, searching for a more comfortable position. "You're already doing that." I lean forward to whisper in her ear. Having her soft, warm body in my arms all day is distraction enough.

Blush creeps into Juniper's cheeks as she turns her head away. I can't stop the smile from spreading across my face.

"Let's play a game."

I lift my brows in surprise. "Cat and mouse?"

A pointy elbow finds my ribs. "Saint!"

"Okay fine." I chuckle. "What game?"

"Truth or dare?"

I'm instantly transported back to my childhood in the orphanage with Roan and Sepehr. This is something we used to do all the time. It helped pass the boredom of scrubbing floors, or the nights when we couldn't sleep.

I tighten my arms around her waist, drawing her closer. "My interest has peaked."

Juniper throws a smile over her shoulder. "I'll go first. Truth or dare?"

"Hmm, dare."

It's too early to start with truths. I need to allow my heart to warm up to the idea of sharing answers Juniper might not want to hear.

In the quiet of the woods, I wait while she thinks. My eyes never leave the shadows, always on the lookout for unwanted creatures or company.

"I dare you to tell me the first thing you ever drew," she finally says.

I eye her warily. "Isn't that technically a truth?"

Juniper throws a smile over her shoulder. "Tell me anyway."

It takes me a few moments to sort through the mess in my mind. I'd been drawing since I could hold a pencil. "It was a dead butterfly that I found in the orphanage garden."

Juniper's soft smile finds me over her shoulder. "I love butterflies. What colour was it?"

"Pale brown, but in the sunlight its wings almost looked gold."

Her head angles to the side. "Sounds like a Sableflare."

"You know your butterflies."

"I try," she replies quietly.

Come to think of it, I've seen a few framed butterflies in the cottage she shares with her mother, and there are certainly plenty in her garden. The more I look at her, the more I realise she is a butterfly stuck in her cocoon—waiting to break free and fly.

Perhaps she just needs encouragement.

"Okay, my turn. Truth or dare?" I say, my voice playful.

Juniper doesn't even hesitate with her choice. "Truth."

I chuckle. "You're brave. Alright . . . Do you want to stay in Meadowbrook forever?"

She tips her head back a little, her glossy chocolate waves brushing her shoulder. "Well, since I have to tell the truth . . . Yes. I'd happily travel if I knew Meadowbrook is where I would always return."

I nod. "Having a place to call home is important."

Silence sits between us for a while as we plod along. We're making good time, so I haven't bothered pushing the horse faster.

Juniper glances over her shoulder again. "Alright, no choice this time. Tell me the truth."

"Well that's hardly fair."

Her sweet laughter rings clear. "No more games, just questions. Have you been pick-pocketing on this trip?"

My hands stiffen on the reins. "Define pick-pocketing."

Juniper rolls her eyes. "You know exactly what I mean, Saint. Stealing. Taking things that don't belong to you. That kind of pick-pocketing."

There's no escaping this. I stand at a crossroads, the choice mine alone. But no matter which path I take, they both lead me further from her.

I shrug lightly. "Then, yes."

Her gaze is fixed ahead, and I feel her body stiffen. Here it comes. The undoing of all the good today has brought. Yet how was I to avoid it? She asked for the truth, and that is what I gave her.

The stitches in my heart holding the tears together began to ache, as if they might unravel the moment Juniper speaks.

"Who, and when?" she asks softly, her voice tinged with disappointment.

My shoulders drop in defeat. "Couple of merchants in the last town, and that pompous bastard who shouldered me at the fair then looked at me like it was my fault—he deserved it."

Juniper glances over her shoulder. "Saint—"

"What? I only take what's necessary. It's not like we're rolling in riches here. And besides, half these people are crooks themselves."

"I get it. I do. I know life hasn't exactly given you or I a fair hand. And I'm not saying I condone every rule, but . . ." Her voice is soft. ". . . Don't you think we should try to do things the right way? At least while we're in this together?"

A small sigh escapes my lips. "There's a right way? The world doesn't play fair, Blue. You know that as well as I do."

Juniper gazes off into the darker parts of the surrounding forest. "Maybe not, but I know there is always a choice."

Her voice holds a hope that I never allow into my heart. It never stays long anyway. Hope is for those who haven't stared into a darkness so absolute, even the pits of hell seem merciful in comparison.

My hands tighten on the reins again. "It's no fun playing this game when you're trying to keep me morally upright."

I can't see her full face, but I swear a small smile forms on her lips. "Someone has to."

The cobblestone streets of Stone's Ridge are quiet at this hour. A few lanterns still lit cast dancing shadows over us as we pass under them. The town is peaceful, but my mind is not. It's suffocating.

Every turn of the road, every familiar creak of leather as the horse steps forward, floods me with memories I thought I'd buried. The orphanage. The river where I used to skip stones. The market stalls where I learned the art of slipping an apple into my pocket without being caught whenever the carers took us to market day.

I want nothing more than to turn the horse around and flee.

Juniper shifts in the saddle, her back pressed to my chest, and the warmth of her body anchors me.

I'm not just doing this for me . . . But for her, too.

I exhale quietly, gathering all my strength to keep pushing forward.

There's an inn here, and I know exactly where it is. In the middle of town, its golden light spilling from windows onto the murky streets.

We pull up out the front. I slide down from the horse's back, handing the reins to a waiting stable hand. "Boarding for one night, please." The male nods as he waits for Juniper to join me. We move into the lobby where a tall, thin elven male with pointy ears and a long grey beard greets us with a smile.

"One room?" he asks, already pulling out his ledger.

"Preferably with two beds, please." Juniper voices.

A pain tugs inside my chest as I flick my gaze to her, but she keeps her focus on the innkeeper, paying him a few coins from her trouser pockets.

Something inside me deflates. I tell myself I shouldn't care, that I shouldn't have expected otherwise—but the disappointment is there, gnawing at the edges of my thoughts. After everything, after all the moments we've shared, have I ruined this? Have I lost whatever it was that had begun to form between us?

I thought after our conversation today everything was alright, but perhaps it wasn't, and I thought wrong. Wouldn't be the first time.

I should give her some space. Heaven knows I need it, too.

The innkeeper slides a key across the counter. "Upstairs, second door on the left."

Juniper thanks him, and I follow her up the steps, forcing my feet to move even as my chest tightens. I tell myself it doesn't matter. But as I glance at her ahead of me, her hair catching in the candlelight, I can't help but wonder if I've already destroyed my chances before they ever truly began.

She unlocks the door and steps into the room, but I don't follow. Instead, I hover in the doorway. "Juni—"

Her eyes find me across the room. "Yes?"

"I think I'm going to get some fresh air . . . Walk around town for a bit."

She nods. "Alright, I'm going to bathe and crawl into bed, anyway." Her eyes are empty. Gone is the glimmer she usually has when she looks at me.

Placing my hand on the doorknob, I run my eyes over her one more time. "I'll knock four times when I return, but don't wait up for me."

Juniper doesn't move. I want her to stop me, to call after me, to tell me everything's okay. But she doesn't say a word. I want her in every way, yet I need her to want me back . . . all of me—not just the good parts.

She dips her head. "See you in the morning."

I turn, closing the door behind me. I have no recollection of making my way out of the inn, down a side street, and into the forest on the outskirts of Stone's Ridge.

The next thing I know, I'm tugging the ring from my hand, placing it into my pocket, and waiting for the shift to happen.

It starts with a shiver. A deep, bone-deep tremor that ripples through me, curling my fingers inward as heat spreads beneath my skin. My breath stutters. Muscles tense. The world tilts, stretching and shrinking all at once.

I close my eyes and let it take me.

My arms shrink inward, bending, twisting, until feathers unfurl from where fingers once were. A sharp pang shoots down my spine as it shortens, as my shoulders collapse inward.

My senses heighten—the distant rustle of leaves sharpens, the scent of damp earth floods my nostrils before my nose reshapes into a curved beak.

Every detail of the night becomes distinct as my sight sharpens—the glint of moonlight on damp grass, the flicker of a moth's wing.

Then, a rumble of distant thunder sounds. Another night. Another storm.

I stretch, flexing my talons against the dirt before shaking out my new form. Lighter. Sleeker. The night air hums against my feathers. With a single beat of my wings, I lift off the ground the wind carrying me effortlessly into the dark—into the shadows where I belong.

# Twenty Four

## MR BRAMBLES OVERGROWN GARDEN

Four knocks at the door break me from the trance I'm in. I'd been staring out the window at the streets below. The ground is still soaked from last night's storm, yet it doesn't slow the bustle of townsfolk beginning their day.

I glide across the floor, my boots barely making a sound. "Who is it?" I call, making sure it's safe to open.

"It's me, Blue," Saint replies.

It's confirmed the moment I crack the door open. I spot his blue eyes, and dishevelled appearance. He looks as if he hasn't slept a wink.

The hinges creak as I open it wider. Saint slips into the room, and I shut the door behind him, locking it again—we can't be too careful. Who knows where Drogos and Riggs are at this point?

"You didn't come back all night?" I state, my voice laced with concern.

He runs a hand through his hair as he makes his way towards the washroom. "Just needed some space."

My heart falls out of my chest, runs across the floor and clings tightly to Saint's leg, refusing to let go. Yet, my body remains rigid on the other side of the room. I don't blame him for needing space, I needed it too. Yet as I watch his back disappear through the doorway, all I see is a troubled little boy who hasn't known the gentle touch of unconditional love.

Despite his actions, underneath the layers of his morally grey ways, he's a good man. And he needs someone to be gentle with his heart.

Perhaps today will give him the answers he seeks. Perhaps he will find a wholeness once he has his own ring. Perhaps he will finally be free.

While he freshens up, I busy myself, gathering my things, ensuring everything is packed and ready. The weight of the day settles over me—it's a big moment for both of us. I will finally have my wicks, and Saint will finally have his ring.

He doesn't make eye contact when he returns, so I leave him be. Perhaps he needs more time. We collect our things and head out of the room. I hand the room key to the innkeeper, offering our thanks. Outside we collect the horse.

The streets hum with life as we make our way through the early morning crowds. Vendors roll up their stall coverings, the scent of fresh bread and coffee drift through the air.

Saint walks beside me, tugging the horse behind him, one hand shoved into his trouser pocket. There's a quiet tension in his posture, and I know that there are words between us not yet said, so I don't press him. Not yet.

"Do you know where the wick supplier is?" I ask gently.

He nods his head. "Up ahead."

My boots tap lightly against the damp cobblestones. I keep the rest of my thoughts to myself. There would be time later to talk.

I focus on the reason we're here. My heart races the closer we get to the supplier's shop. A wooden sign swings gently above the door, the painted lettering slightly faded but still legible.

This is it.

All the anticipation I'd been experiencing quickly exits my body when I realise that the doors and windows are all boarded up. The place looks as though it hasn't been open in weeks.

My heart lurches, a sharp twist of panic threading through my ribs. Surely, I haven't travelled all this way in vain? The silence is thick, suffocating, and suddenly, the months of waiting, of unanswered letters, all make sense. No wonder I haven't heard from them—the place is utterly abandoned.

Saint rests a hand on the swinging front gate. His eyes roam over the building, assessing it. "It seems as if it is closed?"

Tears well in my eyes, and I shake my head softly. "It can't be. I need those wicks."

A warm pressure forms over my hand. I glance down to see Saint squeezing it. I meet his gaze, trying to summon a smile.

"I will ask someone," he murmurs, handing me the reins. "Look, there's a grocer across the street. Wait here."

Saint hurries away, returning shortly. "The owner of the shop lives out the back."

A morsel of hope returns to my chest. Maybe I'm not out of luck just yet.

Saint gathers the horse, and we set off following the narrow stone path that winds behind the shop. My breath catches once more with the sight that lies before us. The garden, if it could still be called that, is a tangle of wild growth—once-proud rose bushes strangled by ivy, herbs gone to seed in neglected wooden planters. A rusty watering can lies tipped on its side, forgotten near a cracked bird bath filled with murky rainwater. The place smells of damp earth, wax, and something faintly sour, like old oil left too long in a lamp.

"Saint—"

He reaches his arm out, stopping me. "Wait here. I will knock first."

I nod, and he walks to the door of the rundown cottage. The shutters hang crooked, one missing entirely, while the thatched roof sags in places as if weary from holding itself together. The stone walls, now green with creeping moss, seem to have lost their battle against time.

Saint knocks a few times on the fading green wooden door, taking a step back while he waits.

My fingers fiddle with the buttons on my blouse. I truly have no idea what I'll do if I can't get my hands on some wicks today. Perhaps I'll have to travel to another town, further from here. A place that takes me further from mother—and the shop. How will I make my debt payments now?

Saint knocks again. A shuffling sound follows, then the slow creak of footsteps across wooden planks. Moments later, a man appears in the doorway, blinking as if the sunlight is an unwelcome guest.

I release the breath I'd been holding in. Someone's home. *Thank the stars.*

The man is older than I expected, with small round wire frames that sit upon his slightly crooked nose. His eyes, sunken but sharp, flick between me and Saint before settling on me with mild curiosity.

"What do you want?" he grunts.

I clear my throat, stepping forward to offer my hand in greeting. "Sir, my name is Juniper. I'm from Meadowbrook, and I usually order my wicks from you."

The man's face softens. He opens the door wider. "You'd better come in."

My mind is a whirlwind of thoughts, and I'm struggling to process all of Mr Bramble's words. I'm thankful for Saint's presence beside me.

"And you're certain it was Donovan's men?" Saints words sound bitter.

Mr Bramble nods. "I only owe debt to him—none other."

Saint stiffens beside me, his entire body going stiff. The shift is so slight, most wouldn't notice, but I do. My fingers inch towards his hand, hesitating only a second before I squeeze. His palm is rough, warm, and though he doesn't squeeze back, he doesn't pull away either.

"I missed a few payments, and they made sure I wouldn't forget again. Had me beaten, locked me in their damn prison for a week. By the time I got out, I was behind on everything—

orders, stock, rent." His voice cracks with emotion. "It's been hard clawing my way back."

My heart shatters for the fragile man.

I pull my hand from Saints and clasp Mr Brambles in my own. "I'm so sorry you've experienced evil in its finest form."

Kind brown eyes find me. "I'm sorry I haven't sent your wicks yet."

I shake my head. "Please don't apologise. You've been through so much."

Mr Bramble pats the top of my hand. "I do have a small bundle I can offer you now though, if that helps?"

Relief washes over me. Even though I don't want to take from the little he already has, I desperately need something to keep me going.

"I'd appreciate anything you have to offer."

Mr Bramble scurries off, dragging one leg behind him. I flick my gaze to Saint. He is quietly fuming. I can feel the heat radiating off his body. The sooner I get him out of here and some place he can vent his frustrations, the better it would be.

Mr Bramble returns, gently pressing a bunch of wicks into my hands. "I will have the rest of your shipment to you in a week's time."

I offer him a friendly smile. "Please don't stress. I can assure you this will last me a little while longer, but thank you all the same."

We bid Mr Bramble farewell and step back into the tangled mess of his overgrown garden, weaving through wild ivy and overgrown hedges towards where we left the horse. With a final wave, we set off towards town, the steady rhythm of hooves on dirt the only sound between us. Saint walks in silence beside me, his expression unreadable, his thoughts locked away behind a wall I can't breach. I want to reach for him, to offer him a space to unburden whatever storm is raging in his mind. But I don't know where that space is—or if he'd even step into it if I did.

So I do the only thing I can think of. I step closer and take his free hand in mine.

# Twenty-Five

## AN OLIVE BRANCH

There it was. The only home I'd known for the first eleven years of my life. It looks smaller than I remember. From up here, it's just a cluster of weathered stone and timber nestled against the rolling hills, the late afternoon sun casting long shadows over its slanted roof.

We've just come from the wick supplier, where I learned—yet again—just how far Donovan's cruelty stretches. Beating an old man, shattering his leg, and ripping away his livelihood without a second thought. Not only that, his actions were now affecting Juniper, and I didn't like that one bit.

The rage in my chest is molten, searing, relentless. I want to fucking kill him. Maybe I will.

And now, I'm here. At the orphanage. The place that made me, yet never truly felt like home. It's too much to process, too much to carry all at once. The weight of the past and the fury of the present press down on me, threatening to suffocate.

I grip the reins tighter, my knuckles aching. I thought seeing it might bring some sort of peace, but all I feel is the pain of living in a place I knew I never truly belonged.

Juniper shifts in front of me, her presence steady, grounding. She says nothing, just waits. The wind tugs at her hair, sending loose strands dancing across her face. I don't want her to see just how much turmoil my mind is in, so I gather them and shove them into the black box.

I exhale slowly. I've come this far. I can go a little farther. "If you don't want to—"

Juniper glances over her shoulder. "I'm coming with you," she says as she rests her hand on my leg. The tender gestures does something in my chest. Suddenly, I have all the encouragement I need to urge the horse forward towards the orphanage.

As we draw nearer, sounds of children laughing greet us. They are scattered in the yard. Some playing with a ball, others taking turns on a rope swing tethered to a large oak. I used to climb that tree with Sepehr, and Roan.

Memories flood into my mind as I pull the horse to a stop just outside the front steps. For a moment, I just sit there, gripping the reins too tightly, my pulse hammering in my ears.

Juniper slides down first, her boots crunching against the dirt path. She looks up expectantly, but doesn't rush me.

I swing a leg over and dismount, my stomach twisting. I spent years wanting to forget this place, yet now, standing here, it feels like I never left.

A young boy, no older than ten, steps out from around the side of the building, a bucket in hand. His gaze flicks between us warily, lingering on me a little longer.

Juniper clears her throat, offering a warm smile. "Hello. We're looking for the headmistress. Is she here?"

The boy nods, setting the bucket down. "You mean Miss Alderidge?" He wipes his hands on his trousers, giving me another once-over before jerking his chin towards the door. "She's inside. You can knock."

Juniper thanks the boy, before we take the steps to the door. My fist hovers over it for a heartbeat, and then I knock.

I wait for what feels like a thousand years before I finally hear footsteps approaching. When the heavy wooden door finally creeks open, I'm greeted with a face I don't recognise. Hazel eyes on a young woman, whose hair is neatly tucked under a yellow headscarf. "Can I help you?" she asks cheerily.

"I'm looking for Miss Alderidge. Is she in?"

The woman nods. "She's in her study. Please, follow me."

She ushers Juniper and I inside, closing the door behind us. All three of us quietly walk the halls, and it's like I never left. Everything feels so familiar, yet so foreign at the same time.

I don't even need to be shown the way to Miss Alderidge's study. I used to frequent it in my younger years. Either because I was being scolded for being caught snatching pastries from the kitchens, or because she needed me to help mend something in the orphanage.

The woman with the yellow headscarf stops outside another door and knocks quietly.

"Come in," Miss Alderidge's voice sounds through the wood.

Hearing it for the first time in so long is like a healing balm upon my wounded soul. The three of us move into the study to find a frail looking, grey-haired woman sitting at a large wooden desk. The younger woman leaves once Miss Alderidge nods, closing the door behind her.

"Can I help you?" Eyes, golden and bright, crinkle at the corners. She has aged so much. It was to be expected, but the kindness she carries is still evident on her face.

I take a small step forward. "Miss Alderidge, it's me—Saint Everhart."

Her eyes widen, and she pushes the chair back to stand. Holding onto the edge of the table for good measure. "Saint? . . . My dear boy! How are you?" She cries as she hobbles from around the side of the desk. Her brittle arms coax me in for an embrace. I have to lean down to reach her tiny frame.

"I am well." I chuckle. She smells of camphor oil, a scent I've never been able to forget.

We pull apart, but she remains close. "It's been so long," she says, reaching up to cup my cheek affectionately. "What brings you here?"

I offer her a gentle smile before taking a step back to introduce the woman standing patiently beside me. "Miss Alderidge, this is Juniper."

The elderly woman grasps Juniper's outstretched hand. "Hello dear."

Juniper smiles. "Pleased to meet you."

After the introductions, Miss Alderidge ushers us to sit, then returns to her side of the desk. I gather my churning thoughts, sorting through what isn't relevant right now. The answers I seek are on the other side of my tongue, if I would just allow myself to ask the question.

With a sigh, I lean forward, clasping my hands on the edge of the desk. "I'm here because I need your help." "I'm looking for my shifters ring, and I was told you have it?"

Miss Alderidge's brow knits in confusion. "By whom?"

My heart begins to beat at an unusual rhythm. "The man who adopted me fifteen years ago."

Her eyes dull, her face falling in sorrow. "Then you've been lied to."

It's hard to hear above the drumming inside my chest. "What do you mean?" My voice is low.

Miss Alderidge shifts in her seat. "Your ring was given to the folk who adopted you."

The world around me narrows as realisation dawns on me. Muffled voices can be heard in the distance, as if Juniper and Miss Alderidge are across the room.

I bring my focus back, despite the rage slowly simmering under the surface of my skin. "Are you certain?"

Miss Alderidge nods. "Yes. I know because I gave it to them myself, telling them that it was a vital part of your life. They assured me you would receive it when the time came."

I'm lost for words. All this time, I thought I would find my ring here. I would move on with my life and finally be free. Yet fate had a mind of its own.

"I take it, you did not receive it?" Miss Alderidge's voice is soft.

I shake my head. "I did not. Though I'm sure there is a reasonable explanation." I try to feign a relaxed smile through gritted teeth.

Her eyes soften. "Tell me, are you happy? How are Roan and Sepehr? Were you taken care of?"

She truly had no idea about what we'd all been through with Donovan. How would she? Once we left the orphanage, we never saw her again. Yet I refused to be the one to tell her what he was truly like. I wanted her to believe I was happy—that everything is fine . . . Even if it isn't.

Juniper shifts beside me, the slight movement sending a ripple of awareness through me. The air in the room feels thick, stifling—whether it's the space itself or the heat crawling beneath my skin, I can't quite tell. All I know is that my pulse is too loud, my thoughts too tangled, and the need for fresh air presses down on me like a vise. Finishing this conversation quickly would serve me well—before I suffocate under the weight of everything.

"They are both great, we have lived a good life," I hum.

Miss Alderidge's eye brighten with joy. "If you're ever in Stone's Ridge again, please stop by."

The sound of my chair scraping on the stone floor echoes through the room as I stand. "I certainly will."

Miss Alderidge walks us to the door, her kind eyes creased with age and wisdom. "I hope you find the answers you're looking for, Saint," she says, voice gentle, but weighted with something unspoken.

I nod, swallowing past the tightness in my throat. "Thank you—for everything."

Juniper offers the headmistress a warm smile. "It was lovely meeting you."

Miss Alderidge clasps her hands together. "You take care of each other."

With that, we step outside; the door closing softly behind us. The late afternoon light stretches long across the courtyard, bathing the orphanage in gold. I glance back once—just once—before pushing forward.

We find our horse tethered where we left him, patiently chewing at a stray patch of grass. Juniper rubs his nose before swinging up into the saddle with practiced ease. I follow, settling behind her.

The ride back to Stone's Ridge is quiet. I'm too lost in my thoughts to speak.

Juniper glances over her shoulder, catching my gaze. "You lied to her . . . Why?"

My shoulders drop, then I reach to brush a hand through my hair. "Because she was the only good in my life, and I didn't want to break her heart."

She nods, returning to gaze ahead. "I'm sorry about your ring. Why do you think Donovan would hide it from you?"

"I'd say it's because he's a fucking psycho." My voice drips with poison. "Because he likes control, and to keep me on a leash."

The simmering rage bubbling under my skin begins to boil. I want to go to Donovan and rip his fucking eyes out. I want to break every bone in his body until he is a trembling heap of flesh.

Juniper places a hand on my leg. The simple touch, grounds me. She becomes the anchor in the storm raging in my mind. "Saint?"

"Yes?" My voice is stiff.

"Would it bother you if I was to ask around about your parents?"

Her question catches me off guard. I don't quite know how to respond. No one—apart from Roan and Sepehr—have ever cared about me, let alone my family too.

I shrug lightly. "I suppose . . . If that's something you'd like to do?"

"It would be."

My arms tighten around her waist, silence hanging between us. I don't know how long it takes to reach the inn again. I don't even remember paying for lodgings, or when Juniper gripped my hand as she led me up the stairs.

It wasn't until we were inside the room that my mind began to focus. I drop my bag to the floor, it lands with a thud.

Juniper's boots scuff lightly as she moves to sit on the bed. That's when I notice it. One bed. Not two. An olive branch. Yet, all I can think about is what happens next.

I promised I would bring her to collect her wicks. Then I would give back her mother's ring and take her home. But things had not turned out according to plan. I still needed my ring, and the one person who truly had the answers resided a few days' ride away.

However, there was a beautiful woman across the room that I felt responsible for, and there was no chance in hell I was going to put her in danger.

"I need to go to Breydon . . . Alone."

# Twenty Six

## AMBER LIQUID IN GLASS CUPS

A sudden flash of white light flickers through the small inn room, followed by a distant rumble of thunder a short while later. Saint stands on the opposite side of the space, hands on hips.

The bed creaks as I shift my weight. My mind churns, struggling to piece together how we went from standing in the orphanage, surrounded by echoes of his past, to him suddenly deciding to leave. It feels abrupt, like a door slamming shut before I even had the chance to step through it. "What do you mean alone? And why Breydon?"

"I'm going after Donovan and my ring. But don't worry, I'm sending you home with your mother's ring." His words are sharp.

My brow pinches. "Saint . . ."

He runs a hand through his hair, pacing back and forth across the wooden floor. "It's too dangerous for you."

Tumultuous thoughts swirl inside my head. Everything is happening too fast. *Too dangerous?* I'm not some delicate thing to be tucked away while he charges headfirst into the fire. I've fought for everything I have. If he thinks he can just send me home when he's done with me, he has another thing coming.

I catch his eye from across the room. "Since when do you get to decide what's too dangerous for me?"

Saint pauses, folding his arms across his broad chest. "Since I know Donovan, and just how cruel he can be."

I don't say a word, trying to digest everything. It's all so heavy, hanging in the air above me like a weight that's about to come crashing down.

"Do you understand the severity of this situation?" Saints voice is low—pained.

My face crumples in frustration. "How can I if you don't tell me?"

Saint rubs a hand over his face, clearly frustrated himself. "I'll have to go into Donovan's estate—the one I escaped from—and take it by force."

My gaze never leaves his, as he takes a small step towards me. "Things could get real ugly, real fast . . . People could die."

Another flash of lightning streaks across the sky, illuminating the small space in a stark, white glow. The porcelain vase on the wooden table trembles, its delicate daisies quivering as the thunder rolls through the air.

I wince at his words. Death is not my friend, but I remain firm on the spot. "Well, I want to make my own choice."

"Why now?"

I stand, throwing my arms open. "Why now what?"

Saint takes a few strides across the room to stand in front of me. "Why now do you want to make your own choices?"

I lift my chin, heat rising in my chest. "Are you saying I don't?"

His blue eyes bore into me. "That's exactly what I'm saying."

For so long, control has never been mine to hold. Life has pulled me in every direction but the one I wanted, forcing me to bend, to adjust, to endure. And now, as helplessness creeps in again, it feels all too familiar—like I'm slipping back into a life where my choices don't matter. Where I am expected to follow, not lead.

Tears well as I push down the lump forming in my throat. "Well, at least the choices I make are carefully thought out, always considering how they might affect others!"

Saint's face becomes unreadable, yet his eyes narrow. "What's that supposed to mean?"

I take a step towards him, my fists clenching by my sides. "You know exactly what I mean." My lips quiver. "I don't have the freedom you do, to just say what I want, do what I want, take what I want."

Saint tilts his head to the side. "And what do you want, Blue?" His voice is low, almost mocking.

I bite my tongue as I shake my head. If I speak, the words will be hurtful.

Patchouli and cedarwood surround me as Saint steps closer. "Not what your father or mother wants. What do you want?" he presses.

"It's not that simple, Saint." My voice trembles. I can't stand to look into his eyes. They search for answers I do not have.

Spinning, I move to stand in front of the window. The glass is clean, framing the streets of Stone Ridge below. Folk scurry about as the first drops of rain begin to fall.

Saint doesn't let up. "Do you want to sell your father's candles forever? Is that your dream or his?"

I fight back the tears, though much more of this, and I will find myself as a puddle on the floor. I turn to face him again, anger pulsing in my veins. "This is ridiculous, Saint. What kind of question is that? I've got responsibilities—people relying on me—"

His boots sound on the floor as he reaches me. "That's not what I asked, Juni."

Tears begin to spill down my cheeks. There is no stopping them now. He speaks to a deeper part of me that responds willingly to his call, yet the other half of me wants to keep the truth hidden away. Somewhere it can always be safe.

"Perhaps you want to be a sailor or go visit the orc colonies or be a baker or librarian? Tell me, Blue," he pleads.

My voice rises, frustration spilling over like a dam breaking. "You think I don't want more? That I haven't dreamed of something different? But dreams won't pay off my father's debt, Saint!" I pause to take a breath. "They don't heal my mother's injury or keep food on the table. When Mama first got injured, I had to take over everything. They always trusted me to be responsible. I've spent my whole life stepping up because there was no one else. No one to take care of Mama, no one to run the business, no one to make sure we didn't lose everything. And that's just it, isn't it? It doesn't matter what I want. It never has. Because I'll be looking after her and this damned chandlery until the day I die!"

My chest rises and falls with a heavy breath. The truth was out in the world now. There was no taking it and stuffing it back into my mouth. It almost felt good to say it all out loud.

Saint steps in even closer, so close I can feel the warmth of his body. "So what do you want?"

I try to summon the anger again, to cling to it, but it slips through my fingers like smoke. "It's not that simple," I spit out.

His eyes soften, flicking over my face. "It should be."

The sting of his words is worse than any insult. I hate him at this moment—for seeing the truth I'd been trying to avoid, for daring to ask the one question I didn't have an answer to. My whole life had been a blur of duties and sacrifices, never stopping to ask myself what I truly wanted.

Silence coils around us like a noose, tightening with every unspoken word. It's too much—his presence, his questions, the weight of his gaze pinning me in place. I'm not ready to face the monsters that perch on my shoulders, whispering their relentless doubts, dictating my every move.

I wipe the tears from my cheeks as I take a few steps away from him, the back of my legs bumping into the bedframe. "I know that right now I would like to be left alone."

Saint reaches for me. "Blue—"

I hold up a hand to stop him. "Please . . ."

The sound of the rain on the slate roof grows louder. Already the sky outside is a dark shade of grey. Another storm—one that matches the one brewing inside my mind.

Saint's shoulders drop, his eyes void of light. He takes a few steps back, his gaze never leaving mine. I keep my posture firm, not wavering. He finally tears his eyes away, scooping down to pick up his bag.

I watch as he moves to the door, pulling it open, he turns with his hand resting on the knob. "Keep the door locked . . . I'll knock—"

I nod. "Four times, I know . . ."

With a sigh, he quietly leaves.

As soon as he's gone, my legs give way, shaking uncontrollably. I collapse onto the bed in a sobbing heap. It only takes the image of my father's smiling face in my mind for the floodgates to the dam of emotions I'd sealed shut to spill forth. For the first time in so long, I cry into the pillow with no intention of stopping anytime soon.

Saint's question echoes in my ears. *"Do you want to sell your father's candles forever? Is that your dream or his?"* Was it my dream? Letting go of the shop feels like letting go of him. Like erasing the last traces of his presence, the way his hands moved with practiced ease as he dipped candles, the scent of cinnamon and clove lingering in the air—his favourite. His methods weren't always efficient—I know that. I have new ideas, better ways to do things. But if I change too much, will it still be his shop? Will I be dishonouring his memory?

I want to make him proud, even from beyond the grave. But how do I do that when moving forward feels like leaving him behind?

Why did he have to leave?

Who knows how long I cry for, but when the sun has truly gone to bed, and the storm rages outside, I lift my weary head. I haven't eaten all afternoon, my stomach clearly letting me know as it growls in protest.

Perhaps I can head downstairs to the tavern inside of the inn. *Stars* know I won't be sleeping anytime soon. I move quietly across the floor to the washroom, where I freshen up as best I can. My red-rimmed eyes can't be concealed though. I would have to deal with them.

As I leave, I make sure to lock the door behind me, pocketing the iron key. The tavern is mostly empty, save for a couple of weary travelers nursing their drinks in the corner. The bartender, a middle-aged man with graying hair and a knowing look, wipes down the counter as I settle onto a stool.

"What'll it be?" he asks, glancing up.

"Something strong," I reply.

He nods, pouring a dark amber liquid into a glass and sliding it across the counter. I wrap my fingers around it, staring at the rippling surface. I never drink whiskey, but father always liked a glass after a long day. I would drink one—in his memory.

I throw back the shot in one swift motion. Fire scorches down my throat, searing its way to my stomach, and I grimace, my face twisting in disgust. Who in their right mind enjoys this? I shove the empty glass towards the bartender. "Another, please."

He pours again, pushing it back towards me. "You look like someone with a lot on their mind," he says, throwing the white cloth over his shoulder to steady his palms on top of the wooden bench. "I've got two good ears, and no place to be if you feel like talking."

I let out a quiet huff, swirling the drink before taking a sip. The burn is a welcome distraction.

"I wouldn't even know where to start," I admit, glancing up to look into his kind brown eyes.

He shrugs. "Sometimes, that's the hardest part."

With a sigh, I lean on the bar, resting my head against my propped-up arm. I run my fingers along the rim of the glass, gathering my thoughts. "Let's say there's someone," I start, pausing to gather the right words. "And they've been through hell. More than most. They don't talk about it much, but you can see it—feel it. Yet they smile through it all."

The bartender pulls the cloth from his shoulder and wipes down the counter, nodding as he listens. "Go on."

I swallow, tracing circles on the worn wood. "This person . . . They need something. Something important to them, something that will help them figure out who they are. But getting it means someone else has to endure something for a little while longer."

"Is the enduring person in pain?"

I shake my head softly. "It's more of an inconvenience."

The bartender nods silently, ushering me to continue.

"I want to help both of them. But helping one means my own responsibilities, and people who need me will feel the pressure. If I help the other . . . it will be my heart that suffers the consequences."

Thunder rumbles through the room, rattling the glassware.

The bartender hums, setting the cloth down. "And you're afraid that if you help one, you might lose the other?"

I nod, my eyes welling with tears again.

He continues. "Will one of them definitely be there for you, no matter what?"

My thoughts travel to Mother. She's not going anywhere, and she would never leave me. Our home is in Meadowbrook, of this I am certain. A silent tear travels down my cheek. I nod as I wipe it away.

The bartender leans against the counter, considering my dilemma. "Sounds like you're torn between duty and your heart."

I let out a hollow laugh. "That's a much simpler way of putting it."

A gentle smile breaks across his mouth, his kind brown eyes crinkling in the corners. "You'd be surprised how many people find themselves at that crossroads. The real question is—what does your heart want?"

There's that question again. What do I want? Do I want to return home, and never know what might have been, between Saint and I? Or do I follow him, help him find his ring so he can truly be free—like Mama.

What about the shop? I didn't have a choice when Papa died, but I can make one now. Deep down, I know the shop is still my dream, but if I want to keep it alive without sinking into debt, I need to take a different path. No more clinging to the old ways out of fear or sentiment. When I get home, it's time to make those changes—to build something stronger, something truly mine.

I glance up at the bartender, who hasn't moved while I'm lost in my thoughts. I offer him a faint smile. "Do you have some ink and paper?"

He nods, moving to the far end of the bar, returning a short while later. He places the stationery in front of me gently. "Follow your heart."

I dip my head in thanks as I reach for the pen. It hovers above the paper while the storm rages outside. It's now or never. Have I decided? And will I truly be happy with this choice? Too long have I been torn between duty and desire, between what's expected of me and what I truly want. But standing at this crossroads, I finally see the path that feels right—not because it's the easiest, but because it's mine.

Saint isn't just someone I care about. He's the person my heart yearns for, the one who has shaken up everything I thought I knew about myself. I'm not following him out of guilt or obligation. I'm choosing him because I believe in him, in us, in what we can build together.

Of course, I'm not going to throw myself into danger—I'm mama's only caretaker. But Saint needs me too. We have to finish what we started. The realization settles deep in my chest, not heavy like a burden, but light, freeing. For the first time, I feel like I'm stepping into my own life—one not dictated by the past or by fear, but by what I truly want. And what I want is *him*.

*Dear Mama . . .*

# Twenty-Seven

## RECKLESSNESS GETS YOU KILLED

I didn't sleep a wink last night. I tossed up whether I should shift, leave her the ring and take off by myself, but I didn't want to be another person who didn't give her a choice. So I walked it off, only stopping to shelter from the storm until it passed.

The pine behind me did little to protect me from the rain, but I'd found the raindrops to be refreshing to my soul. I drop my head back against the tree, closing my eyes to the rising sun. Soon, I'd have to face the day—face her.

My thoughts travel to Breydon. Do I want to return? Do I want to place myself back into the hands of the man I'd spent my life freeing myself from? Do I really need my ring?

A yellow robin flits across my path, its wings a blur of effortless motion. I pause, watching as it dances through the air, unburdened, untethered—free. The sight of it stirs something deep in my chest, a sharp ache that gnaws at the edges of my thoughts. It moves as if to taunt me, a quiet reminder of everything I am not. Showing how free he is, and how trapped I am.

Maybe I just need to accept the fact that this is my life. Forever half in this world, the other in a place that is still me, but I have no control over. Perhaps I'm not destined to have love—a family . . . a home.

I should make sure Juniper gets back safely, and then leave her family be. Maybe I'll find Sepehr and Roan. We can travel to a far off place. Somewhere that Donovan and his sulphurous tendrils will never reach us. Juniper will be free to live her life, and I will learn to live with the one I have.

My shoulders drop. I truly thought the orphanage would have the answers I sought. In hindsight, they did, they just weren't answers I wanted to hear.

Water droplets from the pine needles drip onto my boots. I should really get back to Juniper and beg for her forgiveness. I was out of line last night. I had no right to question her dreams and what she wanted for her life.

It was time to take her home, and I'd make sure she got there safely.

The walk back to the inn feels unfamiliar, as though the town has shifted in my absence, becoming something foreign and unwelcoming. The muffled voices of townsfolk spilling from their homes seem sharper, more intrusive, grating against my already frayed nerves. Or perhaps it isn't them— perhaps it's me, unravelling thread by thread.

Before I know it, I'm standing outside Juniper's door knocking four times.

Eyes framed by lush, dark lashes greet me. The skin around them looks inflamed, as if she's been crying all night. She probably has, and it was all my fault.

She doesn't say anything, but steps aside, allowing me to step into the room. I drop my bag onto a nearby chair, turning to face her. Perhaps I should say everything now, get it over and done with before I change my mind.

I trace her movements as she glides barefoot across the room to sit on the bed. The sheets are twisted, like she's only just woken. I glance around the room quickly and notice that her bag isn't packed.

My gaze flicks to her, and my heart stumbles over itself. She is so beautiful. Golden sunlight pours through the window, framing her body, making her look like she is covered in honey.

I swallow down the feelings rising in my chest. "I don't expect you to choose." The words leave my mouth before I even realise I've made the decision to speak them.

Juniper watches me, a slight furrow to her brow, waiting as if she is bracing herself for whatever I say next. I exhale, running a hand through my hair, trying to make sense of the thoughts tangled in my mind.

"I made a promise to take you home, and I'm going to do that. Because I'm not going back." I shake my head. "I can't. I can't take the risk of being caught by Donovan again or—worse yet—put you in danger."

She opens her mouth, but I hold up my hand before she can argue. My feet carry me back and forth across the room in a frantic way. I can't face her right now, so I drop my gaze to the floor. "I need you to understand something. I've spent my whole life looking over my shoulder, hiding in the shadows, just to survive. But I'm done running. I need to learn to live with what I am . . . Even without my ring."

Movement brings my gaze up from the floor. Juniper slowly stands. "Saint—"

"I don't expect you to choose," I say again, softer this time. "This isn't just about me, it's about you too. Your life, your home, your shop—everything you've spent years holding together." I swallow, my throat tight. "I just . . . You can't put that on hold just for me."

She walks across the room, stopping in front of me. My heart stills. I can't bear being this close to her. Especially when all I can smell is her lavender, and honey scent.

Juniper's eyes search mine. "You have to do this. We didn't come all this way for you to give up now." Her words are soft but firm. "There must be some way of sneaking in to retrieve your ring. We will think of something—together."

I open my mouth to argue back, but I can't find the words.

She takes a step towards me. I catch my breath when her hand cups my face. She's looking at me . . . Truly looking at me. And if I'm being honest, I don't know how to feel.

"You might not expect me to choose . . ." Her thumb brushes over my cheek,. ". . . But I'm choosing anyway, and I choose you, Saint."

"Juni—" I blink a few times, her words registering. "You choose me?" The words come out in a whisper.

Chocolate hair bathed in golden light shimmers as she nods slowly. "Yes . . . I choose you over and over."

I take a step back, dragging a hand over my jaw as I struggle to process the weight of her words. No one ever chooses me. Not when teams were picked for ball games at the orphanage, not even my own family. I'd always been the last option—the afterthought. Yet here was this divine specimen in front of me with the heart of gold, perfectly pink lips and eyes that I longed to take refuge in.

She was choosing me?

Juniper takes a slow step towards me. "Let's go get your ring—together."

My eyes search hers. "But what about the shop?"

With another step she draws closer. "It will be there when I return. I have to trust that other people can run it, and that I don't have to do it all by myself."

I'm struggling to comprehend everything she's saying. It's like a dream that I never want to wake from. This is certainly not how I imagined my morning unfolding as I made my way here from the outskirts of town. I had prepared myself for tension, for uncertainty, maybe even for goodbye. But not this. Never this.

"What about Kamari . . . Her ring?" I ask. My mind is still in disbelief.

Juniper finally reaches me. "I have sent her word—with the wicks. She will understand."

"Blue—" The words leave my lips in barely a whisper.

A glint of joy sparks at the corners of her mouth, turning it up into the smile I've become obsessed with seeing. "You might need to weed all the garden beds, fix all the broken things for free, and maybe even repaint the house, but she will forgive you." She softly laughs.

I can't stop myself from reaching out, my fingers brushing against the silken strands of her hair as I tuck them behind her ear. The way they catch the light, shimmering like spun gold, is almost hypnotic.

But the real question isn't whether I can touch her—it's whether I can trust her words. Could I truly believe them? Could I allow myself to hold on to them, to let them settle into the cracks of my guarded heart without the fear of them slipping through my fingers like everything else I've ever wanted?

I gaze down at her, lost in her peace. "What will you think of me if I really hurt someone?"

Warm, delicate hands rest on my waist, tugging me closer. "We will deal with that *if* it happens. But if I'm being honest, I find it incredibly sexy seeing you go after what's rightfully yours."

Tears form in the corners of my eyes, something I haven't felt in a very long time. I don't do this. I don't let emotions take hold, don't let them weaken me. When you live the life I've lived, emotions are a liability. They cloud judgment. They make you reckless. And recklessness gets you killed.

But then there's *her*.

She looks up at me, and I come undone. "I won't let you give up. I won't let you live in whatever birdcage you put yourself in." Her words are light in my forever darkness. Opening the door to the internal prison I've been locked away in. "We are going to do this," she whispers.

Nothing else needs to be said. My lips find her in a fervent kiss. Without warning, without permission, simply because I couldn't have done anything else. A kiss so passionate that I forget my own name. She tastes like every good thought I've ever had.

Juniper reaches up on her tiptoes, wrapping her arms around my neck, digging her fingers into the base of hair. At this moment, I want all of her—forever. Our mouths collide in a heated dance, nipping, biting, tugging, a battle of desire neither of us wants to win. Every slow, deliberate stroke of her tongue on mine sends a warm jolt through my bones. She's all I've ever wanted.

I pull back gently, needing to look at her. Her face is flushed with colour, lips slightly parted and swollen. My eyes drink her in, all the way down to the floor. "What happened to your nightgown?"

She sinks back onto the balls of her feet as she glances down at the tattered hem of her white cotton gown. "I tore it when you needed your arm bandaged."

My heart pulls towards her, an invisible thread tightening with every breath. She's always giving—her time, her kindness, her unwavering belief in me. And all I've done is take. Take and take, like a man who has never known abundance, only scarcity. But she deserves more than that. She deserves someone who gives just as fiercely as she does. It's my turn to give, and her turn to receive.

I cup her face between my hands. "Why didn't you tell me? I would have got you a new one?"

A smile dances across her mouth. "You mean you would have stolen it?"

"Same thing," I shrug, flashing her a lopsided grin. "I'm sorry that you had to use your own clothes."

Juniper pulls out of my arms to spin around. "Don't you like it this length?"

Desire tightens in my core, a slow-burning heat that spreads like wildfire as I watch her spin. Every movement, every curve of her body, is intoxicating. From the graceful tips of her fingers to the delicate arch of her foot, she is effortlessly mesmerising. A temptation I can't resist. I want her more than I've ever wanted anything.

Even more than my freedom.

I slowly stride towards her. "I'd like it more if it was on the floor."

Juniper pauses, her eyes glittering with mischief. "Why don't you take it off me, then?"

I don't need to be told twice. I'm by her side in seconds, lifting the gown up and over her head. And before it drops to the ground in a discarded heap, my lips find hers once again. She meets me stroke for stroke. Her tongue dances with mine in slow sensual movements, angling her head to allow me better access.

My hands drag up her waist to cup her breasts—her desire makes her nipples pebble like pink pearls. I want to bury my face between them.

Juniper's hands slip beneath my shirt, her fingertips trailing over the ridges of my tense stomach, leaving a searing path in their wake. She moves slowly, tracing idle patterns across my skin, as if memorising every inch of me. When her touch glides over my back, a shiver ripples through me, my muscles instinctively tightening beneath her featherlight caress.

Then she hesitates, her fingers hovering just above the waistband of my trousers—a silent question, a test of restraint. The delicate touch sends my heart into an erratic state, and blood rushing to my cock. I need to feel her skin on mine. I want us to be so close that we become one.

My arms steal around her, and I pick her up, wrapping her legs around my waist. We turn, moving towards the bed. Not once has her lips left mine. She is consuming me, and I, her.

With gentle ease, I lower her down to sit on the edge of the bed. Our kiss finally breaks, both of us gasping for breath.

I reach down and run a thumb over her swollen bottom lip, dragging it down to reveal a flash of white teeth. "Are you sure you want this? Because once I start, I won't be able to stop."

Her eyes are drowsy with pleasure. "I want you, Saint."

My damp jacket hits the floor with a light thud, then I grip the hem of my shirt, pulling it up and over my head in a hurried motion.

Juniper is looking up at me through dark lashes, her teeth gently biting her bottom lip, as she watches. The absence of her mouth on mine is a sin.

I lean down to cup her face in my hands, kissing her passionately. She whimpers when my tongue drags over hers. I trace the tip across the roof of her mouth as I curl it back towards me, flicking her top lip as I exit. Licking her like she's a spoonful of raw honey.

*By the stars*, I must have all of her.

My lips make a path across her jawline all the way to her ear, where I suck her lobe into my mouth. I hear the hitch in her breath and grin as I gently bite down.

Juniper reaches for my belt buckle, pulling it free, before dropping it to the ground in a *clatter*. However, I stop her hand as she reaches for the trouser button. She frowns briefly—confused. I want more than anything to be fully naked for her, but not yet.

I place my thumb under her chin, the rest of my hand gripping the back of her neck. I tilt her head up so she can look at nothing but me. "Let me taste you first."

Pink blush floods her cheeks. She knows what I mean, but there is hesitation in her eyes. So, I wait. Every muscle in my body is coiled tight, every breath shallow as I silently beg for the permission I crave.

And then—finally—she nods.

The air leaves my lungs in a sharp exhale, my knees damn near buckling beneath me. Every fibre in my body wants to ravish her, to lose myself in her completely, but I have to move slowly—for now.

I reach up and wrap my fingers into the edge of her lace undergarments, dragging them ever so slowly down her hips. My cock twitches when I spy the sacred place of pleasure between her legs, hidden by a light dusting of brown curls, waiting for me to explore.

The cream lace drops to the floor with our other garments, and I pull her to the edge of the bed. Juniper gasps softly.

"Are you sure you want to go . . . Down there?" Her voice is barely a whisper.

I pull back, my head tilting to the side. "Has anyone ever pleasured you with their mouth before?" My fingers brush over her warmth, tracing patterns over her skin.

Juniper softly shakes her head as she bites her bottom lip, her fists clenching the fabric beside her. I can't stop the grin from forming on my face. Watching her come undone with the simple flick of my wrist makes my whole body feel like it's on fire. I pause my hand, allowing her time to catch her breath.

Her eyes are soft. "I've had sex before, but it wasn't life altering."

A chuckle leaves my lips. "Oh Blue, by the time we are done, you won't even know your own name."

She gasps quietly at my words.

I kneel between her legs before placing them over my shoulders. I hear Juniper moan as her thighs naturally part for me, exposing her for my viewing. She is fucking perfect. Everything about her is.

While she is still propped on her elbows, Juniper watches me as I dip my head to drag my tongue up her centre. The first taste of her brings a groan from my throat and a whimper from her lips.

She falls back against the sheets, writhing as I tease her with my tongue. My hands grip her thighs, pulling her closer as I find her clit, circling it gently before sucking it.

Juniper cries out softly as she threads her fingers through my hair, grasping it as she thrusts her hips into my face.

I growl against her core, burying my tongue deeper into her until she is bucking off the bed. Sucking, biting, flicking, until she is a trembling heap beneath my touch.

When I feel her thighs shake, I pull back, licking my lips before trailing kisses over her stomach up towards her breasts. Her meadow eyes meet mine, half hooded in pleasure.

"Fuck, you taste so good, Blue," I moan.

Her nipples pebble at my words, as a feral grin rips across my face. She reaches up, her fingers dragging through my hair again, as she tugs me down to meet her mouth. The kiss is wild. As if both of us are letting go of everything that has ever held us back.

My cock strains against my trousers, begging to be free— begging for attention, but I want to make sure she is almost at a breaking point before I take her over the edge.

I reluctantly drag my lips from hers, turning my attention to her breasts. I take one nipple into my mouth, flicking my tongue across it as I palm the other, kneading it gently.

Juniper moans. "Saint, please—"

"Please what, Blue?" I murmur against her warm honey skin.

"I need—" her breath hitches.

I lift my head to look at her. "Tell me what you need?"

Desperate hands run over my arms, her nails digging into the patterns marking my skin. "I need to feel you inside of me."

A deep chuckle ripples up from my stomach as I stand upright. Juniper props herself up on her elbows, looking utterly dazed and delicious. She watches me hungrily as I slowly undo my trousers.

I shove the fabric over my hips to the floor below. My hardened length springs free, bringing a small gasp from Juniper's lips. She swallows, her eyes widening slightly.

I take the opportunity to check in with her again. "Are you still sure?"

She nods. "Yes."

"Do you take a tonic?"

"I haven't, but I'll get one."

She scurries up the bed as I climb onto the mattress, settling on my knees between her thighs. I can't help but brush my fingers over her clit again and Juniper sucks in her breath. "Once we do this, there will be no going back," I warn her gently.

Her legs spread wider for me. "Good, now do it."

A smile plays on my lips. Her gaze never leaves mine as I place three fingers into my mouth, sucking on them before I reach down, and slowly push them into her warmth.

Juni gasps, throwing her head back.

She's tight and warm—but ready.

How is this even real? How do I have Juniper Fairchild in bed with me right now? The moment I laid eyes on her, my heart told me it only beat for her, yet my mind didn't believe it. But here she is, writhing in the sheets as I pleasure her.

I slide my fingers in and out a few times, stretching her, watching her come undone. "You're soaking my hand . . . What a good girl."

"Saint—" Her voice is breathless.

"Yes, Blue?"

"I'm about to shatter."

I lean over her, my fingers still buried in her warmth. "Not yet."

Slowly, I pull out. She watches as I suck all her juices off each finger, one at a time.

The look she gives me turns feral. "Kiss me," she whispers.

Without hesitation, I lean down, capturing her lips in mine. Pain rips up my back as Juniper's nails drag over my skin. The intensity of it mixed with our kiss only makes my cock harder. I pull back, whispering against her lips. "I want you, all of you."

"Then have me."

This is it. This is the moment I'd been dreaming of, the first time I saw her down by the lake, completely unaware of the way she had already begun to unravel me. I'd wanted her then, but never dreamed I'd actually have her. Yet here she is . . . Choosing me. This isn't just a fleeting desire. This is everything. *She* is everything, and I'm going to give her every part of me—including my heart.

I angle myself between her slick warmth. As I press in, Juniper gasps. I lean down, claiming her lips as I push into her all the way.

Juniper cries into my mouth, but I drown out the sound by kissing her with everything in me. She feels like silk as I wait, allowing her walls to stretch around me. When she starts to move against me, I slowly drag out of her inch by inch.

The feeling of her squeezing my cock is mind-altering. I tear my lips from hers, needing to watch. Placing my hands on either side of her face, I watch my length—glistening from her wetness—disappear back inside. I moan, pleasure coiling in my stomach, building the release that I know is coming soon.

The bed creaks in time with our movements, a steady, unrelenting rhythm that drowns out everything else. Juniper's head tilts back, her lips parting on a breathless gasp, and the sight alone nearly undoes me. Every thrust, every touch, binds me deeper to her, until there is no distinction between where I end and she begins.

It hits me then, with startling clarity—I will never want another the way I want her. She has ruined me, branded herself into my very soul. If she asked me to set the world ablaze, I'd strike the match without hesitation.

"You're so fucking beautiful, Blue," I whisper.

Our pace picks up, and I bite my lip, stifling a groan as I watch her breasts bounce. Sweat glistens between them as the heat of the morning sun pours into the room.

Her meadow eyes, heavy with pleasure, find me. "I need more of you."

I don't even stop to think. Rolling our bodies so Juniper is on top, straddling my hips with my cock still buried inside her.

She places her hands on my chest and begins to rock back and forth—riding me. I can't stop the groan escaping my lips this time, and I know for a fact that both of our releases are coming soon. She's so tight around my length as I grip her hips, helping her to slide up and down.

She drops her head back and I watch as the air kisses her lips instead of mine. Oh, that won't do . . . That won't do at all.

With practised ease, I pull myself up to rest my back against the headboard of the bed.

Juni instinctively covers her breasts with her arm while I adjust my position.

A light growl forms on my tongue. "You don't ever need to cover yourself in front of me. I want to see all of you."

She slowly drops her arm. Baring her chest, all for my pleasure. "Am I allowed to see all of you?" She raises a brow.

I trail kisses across her collarbone. "Whenever you wish it of me."

Juniper smiles as she leans forward to kiss me. I claim her right back as she begins to rock her hips.

We lose ourselves in each other as the pace builds. I never take my eyes off her. Not even when she drops her head back, moaning. It only makes me thrust up into her harder. I nip at her slender throat before dipping my head to take a shell-coloured nipple into my mouth.

Feeling the pebbled skin between my teeth sends heat through my core. I almost explode on the spot, but I want to see her come first.

I'd promised her that by the time we were done, she'd forget her own name, and that was a promise I wasn't willing to break.

She whimpers as I grip the back of her neck, pumping into her. My other hand finds her hip.

Her gaze, heavy with pleasure, locks on me. Her back arches elegantly, a figure carved from honeycomb, and fire agate. I feel her slick warmth grip me tighter as she wraps her arms around my neck. With a sweet cry on her lips, she comes, bucking her hips. My fingers dig into her thighs, dimpling the skin as I continue to thrust up into her, carrying her through her orgasm.

Seeing her open mouth gasping for air as the waves of pleasure wash over her is all I need to find my release. My stomach muscles stiffen as my cock spasms. Juniper milks me, her hair falling around us as she gently rocks back and forth.

My vision blurs, the world momentarily darkening as pure ecstasy crashes over me, searing through my veins like wildfire. I can't remember the last time I came this hard—so completely undone that my body feels weightless, boneless, utterly spent. All I can do is surrender to the aftershocks, lost in the sensation of her, of us.

Juniper collapses against my chest, her warm breath coming in gasps. Neither one of us can move. We just lay in each other's arms, soaking in bliss.

"You chose me . . ." I whisper against her hair.

She moves to look up at me. "I'd choose you in every lifetime."

The words are a shock to me. I'm finding it so hard to believe that someone as beautiful and good as her would choose someone like me.

"Even if my past leads you into danger?"

Juniper reaches a hand to twist the silver hoop in my right earlobe. Her gaze travels from my chest to my lips, landing on my eyes. "You're worth saving. You're worth fighting for, because I'm doing it for you right now, and I'm not going anywhere."

Juniper presses a lingering kiss to my lips before flopping onto the bed, her body sinking into the sheets. She turns onto her side, propping her head up with one arm, watching me with those deep, meadow eyes. The glow of the sun casts soft shadows across her skin, tracing every curve and dip. She looks like something out of a dream.

"Don't move," I say, my voice rough with intent.

Her brows lift in curiosity, but she stays as she is, watching as I cross the room. I dig through my bag, fingers brushing over the familiar leather of my sketchbook. With a pencil in hand, I pull up a chair beside the bed, angling it so I have the perfect view of her.

Her lips twitch into a smirk. "Do you plan on selling that, or keeping it all to yourself?"

I glance up briefly, meeting her gaze before dragging my pencil across the page, already lost in the lines of her.

"This is for my eyes only, Blue."

# Twenty Eight

Life has never been kind to me. Not until this very moment.

Perhaps all the pain and suffering I'd endured was leading me here, so I would know beauty when I touched it.

She has become my everything. I've been so lonely, and then she came along, changing everything I ever thought I knew. We've become so close, and I can't imagine being apart from her again.

I have a colossal urge to never let her out of my sight.

Golden morning sun bathes Juniper's skin as she sleeps peacefully by my side. The sheets barely cover her honey-coloured skin. I have to hold myself back from reaching out to drag my fingertips across her hip.

The steady rise and fall of her chest brings back memories of the way she gasped as I made her come. More than once.

We'd spent the entire day—until the moon rose—in bed. Exploring one another's body. The rest of the night we'd both slept. Our bodies spent.

Now that she was sending the wicks to Kamari, and we were locked in a room together out of the public eye, we both agreed we could take a day to breathe. Not spend it looking over our shoulder or travelling on the back of a horse.

Though I would have to wake from this dream of bliss soon. Just because Juniper had secured some wicks, it doesn't mean the journey ends here. I still need to get my ring, all the while keeping her out of danger. How I was going to manage either of those, I was still unsure.

Juniper stirs awake, her eyes blinking slowly as she focuses on my face.

"Morning, Blue."

A smile breaks across her face, her arms stretching above her head like a cat who's just woken from a nap in the sun. "What time is it?"

"It's still early." I gently roll on top of her, trapping her in place, kissing between her breasts, all the way up until I reach her throat. Her pulse flutters beneath the warmth of my lips.

A light laugh escapes her as I linger on her neck. The sound of it ignites a fire in my soul, cultivating a peace that I will protect at all costs.

"How long have you been watching me sleep?" Juniper cups my face, bringing me up to meet her gaze.

I place a tender kiss upon her lips. "Long enough to know that you are the most beautiful woman in all of Sapphire Vale."

She reaches up to brush her thumb over the three black lines tattooed under my left eye. "I've never met anyone like you before."

I grin down at her. "Is that a compliment?"

"I let you ruin me—twice—I'd say it's a compliment," she whispers.

My jaw tightens as my lips part, my tongue slowly gliding across my bottom lip. I'm trying to hold back the smirk that wants to break free. "I can't help being an exceptional lover."

A pink flush creeps into Juniper's cheeks. "When do I get to see this list?"

"You've already seen the beginning, but we can continue the rest if you like?" I hum against her mouth, my hands finding their way down between her legs.

She gasps when I find the tender spot that makes her toes curl. I want to ravish her until we're both spent. There isn't enough time in the world for the things I want to do and feel with her. We could *fuck* all day until we were raw, and it still wouldn't be enough.

"Perhaps we should have breakfast and talk about a plan." Juniper's words float through the air.

I groan softly, rolling to the side until my back is against the sheets. "Fine, but after that, we're having some fun."

With a melodic laugh, Juniper rolls on top of me, folding her arms to rest, on my chest. Her breasts brush my skin, sending a shiver up my spine. "Careful, or I won't be able to wait until later."

She smiles before reaching to touch the three lines marking under my eye. "What does this stand for?"

"It's symbolic of me, Roan and Sepehr. The three brothers," I answer softly.

"How long have you had it?"

I place a hand behind my head, looking to the ceiling as I recall when I'd received it. I had that many tattoos that it was sometimes hard to remember where and when I got each one done. "I think I was eighteen. All three of us got it at the same time, although only I have it on my face."

Juniper drags her nails across my chest. "What about all these other ones?"

I reach out to bury my hand in her hair, my palm resting over her ear. "Over time, I've just slowly collected them."

"And your piercings?"

My hand drags down her jaw, my thumb brushing over her lips. I'm finding it very hard to concentrate on her questions, especially when her eyes are glittering with mischief.

"The ones in my earlobe I've had for years. Donovan never cared if we did things like that—hell, he'd offer the services for free at the celebrations he held. The ring in my septum, though, that was a dare."

Juniper flicks her gaze down to it before bringing it back to me. "Who dared you?"

A grin spreads across my face. "Roan. He dared me to run down the spiral stairs, and back up at Donovan's estate before the hourglass ran out. And as you can see, I failed miserably."

Juniper's eyes crinkle at the corners as she smiles. "Do you regret it?"

I shake my head softly. "Not at all. Sometimes I forget it's even there."

There are many things in my life that I wish I could change, but never the cosmetic ones. They moulded me into who I am today. It is the only control I have over my body—something Donovan can never take from me.

Juniper lowers her head to my chest, folding an arm over my waist. I still can't believe she's here in my arms. Maybe she's not. Maybe this is all a dream, and soon I will wake.

Her warmth breath tickles my skin as she traces her fingers over the black vines marking my chest. I glance down to watch her. Instantly, my cock begins to throb, blood rushing to it when I see her naked body against mine.

This is definitely not a dream.

She tilts her head, her gaze meeting mine, heavy with the same reluctance I feel. Neither of us wants to move, to break the fragile sanctuary we've built between these sheets. Reality looms just beyond the closed door—Donovan and his men, the road stretching ahead, the unknown waiting to sink its teeth into us. My chest tightens at the thought of taking Juniper into Breydon. She has no idea what waits for me there—hell, even I don't. But if there's one thing I'm certain of, it won't be anything close to mercy.

I fight the desire building in my core the longer her gaze lingers, or her fingers wander. "You keep looking at me like that, Blue, and we're never leaving this bed," I whisper.

A smile tugs the corner of her mouth. "We really should get up. The innkeeper might think we've vanished."

I prop myself up on my elbows. "It's cruel of you to expect me to function after the night we've shared."

Juniper's grin grows wider, one brow arching in playfulness. "The quicker we get your ring, the quicker we can find the time to fulfill the *list*."

I swallow down the desire clawing at my throat, my mouth parting slightly as I drag my gaze over her body. I reach for her, but she is too quick, scurrying out of my grasp before she lightly dances across the floor into the washroom with laughter on her lips.

It doesn't take long to pack our things and head down into the tavern for some breakfast. After leaving the letter, and wicks to be sent off to Kamari, we pay for our lodgings before heading outside to the bustling streets of Stone's Ridge.

My gaze flicks all over the place—searching the shadows, making note of any watchful eyes. It's been a few days since Drogos, and Riggs caught us at the bridge, and they wouldn't know what road we have taken, but I still can't be too careful.

Instinctively, I reach for Juniper's hand, lacing her fingers through mine. The marketplace hums with life. Vendors call out their wares, their voices blending into a constant murmur against the shuffle of boots on packed dirt. The air is thick with the scent of spices, ripe fruit, and the occasional whiff of something fried.

"Saint?" Juniper tugs on my hand. "We need some extra food for the road."

I nod, glancing around, scanning the market with a wary eye. Everything appears normal—children weaving between carts, a woman haggling over the price of fresh bread, a merchant unloading crates from a wagon. No shadows lurking. No eyes that linger too long. It feels . . . Safe enough.

"Alright," I say, forcing myself to step back. "I'll get the horse and meet you here in a few moments."

Juniper stands on her tiptoes, kissing me briefly on the cheek. "Hurry back." She flashes me a grin before heading into the market stalls.

The thought of letting her go alone sends an uneasy pang through my chest. I almost tell her to wait, that I'll go with her, but I shake it off. I'm being overprotective. She can handle herself. Besides, I'm only down the street.

I turn away, heading towards the stable yard. The further I walk, the heavier the unease settles in my stomach. It's nothing,

I tell myself. Just my nerves. Just the habit of a man who's spent too much of his life waiting for the worst to happen.

After paying the stable hand a single copper coin, I saddle up the horse and begin my trek back towards Juniper. Perhaps leaving this town and seeking sanctuary in the quiet of the forest is best—even if there is a chance of encountering Galanthors or Lycans.

I reach the place I'd left Juniper, but she isn't here. No need to panic though, I was probably quicker than she thought I'd be and there is a good chance she's still purchasing goods.

A few minutes pass by, and she still hasn't returned to my side. I don't let myself panic, but I do start to shift uneasily on the spot. My eyes are scanning the crowds for her glossy chocolate hair and the soft blue gown she'd put on this morning.

Only when I don't spot her after a few moments do I allow my heart to quicken. Something isn't right. She wouldn't leave me here—would she?

Of course she wouldn't. She chose to come with me, and out of the two of us, Juniper's the one who keeps her word. Perhaps she got distracted by something and wandered off farther than intended.

I don't want to leave the meeting place we agreed on, but something doesn't feel right. Something in my gut tells me that I should go looking for her—so I do.

I push through the bustling market, dodging merchants and customers, my chest tightening with every step. Scanning the crowd, I search for a flash of blue, for the familiar sway of her stride. If something has happened to her, or someone has taken her—I will never forgive myself.

Each street I pass, my heart beats faster. Where has she gone?

I want to stand on the water fountain and shout her name, and if it comes to that, I will.

Then I see her.

Down a narrow alleyway, shadowed by the looming stone walls. Juniper is pressed against one, her back rigid, shoulders squared. Two men stand before her, bodies angled to block her in.

*Fuck.*

Brogos and Riggs. Donovan's men.

My breath leaves me in a rush, my pulse roaring in my ears.

Without thinking, I shove the reins into the hands of a startled villager. "Watch him," I snap, my voice tight.

Then I move.

I keep to the shadows, not wanting my presence to be noticed just yet. Juniper's face remains emotionless, like she's trying to keep herself together. *"Good girl,"* I whisper under my breath. *"Don't give them anything."*

The blade I keep concealed in my boot feels like a weight. I want to pull it out and throw it at the back closest to me—Riggs. Yet, I would hate to hit Juni, so I keep it hidden.

As I approach, I step out of the shadows. "Donovan might allow you to touch things that aren't yours, but I certainly won't. If you value your sad pathetic lives, I'd watch where you place your hands. I'm in a . . . *Killer* mood."

Both men spin to face me, their eyes ablaze with fury. I can't help the smirk appearing on my face. "Hello, boys. We meet again."

Riggs's top lip turns up in disgust. "Well, look who we have here . . . Donovan's Scum."

I clutch at my chest, faking a punch to the gut. "Your words wound me."

"Where have you been hiding? We've been looking for you ever since you left us at the bridge," Rigg's practically spits.

I throw Juniper a glance, trying to reassure her that everything is going to be okay. She doesn't need to say anything, but her eyes say it all. She trusts me.

Brogos takes a step backwards towards Juniper, as Riggs takes one towards me. They might be ugly brutes, but they are strong. I'm going to need to pay attention to all the details. Lucky for them—I'm good at that.

"Sorry, I didn't make things harder for you. If you'd like, I'll let you count to ten while we hide, and you can try again?"

Rigg scoffs, folding his arms across his chest. "You're not getting away this time. We've got your lady friend. And do you know what's really funny?"

"Oh, do tell."

"It seems as if we've met her before, yet I recall she didn't know where you were. Now we are in the company of two liars."

I release a chuckle from my lips. "So no better than the company you keep daily."

Drogos, and Riggs snarl almost in unison. I really need to wrap this up. The longer I stand here, the more pissed off I'm becoming. "Come on girls, aren't you sick of sniffing Donovan's arse? Let the lady free, and we can all go our separate ways."

Riggs advances towards me. "Look who's trying to play the hero now. Doesn't suit you, Saint."

My brows arch. "Me? The hero? Oh, you've got me all wrong Riggs." I step towards him, a feral grin plastered on my face. "See, in your story . . . I'm the villain."

Riggs with a dopey look on his smug face, lunges first. I sidestep, but his fist clips my ribs, and pain bursts through my side. With gritted teeth, I spin, elbowing Riggs in the stomach, driving the air from his lungs. He doubles over with a grunt. He wasn't out, but he'd be unable to focus for a few moments.

A cry from Juniper whips my head in her direction. Brogos is grabbing at her wrists. She yanks free, stepping back—but not fast enough. He snatches at her hair, jerking her backwards. Her shrill cry sounds through the air.

Fury blooms through my blood, turning it from red to black. Brogos touched her. I warned him.

I sprint towards her, but Riggs barrels into my back, sending me sprawling to the ground. Not wanting to snap my wrists, I twist my body, landing on the shoulder with the arrow wound. I cry out in pain as the skin tears apart. That's gonna need attention.

Riggs descends upon me, so I kick my leg out, catching him under the chin. I swear I see a tooth go flying, as I hear his jaw crack. Blood sprays across the sky.

I scramble to my feet just in time to see Juniper lash out at Brogos. Her knuckles crack against his cheekbone. Brogos stumbles, snarling—but so does she, shaking her hand with a hiss of pain.

"You bitch!" Brogos cries out.

I launch myself at him, slamming my shoulder into his gut. We hit the ground hard. My cold, hard eyes stare into his as I fist his shirt in my hands. "I warned you not to touch her." My knuckles crash against his jaw once, twice, before rough hands yank me backward.

Riggs.

His arm hooks around my throat. My vision spots as he squeezes, cutting off my air. My boots scrape against the cobblestone, searching for leverage.

Then I find it.

I slam my head back. Bone crunches under my skull—Riggs's nose. He howls, his grip loosening. I tear free, sucking in a breath just as Brogos drives his fist into my ribs.

Pain rips through me. My knees threaten to buckle, but I catch myself, jamming my elbow deep into his stomach. He doubles over, and I drive my knee up into his face. Drogos crashes to the ground, blood spilling from his mouth staining the street.

I barely have time to spit before Riggs is on me again. He lands a punch to my jaw, my head snapping sideways. Stars burst behind my eyes as a metallic taste seeps into my mouth. I spit the blood onto the stoney surface, holding my arms up to protect my face as he jabs his fists towards me again.

He swipes. I dodge.

This needs to end. Already too many have gathered to watch. I swear I can hear the whistles of law enforcement approaching. I need to get Juniper out of here.

With a final swing, my elbow connects with Riggs's jaw. His eyes roll back in his head as I grab him by the collar and slam him into the alley wall. He slumps, groaning.

I don't even bother to wipe the blood from my lip, as I race to Juniper's side. She's shaking, breathing hard, holding her injured hand. "Are you alright?" My chest heaves as I gulp down fresh air.

She nods, yet her meadow eyes are brimming with tears.

I grip her hand in mine, hurrying down the street back towards the villager holding the horse. I thank him profusely before helping Juniper up into the saddle.

The sound of a shrill whistle grows louder. I'll leave the law to deal with the two idiots in the alleyway.

Kicking the horse into a trot, we make our way through the large crowd that has gathered and out of the town gates, heading for the safety of the forest.

Dread seeps into my soul. What if things had been different? What if the men had overpowered me for even a second? This could have been a whole different scenario. How was I supposed to take her into Breydon and keep her safe?

Smudges of brown, and green whip by us as I push the horse faster. The urgent need to be away from Stone's Ridge grows more intense with each moment that passes by.

Who knows how long we ride. All I care about is the woman in front of me, that I'm clutching against my chest, and the distance we are putting between us as the men we've left behind.

Only when I know the horse is exhausted, do I pull him to a walking pace.

My defence hasn't dropped, yet my heart has slowed. The sun is beginning its descent for the evening, which means we will need to find shelter soon.

Juniper shifts in the saddle, and my instinct is to draw her closer. She flicks her gaze over her shoulder. "So," her voice is soft. "I'm yours?"

For the first time in my twenty-six years of life, I feel hesitant in my confidence. Had it been a poor choice of words? I'd meant every word when I'd threatened Brogos, but perhaps in the moment I'd been too presumptuous?

I drop my gaze, fiddling with the blue fabric of Juniper's dress. She waits patiently for my answer. I drag my gaze back to hers, swallowing down the fear of rejection that is knocking at my mind.

"Blue, I didn't mean—"

"So, I'm not?"

I sigh, running my hand through my hair. This was not turning out well. How do I explain to her that I hadn't meant it in a way that might make her feel owned, yet I needed her to understand that what I feel for her is borderline possessive.

She flashes me a grin that tightens that invisible tether joining me to her. "What if I want to be?" she grins.

My brows raise slightly. Time slows as my heart rate builds into a pace that is hardly sustainable. Does Juniper Fairchild want me to claim her as mine? Because in my mind, I already have.

Her eyes that I find myself lost in over and over again travel over my face. My arm around her waist tightens, yet she's still not close enough. "Oh, Blue." I nuzzle my face into the back of her neck, inhaling her sweet scent. "You were mine the moment your meadow eyes, soaked in sun, looked at me."

I hear the sharp intake of her breath as she drops her back onto my shoulder. If only I wasn't sitting on a horse, riding through the forest, covered in blood. For I'd very much like to kiss her right now.

She brings her head back up, twisting in the saddle to face me. "I was hoping you'd say that. Now, I just have to make sure you never change your mind."

I can't hold back any longer. Who cares about my busted lip or the stinging pain in my shoulder. None of it matters when it comes to her. Pulling the horse to an abrupt stop, I gently grip the back of her neck, angling my head so I can pull her lips to mine. All the adrenaline I'd been feeling channels itself into the kiss. It's hungry, devouring, full of passion, and she meets me with everything she has.

We sit atop the horse in the middle of the forest, entwining our souls together until I have no idea where mine ends and hers starts.

I gently pull back, resting my forehead on her temple. "You'd better hold on tight, Blue—because I'm not letting go."

# Twenty-Nine

## WRAITH WOODS

"If we take the path through the Wraith Woods, I doubt Drogos or Riggs will follow us," Saint mutters.

We've come to a fork in the road, and he's standing just down from me at the mouth of the woods. I swallow the dollop of fear rising in my throat at the sight of it.

To the right, the road is well-trodden, and muddy beneath the golden light of the morning sun. Wagon tracks and deep hoofprints mar its surface, proof of travellers constantly passing through. It stretches towards a distant town, too far to be seen.

I glance at the map in my hands before finding Saint again.

To the left, the path is no more than a whisper through the trees. The entrance to the Wraith Woods is a dark gash in the landscape, the thick canopy swallowing the light before it even touches the forest floor.

The path that takes us to the next town is the safe choice—the obvious one. A place that Donovan's men would expect us to go.

I flick my gaze to the dark entrance on my left. Shadows shift unnaturally between the trees, and an eerie quiet settles over the path, as if the woods themselves are waiting. Watching.

Neither path is safe.

Saint walks back towards me, his boots squelching with each solid step. It stormed again last night. I'd spent most of it huddling inside the tent plastered to his side. Neither of us got much sleep—and it wasn't for enjoyable reasons.

His jaw is set, the look on his face unreadable.

"What are you thinking?" I ask when he reaches my side.

Saint exhales sharply, dragging a hand through his pale hair. "When I came through here a few moon cycles ago, there were no wraiths to be seen. I know for a fact that they don't come out in the daylight. If we can make it through before sunset, it should be alright."

I roll the map back up, shoving it into my bag. "So we will go that way then."

He shakes his head—unsure. "But after what we've been through, I feel like a quieter path is the wiser choice."

I glance at him, my fingers finding the reins on the horse beside me. "So," I murmur, swallowing the unease in my throat, "what's it going to be?"

Saint exhales again, glancing both ways. "Either way, we're walking into trouble." He looks at me then, his blue eyes searching mine. "But only one of these roads gives us a chance to disappear."

The woods.

A chill runs down my spine, but I nod. "Then we disappear."

He turns to cup my face. "Are you certain? I can't promise you safety that way."

I nod again. "We will do it together. We just have to move quickly. You said they don't appear during the day, and the sun has only just risen. We have time."

Saint gently kisses my forehead, sending a shiver down my spine, yet this time it also ignites a heat in my core. His touch is doing a lot of that lately.

"Then let us fly, Blue."

I take in a deep breath before pulling myself up into the saddle. Once Saint settles behind me, we began to move.

The moment we step into the Wraith Woods, the world changes.

Light from the morning sun barely makes it past the thick canopy. The air is damp, clinging to my skin, laced with the scent of moss and decaying leaves. Every step our horse takes is muffled by the thick layer of fallen pine needles or the drenched soil beneath its hooves. The further we go, the quieter it becomes.

No birds. No insects. Just the sound of my heart thudding in my chest. The pine trees seem taller here, their limbs twisted to match the eerie feel surrounding us. It's going to be alright . . . Right?

I swallow. "Saint—"

"I know." His voice is low, careful. "I'm here."

He keeps a hand on his knife. I don't blame him for being uneasy. I am too. But we have to do this. We've already been through so much together. We will get through this too, I try to convince myself.

Perhaps all we need is a distraction.

"How's your arrow wound?" I throw over my shoulder quietly.

Saint's grip around my waist tightens. "The pain is bearable. How's your hand?"

I glance down to the red and purple welts blotching my knuckles, rubbing my other hand over them gently. "It hurts more now than it did before, but I'll be alright."

He pulls me closer, his chest a warm comfort on my back. "I'm sorry that you had to go through that," he says quietly.

I reach to squeeze the arm he has wrapped around my waist.

"I feel like I should come with a warning label," he continues.

A smile tugs at the corner of my lips. "I'd read it, and still take my chances," I say over my shoulder.

Saint huffs, and even though I don't turn to look, I can feel him smiling.

For a few moments, we don't speak. There is something about this place that makes even talking eerie. I thought my journey to Stone's Ridge to collect the wicks would be an adventure, but not this . . . Never this. My mind is restless, though, thoughts spinning back to the fight in the alleyway.

I glance behind me at Saint, at the bruises darkening along his cheekbone and jaw, the faint line of dried blood near his bottom lip. He took some hits, but I noticed something when he fought.

"You rarely used your fists," I murmur.

Saint's eyes flick to me before returning to the path ahead. His fingers tighten slightly around the reins. "That's correct."

"Why?"

A breath escapes him, more exhale than sigh. "I've always had to take care of my hands." He flexes his fingers as if testing them, making sure they still work the way he needs them to.

"When I was a kid, I learned to protect my hands. Most of my livelihood depended on my ability to take what I needed to survive. I never broke the habit—I learned to be careful. A broken knuckle, a sprained wrist—that could ruin me."

I frown, thinking back to the way he fought—using his elbows, his head, his entire body in ways that let him keep his hands mostly out of it. Clever. Efficient. "So you've trained yourself to fight like that?"

A ghost of a smirk plays at the corner of his mouth. "Something like that."

I watch him for a moment longer before turning my gaze forward again, letting the conversation settle between us. The Wraith Woods stretch endlessly ahead, a twisting maze of trees and mist. We have miles to go before we're clear of them. The ground is also becoming much softer. I worry that soon it will turn to bog.

I shift slightly in my saddle. "What's Breydon like?"

Saint huffs quietly. "Compared to Meadowbrook? Bigger. Louder. A place I'd rather not see again."

"That bad, huh?"

I hear the pain in the exhale of his breath. He doesn't need to say another word. I understand. "We will find a way to get your ring, and then we will leave, never to return again— unless you want to."

He pulls me closer. "Thanks, Blue."

I smile in his embrace. I might be fearful of the unknown— of what waits for Saint in Breydon, but I believe in him, and for now, that's enough.

It's dark, yet I know in my bones it's only midday. That's how dense the canopy is above us. We'd been travelling for hours, eating on the go. Neither one of us wanting to stop. The sooner we were on the other side of these woods, the better.

I haven't spotted a single animal. It makes me even more nervous of what lurks here when the sun goes down. Wraiths weren't common everywhere, but I'd heard of stories from travellers in the taverns back home. Never did I think there was a place like this so close to Meadowbrook.

Shows how little I know of Sapphire Vale.

The horse stumbles forward, losing its footing. Saint's grip tightens around my waist as I lean to the side to assess the ground in the dim light. The ground is changing. I can see the dark patches up ahead. They look more like deep holes in the road than actual surface. With the amount of rainfall we've had lately, it doesn't surprise me.

"We need to be careful going forward. The ground is becoming softer." I straighten, twisting to look at Saint.

He presses his lips into a thin line. "I'll try to go around the worst parts."

I nod, and we keep moving. Another hour passes by, thankfully we have avoided most of the mud. In fact, the trail almost seems as it's cleared up the deeper into the forest we move.

My body aches from the hours of sitting on horseback. What I'd give to rest for a while. I lean my head back, finding Saint's shoulder. It's not the most comfortable headrest, but feeling the warmth of his body, and the way his muscular arms wrap around me makes me feel so safe, that I could quite easily fall asleep.

"Rest, your eyes for a while. I'll keep watch," he hums against my hair.

I don't need to be told twice.

Sleep doesn't find me straight away, though. Mostly because I can't stop thinking about the things Saint and I did together. The way his hands brought me a level of pleasure I have never felt before.

He's definitely more experienced in the bedroom than I am, but surprisingly, it doesn't bother me. As long as he is all mine, and shares his knowledge with me, then I have no reason to complain.

In fact, I'll insist he show me all the things he can do.

My mind is deep in the memories of Saint and his mouth when suddenly chaos erupts around me as the trail beneath us dissolves.

The horse lurches forward with a sharp, startled whinny, its front legs sinking knee-deep into the muck. And I fly through the air to land in the bog.

"Juni!" Saint's sharp hiss sounds through the forest.

A sharp gasp escapes my lips as I struggle to find my footing, my boots sinking under me until I'm knee deep.

"Whoa!" Saint yanks the reins, trying to steady the animal, but the more the horse struggles, the deeper it sinks.

He jumps from the saddle, landing on harder ground. "Stop moving," he cries out, racing for a large dead log lying on the side of the trail.

With a heave, the log shifts as Saint' drags it towards me. He shoves it onto the surface of mud, laying his body over it as he crawls forward. "Take my hand," he exclaims.

His hands clamp around my arms, fingers curling tight.

"Hold on, Blue." His voice is strained as he braces himself and pulls.

Panic is quickly rising in my chest. The last thing we need is to be stuck in the Wraith Woods come nightfall. Not only am I stuck, but the horse too.

The bog doesn't want to let me go. It clings to me, sucking at my legs with every inch I'm lifted. I try to twist my legs free, but I end up twisting my right foot too far around, causing a hot, sharp pain to erupt.

"Ahh!" I cry out.

Saint grips my hand tighter. "Juni—"

"I'm alright, just twisted my ankle."

My brow pinches in frustration, and I grip Saint's hand in mind. "Go again."

My breath is coming too fast, panic tightening my chest, but Saint doesn't stop. He yanks harder, his grip solid and unyielding, until finally, with a sickening squelch, I'm free.

I stumble forward, landing against him. His arms tighten instinctively, holding me upright.

"You okay?" he asks, breathing warmly against my temple.

I nod against his chest, still shaking. "I'm alright—thank you."

We lay in each other's arms for a moment, allowing the adrenaline to pass. Tears spring to my eyes. Saint has saved me in so many ways, not just physically, but mentally too, and I'm not sure he even knows it yet.

When my heart calms down to a normal rate, I lift my head to look at him. "We need to get the horse free."

He sits up, bringing me with him. "Let's get to work, or we will be here all night."

"No thank you," I whisper.

It's gruelling—freeing such a large animal from a pit of mud. And so many times I want to give up. We work together, trying everything—loosening the ground around the horse's legs, coaxing it to shift its weight just right. Every failure makes the task feel impossible, but we don't give up.

An hour passes. Then another.

By the time the horse finally heaves itself free with a mighty pull, all three of us are exhausted. I collapse onto a dry patch of grass, wiping my mud-streaked face with the back of my arm.

Saint stands beside the horse, chest rising and falling with heavy breaths. His shirt is soaked through, hands and forearms covered in mud. He lets out a low, breathy chuckle, shaking his head.

Despite his appearance, he's still the most beautiful man I've ever had the pleasure of knowing

"That," he says, running a hand through his filthy hair, "was hell."

I groan, flopping onto my back. "Tell me about it."

Then silence. The weight of our situation settles in. We glance at each other, then at the dense, never-ending trees surrounding us.

We don't even need to say the words. He knows that I know we're not making it out of here before nightfall.

"So, what are we doing to give ourselves the best chance of staying hidden for the rest of the night?" I whisper.

Saint looks defeated. It seems we can't catch a break at the moment. Wicks, orphanages, rings, his past, and now wraiths. I reach for his hand, squeezing it gently. "Saint?" I press quietly.

He focuses on me, taking a breath. "We need to find water. Wraiths hate water."

I nod, taking the reins in one hand, his in the other. Surely there is a dam, or stream, somewhere that we can hide by for the evening. One glance in Saint's direction tells me that he's exhausted and overwhelmed right now. I can see it in the way his eyes are glazing over. He's not focused—barely speaking. The last week has been quite traumatising for both of us.

With a slight limp, my feet carry me forward as if they have a mind of their own. I have no idea where we're going, but I know Saint needs me to lead right now. I just hope I'm going in the right direction.

Night has truly swallowed the woods by the time we find water. A small glassy pond, tucked between gnarly pines, its surface hinting at the canopy of stars above the trees. It's not like the lake back home, but I'm grateful we found something.

We set up camp in silence, our movements efficient and practiced. No fire. Not here. Not when we know what lingers in these woods. Instead, we eat in hushed tones, keeping our voices low, our ears pricked for any sign of movement beyond the trees.

I'm trying my best to keep the fear of the unknown from my mind, but it is slowly creeping in, no matter how hard I try to shove it away.

I sit with my back against a fallen, decaying log. Saint is beside me, his dagger balancing expertly on his knee—just in case. I can barely make out the lines of his face, but I know he's looking at me every now and then. This is not what either of us thought would happen.

My body is exhausted. All I want to do is sleep. I fight it. I really do, but the struggle is real. If only I'd had better sleep the night before, perhaps I would have lasted longer.

The horse is tethered to a tree close by. Even he looks exhausted. Being stuck in a bog will do that to you, though. I'm glad he's alright. I would have hated telling Theon his horse was injured—or no longer with us.

My blinks grow slower, eyelids heavier. My body slumps where I sit.

Saint exhales through his nose. "Go to bed, Blue."

I shake my head, trying to muster a glare, even though he can't really see me. "I'm fine."

He leans down to press a kiss against the side of my head. "I'll keep watch."

I press into his side for a moment, knowing that it's useless to argue with him. With a reluctant sigh, I crawl into the tent beside us, curling myself into a ball as my body finally gives in.

I don't know how long I sleep before the horse's frantic neigh sounds through the air. My eyes snap open, my heart instantly beating furiously. For a second, I just listen. I can hear Saint's soft whispers, trying to calm the horse.

Thrashing hooves stamp at the ground. Fear sets in. If this noise keeps up, we're doomed.

Hesitantly, I inch towards the tent opening, not wanting to know what waits on the other side, but whatever it is, I won't let Saint face it alone. I drag back the fabric to find him standing by the horse, stroking his neck, trying to calm him.

Then a blood curdling sound travels through the murky shadows. A screech so cold it would cause the dead to turn in their graves. I shudder, swallowing down the bile rising in my throat.

It certainly wasn't a human sound, nor animal. No . . . It was something in between.

The wraiths.

I scurry out of the tent to stand by Saint, who automatically gathers me to his side, both of us staring at the canopy. A flicker to my right draws my attention. Shadows—neither fully dead nor truly alive drift between the trees. I bite back a scream at the sight of them.

"Saint . . ." My voice trembles.

His head snaps in the direction of the shriek that slices through the air. My stomach drops, and my knees nearly give way.

Saint brings his attention towards me. His eyes find mine, dark and serious. "Hide. Get in the water. Do not let them see you."

I shake my head. "Saint, no. I'm not leaving—"

He grabs me by the arms and softly shakes me. "Please, Blue. Trust me."

He doesn't give me time to argue. In one swift movement, he yanks mother's ring from his finger and throws it towards me.

I barely manage to catch it before he's gone. Not gone, but not himself. In a beautiful transition that is more magical than I can even comprehend, he changes. Where Saint had been standing was now a large white owl, with big black eyes.

He leaps from the ground, taking flight, wings cutting through the inky night.

The wraiths screech louder, their twisted bodies unfurling from the shadows, bony fingers reaching for him. One turns its sunken eyes on me.

I freeze. My breath catches.

The lake. I twist my body, sprinting for the water. As soon as it hits my boots, I will my siren form to come forth. She hears me as if she already knew I needed her. My feet push off the water's edge, and before I hit the surface my legs and dress have disappeared, and in their place is my glittering, scaly tail.

It's dark down here—deeper than my lake at home. The murky waters are hard to navigate, with patches of reeds scattering around the dam. I flick my tail, heading for the surface, clutching my mother's ring tightly in my hand. I can't afford to lose it.

I wipe the water from my eyes once I break free. More screeches sound through the darkness, and I force the tears back as I watch Saint dodge and weave through the tree trunks, like a white smudge against a black tapestry.

Saint swoops down, striking a wraith. It shrieks, its skeletal form twisting violently as it swipes at him with razor-like claws. He dodges, wings flaring wide, but the other wraiths are closing in.

There are at least four of them.

Tall, looming creatures. Their bodies a tangle of bone and decaying tissue, draped in wisps of tattered darkness that replicate shredded fabric. Hollow, sunken eyes that glow with an eerie, cold light. My body shudders at the sight of their long, clawed fingers that curl like the gnarled roots of the trees they haunt. And when they move, it's as if they are born from the shadows themselves, floating with unnatural swiftness, their forms flickering in and out of sight.

I feel utterly helpless out here in the middle of the dam, but I know that on land I'd be such an easy kill, and that is not something I can afford to be. Not when Mother needs me . . . Not when Saint needs me.

He glides through the air effortlessly. If I didn't know how important it was for him to control his shifting, I'd almost argue that he was born to be a bird for a reason. He is the most graceful creature I have ever seen.

With each attacking swoop of his sharp talons, he manages to scare two of the wraiths away, but the last two are relentless.

A scream carries through the air, as cold, hollow eyes find me, and though I know it won't reach me in the water, that won't stop it from tormenting me with its soulless gaze, or its deathly cry. It heads towards me, so I push myself further back into the middle of the water, preparing myself to swim to the deepest part if I need to.

Saint screeches near the shore, swooping past the wraith, drawing its attention away from me. It works for a moment, but as he turns to attack it again, the other catches him mid air.

A strangled cry—more human than owl—rips from him as he tumbles from the sky, hitting the water with a sickening splash.

"Saint!"

Panic crashes over me like a wave.

My body kicks into gear as I dive in after him, swimming as fast as I can. The water is ice cold, and I make sure to splash my tail against the surface in hopes the water will reach a wraith, warning it of what will happen if it tries to come closer— their dead flesh would fall off their already dead bones. The water won't kill them, but it would certainly slow them down.

Icy, murky water swallows me whole. I kick downward, searching. My hands brush against feathers, as I yank Saint towards me, gripping him in my arms.

As I swim back to the surface, he flaps about, taking in air, his feathered chest heaving in and out. Tears threaten to spill again at the sight of his small helpless body. So different from the strong male I usually see.

His owl form is limp in my arms, wings dragging in the water.

"No, no, no," I whisper, pushing his soaked feathers from his face. He's breathing—but barely.

I open my fisted hand, revealing my mother's ring. My fingers tremble as I go to slip it on to a feather on his wing. Perhaps if I help him to shift back, he will have more control. With all these feathers, I don't even know if he's been injured or not—it's too dark to tell.

His large eyes open, focusing on me, before looking down at the ring. He weakly flaps his wings, pushing away from me.

My brows knit. "Saint—"

He does it again. Shaking—but insistent.

Realisation hits me. He doesn't want me to put the ring on.

The two wraiths screech at the water's edge, but they don't dare to come across the dark surface. And even though I am absolutely terrified, I do feel I have a sense of control being in the water. I can stay out here for hours if need be. As soon as the sun rises, the wraiths will be gone, for light will obliterate all forms of darkness.

Just wait until Dove hears about this. She's going to be so jealous of all this adventuring I'm doing. The thought of her silver eyes and bright smile keep me going. I have to. For mother, for Theon, for my shop . . . For Saint.

The wraiths stalk the shoreline, their hollow eyes scanning, searching. They're patient. Watching. Calculating how long before exhaustion drags me under, before my grip on Saint falters, before the cold steals the strength from my limbs.

One attempts to reach me. I lay on my back, cradling Saint against my chest as my tail flicks water in its direction. In the dark, I hear the sizzling sound of flesh melting. The Wraith screams, jerking back towards the forest.

My stomach turns over. Such horrid creatures.

I press my lips to the damp feathers of Saint's head and whisper, "Just hold on, okay?"

Who knows how much time passes. Every second is torment, as I fight fatigue. A few times my head drops, hitting the water's surface. The cold is enough to wake me for a while, but it's not long until my head is nodding once again.

My body aches, and even though I'm in my siren form, pain throbs in my tail. No doubt my ankle. Even my arms are in agony as I hold Saint above the water. I flick my tail, struggling to keep us afloat in the murky depths. The cold seeps into my bones, the dark water swirling around us like an unforgiving abyss. My breath comes in ragged gasps, but I tighten my grip, refusing to let exhaustion win.

And there, in the dark, I stay awake. Holding him. Protecting him.

Until the morning comes.

# Thirty

Something warm brushes across my face, stirring me from slumber. Early morning sun. I must have drifted off at some point in the night, though I'd tried ever so hard not to. Screeching howls reserved only for my memories sound in my mind. My eyes shoot open as I recall the wraiths readying myself for their hollowing stare. Yet, it's not them I see, but Juniper's knitted brow, and eyes full of distress. Her arms are wrapped around me, her expression tight with exhaustion, with relief.

I barely register the feeling of damp earth beneath me, the sharp contrast between the cool morning air and the water still clinging to my skin. My limbs are sluggish, heavy, like they don't quite belong to me anymore. The world drifts in and out, my body weighed down by exhaustion, by pain, by the icy grip of whatever hell last night dragged me through.

"Blue—"

She wipes a tear from her cheek, leaving droplets in its place. They shimmer like glass as the sun peaking through the canopy touches them. "We made it, Saint."

I swallow, my throat raw, every part of me aching. I try to move, to push myself upright, but my body protests with sharp, punishing pain. A groan slips past my lips, and instantly Juniper's grip tightens.

"If it's too painful to move, then don't. I can hold on a little while longer," she breathes, her voice raspy, thick with fatigue.

My head moves without a second guess. "No, we need to get out of here. You've already held on for so long."

She brushes hair from my face before helping me to sit up.

"Thank you," I whisper.

Once she's certain I'm not going to topple over, she closes her eyes. What happens next is nothing short of magic. The transformation is seamless—one moment she's a siren, a being from another world, then next, she is my beautiful Juniper again. A woman who has given me more than I deserve.

I shakily get to my feet. She stumbles slightly as she moves onto solid ground, her body trembling with exhaustion. My hands reach for her, just as she collapses in my arms.

"You're shaking," I rasp, my voice barely more than a whisper.

Juniper looks up at me with a lopsided grin. "So are you."

She's not wrong. I'd like to think that I have the strength and stamina to handle most things life throws at me, but even I have limits. Both of us are going to need a week of sleep once we make it out of these woods.

The wraiths are gone. The sun has begun its slow ascent, filtering weak golden light through the twisted branches overhead. The nightmare of the night before is over. But as I look at Juniper—her lips pale, her arms covered in goosebumps, the shadows under her eyes dark with exhaustion—I know the cost of surviving it.

Once her feet are steady, I gently let her go so I can check on the horse. I find him a few feet away, his reins tangled in some bramble bushes. Relief washes over me; the last thing I needed was to have to travel on foot.

Returning to the water's edge, I find Juniper standing there. Her face is void of feeling, her arms wrapping around herself.

She sees me approach, but the light in her eyes is gone.

"Come here." My voice is soft as I reach for her. I don't know what I plan to do—whether to hold her, to thank her, to somehow take away whatever weight she is carrying—all I know is that right now, she needs to be held.

She collapses into my arms in a sobbing heap. This strong, yet fragile woman, who's had to hold it together for so long. We stand in the quiet forest, and I hold her tightly while all the pain, frustration, and fear pour out onto my chest.

"Thank you . . . For saving me. For being so brave," I whisper into her hair.

Once the tears have subsided, and breathing becomes smooth, I place an arm around her shoulders as we head for the horse.

In silence, she attends to the arrow wound on my arm, making sure I'm not bleeding out. I'm grateful for her tender touch and the knowledge she carries about keeping wounds clean. Without her, I would most certainly be lying in a ditch somewhere with gangrene.

I reach for her hand when she's done. "How's your ankle?"

Juniper glances at it, then back at me. "I think the icy water helped with the swelling. It's much better this morning."

I nod. "Let me know if you need anything."

She climbs into the saddle while I gather our things scattered about the forest floor, then I join her.

The ride through the forest is silent beside the horses hooves crunching the bracken strewn across the narrow pathway. As much as I want to get my ring back, I think it would be wise if we take a day to recover. Perhaps the next town will offer some sanctuary where we can rest. Though funds are dwindling, I have to be frugal with the lasting coins—especially now that I am trying to live a different kind of life.

My right hand flexes on the reins. The absence of Kamari's ring makes me feel naked—vulnerable. Not only that, but dread seeps into my soul. I'd thrown it at Juniper when the wraiths attacked. Now that she had it in her possession, would she give it back?

Juniper shifts in the saddle, reaching for something in her dress pocket. She pulls out Kamaris ring, placing it on my finger without saying a word, as if she read my mind.

I lean forward to rest my forehead against the back of her head. "Thank you," I whisper, not knowing what else to say. I certainly don't deserve the kindness she offers me.

It's midday by the time we reach a small town on the map Juniper keeps stashed away in her bag. Despite how much anxiety maps give me, I'm grateful that she has one. I know my way around most places, but there are a few I've never been to.

We crest the last hill, and my gut tightens the second I lay eyes on the town. It's small—too small. The kind of place where strangers stand out, where townsfolk pay attention, where faces are remembered. I don't like it.

Juniper shifts in the saddle in front of me, wiping sweat from her brow. "It looks quiet," she murmurs.

"Too quiet," I reply, scanning the streets below.

A handful of people move between the diminutive wooden buildings, some gathered outside a tavern, others hauling sacks of potatoes from a supply cart. A middle-aged woman throws a bucket of wash water into the dirt road, and even from here, I see the way her eyes flick towards us, lingering too long.

The hair on the back of my neck stands up.

"We should keep moving," I say, tightening my hold on the reins. "Next town's bigger. More places to get lost."

Juniper glances back at me, her brows furrowed. "Are you sure? You look like you're about to fall off this horse."

I huff a quiet laugh, though my body does protest every movement. The fight, the wraiths, the night spent half-drowned in a lake—I feel it all. But stopping here isn't an option.

"We'll rest when we find a place safe enough to do it," I tell her. "This town's too small. Too many eyes."

She studies me for a moment, then nods. "Alright. Let's go."

With a gentle squeeze of my legs, I steer the horse away from the road leading into town, guiding it back onto the trail that skirts around it. My muscles ache, exhaustion pulling at my limbs, but I push it down. We need distance. We need to disappear.

We reach another forest. It swallows us whole as we enter. My eyes never rest as I keep watch on our surroundings. Though no matter how deep into the forest we go, I can't shake the feeling of being watched.

Back at the town, I could see Danden Mountain in the distance. Breydon was on the other side. So the chances of travellers between here and there that might recognise me grow higher with each passing moment.

Movement to my left catches my eye—a flash of tawny fur darting through the underbrush. A deer, startled, bounding deeper into the woods. Overhead, a flock of birds erupts from the treetops, their wings slicing through the air, shrill cries echoing in the vast silence.

Every instinct in me screams to push the horse faster, to put more distance between us and whatever might be lurking behind. But Juniper slumps against me, her breaths slow and even, her exhaustion pulling her under miles ago. She needs the rest.

I don't always remember the things I do when I'm in my owl form, especially if it's hours into the shift, but I can recall the way she searched for me when my body hit the water. The way she held me above the water's surface all night. My chest tightens at the memory. Not only has she chosen to come with me, she chose to save me, too.

In my story . . . She's the hero.

Her honey scent bathes me—making me feel as though I've fallen asleep in a field of wildflowers where the bees roam carefree. As much as I would like to stay inside this daydream, I simply don't have that luxury.

The sound of a twig snapping draws me from my thoughts. I grip the reins, stopping the horse. Juniper stirs awake—rubbing the sleep from her eyes.

Tiny hairs stand upright on the back of my neck. I know for certain now that we are being followed . . . But by what—or whom?

"Saint?" Juniper's voice is soft from slumber.

I quickly place my hand over her mouth, silencing her. "Don't move," I whisper, dragging my hand away.

With gentle ease, I slip from the horse's back. My hand flexes by my thigh, ready to reach for my dagger, should I need it. I was exhausted, but if either one of Donovan's men steps out of the shadows, they're going to find a blade between their eyes.

Juniper's cry slices through the air, sharp and desperate, a warning that comes a second too late.

A blur of darkness hurtles towards me, and before I can react, it slams into my chest with bone-rattling force. The impact rips the ground out from under me, my back colliding with the earth in a brutal crash. The breath is stolen from my lungs, leaving me gasping for air that won't come. My vision wavers, stars sparking at the edges. My body screams in protest, but I have no time for pain. No time for weakness.

Because whatever just hit me—isn't finished yet.

"Saint!" Juniper screams my name, as I go tumbling down the slight decline.

The figure rolls with me. Twigs snap beneath us, the earth unyielding as I fight to gain control. If I don't find my footing now, I'll end up with a branch through my skull—or worse, dead. My fingers claw at the fabric of my attacker's cloak, twisting into the material as I summon every ounce of strength. With a guttural growl, I shift my weight, using the momentum to roll us. A sharp rock digs into my ribs, but I don't stop—not until I'm the one on top.

My dagger flashes in the dim sunlight, raised high, ready to strike. My chest heaves, muscles burning as I press the blade closer.

Laughter erupts from beneath the hood of the darkened figure, freezing my hand in place. I'd recognise that sound in a crowd of people.

I rip the hood up, revealing a face I've spent the last twenty-six years looking at.

"Sepehr?"

His silver eyes peer up at me, accompanied with a grin. He lifts his head, sniffing the air. "Smells like a wet dog around here."

I grab him by the scruff of his neck and yank him into an embrace. "I've missed you, brother."

I rise to my feet, pulling Sepehr up with me. A thousand questions swirl in my mind, words pressing against my tongue, but there's no time—not yet. I've left a very frightened woman on a horse. I head back up the hill, my pulse still racing from the shock of reunion, Sepehr in step beside me.

I reach the horse's side and squeeze Juni's leg in reassurance. "Juniper, this is Sepehr."

She reaches down to grasp his hand in greeting. "The famous Sepehr . . . What an entrance."

Sepehr bows low in respect, before straightening with a grin. "An honour to meet you Juniper, though how you are stuck with this old man is a story I'm dying to hear."

I glance towards the sky. There is still enough light to travel to the next town, so I have time to explain some things here in the forest. *Stars* know Sepehr will want to know everything.

"What are you doing here? I thought we had another moon cycle before the meeting place?"

He's early. It's not a good sign. I brace myself for news I don't want to hear.

Sepehr exhales, rubbing the back of his neck. "I decided not to wander too far. I've been lying low, keeping out of trouble. Spotted you back in that small village." His lips twitch into a smirk. "Thought I'd surprise you."

And that he did. He was never one to stray too far, even at the orphanage. He was a homebody, but a damn good one. Knows how to stick to the shadows—makes himself almost invisible.

"Surprise is one word for it," I mutter, shaking my head. "You've got some nerve sneaking up on me like that."

"Didn't expect you to try to stab me, though. My face isn't that forgettable, is it?"

"It's lovelier than Saints," Juniper chimes in.

I turn my head slowly towards her, one brow raised in question. She flashes me a grin, and I flash her a look that makes her squirm in the saddle—in a good way.

Sepehr shifts his weight, folding his arms across his chest. "If the meeting place isn't for another moon cycle, then why are you headed this way?"

I sigh, running a hand through my hair. "It's a long story, but to sum it up. I stole Juni's mother's ring because she's a shifter. I needed it so I could join Juni on her trip to Stone's Ridge. She needed wicks for her business, and I needed to go to the orphanage to get my ring, so I could give the one I stole back."

"Saint—"

"I know, I know . . . But the orphanage didn't have my ring, and now we are going to get it from Donovan," I finish with a sigh.

Sepehr looks baffled, his gaze flicking between me and Juniper. "And you're okay with all of this?" he asks her, while pointing at me.

Juniper shrugs. "He kinda stuck, and now I don't want to let him go."

A grin breaks out across Sepehrs face. "Saint . . . you dirty dog."

I roll my eyes at him before flashing a grin at Juniper. Her words bring a peace that my soul longs to hear.

"Donovan's men have found us twice, though."

Sepehr's expression hardens. "Twice?"

I nod. "Almost lost Juniper to them the second time." My fingers tighten into fists at the memory, the helplessness of that moment still fresh. "We barely got away."

His jaw clenches. "Bastard doesn't give up, does he?"

I shake my head.

Sepehr glances at Juniper. "So where are you from, Juniper?"

Her eyes light up at the question. "Meadowbrook."

"That's quite a ways from here, yes?" Sepehr's brow knits.

I nod. "We've been travelling for over a week. Spent the night in the Wraith Woods last night, nearly died, you know— all that good stuff."

Sepehr's eyes grow wider with every word that tumbles from my lips. "You two have really been through it."

The horse shifts, dancing on the spot, eager to keep moving. I can't blame him, I am too. Juniper reaches for the reins, trying to steady him.

"Have you seen or heard from Roan at all?" I ask.

Black hair shimmers in the sunlight as Sepehr shakes his head. "Haven't seen him."

Relief and dread wash over me. "Hopefully he did what I told him to, and stayed out of sight. Perhaps he's found some lovely, hospitable girls, and they're taking care of him."

"That's the dream, isn't it?" Sepehr chuckles.

I throw my glance in Juniper's direction. "It sure is."

Her face turns pink under my gaze.

Sepehr tilts his head. "So when do we leave for Breydon?"

I arch a brow. "We?"

Sepher grins. "There is no way I'm letting you have all the fun—besides, you could use the extra help."

It's true. I had no idea how I was going to keep Juniper safe and steal my ring back. I'd be a fool to turn down Sepehr's offer. With him by my side, I might just have a fighting chance. And if we find Roan along the way? Then, for the first time in a long time, I might finally feel whole again.

# Thirty One

KISS ME

Hearing Saint laugh with Sepehr is probably the highlight of this whole trip—that, and his cock—for a lack of better words. I'd never thought I'd find pleasure in a male like I do with Saint. One glance in his direction, and my body awakens—craving his touch. Too bad I'd have to wait a little longer.

The warmth of the inn is a stark contrast to the chill of the night air outside. The scent of roasted meat and fresh bread lingers in the space, mingling with the tang of ale and the low drawl of voices. The tavern isn't crowded, but enough people fill the room that we placed ourselves in a far corner—the darkest part of the tavern.

I stir my spoon through the thick stew in front of me, my stomach growling at the smell, but my mind is too distracted to eat, yet I know that I need to rebuild my strength, so I force it down.

Saint sits next to me, his gaze flicking towards the door every now and then. He finished his food already, and is discussing all things Donovan with his brother over a pint of golden ale.

Sepehr, on the other hand, has no such reservations. He leans back in his chair, a half-smirk playing on his lips as he tears into a hunk of bread. He eats like a man who hasn't had a decent meal in weeks, which, from what I've gathered, might not be far from the truth. He's more relaxed than Saint, but there's a sharpness in his gaze, a calculating glint that tells me he's aware of everything happening around us.

Sepehr's eyes reflect the dancing flame from the red candlestick on the table. The sight of it tightens my chest. How is my mother? Is she coping alright without me? My heart feels heavy in its bone cage—torn between home and the male beside me.

Sapphire eyes find me. I smile at him softly, squeezing his leg under the table. A little reminder that I'm still here, and I'm still choosing to be.

"We can't just walk into Breydon blind," Saint mutters, before downing a mouthful of drink. "Donovan will be expecting me to come for the ring. If his men found us twice already, they'll be watching."

Sepehr nods. "And he won't have it somewhere on display."

I watch them talk, my heart feeling heavy. This is going to be so much harder than I thought it would be—not that I thought it was going to be easy. "Then how do we get it back?" I ask.

Saint exhales sharply, leaning back in his chair, arms crossed. "Haven't figured that part out yet."

Bellowing laughter a few tables behind me makes me jump with fright. Saint notices and places his hand on my leg. His touch sends a warm sensation over my skin. I long for a quiet room where it's just him and I tangled between the sheets. I know he needs to discuss things with Sepehr, so I'll be patient, but as soon as I'm alone with him, and we've both refreshed ourselves, he'd better be ready to mark something off the list.

"What about Roan?" I murmur, tearing off a piece of bread before eating it.

Saint runs a hand over his face. "If we go to Breydon without him knowing, and something happens to us . . . He might never know."

Sepehr's expression darkens slightly. "And we can't wait around here for him, can we?"

The question hangs in the air between us. I go to answer, but Saint cuts in. "No, we can't. I've already asked so much of Juni."

My heart melts towards him. He's thinking about me and my needs . . . Not his own.

"Then we leave a note here with the innkeeper. If he comes through here, we'll tell him where we've gone. That's all we can do." Sepehr shrugs.

Silence settles between us for a moment, heavy with the weight of everything ahead. We have to come up with a plan. It's what I do best. When faced with a problem, I won't rest until I can find the solution to fixing it.

I square my shoulders. "Tell me what I can do."

Saint's gaze snaps to mine, something unreadable flickering in his eyes. "Juni—"

"No." I shake my head. "I'm not sitting on the sidelines. If we're doing this, I want to help."

Saint sighs, rubbing his temple. "It's not that simple."

Sepehr grins. "She's got fire, I like her."

Saint glares at him. "Not helping."

I cross my arms. "I can be useful. You two can't do this alone. Besides . . . I have skills that neither one of you have."

Sepehr's brows arch in curiosity. "Pray tell?"

I steal a glance at Saint. He leans lazily against the table, his elbow propped up as he rests his head on his hand, that ever-present smirk tugging at his lips. His eyes glint with amusement. The tavern has begun to settle, the once lively chatter dwindling to murmurs as patrons trickle out or slump over their drinks. The fire crackles softly in the hearth, casting flickering shadows across the wooden beams. I lower my voice, instinctively cautious. We can't afford to draw any unwanted attention—not tonight.

"Well, I'm half siren. So I can breathe underwater, and I can swim faster than both of you, I'm sure."

Sepehr's eyes widen. "I've never met a siren in real life. Though I know a few live in the lower regions of Breydon, closer to the sea."

I smile at him softly. "Surely I can be of help somehow?"

Saint studies me for a long moment, his lips pressing into a thin line. Then, finally, he sighs. "Fine. But you follow my lead."

A thrill of determination sparks in my chest. "Deal."

Sepehr raises his mug. "Then it's settled. We steal back the ring, rob Donovan blind, and find Roan. Should be easy, right?"

Even though we're all in agreement, a nagging feeling twists in my gut—none of this is going to be easy. I might be all in with Saint, willing to risk more than I ever thought possible, but I can't afford to be reckless. Not when I have a mother back home, waiting for me, counting on me. No matter how deep I'm in this, I can't lose sight of that.

I smile softly at Sepehr as he bids us goodnight, promising to return in the morning. Even though I'm sad to see him go, I'm eager to have Saint all to myself.

The stairs creak as we head up to our room. The tavern is almost empty, save for a few drunk patrons at the bar. We leave their boisterous laughter behind as we find our door.

Saint unlocks it, and we head inside. He quietly closes it after I've passed through the doorway. When it's shut, he leans his back against the wood, eyeing me. His gaze is assessing, like he's trying to figure out where my head is. Usually I would tease, make him beg for it, but not tonight. I nearly lost him in the woods. I won't waste a second when I'm with him.

"Kiss me." My voice is soft but filled with urgency.

Within seconds, he's crossing the floor to grasp my face between his hands, trembling with need.

A moan escapes me as his lips find mine in a hungry kiss. He's everywhere, and all at once. In my mind, in my soul, in my mouth. I can't get enough, as I slip my arms around his neck, standing on the tips of my toes. He tastes like all my dreams coming true.

His tongue explores my mouth, and I explore his. The kiss has warmth pooling between my legs, the ache for his touch becoming more than I can bear. I don't want his hands on my waist; I want them between my legs.

In fact, I want more than that. Reluctantly, I pull back, my breath coming in short gasps. I keep my arms locked around his neck, my gaze on his. "I'm going to freshen up, and then I want to do another item on your list."

Saint's eyes darken, a smile playing on his lips. "Are you sure? Wouldn't you like to sleep?"

"I'll sleep when I'm done with you," I whisper against his mouth.

His gasp is barely audible, but I catch it. "You'd better hurry then, Blue." He grins.

I dance away from him before he has a chance to kiss me again, a grin flashing between us. He will want to use the washroom too, so I don't linger. Besides, I've had more than my fill of water lately. Half siren or not, I can appreciate the luxury of being warm and dry.

When I return, I find him sitting by the window, dressed only in his trousers. The silver light of the full moon spills over his skin, tracing every sharp angle and defined muscle, making him look almost untouchable. I pause in the doorway, caught in quiet awe. How did I get so lucky? To have someone like him—someone so beautifully untamed—look at me the way he does or want me the way he does? The thought sends a warmth curling through my chest, soft and consuming.

His head swivels around as I step inside, his sapphire eyes glinting in the low light. Slowly he leaves the chair, and as he passes me, he grips my chin, planting a fierce kiss on my mouth before striding into the washroom.

The intensity makes the desire already building in my core come alive. I'm on fire, and Saint holds the match.

I pace the room quietly, waiting for his return. I'm so consumed by my need for him that I can't sit still. How should I be when he returns? Should I sit on the bed? Perhaps I could sit in the chair as he did. Or maybe I'm overthinking it altogether.

The silver light from the moon beckons me to sit upon the window sill. So I do—pulling my feet up under me. A canopy of stars glitter in the inky sky. This is the first night in a while that it hasn't stormed. I'd almost forgotten what the night looked like.

It's not long before I hear the creak of the washroom door. My head swivels around, meeting Saint's gaze. His eyes take their time tracing the outline of my figure.

I ease from the window, taking a few steps towards him. He takes a few as well, but stops when I pull my nightgown up and over my head, dropping it to the floor in a crumpled heap.

His sharp intake of breath brings a flush to my cheeks, and suddenly I don't feel so bold. This is so not like me, but I can't seem to help myself. The way he looks at me gives me a confidence I've never known before.

"So, what's on your list?" My voice is low as I take another step.

Saint watches me, his lips parting slightly as he runs his tongue on the seam of his bottom lip, deciding what to do with me.

I pause when I reach him, fully naked—his to command.

Slowly he reaches out a hand to run a finger along my jaw, gripping my chin to pull it down every so slightly. "I have dreams where you're on your knees for me."

My breath catches, but I keep my gaze locked on him.

He slides his thumb into my mouth, forcing me to suck it, sending a thrill down my spine.

"Would you like to be on your knees for me, Blue?" His voice is guttural.

There is no hesitation on my behalf. I nod before slipping to the ground in front of him.

His eyes darken to a shade of blue I've not seen before. My fingers shake a little as I reach for the button on his trousers. They come loose, and I grip the top slowly sliding them down his hips. His muscular thighs are sprinkled in silky dark hairs. I turn my focus to his skin, not the erect hardness in front of my face. With every drag of my hands across his skin, his cock twitches, and my mouth waters.

I look up at him. Taking his length in my hand.

Saint tucks a strand of hair behind my ear. "Open your mouth."

The thrill I feel when he gently demands awakens a side of me I didn't even know I enjoyed. For once, someone else was taking control . . . And it wasn't me.

I shove down the fear of being inexperienced, and part my lips. At first I just suck the tip, running my tongue around the head. Saint moans softly, so I do it again, before taking him further into my mouth.

"*Fuck*, Blue," he whispers.

I keep one hand on his thigh and wrap the other around his shaft, gripping it tightly. My head bobs back and forth slowly, easing him in and out of my mouth. The ache between my legs grows with every passing second—I *need* him. All of him. Every day, for the rest of my life. Not only do I desire his body, I desire his company, his mind, his soul.

My mouth pops off the tip of his cock. It bobs, glistening in the low light. Saint's face has this feral look about it, like he's about to burst at the seams, and ravish me. So while I have his gaze, I lick from the base of his cock all the way to the tip.

It's his undoing.

He reaches for me, his hands firm beneath my arms as he hauls me up with effortless strength. Instinctively, I wrap my arms around his neck, my legs locking around his waist. A low chuckle rumbles from his chest as he strides across the room with purpose, his grip possessive, claiming. And then—he tosses me onto the bed, the mattress dipping beneath me as I land with a breathless gasp.

For the next hour, nothing else exists. Just us. Two lovers tangled in the sheets, mapping each other's bodies with lips, hands, and whispered names. Flesh against flesh, soul against soul—until there is no space left between us.

Silver light spills across the sheets, casting a soft glow over our tangled limbs as we lay together, breathless and spent. My body is utterly boneless beside Saint, exhaustion humming through me—a sweet, lingering ache from the pleasure he's left in his wake.

"When I first saw you . . . I wanted you to fuck me," Saint whispers into my hair. I turn to look up at him, so he continues. "But then I got greedy, and now I want you to love me."

I twist in the sheets so I'm sprawled across his chest. He watches me. His face filled with fear, and something else . . . Hope. My heart is racing in my chest at the thought of Saint wanting me to love him. I didn't even need to think about it.

Propping myself up, I trace a finger across his jaw. "I *think* I loved you the moment you stepped into my shop. I *knew* I loved you the moment I found the new wheel on my cart."

Saint sucks in his breath, flipping us, until I'm safely tucked under the weight of his body. A small tear slips from the corner of his eye, so I reach up to brush it away. "You love me?" he whispers.

I bring my head up, grazing my mouth against his. "I love you, Saint Everhart."

With a gentleness that I've only ever felt in his arms, he leans down to nuzzle his face in my neck. We lay there, just holding each other. "I love you, Juniper Fairchild," Saint whispers into the dark.

I never set out to find love, but some things are written into the very fabric of our souls. A heart knows when the search is over—when it has found its home. And mine had, because I found him.

# Thirty Two

## RETURNING TO BREYDON

Nothing could have prepared me for the feeling of returning to Breydon. My skin crawls with every step that brings me closer to the home I'd known for fifteen years. Sepehr is tight-lipped beside me. I know he's feeling the same. Neither of us want to be here. Yet I know that if I don't take back what's rightfully mine, I'll never know peace. Donovan will not hold power over me anymore.

The inn room is small, barely big enough for the three of us. A single window lets in the dull, late-afternoon light, casting long shadows across the wooden floor. And the scent of stale ale lingers in the air, mixing with the faint mustiness of old linens. I try to keep my voice down, because the walls are thin. If I can hear the murmur of voices from the tavern below, the occasional burst of laughter, or the shuffle of footsteps in the hall—who knows who is listening to us.

Sepehr leans against the fireplace mantle, fiddling with a matchstick between his teeth, hands shoved into trouser pockets. His face is troubled—probably because we're back in the place we fought so hard to leave.

Juniper plonks herself down on the edge of the bed. Her ankle has been giving her more grief that she'd dare to admit. I will definitely be attending to that soon.

I'm pacing the room, eager to figure out what the hell we're actually doing. "So, what did you hear?"

Sepehr pulls the pick from his mouth. "Donovan is throwing another one of his parties tomorrow night."

I nod, folding my arms across my chest to try to keep me from vibrating out of my skin. I've never felt more restless than I do right now. "Yeah, I heard that too." I pause in the middle of the room, hands on hips. "Perfect time to go in disguised as suppliers—"

Sepehr drops his gaze to the ground, scuffing his boot. "That's not all I heard."

My brow creases, and I flick my gaze between him, and Juniper. She shrugs lightly—she doesn't know anymore than I do. "What do you mean?"

The heavy sigh the Sepehr releases grips my heart. Something isn't right.

"Donovan's got Roan . . ." Sepehrs voice is filled with emotion.

If the room wasn't spinning before, it is now. I grip the top edge of the sofa chair next to me, using it as a crutch to steady my weight. How? . . . How could this happen?

"Who told you?" I barely manage to whisper.

"Street kids." Sepehr throws the half-gnawed pick into the cold hearth. "They hang out by the guards at the gates, eyes and ears of this city. Give them something shiny, and they'll tell you everything."

It was true. Many times I've called upon their knowledge when I needed information that only someone on the ground would be able to acquire.

"Fuck!" I begin my pacing again, running my hands through my hair. "This changes everything."

The stakes were getting higher by the second. Did I have the balls to face the oppression hanging over my head? Was my ring worth the life of my brothers . . . Of Juniper?

I run my hand over my face, stifling a groan. "Not only do we have to find the ring, we will have to get Roan out, too. As long as he's—"

Sepehr takes a step towards me and places a hand on my shoulder, giving it a reassuring squeeze. "He'll be alive . . . Donovan knows we will come for him."

My top lip rises in disgust. "Doesn't mean he will be in one piece."

The room is quiet—too quiet. The kind of silence that creeps in when the weight of a thousand unspoken worries settles over a space. I flick my gaze towards Juniper. Even in the dim light, she's a beacon, something steady in the storm. So quickly, she's becoming one of the most important people in my world, and I'd do anything to keep her safe. But how? How was I supposed to protect her while reclaiming what was mine? How was I supposed to keep her out of Donovan's grasp while destroying the ghosts of my past?

The weight of it all coils in my chest, tightening like a vice. Too many unknowns. Too many risks. And not nearly enough time.

Juniper stands from the bed, slightly limping as she makes her way to my side. She grasps my hand firmly in hers. "Now that we have this information, it's time to make a plan." Reaching up, she cups my face. "Perhaps you could draw the layout of his estate?"

Her scent anchors my thrashing mind. I pull her, twisting her so her back is against my chest. Cradling her in my arms, I breathe her in. I don't even care if Sepehr feels like the third wheel. I *need* her.

Sepehr sighs again, dropping into the single sofa chair. "No doubt he will be keeping Roan in the high tower."

I shiver at the memories of being trapped there as a child. One wrong move, and that's where we'd be sent— punishment—no food and little water for days. Not to mention the thrashing we would get. I pull Juniper closer, trying to lose myself in her essence. Because if I don't calm down, I'm going to tear this inn room apart.

"He will be expecting us to look for him there," I murmur. "Maybe I need to shift tonight. Circle the place and see if I can find out where they might be keeping him."

Sepehr nods. "Wouldn't hurt, and I doubt Donovan will be expecting it."

Juniper shifts in my arms, and I'm suddenly very aware that she's standing on her injured ankle. I move so I can sit in the chair opposite Sepehr, pulling her onto my lap. "What if we split up? You focus on Roan, and I'll get my ring."

Sepehr eyes me warily. "Is that wise?"

I shrug. "Probably not."

Juniper shifts in my lap, placing an arm around my neck. "I think we should stick together. We'd have greater power in numbers."

I glance at her beautiful meadow eyes. Melting at the way she looks at me. "We?" my brow lifts.

She nods. "Yes, all three of us."

A low chuckle escapes me. "There is no way you're coming inside the viper's lair. It's not safe, Blue."

She looks at me crossly. "If I wanted to be safe, I wouldn't have followed you here."

"She could be of use, Saint," Sepehr pipes in.

I reach up to tuck a strand of hair behind her ear. "Not if I have to be thinking about her safety. I won't be able to concentrate, Blue."

I didn't want her to feel like she was useless, because she wasn't. She was far from that. But the thought of her getting caught in the crossfire? That was a weight I couldn't carry. She was a part of me now, woven into the very fabric of my soul. If something happened to her . . . If I lost her . . . There would be no coming back from that. No healing. No moving on. Just an endless, hollow existence where a piece of me was forever missing.

Juniper nods, but her eyes are misted. "I want to help in some way, though."

I offer her a soft smile. "Fine, but you're not coming into the house."

Sepehr stares off into the distance. He has his thinking face on. I should too. We are running out of time. Who knows what Donovan will do to Roan, and who knows how long Roan will last.

*We're coming for you, Roan.*

I close my eyes, letting the silence of the room settle over me, dulling the chaos in my mind. But even in the quiet, my thoughts refuse to still. I picture the estate—the winding halls, the shadowed rooms, the countless places Donovan could have hidden Roan. My gut tightens. If he's even still there. If he's even still alive.

"I'm thinking our best shot is to sneak in under the disguise of suppliers for the party. Find Roan, and the ring, and then if we can sneak back out, great—if not, we'll have to either leap from the balcony or chance the spiral staircase in the tower—I think Donovan blocked it years ago."

Sepehr's brows raise so high I fear they will slip off his forehead. "Leap off the balcony? Are you insane?"

I shrug. "It's that, or chopped liver?"

Juniper's head snaps around with a gleam in her eye. "I could wait in the ocean below. When you jump, I'll tie a rope around you all and swim you to shore?"

I smile at her eagerness to help. Perhaps it'll be good to have her with us after all. "There we go. It's settled then."

Sepehr scoffs. "I doubt it'll be that simple."

I drop my head back against the chair, releasing a sigh. "It never is."

# Thirty-Three

## FIND THE RHYTHM OF LOVE

I haven't moved from the safety of Saint's embrace. Sepehr left not long ago, giving us some privacy to say our possible goodbyes. I shuddered at the thought of the word. It wasn't an option—saying goodbye to half of my heart *wasn't* an option.

The room was quiet—dark. Most of the inn's patrons had finally fallen asleep. Both Saint and I should be sleeping too, but there's still too much that's been left unsaid. Who knows what tomorrow will bring. I have to say it all now while I have the chance.

"Promise me something," Saint whispers into the side of my head. His warm breath caressing my cheek.

I close my eyes, not wanting to hear his next words, as I nod.

Saint pulls me closer to his chest. "Promise me that if everything goes bad, you'll swim away."

Tears well, threatening to spill. "Saint, please don't—"

He grips my face, turning it to look at him. "Get out of Breydon and don't look back." His voice is firm, but his eyes are soft.

I lock my gaze with his, refusing to look away. Every part of me wants to deny him—to tell him that dying is not an option, that I won't let it be. But the words lodge in my throat, tangled in the storm of emotions raging inside me. I bite down on the inside of my cheek, grounding myself, forcing back the tidal wave of fear and turmoil threatening to pull me under.

Saint rubs a thumb over my chin. "If I don't come back, you have to promise me you'll leave. Forget about me, forget about this, and live your life." His voice is barely a whisper.

Sapphire eyes sweep over my face, silently pleading for me to agree. But I can't . . . I won't. His scent—earthy patchouli and rugged cedarwood—wraps around me, sinking into my skin, branding me. How do I hold on to this moment? How do I weave him into my very being, or soak myself in him so no matter where I go, he comes too?

I shake my head. "I'll run if I have to, but don't ask me to forget you. You're a part of me now."

His forehead drops to mine, and we simply sit in each other's arms, neither one of us wanting the peaceful spell to break. Right now, he is here, all in one piece, and he is mine. There is no way on this beautiful green earth that I'm going to take that for granted.

"When you find Roan, and your ring, you will return to me, and we're going to live happily in Meadowbrook," I whisper into the dimly lit space.

Saint huffs softly. "And what am I going to do in Meadowbrook to support this beautiful life?" Saint nuzzles my neck.

"You're going to have a sign painting shop, of course. You'd be so good at it, and there is only one other on this side of Sapphire Vale."

My breath catches as Saint's teeth gently scrape against the column of my throat. I know what he's trying to do—distract me, and himself, from the looming threat that tomorrow brings, and if I'm honest, I'm going to let him.

His fingers dig into my rib cage, crushing me against his chest. "I love that you have it all planned out."

"Don't you think it's a wonderful idea?" I'm breathless as he licks up my neck, nipping at my earlobe. Desire pools between my legs. He wants this just as much as I do.

Saint dusts kisses across my jaw. "I think it's brilliant."

I let my head fall back, closing my eyes, while Saint trails his lips up the other side of my jaw, his hands finding the buttons on the front of my gown.

"So that's a yes?" I whisper.

He cups my face, forcing me to look at him. "It's a yes. I wouldn't want to do anything else."

I grin then, before claiming his mouth in a heated kiss. His fingers find my buttons again, hurriedly tearing my dress from my shoulders as I dip my tongue between his lips. He moans from the back of his throat, so I kiss him deeper.

My breasts are exposed to the air as Saint palms one gently, kneading it before rolling my nipple between his thumb and finger. Instantly, my skin pebbles over with pleasure. I cup Saint's face, angling my head so he can kiss me deeper. There's nothing I'd rather be doing right now, than finding pleasure in his arms until both of us are spent.

I rip my lips from his, my breath coming in short gasps as his touch quickens my heart.

He leans down, capturing a nipple into his mouth, flicking his tongue over it. I arch my back, forcing my breast deeper into his mouth, digging my fingers into the back of his neck as he licks and nips at my breast.

This isn't enough . . . I want to climb inside him and wear his skin. I want to be so close that we become one.

Saint pulls back, his gaze flicking between my mouth and my eyes. I slowly ease from his lap, the top half of my dress hanging at my waist. "Come," I murmur, holding my hand out to him. He takes it, eyeing me warily as he stands.

My fingers find the buttons on his shirt, undoing them one by one. Once it's free, I ease it from his shoulders, taking my time to drag my fingers down his warm, sculptured chest. When I reach his racing heart, I place my palm over it before meeting his gaze. "If I recall, you said that you'd fuck me on every flat surface you could find."

Saint's eyes darken, a barely audible growl escaping him as he reaches for me. I can't stop the grin forming on my face as he grips it, bringing his lips crashing down on mine. I grip the edge of the trousers slung low around his waist, holding on as he walks me backwards. My ass hits the edge of the wooden table in the room, and suddenly my internal desire manifests into reality.

Heat travels into my core instantly at the thought of how the rest of this evening is about to unfold.

I suck Saint's tongue into my mouth before dragging my teeth to bite his bottom lip. It draws another growl from him as he hungrily kisses me back. His mouth devours mine as our breaths become one.

The absence of his lips is more than I can bear as he slips to kneel in front of me. My chest expands in and out in anticipation of his next move.

Without a word—his gaze on me. He slowly lifts my skirts to my waist until I'm fully exposed—just for him. He flicks his eyes down, then drags them back up my body to meet me, a brow arched in surprise. "Were you planning on seducing me tonight?"

A smile plays on my lips. "The thought had crossed my mind."

The corners of Saint's mouth turn up as he leans towards me, his eyes never leaving mine. My mind fractures when he flattens his warm tongue, running it up my centre. The act is so powerful that I have to grip the edge of the table on either side of me to stop myself from collapsing to the floor in pleasure. His deep chuckle vibrates my warmth as he begins to have his way with me.

I drop my head back, closing my eyes as he flicks his tongue across my clit. "Saint—" I breathe.

Fingers dig into my thighs as he presses his face into me, lapping at the slickness that my body can't help but provide for him. A feast that only lovers know the taste of.

He finally pulls away, standing once again. I bring my head back to meet him, not knowing up from down. My mind is lost to the cloud of pleasure that's settled over me.

Saint steps closer, placing a tender kiss on my lips as his grip on my hips tightens. "Last chance to change your mind, Blue," he hums against my mouth.

I slide my hand down the front of his trousers, palming his hardened length, hearing the catch in his breath. "Fuck me."

A gasp escapes me when without warning he flips me so my palms are face down on the tabletop. He drags his hand up my spine, adding pressure until my chest is flat against the wood, my breasts scratching against the rough surface as I stretch my arms out in front of me.

This is not something that would have happened with Wesley. He was too small-minded, he also only ever thought of himself, and always managed to reach the finish line before me. Unlike the delicious man behind me who always made sure I finished first.

I feel the cool air against my backside as Saint lifts my skirts up to gather at my waist. The idea of being fully on display for him brings another wave of pleasure to my core.

His fingers brush against my entrance, drawing a moan from my lips. "You're so wet for me, my love."

I glance over my shoulder. "Please, Saint."

He grins, and I hear him fumbling with the belt on his trousers, before my world suddenly explodes around me as I feel his cock thrust into my warmth. My eyes roll back in my head at how deep he is, and I can't stop the moan that escapes me.

Saint reaches his hand around to place it over my mouth, forcing me up—while still buried in me—so he can whisper into my ear. "Careful, Blue . . . These walls are paper thin."

I don't care who sees or what they think. Let the whole world know—I am his, and he is mine. Nothing and no one could ever change that. No other touch, no other soul, will ever satisfy me the way he does. He is the fire, and I am the wick, the only one I burn for, the only man I will ever need.

He keeps his hand over my mouth as he starts to pound into me. The table legs scrape on the wooden floor with every thrust, and I can't help but whimper into his palm each time he sinks back in.

His other hand grips my hip, fusing our bodies together. Pleasure coils tightly in my stomach, every drag of his length on my inner walls feeding that pleasure.

My breasts bounce as we find the rhythm of love, diving into a place where only we exist as we bring each other to new heights of ecstasy.

"You feel so good, Blue," Saint moans softly into the night.

His hand shifts from my mouth to grip my slender neck. The thrill it brings as fingers wrap around my throat is not something I've experienced before, but I'm not scared. In fact, it heightens my senses, making my whole body come alive for him.

I can feel my orgasm building, readying itself to tear from my skin in the form of stars and heat. I let myself go, riding the waves of pleasure.

"Saint, I'm going to come," I pant.

His thrusts come in faster, harder when he hears my words, and it's enough to draw a cry from my lips.

"Sing for me, my love," Saint says, his voice low.

One more thrust and I'm flying . . . Over the edge of pleasure and into the world of ecstasy. My back arches as wave after wave of my climax washes over me. I push up on my tiptoes, angling my hips so Saint can drive into me deeper. It's all he needs to leap into the stars with me.

I hear his grunt, and both his hands grip my hips tightly as he shatters inside of me, my warmth clinging to him— milking him of everything. Saint gently collapses on my back, his palms resting either side of my chest.

I turn my head, meeting his lips in a slow, lingering kiss. A kiss that speaks of devotion, of a love so deep it leaves no room for doubt. While he is still buried inside of me, our bodies entwined, we seal this moment—this quiet, breathless surrender—binding ourselves to each other in a way that words never could.

I'm not sure how long we stay like this, lost in each other. Only when my ankle starts to throb, do I tap his arm gently. He pulls out, then twists me so I'm facing him before cupping my cheeks. "I love you."

Hearing his words is life-giving. For so long I'd put love on the shelf, hiding it away for a time I thought may never actually come. And yet, here he is. He's the man I thought I would never find. The one that steps up in every place every other man stepped aside. He's the rock that never breaks, and he's mine.

I wrap my arms around his neck, drawing him down to brush his lips. "I love you, Saint, and no matter what happens tomorrow, you've given me something I never thought I'd have—love—so, thank you."

# Thirty Four

The early morning is a blur. Waking Juniper felt cruel, her face so peaceful in sleep. Yet, if we didn't move fast, there was a good chance I was going to talk myself out of this whole thing. Well—the ring part, not the part where I find Roan and lug his ass back to safety.

Juniper and I move through the motions, changing, packing our things, and leaving the safety of the room to pay the innkeeper.

Outside the inn, Sepehr is waiting. He nods once when he sees us, his expression serious. No words are exchanged—we don't need them. Instead, we fall into step, weaving through the streets of Breydon. The city is beginning to stir, merchants setting up stalls, the scent of baking bread curling through the alleys, but none of it matters. The closer we get to Donovan's estate, the heavier the air feels, like a noose tightening around my throat.

Juniper's hand feels small in mine, and I want nothing more than to flee this place, with her at my side. But I know if I don't face Donovan now, he will be a constant shadow, always lingering in the corner of my mind.

Today that all ends. It has to.

Before we reach the edge of the property, I stop. Juniper turns to me, her brows furrowing.

"This is where we say goodbye," I murmur, pulling her away from the street and into the shadows of a nearby alley. Her lips part, a protest ready on her tongue, but I silence her by placing something small and familiar in her palm. Her mother's ring.

Her breath catches. "Saint—"

"Take it," I say, wrapping her fingers around it. "Don't forget our promise. Run if you have to, and be careful out in that ocean, alright?"

Tears well in her eyes as I brush my lips across her forehead.

I swallow hard, my next words coming out hoarse. "I love you."

She bites back a sob, throwing her arms around my neck. "I love you. Please be careful."

I nod, pulling her close one last time before taking a step back. She looks up at me, her eyes pleading. "Come back to me, Saint."

I nod. I have to.

She pulls away, hesitating for only a second before slipping into the nearest alley and disappearing towards the sea.

I watch until I can't see her anymore. Only then do I turn back to Sepehr. "Let's go."

Without the safety of Kamari's ring on my hand, I feel exposed. I know I won't shift in the middle of the day, but without the ring's control anchoring me, my own skin feels unfamiliar, like I'm wearing someone else's body and it doesn't quite fit.

Sepehr and I move quickly, keeping to the shadows as much as possible as we approach the estate from the side closest to the mountainside. It's quieter here. Only two guards patrol the area.

I hold up my hand, signalling him to halt. Scanning the area, I make sure it's just the two men, before I give Sepehr the look, he nods in understanding.

Like the shadows we were trained to be, we strike. I take the one nearest to me, using the element of surprise to our advantage. Sepehr takes the other. It's over in seconds— on choked-out gasp, a muffled struggle, and then silence. Thankfully, both went down easily, and I didn't need to use my blade. They'd be out for a few hours.

We drag their bodies out of sight behind some bushes, and after stripping them, we bind their hands and feet with their belts. The uniforms smell like sweat and ale, but it will have to do. Once we're dressed, I adjust my blade, hiding back into the side of my boot.

Sepehr pulls his long black hair back and tucks it on the inside of his tunic before placing the helmet on his head. "That was surprisingly easier than I thought it would be."

I huff lightly. "Let's hope the luck continues."

Once my helmet is in place, we head for the side entrance, waltzing through as if we never left.

The scent of roasting meat and fresh bread engulfs us as we step into the kitchen. The staff barely spares us a glance, too busy with the party preparations. They'll be at this all day no doubt.

I try to keep talking to a minimum, only doing it when needed. Instead Sepehr and I communicate with our eyes. We'd already decided that we wouldn't split up, so together we headed for the dungeons in the lower half of the estate. If Roan wasn't there, then he would definitely be in the tower.

Our steps echo down the stairwell, the hairs standing on the back of neck the further down we go. Familiar smells reach me, and I almost gag. The dungeons stink of vomit, faeces, and old blood—you name it, it's down here. Donovan doesn't take nicely to those who don't pay their debts. I've seen it time and time again.

This space is usually reserved for those folk, but it would be wise to look for Roan here—just in case.

A guard, whose figure was short yet muscular, peers at me with beady eyes. "What are you lot doing down here?"

I haven't even made it to the cells yet, and already I need to do what I do best—lie. "Donovan needs you out at the front gates. He said something about suppliers causing issues and sent us to take your post."

The guard's eyes squint to the point I wonder if he can actually see me before he grunts, spinning on his heel to march up the winding stairs to the ground level of the estate without argument.

The flickering torchlight barely reaches the furthest corners, where rusted shackles dangle from the walls like cruel ornaments. Every step echoes, but Sepehr and I move swiftly, pressing ourselves against the shadows as we check every cell for our copper-haired brother.

Then I see him.

Roan.

He's slumped against the cool stone wall at the back of the cell. Rusted chains strewn upon the floor, thankfully not attached to his limbs. Dried blood crusts at his temple, and his clothes are filthy, hanging off him in tatters. He blinks sluggishly at us, as if convincing himself we're real. When recognition dawns, relief floods his weary gaze.

"Saint?" His voice is hoarse, disbelieving.

A tight knot unfurls in my chest. "Took us long enough, huh?"

My fist clench at my sides at the sight of him, so broken, and exhausted. Crimson clouds my vision as I imagine slitting Donovan's throat before watching him bleed out on the carpet.

Sepehr scans the cell door. "Damn," he mutters under his breath. "The guard had the keys."

We don't have time to chase after him. I drop to a knee, pulling my dagger from my boot. I flip it in my palm, slide it between the iron bars of Roan's cell, and start working the lock.

Sepehr keeps a watchful eye for any intruders. Thankfully, most of the guards would be attending to the suppliers, making sure no busybodies or encroachers enter.

"Saint—" Roan's voice is a hushed whisper.

"I got it," I mutter, jiggling the dagger in the rusted mechanism.

The lock gives a stubborn click, and I wrench the cell door open, losing a relieved breath. Roan stares at us, half in awe, half in disbelief. "You came for me."

Sepehr and I support his weight from either side of him. "Of course we did you buffoon, you're stuck with us until the very end."

He sags against us as we help him up, his body weak but his spirit unbroken. We move quickly, scaling the stairs, weaving through the corridors, sticking to the blind spots. Somehow, miraculously, we reach the ground floor without being spotted.

But I know we're not done. I still need to get him to the balcony, and then I have to find my ring.

Hushed voices approach, and without speaking, Sepehr and I duck into an alcove just as two guards pass us, heading down the hallway. I don't move for a few seconds, waiting until they are gone before I glance around the side of the stone wall.

"Coast is clear," I whisper to Sepher.

He nods, and we resume our escape. Down familiar corridors, around corners that I no longer wish to hide behind, and up the staircase that will hopefully offer our freedom once and for all.

As soon as I step out onto the semi-circle balcony, strung high above the ocean, salty sea air fills my lungs. Probably the only thing I miss about this place.

It's hard to stick to the shadows up here, but we do our best to keep out of view from anyone who might be watching. Sepehr and I move in sync as we sit Roan against the stone wall.

I glance around, making sure that we haven't been followed before turning my attention to Sepehr. "Stay here."

Despite his condition, Roan frowns. "What?"

Sepehr's expression darkens. "Saint—"

"I have to find my ring." My voice is low but firm. "You know that is part of the plan."

"Yeah, but I thought I'd be executing it with you!" Sepehr hisses.

I point to Roan, who keeps falling in, and out of consciousness. "You see the state he is in, he can't be left alone, so we need to pivot."

Sepehr sighs, but nods. "If we're pivoting, what's the new plan?"

I run a hand through my hair as I gnaw at my bottom lip. Really, there is no backup plan, but I can't tell them that. I don't even want to admit it to myself. I just have to act—and fast.

"I'll go in, find my ring, meet you back here, and then we'll plunge to our debt—free lives," I end with a grin.

Sepehr stares at me silently for a moment. "I mean, it's been pretty easy so far, so who says the rest won't be?"

A grin spreads across my face. "That's the spirit."

Without another word, I slip into the shadows, the weight of their stares following me as I disappear into the depths of Donovan's estate.

I truly don't even know where to start looking for my ring. There's a good chance Donovan flung it into the ocean the moment he returned from the orphanage the day he brought me here. But if I was going to look anywhere, it would be his trophy room. The place he keeps all his fine possessions.

Every silent step carries me closer to half of the piece of me that has been missing for so long. The other half is in the ocean now, waiting for me to plunge from the balcony and into her waiting arms.

*I'll be there soon, Blue.*

The hairs on the back of my neck prickle the closer I get to Donovan's prize study. It all feels too easy. I haven't spotted or heard him once, and that alone is a major concern. Where is the bastard?

I slink along the quiet corridors until I reach the dark, mahogany door with the gold nameplate that reads 'Private.' I glance both ways before placing my ear on the wood. Nothing. It's quiet. With a gentle grip, I turn the handle before slipping inside.

The room is dark, perfect for blending in. I flick my eyes around the sacred space, seeing if there is any obvious place I might look first. Growing up, I was never allowed in here, though that never stopped me from sneaking in from time to time.

I leave the door ajar to let the light in. Exotic liquors line a shelf to my left. Rare books, fine porcelain, glassware, and perfumes adorn a large oak shelf to my right. Then there was the large chest of gemstones, gold, and silver coins that proudly sit on a table behind his desk. I run my fingers over the smooth coins, remembering all the times I collected money for him. All the bloodshed and lives lost, just so Donovan's thirsty greed could be quenched.

If I could, I'd pile up all his treasure and force him to light the match, burn it all to the ground. But if I can't do that, I'm going to take it one last time.

There's enough here that I could help some folk that were hurt in the process. Not only that, I could retire—my brothers too. Surely Donovan wouldn't notice if a few glittering items went missing? He deserves so much worse than a few stolen coins. Perhaps that fate will still find him.

I need to find my ring—nothing else matters. But the hardest part? I don't even know what I'm looking for. Will it be the same as Kamari's? Or should I be searching for something totally different? The uncertainty gnaws at me, but

I don't have time for doubt. I just have to find it—before Donovan finds me.

Nothing in the room screams, '*I'm a place a hidden ring could be, come find me*', so I begin with the first place my eyes land. Donovan's desk. The top is littered with papers, and the ledger he always keeps the records of who owes him what—in pristine condition, of course.

I start pulling the drawers open, keeping one eye and one ear on the door. The drawers hold nothing of value. I run my fingers gently on the underside of the table until I feel a slight bump in the wood. A grin forms on my mouth.

Pressing it, I hear a faint click, and then a small wooden door pops down from under the table. A hidden compartment, and inside is a single black ring box.

Slowly, I open it. My breath catches as I view a gold ring with a flat oval surface. On it, an owl has been engraved. It feels heavy in my hand, not because of the weight of the ring, but because of what it means. For so many years I thought I would never find control of my own body.

And here it is.

I slip the ring from the satin crease, snapping the box shut with a quiet finality before sliding it onto the middle finger of my right hand. The moment the metal meets my skin, a sharp sting shoots up my finger, spreading through my hand like a pulse of recognition. It isn't pain—it's something deeper, something instinctual. A missing piece locking back into place. My body exhales in relief. For the first time in too long, I am whole again.

"I always knew you'd come crawling back . . . Like a dog to its master."

The chill that creeps down my spine freezes over my heart. I'd been so focused on the ring that I hadn't noticed Donovan standing in the doorway. Fear threatens to settle in my chest, but it's not welcome. I shove it away, feigning a smile as I look up.

"Sorry to disappoint you D, but I really can't stay." I keep my voice as smooth as possible.

He steps into the room, his hulking figure clad in a red fur cloak—even though it's nearing the end of summer—with eyes so dark they look as if he's plucked them from hell itself. Behind him loom two other figures. Brogos, and Riggs—both looking a little worse for wear.

Donovan shoves his hands behind his back, striding a few steps further into the space. "My expectations were low, Saint. We both know this is all you were ever good for."

I swear the room is warmer than it was before. With sleight of hand, I slide the box back into the hidden compartment before easing my hands into my trouser pockets. "I'm only taking what is mine,"

Donovan scoffs. "Yours? You forfeited any claim to anything the moment I took you in. Everything you have, everything you are, is because of me. Without me, you'd be nothing. Just another orphan starving in that forsaken hovel."

My fists curl, nails biting into my palms. Drogos, and Riggs sneer behind their master. I'm strong, but even I know that three against one is a little unfair.

Especially for them.

I huff. "Don't you dare twist it. You didn't save me—you enslaved me. You took a scared kid and turned him into your pawn. I was nothing more than a tool to you, and you broke me over and over."

"Broke you?" Donovan's brow pinches. "I *forged* you. Look at you now. Strong. Clever. Dangerous. All because of me."

I mockingly laugh at his statement. "Dangerous, sure. But not for the reasons you think," I mutter, taking a few steps towards the side of the desk. The two idiots behind Donovan slowly slip sideways, trying to corner me . . . The longer I stand in this room, the harder it's going to be for me to escape.

And I have to escape. I've got a piece of my heart waiting in the ocean below, and another two pieces on the balcony above.

Donovan sucks air between his teeth. "What was your plan boy? Storm my fortress, steal a trinket, and vanish into the night? You're predictable—like the scared little owl you've always been."

I chuckle. "Predictable—maybe. Yet I still slipped past your guards to free the people you've kept chained, to expose you for the coward you are. You think your power makes you untouchable, but it's just a mask for your fear."

His dark eyes bore into me, but I'm not scared of him—not anymore. I have my ring. I just need to get out of here.

Donovan takes a step towards the desk. I take the opportunity to glance down to see what I could use as a distraction or possibly a weapon. His scent makes my gut turn. Not that it's a horrible one—just one that I'd rather not be reminded of.

"Fear?" he sneers. "The only thing I fear is wasting my time on disappointments like you. Do you really think anyone cares about your sob story? You're nothing but a shadow, Saint. A failure."

His words try to find purchase in my heart, but the moment they near my heart, they smash against the cold that is only reserved for him and melt away.

I slowly pull my hands from my trouser pockets, flattening them on the wooden desktop. "Then why are you trembling, old man? You're afraid because you know your time is up. You've built your empire on stolen power and shattered lives, but it's crumbling—and that frightens you."

Donovan's top lip turns up into a snarl. "I'm done with you . . . Get him."

Drogos, and Riggs don't need any further instruction as they both leap into action. Time slows around me, my mind showing me every option I have, and every possible outcome. I choose the one that gets me the girl, and my friends.

My fingers tighten around the edge of Donovan's desk, my heartbeat a war drum in my ears. The moment stretches, as the men close in on either side of me. Without taking my eyes off Donovan, I muster all my strength and flip the desk. Ink bottles, stacks of paper, and coins fly through the air, crashing down onto the floor.

The men recoil, just as I snatch up a heavy ledger and hurl it straight into the nearest one's face. Papers swirl through the air like a storm of distraction.

"Son of a—" One of them stumbles back, shielding his eyes.

It's all the opening I need. I lunge forward, shoving past their disoriented forms, my shoulder colliding with someone's ribs. A sharp grunt follows, but I don't stop.

The door. That's all that matters.

I barrel through it, boots pounding against the marble as I race down the hall, Donovan's curses chasing me like a shadow.

I have such a small window of time to get back to the balcony and over the edge. There is no way I'm running through the house drawing more attention to myself.

The shouts behind me grow louder as Riggs gives chase. I throw a glance over my shoulder; even Donovan is keeping up, but the ledger must have knocked Drogos out cold. I chuckle to myself.

"You won't escape me again, Saint!" Donovan roars.

I throw him a grin. My breath burns in my lungs, but I don't slow—I can't. The hall ahead stretches long and empty, the only light spilling in from the tall, arched windows lining the walls. At the very end, the stairway curves upward towards the outdoor balcony. Towards Sepehr. Towards Roan. Towards Juniper. Towards escape.

Almost there.

A sharp whistle cuts through the air, and instinct screams at me to move. I twist mid-step, and a dagger sails past me, so close I feel the bite of displaced air against my cheek. It buries itself in the wall with a solid *thunk*.

I don't have the luxury of stopping. So I don't.

Another step, another breath, my legs pumping as I take the stairs two at a time. More shouting. More footsteps. They're closing in.

I shove through the balcony doors, chest heaving. Sepehr whips around at the sound. Roan still looks terrible, but at least he's standing.

"Time to go!" I bark.

Sepehr doesn't hesitate. He grips Roan's arm, supporting his weight just as I hear the first pursuer hit the stairwell.

I spin on my heel, grabbing for the dagger in my boot, buying Sepher and Roan time to leap over the balcony. I throw a glance their way. "Take flight, boys—tell Juniper I'm coming."

Sepehr nods, his eyes lingering on me, before he leaps with Roan into the crashing ocean waters below. I could follow them. Leap to safety, but something stops me. I know deep down that if I don't end Donovan now, I'll never live in peace. I need my past to die, so my future can live.

I plant my feet, turning to face the men spilling onto the balcony. My chest rises and falls with each sharp breath, my grip tightening around the dagger in my hand. Riggs steps forward first, his mouth curled in a sneer, and behind him, Donovan strolls onto the stone terrace as if he owns the world itself.

Donovan drawls, clasping his hands behind his back. "You really are a stubborn little bastard, aren't you?"

I roll my shoulders, shifting my stance. "Obviously, I learned from the best."

It's now two against one, and I'm so okay with that. I don't wait for Riggs to make the first move. Instead, I send my mind to the happiest memory I own, letting it fuel me, steady me. Then I let go.

I dance to the song of fury, my blade the instrument, my body the rhythm.

# Thirty-Five

FIGHT FOR SOMETHING REAL

Seeing the bodies of two men falling from the balcony reminds me of leaves tumbling in the gentle winds of autumn. There is something beautiful in the way their hair catches the morning sunlight like glittering jewels. Two bodies, but there are supposed to be three.

Saint must still be on the balcony. My heart feels like it's being crushed inside my chest. He has to make it out . . . He has to.

I plunge into the cool, blue depths, the water swallowing me whole as I cut through the waves, swimming towards Sepehr and what I can only assume is Roan. The ocean is nothing like the lake back home—it's restless, unpredictable, its currents shifting with an untamed will of their own.

I prefer the lake.

The lake doesn't push and pull—it simply exists. Steady. Constant. Safe.

But the ocean? The ocean demands something from me, testing my strength, my endurance, as if it knows I don't belong here.

It's much darker down here too, and who knows what creatures lurk on the seabed. Thankfully, I won't be around long enough to find out.

The rope slung around my body drags against my skin, rubbing my flesh as it soaks in salty water, becoming a weight. I just need to get to the boys, get them safely to the shore, and then I can turn my focus on Saint.

As I near where the Roan and Sepehr hit the water, I see a dark head bob up from beneath the water. "Sepehr, grab the rope!" I call out before flinging one end to him, while the other is tied securely around my waist. I might not have the strength they do on land, but in the water, it's completely different.

Sepeher takes hold of the rope, his face marred in worry. He points to the water. "It's Roan, I can't reach him!" he shouts across the sound of the crashing waves on the rocks.

Panic surges through me. I nod and plunge into the water. Darkness swallows me as I dive, the world above fading into a distorted blur of silver and black. Everything feels so unfamiliar. The deeper I go, the heavier the water presses against my ribs. I try to suck the water through my gills, filtering out the oxygen I need. It even tastes different.

My eyes dart all around, trying to find Roan. I have one job: get the boys out safely, and already I feel like I'm failing.

I spot him. A shadow sinking fast, limbs slack, hair swirling like molten copper in the water.

Roan.

I flick my tail harder, arms outstretched, but the current tugs at him like greedy fingers, pulling him deeper, deeper—too deep. But I force myself down, muscles screaming, the cold seeping into my bones. I have to reach him before the rope tethered to Sepehr goes taunt.

When I reach him, his eyes are closed. No bubbles escape his lips. Blotches of purple, brown, and red bruises cover his face. He's already been through so much.

No, no, no.

I grab his arm, hauling him to me. His body is dead weight, unresponsive, lifeless. A cold dread grips me tighter than the water around us.

"Don't you dare give up on Saint," I growl through gritted teeth, wrapping my arm around his chest and flicking my tail hard, dragging him towards the light above.

The surface seems impossibly far away. My lungs burn from all the water I'm consuming and filtering, my strength waning under his weight. But I refuse to let go. I break through the salty depths, finding Sepehr treading water not far from me.

"Come on," I rasp, keeping his face above the waves. "Breathe, damn you!"

But he doesn't.

Sepehr swims over to me, the worried look on his face still present. "Is he—?"

"We need to get the water out of his lungs," I shout above the waves.

I pull Roan back against my chest, wrapping my arms around him—then I squeeze him as hard as I can in jerking motions. "I need—to get— the water from—his lungs."

Sepeher can barely keep his head above water, but he does his best. I can't keep both of them afloat, and Roan takes priority first.

I can feel the faint thrum of his heart against my arm. "Come on, Roan, wake up!"

With all the strength I can muster, I crush his chest. The gurgling sound is like a symphony to my ears. Next, he's coughing up water, the colour returning to his face as he sucks air into his lungs.

Relief washes over me. He made it. Now I have to get them to land.

Sepher treads water while tying the rope around Roan's waist. "There is a small island over there, much closer than the shore. Take us there."

I nod without a second thought. There isn't time for that, I need to find Saint.

The current fights me with every stroke. The ocean might look beautiful and innocent from the shore, but out here in the waters, it's a ferocious beast, never to be tamed.

Sepehr gasps for air beside me, dragging Roan's barely-conscious form through the water. His face is twisted with effort, but exhaustion weighs on him, just as it does on me.

The small island—a cluster of jagged rocks jutting from the water, surrounded by sandy shores. It's not much, but it's solid ground. With one final push, I haul my body against the sand, dragging the rope as Sepeher scrabbles at the rocks. He shoves Roan up first, his arms trembling, and together we drag him onto the island. He coughs weakly, but he's alive.

I collapse for a breath, chest heaving, hands shaking.

"Juniper, I can't thank you enough," Sepeher utters through gasping breaths. "If it wasn't for you, we'd surely be dead."

"I'm glad I was there for you. Now, I need to help Saint."

Sepehr's brows knit in worry. "He's still up there with Donovan. Wouldn't let me stay and fight."

Why does that not surprise me? He might have been taught to think only of himself when it comes to strangers, but for his brothers, he'd do anything to keep them safe.

My head snaps towards the estate, towards the balcony where I last saw him. The water between us churns, dark and foreboding, but I don't hesitate. I turn back to Sepehr, nodding towards Roan. "Stay with him."

And then, I dive.

Barrelling through the water, I swim for the side tower that descends into the ocean. I recall Saint saying something about a secret door that leads to the stairwell.

If there was one, I would find it.

The base of the estate disappears into the rocks as if it is carved from the mountain itself. Waves crash against the aging fortress as I scour the best place to dive back under.

My eyes follow the lines of the tower as it disappears into the sea. This is my best chance. I close my eyes, thinking of Mama, and Saint, the two people that I love beyond words. Once this is all over, I'm going to make my dream become a reality—I'm going to create the candles I want, and I'm going to spend every minute I can with the people I love.

With one last glance towards the balcony above me, I dive into the glassy blue waters.

Down, down, down I go until the stone of the tower turns to actual rock. I must be at the bottom. Placing my hands on the flat outer walls feeling for some sort of entrance or doorway.

My fingers graze on a rough surface. The iron door looms before me. Hope fills my chest, but quickly diminishes when I see what's lodged in front of it.

A large rock.

Saint was right, Donovan blocked it off. My pulse pounds in my ears as I circle it, searching for something, anything, that can help.

Then, in the dim light filtering through the water, I spot it. A thick, frayed rope, caught between two jagged stones. It looks as though it's been down here for centuries. My fingers are raw as I pry it free, but when it finally comes loose, I don't waste a second.

I loop the rope around the boulder, my hands fumbling, the current tugging at my body. Tightening the knot, I swim back, gripping the other end, and knot it around my waist.

I close my eyes, drawing a deep gulp of air and water into my mouth, and out through my gills. This is going to hurt.

Then I kick. Hard.

Pain rips through my body instantly, a cry leaving my lips, muted by the density of water. The resistance of the rock threatens to tear my torso in two, but I grit my teeth and pull harder, beating my tail with everything I have. The rope bites into my skin, but the boulder doesn't budge. I want to scream in frustration, but that isn't going to help anyone. A vision of sapphire eyes spur me on. I will not leave him there to fight alone.

Again.

I swim back, gathering momentum before surging forward, the force jerking through my body. My tail screams in protest, but this time—I feel it shift. Just a little.

Again.

My vision swims from the effort, but the rock groans, scraping against the stone. Hope springs forth.

One more—I can do this.

I shove forward with a final, desperate push. A shock of pain lances through my tail, but the boulder lurches free, rolling away with a deep, thunderous crack.

I clutch the iron bars, gasping, trembling. The entrance is open. All those years of cleaning out pipes, and dislodging rocks in the lake, finally pay off. With skilled fingers, I rip the rope from my waist before I yank the iron gate open, swimming through.

My body shakes as I reach the surface, breaking it in time to see Saint stumble through a doorway that must come from the balcony I saw him on earlier. He's shuffling backwards down the stairs, battling a man in a red fur coat. Why on earth is he wearing that? It's much too hot for summer.

I keep hidden in the shadows; it's only the three of us down here, and I don't want to distract Saint. I'll stay hidden unless he needs me.

The man lunges at Saint, knocking the dagger from his hand. I hear Saint's muffled curse, my breath catching. I watch as the blade plunges into the waters.

"You've always been a fool, Saint. A naive little boy who thinks he can change the world. Let's see how that hope serves you when you're bleeding on my floor," the man—who I can only presume is Donovan—sneers.

What a delightful man.

Saint is holding his stance, yet now he has no weapons to defend himself. "Maybe I'm a fool. But at least I fight for something real. You fight for control, for greed—and it's slipping through your fingers."

Donovan takes a step down, and Saint matches his movement, keeping two stair lengths between them.

"I made you. You're nothing without me!"

Saint chuckles. "No, you're wrong. I'm nothing because of you. And I'm done letting you control me."

Before anyone can notice me, I slip beneath the surface again. Saint needs his dagger, and I'd be the one to find it for him. It's so dark down here. No light penetrates these waters, but I'd run my fingers along the seabed until I find his blade.

Just hold on Saint, I'm coming.

I swim to the sandy floor, searching for anything that resembles a knife blade. If only I had some light to reflect on the metal. I use my tail to brush away some of the sand, swimming round and round frantically.

I'm about to think all hope is lost when I spy something silver in the corner of my eye. With a sharp intake of breath, I surge forward, collecting the blade in my hand, and swimming to the surface all in one breath.

I break the surface just as Donovan lunges towards Saint again.

"Saint!" I call out.

His head whips towards me, a look of surprise written all over it. I throw his dagger up towards him, and with the practiced ease of a fluent fighter, he reaches for it.

Donovan snarls, "You think killing me will set you free? You'll always be a monster, Saint. Just like me."

I bob in the water, fighting back the tears threatening to spill as I watch half of my heart face his demons. I want to reach for him, pull him into the water and let it carry us both away to safety, but I keep my mouth shut. He can do this.

The chuckle that leaves Saint's lips sends a shiver down my spine. Donovan's comment really hit a nerve. "You're right. I've done terrible things. But I'm not you. I have something you'll never have—hope. And people who believe in me."

The rage on Donovan's face is palpable. I can almost taste it in the air. He lunges for Saint. "FOOL!" he screams.

Bodies collide in a blur of red and black. I bite back a strangled cry, when I can't tell what's fur coat, and what's blood. The two men go tumbling into the water on the other side of the spiral staircase.

My heart shatters.

No . . . Not Saint.

I hesitate, my breath hitching as I float in place, the saltwater stinging my eyes—but not nearly as much as the fear clawing at my chest.

This can't be the end.

I force myself to move, swimming towards the spot where they disappeared. Tears blur my vision, mingling with the sea, but I make no effort to stop them.

The water is eerily still. No ripples. No movement. No sign of life.

I hover, torn between hope and dread, my body trembling. I should dive, should search—but what if I find only silence waiting for me below? What if I find death?

Something snatches my tail, yanking me back with enough force to steal the breath from my lungs. A scream rips from my throat, bubbling into the water as panic floods my veins. My heart hammers against my ribs, a wild, desperate rhythm.

I twist, ready to fight, expecting the flash of red fur—but instead, I'm met with sapphire blue.

"Hello, love," Saint purrs with a grin.

Without a second thought, I throw my arms around his neck, slamming his body against mine. Tears drip from my cheeks, mingling with the salty water surrounding me, as I hold on to Saint, my tail keeping us steady.

He pulls back slightly to rest his forehead on mine. "You saved me. Again," he whispers.

I glance up to meet his gaze. "You'd do the same for me."

The hand on the back of my neck tilts my neck, forcing my lips to meet his. "I'd do it a thousand times over," he murmurs before claiming my lips in the most tender kiss I've ever experienced in my life.

A kiss so powerful that I forget my own name.

# Thirty Six

The smoke from Meadowbrook drifts in the near distance. It won't be long until we're finally treading familiar ground. I can see how excited, and relieved Juniper is to be home. Her eyes hold that sparkle that I've only ever seen in Meadowbrook.

Afternoon sun seeps through the thick forest canopy. Coating us in liquid gold. Every inch of its warmth is a welcomed embrace. Sepehr and Roan trudge behind me. Their footsteps light, though I can hear the slight limp that Roan still carries. His healing is going to take a little while longer.

I flick my gaze to Juniper who's walking beside me on Theon's horse. Her smile is subtle, but it's there. She has this glow about her that is very hard not to miss.

"You must be so excited to be home, Blue." I smile up at her. Meadow eyes meet mine. "Can you tell?"

A small huff escapes me. "I think the whole forest can."

Juniper grins, and I can't help but mimic her actions, despite how heavy my heart feels. It's one thing to be on the road together, making love, laughing, finding comfort in each other's arms, and sprouting words of affection. But once we face reality, will it all change? Will she still be able to love me after she sees the hurt on Kamari's face in person?

The town gates appear from around the bend. I might be nervous about what awaits me once I'm inside, but I'm still looking forward to a hot bath, and a good meal.

Sepehr, and Roan pick up their pace, they too are keen to find the inn or a tavern. Yet before any of that can happen, there are two things that I need to do.

Juniper pulls the horse to a stop. I hold the leather reins still, her boots crunch softly as she slides to the ground. "Is everything okay?"

She nods. "I just want to stretch my legs. As soon as I step through those gates, this adventure is over, and I will have to go back to everyday life."

I reach for her hand, squeezing it. "Would you like to turn around and go back the other way? We could begin on a whole new adventure."

Juniper's eyes crinkle in the corners. "That does sound wonderful, but perhaps we return Theon's horse first?"

First item on my to-do list. Face the male who received a broken nose at my hand. I didn't feel the need to apologise to him, but for the sake of his, and Juniper's friendship, I owe it to them to be amiable.

The familiar clunk of a hammer against the blacksmith's anvil, sounds through the air. The scent of burning coal and hot iron float along the breeze. Sepehr and Roan are already paces ahead, taking part in the town sights.

Juniper squeezes my hand back as we walk towards Theon's shop. I can tell she's aware of the tension that still lingers between Theon and me. I grip the reins of his horse a little tighter, feeling the weight of unspoken words pressing between us.

Theon steps out from the forge before we even reach the entrance, wiping his hands on a rag. His sharp gaze immediately finds me, yet softens as it shifts to Juniper. I don't feel threatened by the look he offers her. I know she's mine in every sense, yet I can't help but be a little jealous of their friendship.

Juniper runs a soothing hand along the horse's neck before speaking. "We took good care of him," she says, her voice steady over the noise of the forge, then she adds, "Thank you for trusting us with him."

Theon nods with a smile, taking the reins from Juniper's outstretched hand.

He flicks his gaze towards me. There's no hostility in his look, but there's still something weighing between us. A quiet assessment. A measure of trust.

I don't flinch under it. I just hold my ground, letting him decide whatever it is he needs to.

After a long moment, he gives a small nod. It's not an invitation, but it's not a rejection either. A mutual understanding.

I nod back. "Thank you, he's a fine steed."

Juniper watches the exchange but doesn't comment. Instead, she gives Theon a small, appreciative smile before stepping back towards me. "Have you spoken with Mama?"

Theon nods. "I saw her yesterday. She told me everything. I'm sorry if I made things difficult . . . For both of you."

Juniper reaches out to squeeze his hand, but never lets go of mine. "It's all in the past now."

Theon offers a smile towards both of us. The tension may not be completely gone, but it no longer feels like a heavy weight between us, and for now, that's enough.

Juniper brushes her fingers against my arm, a silent signal that it's time to go. Theon leads the horse towards a small stable behind the blacksmiths as we turn and walk away.

Roan and Sepehr join us, commenting from time to time about how big and beautiful Meadowbrook is. I can see the pride beaming on Juniper's face as she points out things to them.

It still hasn't sunk in that Donovan is dead, and it wasn't even me that killed him. When he lunged for me on the stairwell, we both fell into the water. I missed the rocky outcrop—he did not. He hit his head, and never came back to the surface.

Now, I was free from him. I had my ring on my finger, and Juniper in my arms, yet something still gnawed at me. Perhaps I just wasn't used to having my own freedom.

As we near the chandlery, my chest tightens. I know I have to right my wrongs, I just hope it doesn't cost me my future.

The familiar scent of beeswax, and lavender wafts through the air, I glance down at Juniper by my side. Her smile is full, and her steps are quickening. She's eager to see her mother, and I don't blame her. I too would want to see my mother if she were alive.

Before we even step through the door, a high-pitched squeal shatters the calm.

"Juniper!"

Kamari bursts from the shop like a bundle of sunshine, her dark waves, streaked with silver, bouncing wildly as she flings herself towards us. Juniper barely has time to brace herself before her mother collides into her, wrapping her in the fiercest hug I've ever seen.

"Mama," Juniper whispers.

Kamari pulls back just enough to hold Juniper's face between her hands, her sharp eyes scanning for any sign of injury. "You're home."

"Yes, and I brought some friends." Juniper grins as she steps out of the way. "Mother, this is Sepehr and Roan, Saint's brothers."

Kamari hugs both of them, a beaming smile on her face. "More people to love!" she laughs. "Come inside, all of you."

As we enter the shop, I find myself enveloped by a sense of comfort, but I'm still nervous of what Kamari is going to say to me. I step out of the way so that Juniper can view the shop, and speak with her mother. Sepehr and Roan take a fancy to the collection of candles on the shelves, picking them up to smell the scents.

Kamari throws her arms back around Juniper, squeezing her tight.

I should be smiling. I should be laughing along with them, basking in the warmth of a reunion that was nearly stolen from them.

But as I watch them—two souls bound by something unbreakable—I feel a weight settle in my chest.

There is love here, pure and untarnished. A love that has survived distance, uncertainty, and fear.

And I'm on the outside looking in.

I swallow hard, shifting my weight as an unfamiliar ache coils in my ribs.

This is what family should feel like.

Yet standing here, surrounded by people who care, I wonder—will I ever truly belong?

Juniper turns then, her gaze finding mine. There's something soft in her eyes, something knowing. She reaches for me without hesitation, fingers curling around my wrist, grounding me. I savour her warmth.

"You're a part of this too," she says, like she can hear the war in my head.

Kamari finally glances over, her eyes flicking between us. "I believe I owe you something."

A lump forms in my throat as I read myself for the verbal bashing. It's to be expected. I did the wrong thing, and now it's time for the consequences.

"Kamari, let me explain—"

I'm quickly silenced when Kamari loops her arms around me in a fierce embrace. My brow knits together. She's embracing me? For a moment I don't know how to respond. I'm tense, waiting for the backlash of words to spill forth. Yet she just holds me.

"You don't need to say anything. Juniper explained everything in her letter," Kamari murmurs. "I understand why."

My body softens, but I don't let my walls all the way down. I don't know how to do that—especially around a mother figure.

Guilt and shame have followed me around like monsters on a leash, nipping at my heels. I deserve all her anger—all her wrath.

Kamari finally pulls back. Her green eyes are gentle. "You've been carrying a weight for so long that should have never been yours to carry alone." She reaches up to cup my face. "Would you like to put it down?"

Tears threaten to cloud my eyes. I nod silently.

"You're part of the family now," she continues.

*Family.*

The word is foreign to me. Yet it's that unit of measure that my heart longs to be a part of.

I fish around in my pocket until I feel the cold touch of metal. Pulling it free, I hand it to Kamari on my open palm. "I'm sorry I took it." My words come out softly.

She takes it from me, placing it on her finger before looking back up at me. "Saint, it's okay. I forgive you."

My brows pinch again in confusion. "You're not mad?"

She shakes her head. "Not at all."

"But I took your ring?"

Kamari smiles at me before glancing at Juniper. "Yes, but you also brought my Juni back, and the sparkle in her eyes."

Juniper pulls herself into my side, looking up at me through her darkened lashes. I resist the urge to lean down and kiss her perfectly pink lips.

"I don't know what to say," I say, glancing back at Kamari.

Sepehr and Roan are awfully quiet behind me, but I know they're respecting this moment.

A grin spreads across Kamari's face. "Welcome home, Saint."

The words have barely left her lips with the door to the chandlery bursts open so ferociously that the shelves rattle, nearly sending a row of candles toppling over.

"Juniper Fairchild, how dare you leave me for so long!" Dove cries, throwing herself into Juni's arms.

"It's only been just over a full moon cycle." Juniper chuckles.

Dove pulls back, eyes shining. "You took your time. What, did you swim the whole way home?"

Juniper laughs, shaking her head. "Something like that."

I lean against the counter, arms crossed, watching the reunion unfold. There's something nice about seeing Juniper with the people who love her—watching the way she softens, how she lets herself be held.

But then my attention shifts, because Dove's gaze finally slides past Juniper—to the people standing behind her.

I don't miss the way her breath catches when her eyes land on Roan.

It's quick. Subtle. Barely even there.

But I see it.

I see the way her fingers twitch, like she's resisting the urge to smooth down her clothes.

I pull Juniper closer to my side. "Dove, these are my friends. Sepher, and Roan."

My brothers straighten their posture, Roan grinning just a little bigger than Sepehr at the blue-haired bundle of sunshine.

"Hello, boys," Dove coos.

A light chuckle forms on my lips. I think Meadowbrook is going to be a lot of fun.

The sky is a blanket of ebony and diamonds. Not a cloud in sight as Juniper and I lay on the banks of the lake. The grass is cool beneath my back. The scent of honey clings to the crisp autumn breeze. It was nice to have a change in the weather. No storms lingered on the horizon.

Juniper rests beside me, my arm under her head, cradling her neck. Her breath is soft and steady. The lake stretches out before us, dark and endless, reflecting the sky like a mirror.

A streak of silver cuts across the velvet sky.

I hear Juni's sharp intake of breath. "A shooting star," she murmurs.

I glance over at her, catching the way her lips curve into a small smile, her eyes reflecting the heavens above.

"Make a wish," I say.

Her eyes find me. "Everyone knows stars don't grant wishes," she laughs softly. "That's just folklore."

"We could always pretend?"

She nestles in closer to my chest. "I don't need to."

I lean down to press a kiss to her hair. "No?"

Juniper shakes her head, rolling onto her side to face me. "Everything I want is right here."

For a moment, I don't say anything. I just look at her—the way the moonlight catches in her hair, the way the wind toys with the loose strands. She's always been beautiful, but here, like this, she's something else entirely.

How did I get so lucky? How did I get the girl?

I press a kiss to her forehead. For the first time in a very long time, my heart is at complete peace. No one is coming after me, there is no need to look over my shoulder every five minutes, and perhaps it's time to come out of the shadows, and into the light.

Reaching into my pocket, I feel the weight of the small pouch nestled there.

"I have something to show you."

Juniper's brow creases as she watches me sit up. I untie the pouch strings and turn it upside down. Gems spill onto my palm, catching the light—deep blue sapphires, crimson rubies, and dark emeralds.

Her eyes widen. "Saint . . ."

I tip my hand so she can see them better. "From Donovan's private stash."

Her lips part in surprise. "We talked about stealing—"

I chuckle. "This wasn't stealing."

She gives me a look that says, *prove it.*

I sigh, placing the gems back into the pouch. "Alright, so maybe it was, but I was owed every damn gem. Not once did Donovan pay me while working for him. He figured as long as I had a roof over my head and food in my stomach, that was payment enough."

Juniper's eyes soften. "I wish he'd lived just a little longer, so he could have discovered it was gone."

My hand covers hers. "I wish he'd been able to witness his downfall many times, Blue. But now we don't have to worry about debt. I'll sell these, and we can start fresh." I reach out to brush her cheek. "I can open my shop. You can make all the candles your heart desires."

Tears well in her eyes. "No debt? Do you really mean it?"

I nod. "I have no reason to run anymore. No more collecting, no more weight hanging over you. Just . . . a life. One with just the two of us."

She stares at me for a long moment, then shifts closer, lifting a hand to my cheek. Her thumb brushes my skin, slow and reverent, and my breath hitches.

"Sounds pretty magical to me," she whispers.

The autumn wind dances around us, but I don't feel the chill. Not with her this close. Not with the weight of the past finally slipping from my shoulders.

# Thirty Seven

## HOME

I decide to check the letterbox while I wait for Saint. He told me this morning before he left for work to be ready by noon for a surprise. It wasn't unusual—he'd been showering me with little surprises for the last five moon cycles.

Bright winter sun tries to warm me with its rays, but the breeze holds a bite, so I wrap my cloak around me tighter as I head down the garden path. Most of the flowers are asleep this time of year. Too cold for their pretty little heads.

I reach the wooden box mounted on the fence that mimics a smaller version of my mother's cottage and pull the door open. Inside is a handful of cream-coloured envelopes. One catches my eye and is addressed to me. I turn it over and my heart stops as I recognise the name on the back. Movement down the road pulls my attention away. Saint is approaching, so I quickly shove the letter into my dress pocket and put the rest back inside the letter box.

A grin spreads across my face at the sight of familiar blond hair, and blue eyes so bright, I can see them from here. We often sneak away together, trying to find alone time from the rest of the world. He's been sleeping in the spare room, but with Mama around most of the time, it's hard to have time for just the two of us.

I flick my gaze towards the cottage, its walls freshly painted white. Saint had offered to do it because he felt bad about taking Mama's ring, and she was more than grateful to accept, even though she tried to convince him it wasn't a necessity.

The gate swings open effortlessly as I walk to meet my heart.

He grins as he reaches me, leaning down to cup my face, planting a fierce kiss on my lips.

I swear I will never grow tired of his kisses. They are the air I breathe.

"Hello, my love." He grins.

I smile up at him. "How was the shop this morning—busy?"

True to his word, Saint had sold the gems he'd taken from Donovan to a jeweller, collecting a hefty sum of money. With it, he'd cleared the chandlery debt . . . which changed my life. No longer did I wake in cold sweats at night, thinking of how much money the shop still owed. I was no longer bound by debt, and it was liberating. Word had reached us that someone from Breydon took over Donovan's business. Someone less . . . Evil. He'd also shared some with Sepehr and Roan before buying a vacant shop a few down from the chandlery. So far, he was the most sought after shop sign painter in all of Meadowbrook.

"You've got to stop telling people about my shop, I'm not sure I can keep up." Saint presses another kiss to my mouth.

"Never," I whisper against his lips.

He chuckles, taking my hand in his.

"So did you check on Roan on your way past?"

Saint nods. "He's fine. Dipping the candles just like you taught him."

My heart releases a sigh. Roan had taken a liking to the candle making process a few moon cycles ago, and I'd been more than grateful to have an apprentice alongside Wilson— the boy who helped while I was fetching wicks.

Now that Donovan was gone, and the new debt collector was in control, Saint cleared up all the debt, which meant I could finally breathe, it also meant I was designing new candles and scents, which were becoming my most popular orders.

Sometimes I had to pinch myself. I still had my father's shop, and now I get to make the kind of candles I'd been dreaming of.

I glance up at Saint. "So, where are you taking me?"

"Secret," he says, with a wink.

Rolling my eyes, I huff. I know better than to try to argue with him.

We stroll along, heading towards the outskirts of town, towards the forest. The winter air is crisp, biting at my cheeks as Saint leads me deeper into the woods.

It's not cold enough for snow yet, and some of the trees have lost their leaves, but there are some who still stand tall and proud, covered in greenery.

Saint walks ahead, his hand warm in mine, his thumb brushing over my knuckles absentmindedly. I watch him, the way his breath clouds in the air, the way his shoulders seem lighter than they've been in days. Whatever he's planning, it means something to him.

The deeper we go, the more perplexed I become. There is nothing but dense forest here.

I'm about to question him again when he stops in front of a curtain of vines. He pulls it to the side slowly before glancing over his shoulder to look at me. With a gentle tug on my hand and a smile on my lips, he pulls me through.

Then, with a sudden rush, the ground erupts in a flurry of motion.

A cloud of blue bursts upward, filling the air with shimmering wings. I gasp, stepping back into Saint's side as dozens—no, hundreds—of butterflies take flight all at once, their sapphire wings catching the pale light filtering through the trees. They swirl around us like a living storm, their delicate forms brushing against my skin, fluttering past my cheeks.

I release his hand to take a step forward, my jaw open in shock. Never in my twenty-five years have I ever seen something so beautiful. I can't even form words.

Wings brush against my face, my hair, my skin. I close my eyes and tip my head towards the sun. I never want this moment to end.

The butterflies dance through the air, their movements weightless, effortless. Some settle back onto the mossy ground, while others continue their wild ascent towards the branches above. The whole grove feels alive with them, like we've stepped into something untouched, something sacred.

I turn around to face Saint, only to find him on one knee with an open box in his hand.

Nothing can stop the tears from forming now. I slap my hand over my mouth, fighting back the emotions, as I take a few steps towards him. His eyes are brimming with excitement as I reach out to take his free hand.

"Saint—"

He clears his throat. "Juniper, my love. I have stolen many things in my life, but your heart is the one treasure I promise never to return. And if you'll have me, I'd like to spend the rest of forever drawing our story one sketch at a time."

A silent tear slips down my cheek. I can't pull my gaze away from his, transfixed to the spot. How did I get so lucky? How did I get him?

I brush the tears aside, nodding, because there is no other answer.

"Yes," I manage to whisper.

Saint grins before reaching inside the box to pull the ring from it. My breath is snatched from my lungs as I view it. A black opal, surrounded by tiny blue sapphires on a thin gold band.

He knows me so well.

Saint rises to his feet, his hands steady as he slides the ring onto my finger. It fits perfectly—like it was always meant to be there. A shiver runs through me, not from the cool evening air, but from the overwhelming certainty that this moment is changing everything.

He cups my face with such reverence it nearly breaks me, his thumbs grazing my cheekbones as if memorising every detail. My fingers clutch his shirt, pulling him closer, needing to feel him against me.

Then his lips find mine, and the world around us fades. This kiss isn't just passion—it's a promise, a silent vow of forever. His warmth, his love, his devotion pour into me, and I give him everything in return. It's the most intimate kiss we've ever shared, and in this moment, I know with absolute certainty that I am his, and he is mine.

We gently pull apart. His forehead rests on mine. "I love you, Blue."

I look up to place a soft kiss on the bridge of his nose. "I love you."

Who knows how long we stay there in the woods, locked in each other's embrace, watching the butterflies flit around us. It's like a dream, one I never want to wake from. Only when the sun begins to set, do we leave our secret place in the woods.

"Wait until Mama sees this," I utter softly.

Saint wraps an arm around my waist, pulling me close. "She's already seen it."

My mouth drops open.

Saint chuckles. "What did you expect? I had to ask someone for your hand in marriage."

I nestled into his side, a smile on my lips. "I hope she said yes."

Saint halts, spinning me to face him. He drops his head until his lips barely graze mine. "She definitely did."

I can't bear to be apart from him. I push up on tiptoes and kiss him with everything I have. He matches me with fervency.

Once I feel as if I might pass out from the lack of air, I pull back. "I want you to meet someone," I whisper.

Saint's brow creases, but he doesn't release his grip on me. "At this hour?"

I nod before taking his hand in mine.

We step onto a well-worn path that cuts through the meadows, heading for a small hill in the distance, leaving the forest and its magical butterflies behind. The cold wind brushes over the long, pale grass on either side of us, our boots almost silent with each step.

The sun is sinking behind the trees, painting the sky in strokes of amber and violet, casting long shadows across the ground.

We reach the top, and Saint's breath catches. I glance up at him, watching as he takes in the sight. My fingers tighten around his hand, drawing him closer.

The graveyard is small, nestled at the top of the hill. The headstones are weathered, some leaning with age, some standing strong. I've made this walk more times than I can count, but tonight it feels different. Tonight, I'm not alone.

I stop in front of the stone that bears my father's name: *Vern Fairchild.* The hand carved letters are still fresh compared to others. I crouch down to run my fingertips over them, tracing the familiar grooves. "I wanted you to meet him," I say softly, glancing at Saint. "I wish he could have met you."

Saint crouches down beside me, resting one hand on the earth beside the stone. "I would have loved that, Blue."

"Papa, this is Saint—my love—he just asked me to marry him, and I said yes," I manage to murmur.

A lump rises in my throat. The wind picks up, rustling through the grass and stirring the leaves of a nearby tree. For a moment, I let myself imagine my father here, standing beside me, nodding in quiet approval.

Saint places one hand on my knee, the other on top of the headstone. "I never had the chance to meet you, sir, but I see you in Juniper every day. Her strength, her kindness, the way she carves, and dips candles—her resilience." He squeezes my knee. "I want you to know that I can never replace you, but I promise to take care of your girls for as long as I live. I promise to love Juniper fiercely until my very last breath . . . Thank you for giving me the gift of her."

I can't hold back the emotions anymore. They flow from me in a raw and guttural way. I grip Papa's headstone as the tears pour out onto the grassy surface. Saint has his arms around me in a heartbeat, holding me tight as I mourn the loss of my father.

"I'm here," he whispers into my hair. "And I always will be."

When the tears subside, Saint gathers me in his arms in a warm embrace before we start the journey home. I'm eager to see Mother and share the news.

The path home is quiet, the cool dusk air curling around us as Saint and I walk side by side. The weight of the evening still lingers in my chest—grief and love, loss and hope, all tangled together.

But then, Saint slows.

I frown, watching as he stops in front of a small cottage a few doors down from my mother's house. The Flannigans' old place. It's tiny but cosy, with ivy creeping up the stone walls and a little garden patch out front, overgrown from neglect. I glance at him in confusion.

"What are we doing here?"

Saint doesn't answer right away. He watches me, a small, knowing smile tugging at his lips before he finally speaks.

"This," he says, gesturing to the cottage, "is ours."

I blink. "What?"

"I bought it," he says, turning fully to face me.

A sharp breath catches in my throat. I'm not sure I can take many more surprises today. I'm running out of tears. I look at the cottage again, the freshly painted wooden door, the small stone chimney, the bay window that glimmers in the lantern light from the street.

I've dreamed of owning my own home, but never thought it would come true this soon.

"You . . . You bought this?"

Saint nods, stepping closer. "As much as I love your mother and her hospitality, I'm tired of sleeping alone in the spare room. I want you in our bed every night for the rest of our lives. I told you once before, I don't like to share."

I throw my arm around his neck, breathing in his patchouli and cedarwood scent. I can happily say that I'm obsessed with this man. "Thank you," I whisper into his skin.

Without another word, Saint scoops me up into his arms, carrying me through the front gate, up the garden path, and over the threshold of our new home.

Inside, I expected to find it empty and dark, but once again Saint has outdone himself. The small living room floor is scattered in hundreds of candles. A trail of white rose petals threads its way from room to room.

"Saint—you've outdone yourself."

He throws me a boyish grin. "I couldn't have done it without Dove. She's the talent here."

My feet gently touch the ground as I slip from Saint's embrace. He reaches for my hand as we slowly stroll around the cottage. That's when I observe the walls. I was in so much shock when I came inside that I didn't notice until now.

They're lined with wooden frames filled with Saint's sketches. There's me as a siren, me dipping candles; me sleeping peacefully as I'm wrapped in the bedsheets. That one brings a blush to my cheeks.

I reach to touch them. "Saint, these are so beautiful."

He comes up behind me, placing his arms around my waist. "I'm glad you like them," he whispers into the side of my neck.

Little bumps form on my skin as his warm breath caresses me. I spin in his arms to face him. "Thank you . . . For everything."

There is a glint in his eyes. "Want to try out the bedroom?"

My eyes widen, but so does my smile. "There is no furniture in here?"

Saint's brow arches. "I may have bought a bed too."

"Saint!" I playfully swat his chest. "Glad to see where your priorities are."

He grins at me. "You can't blame a man for wanting his beautiful woman, every second of every day."

I stand on tiptoes to kiss him lightly. "Well, before we do that. I have a surprise for you."

"For me?" Saint asks, confusion washing over him.

I reach into my pocket, pull out the cream envelope, and hand it to him. "I haven't read it yet, but I believe this is for you."

Over the last few weeks, I'd been helping him with his letters. Every day, he was getting more and more confident in reading. I'm so proud of him.

He takes it gently, his fingers brushing against the paper. Tearing the seal, he pulls out the folded parchment. A small image slips free, but he doesn't look at it yet. His eyes scan the letter first, and as he reads, I watch the shift in his expression— the way his brows knit together, the way the colour drains from his face.

I begin to panic. Is it bad? Have I done the wrong thing? Perhaps I should have read the letter first before giving it to him.

I don't breathe as he lifts the photograph, his fingers tightening around the edges.

Glancing over at his hand, I know what he's looking at. The image is old but clear enough—the man with the sharp angles of Saint's face, the woman with a softer gaze and golden waves of hair. His parents.

"What does the letter say?" I whisper.

Slowly, he hands it to me, and I run my gaze over it. My heart beats wildly in my chest. It's from his aunt and uncle who still live in Sapphire Vale. They want to meet him.

Tears well in my eyes as I glance from the letter to Saint.

He finally looks at me, and it's not anger or resentment I see, but hope.

"How did you find them?" he whispers.

"I've been doing some digging," I say softly, "because I wanted to give you something real to hold on to."

Pools gather in his sapphires. "They want to meet me?"

He says it like a question, as if he almost doesn't believe it.

I nod, my chest tightening. "You deserve to know where you come from, Saint."

He exhales sharply, blinking fast, his hands trembling as he clutches the photograph like it's the most precious thing in the world. And to him, it is.

His gaze flicks back to me, and I can't help but melt under his loving expression. "Thank you," he says softly.

I wrap my arms around his neck. "Now, how about we try out that bed?"

Laughter erupts from Saint's stomach as he lifts me, twirling me around the room. When he places my feet back on solid ground, he captures my mouth in a delicious and passionate kiss.

I crave his taste and his touch. With a gentle scoop he lifts me so I can wrap my legs around his hips. Then he marches us to our new bedroom, where I find a beautiful four-poster bed already made with white and blue linens.

"How do you just keep getting better and better?" I whisper into Saint's neck, nipping and licking at his skin.

He moans softly with every kiss I place on his skin. We stop beside the bed, and he leans back to look into my eyes. "Because for you, Blue, I can be nothing else."

I squeal when he throws me onto the bed, my hair fanning out around me. He leaps on top of me, rolling us into the softness of the blankets. At this moment, I have never been happier. I've found my home, where my heart goes to rest . . . And it's *him*.

Saint hovers over me, hands on either side of my head. Desire coils low between my legs, a familiar ache that only he can satisfy.

"Now, this house is far enough away from others that I want to hear all your pretty moans and whimpers as I make love to you." He leans down to brush a tender kiss on my lips. "Don't be shy, Blue."

I bite my bottom lip as he hurriedly removes his shirt while I unbuckle his belt. It's been too many weeks since I had him completely to myself. Right now, I need him more than I need air.

"Your turn, my love." Saint leans down to nuzzle my neck.

My fingers can't grasp the hem of my dress quick enough. He has to help me drag it up and over my head.

His eyes darken as he takes in my naked body. The only light in the room comes from the moon outside. Bathing us in a wash of silver light.

"What are you waiting for?" I whisper.

The corner of Saint's mouth turns up in a grin as he reaches his hand down between us, finding my warmth.

His mouth parts softly as he sucks in a breath. "You're so wet for me."

I whimper, throwing my head back into the mattress as he plunges two fingers into me. "Only for you," I whisper.

Slowly, he drags his fingers out, before thrusting them back in. "Good girl."

Ecstasy and desire wrap around my senses as Saint pleasure's me with his hand. I will never tire of our lovemaking. Every time I'm with him, it only makes me want him more.

He pulls his hand from between my legs, and I moan softly at his absence. "Look at me," Saint gently demands.

My eyes find him just as he lines his cock up, plunging it into my warmth. I can't stop the sounds escaping my lips, and the louder I get the darker Saint's eyes become.

He takes me to a different world with every thrust of his hips, every stroke of his hardened length, every whisper of my name on his lips. Tonight is not about the slow and sensual, it's about the hunger, and the passion we have for each other.

My hands grip his waist, fingers digging into the hard planes of his back as if holding on for dear life. My nails rake over his muscled shoulders, desperate to anchor myself to him, to this moment. My legs tighten around his hips, pulling him closer. A low, guttural groan escapes Saint as I draw him deeper, his breath hot against my skin, his body a perfect fit against mine.

He buries himself into me, deeper, harder, faster. "*By the stars*, you feel so good."

I moan his name, not caring who might hear as my pleasure builds.

"That's it, Blue. Tell the world who you belong to." Saint leans down to capture my mouth in a kiss.

I meet it with passion, my tongue dancing with his. Heat coils in my stomach as he pounds into me.

"Saint—" my voice is breathless.

"I'll come when you do, my love."

My eyes roll back into my head as he thrusts into me, sending me into the dark abyss of ecstasy. I vaguely hear him grunt and feel him stiffen as he follows me over the edge.

A few more gentle thrusts, and he's collapsing beside me in a boneless heap. Neither one of us says a word while we ride the waves of our orgasms. This day could not have ended any more perfectly. Never has my heart felt more at peace than it does right now.

I slowly roll over, smiling at the soft rise and fall of Saint's chest. His eyes remain closed, his body utterly relaxed, draped in the quiet aftermath of happiness. I trace idle patterns along his skin, memorising the warmth of him.

"Thank you for everything," I whisper into the silvery light of the room.

A little smile dances on his lips. He stirs, propping himself up on an elbow, sapphire-blue glittering in the low light. "Thank you for choosing me," he whispers back.

I reach up to brush my thumb across his bottom lip. "Mine," I whisper.

"Yours," he breathes.

# Acknowledgements

I remember when I was younger; I wrote a book that had about five words on each page and my friend Anna drew the pictures for me. To this day, I still have it.

I always knew I wanted to write stories from a very young age, it just took until I was thirty-six to find the stories inside me. The day I took the leap into making this happen was the day I finished reading a fantasy romance I'd randomly bought in a bookstore one day. That book helped me rediscover my love for fantasy and the endless worlds that could be imagined. Magical tales woven with romance, action and mysteries. A place where powerful men and women went on adventures, and where I could escape reality and join them.

**To my readers.** I hope you know that no matter what stage in life you are at that you are always worthy of love. I hope you read this and find joy, spreading it to others around you. Thank you for encouraging me to keep writing.

**To my husband Jared.** My rock and my safe place. You have held me when I've cried and almost given up. You have encouraged me to keep going and always supported my dreams. Thank you for believing in me, even when I didn't believe in myself. You have shown me that the men I write in my stories are actually real. You are my perfect man. Without you, I wouldn't be where I am today. Thanks for all the donuts. I love you.

**To my beautiful children, Charleston and Meadow.** Thank you for being patient with me through the tough times. You are both sunshine in my days and I love the joy you bring to everyone around you. Never give up on your dreams. I love you both so much.

**To my editor and friend Megan G. Mossgrove.** I would need thousands of pages to write everything I would like to say to you. You've changed my life in ways I can't explain and have been with me from day one. Thank you for walking with me on this journey, for your endless support and your beautifully intricate mind. Thank you for every word you suggested and every comma you added to this story. It wouldn't be where it is now without you. You are pure sunshine. I love you.

**To my Alex (AllyCat).** My emo bestie, my bosom friend. Who would have thought that an image of a Motionless In White concert would join two souls together. Both have a love for emo music, writing and staying indoors with a cosy book. You have kept me sane throughout this entire process and have made me laugh every day. Thank you for always encouraging me and cheering me on. I'll always leave the light on for you. I love you.

**To my incredible street team.** Noelle, Erin, Kelly, Ana, Meg, Erin Rose, Alex, Kirsten, Letitia, Amarie, and Brittany. The constant support you all show me is magical. I appreciate each and every one of you, and honestly can't thank you enough for the hype you give me and my books. Thank you, thank you, thank you. From the bottom of my heart, thank you.

Sarah Davies lives in a cottage by a stream that runs through a meadow at the base of a grassy hill. Her garden is filled with every flower imaginable and white ducks with orange beaks and webbed feet, pitter patter in puddles of mud. A beehive is nestled beneath the branches of a pink crepe myrtle tree that provides shade for all her cats and inside her kitchen, the kettle is always warm.

She doesn't really live there, but in her mind, that's where she goes to find inspiration. It's in that magical place where all her stories are formed and she puts them down on paper. One day she hopes to make this dream a reality, where she will live peacefully with her husband and two children.

Sarah is a romance, fantasy author, writing predominately standalone romantasy's from her home in Queensland, Australia. When she's not dreaming up a new story or chipping away at current ones, you can find her sipping on tea, or simply being with her family.

# Other books

KDP AMAZON ETSY

IF YOU HAVE READ ANY OF MY BOOKS I WOULD
TOTALLY APPRECIATE A RATING OR REVIEW. YOU
CAN DO SO ON GOODREADS OR AMAZON.
EVERY LITTLE BIT HELPS INDIE AUTHORS AND I
APPRECIATE IT SO MUCH.